VICHY WATER

a novel

Calvin Barry Schwartz

Copyright© 2007 by Calvin Barry Schwartz

ISBN 978-0-578-03858-2

Published by Earthood Media, LLC Publishers
    2 Nancy Road
    Marlboro, New Jersey 07746

Cover art and design by Joe Carroll

For information regarding special discounts for bulk purchases please contact
Earthood Media Special Sales at 732-617-0612 or earthood@gmail.com
www.vichywater.net

Signature Book Printing, www.sbpbooks.com

DEDICATION

To Mollie, you molded and instilled.
To Fran and Neil, you love and support.
Always and in all ways.

ACKNOWLEDGMENT

Here's where I depart from mainstream. Spiritually, I've had help all along life's journey and I wrote about this angelic spirit. A poignant "thanks" and "love" to my grandfather Colman who passed in 1937. At this juncture, I always find the need to say I'm perfectly normal, after all I go to fifty Rutgers sporting events a year, play beer pong and did a keg stand.

Perhaps the most satisfying part of the process, because writing years are behind, the acknowledgement still challenges thought. In beginning days, Alan Frankel read and passed my writing to a higher authority where just a few critical words helped me to reinvent. Ann Kugel was like an editor in the formative stage.

Dave Zeak and Joel Schlossberg nudged me for years about my writing and I needed that. Writing a novel is like birthing a child for a guy, so I always thought, and then I find out Norman Mailer said the same thing more eloquently. Early on, after finishing that pre-historic first draft on 'Vichy Water,' Doug Dolan and Dr. Michael Kerner went where no one has gone before, read the novel and reinforced confidence levels and that meant everything to me and "my child." Then Dr. Kenneth Schwartz and Margie Schwartz (no relation whatsoever) nursed me along after the birthing.

Family can be a wonderful word. The more the merrier, especially for networking and support. Of course I've already dedicated this work to Fran and Neil. Hildy Abel climbed on top of the Empire State Building when I finished writing, stood right where Fay Wray was in 1933, and yelled to the city, that her brother (me) finished his first novel and who wants to represent or publish me? Saree Block did the same thing using a cell phone. Michael Block is my constant promulgator. Public relations wise, I still run up and down the aisles of New Jersey Transit trains, telling annoyed passengers that I wrote a novel. Joe Schwartz left something practical and Stuart Schwartz, a friend, cousin and Texan, got it to me and that helped with the final stages of a novel's birth.

Perhaps you're never done writing a novel as I'm learning. There's always another read through. Maybe it's like sending your child off to college, when you find a dozen reasons to re-inspect their dorm room, not wanting to leave them or yourself. At this stage of the process, I found a group of people as in focus group who read the manuscript and sat down with me and "my child" and gave feedback; the nourishment and critical awareness that was so needed. To these early settlers and colonists, I salute you. Don Olsen. David Pone. Gene Battifarano. Dave Samuels. Lois Weinstein. Toby Greenberg. Barbara Michaels. Dr. Martin Nagel. Joel Potter.

There's a business aspect as well and it's like a child's crib. Robert Feldman nurtured "my child" with conceptual advice akin to a birth announcement, the internet. Jason and Kenneth Beckerman; you walked me by the hand (and still do) into the new world; otherwise I'd still be sitting in a dimly lit public library doing research until I'm an octogenarian. All of the above is wonderfully heartfelt, filled with endless gratitude, a most powerful, enduring emotion.

Calvin Barry Schwartz   October, 2009

ONE

2003

Two middle aged men, dressed in mountain hiking gear, strolled thru Cathedral Square in Belluno, Italy. Late June mornings were cool, sweaters compensated. Towns in the Piave valley, fifty miles from Venice, still had medieval feel, resisting change, defining European allure.

They spoke in Italian.

"A little God now?"

"Where?"

"Church of San Rocco."

Antonio knew the area well.

Vito pointed to a facade. "Old, simple, historic."

"Sixteenth century."

At the church door, a young woman emerged, kerchief nearly containing jet black hair, but chest noticeably uncontained. The shorter man smiled, about faced, followed her, and abruptly turned back.

"No bra and she was in church praying. Does that make any sense?"

"Maybe she was praying for God to forgive the no bra?"

"No, asking God why such a chest is wasted in Belluno of all places."

"Do you think she got an answer inside?"

"No, but she told me to drop dead and stop following her. That was the quick about face."

"And you listened without putting up a fight. Did you tell her that you made special movies in Sweden?"

"Something told me a husband or boyfriend was too close, besides, what would I do with you?"

The church was empty. They sat a few pews apart but on opposite sides for fifteen minutes. Friends have a certain sense, knowing time to move on. A late model blue Punto waited a few blocks away with a rear filled with hiking gear, tents, food, extra boots, a case of water from Belluno, highly regarded in Italian water circles. Exaggerated mountain hats, with blue feather, lay on front seats.

"No balls to wear the hat."

"You too, no balls."

On the drive to Bellunesi Dolomites National Park for a first day of holiday hiking, twenty minutes out, was a tourist overlook. "Five minutes; I need a rock that won't mind being pissed on."

"Me too."

Both headed opposite for the same urgency, able to hear voices clearly.

"Hey Vito, pissing on rocks in the middle of nowhere under a perfect blue sky is almost meditative, religious."

"We should do it more often."

"We've got a week to piss on rocks and not think of anything."

"Don't say anymore, that's our agreement, no mention of work."

"By the way that was a magnificent chest back there. It just hit me. I should've done more, been aggressive, dropped to my knees or offered that Belluno maiden some money."

Reuniting, they found a boulder, smoked without a cloud in sight. "Why, no clouds?"

"We prayed for good weather. Somebody listened."

"Saint Anthony?"

"Maybe. You love that Saint, don't you?"

"Wish I could use him for more things."

Approaching the car, disbelief and horror struck like a lightning bolt, freezing both like deer caught in a sinister light beam. Four police cars formed a semi-circular ring around the Punto; police used open doors and car bodies for shields. Guns and rifles were aimed. Disbelief leads to outrage at obvious mistaken identity. Antonio and Vito wildly flailed hands, both yelling, "We've done nothing except piss in the woods. Mistake, mistake!"

Hands moving too close to waists where guns could be drawn from provoked cops to open fire, striking them dead. When the Punto was searched, a white opaque plastic bag filled with cash from a robbed Belluno bank was recovered.

Bank employees positively identified the car but bank robbers wore masks. The case was eventually closed. Cops received commendations- the ones who opened fire first and the decoy at the church.

1960

Vacant lots in the Weequahic section of Newark were hard to find, disappearing into two family houses, gas stations or small synagogues that became churches after the riots. One lot, bordered by Clinton Place, Shepard and Goodwin Avenues had scattered trees, grassy, weedy overgrowth and probably poison ivy except no one was sure what it looked like. Motherly fear of strange multi-leaf plants kept the incidence of itchy rashes near zero.

Some assumed the lot dated back to colonial times without evidentiary traces of mankind, then a few years back, cylindrical pieces of cement were uncovered by street urchins. A local patriarch decided the lot might've been a miniature golf course back in the twenties, reasoning forty years was enough time for overgrowth to play hide and seek.

The longest day of the year made a group of boys wait until nine p.m. to gather where three trees formed a canopy. There was a fourth tree; a decaying log with a saprophytic dank smell. After gathering handfuls of dried twigs and branches, the boys log rested.

"Who has matches?"

"I hope somebody has."

"Hey Sandy, are we waiting for anybody else?"

"Yeah Cohen, that new kid I told you about."

"So where the hell is he?" Cohen yelled, jumped on top of the log, pretending lookout, then grabbed his crotch in symbolic frustration.

"Across the street, behind the gas station." Sandy had a hard time finishing a mile run during gym class, and over compensated for physical deficiencies by organizing events he felt he could win. Some of the guys recognized that as a character flaw.

Cohen's shrill voice irritated. "Are you serious; that kid with a telescope?"

"None other."

"Why?"

"Why not, he lives a block away." Sandy's hand, with lit Pall Mall cigarette, pointed due east in the direction of Newark Airport then returned the crotch grab, making sure Cohen saw him, while cigarette now dangled precipitously between lips.

"Shoot, here he comes. *Dis-fucking* belief, you invited a stranger." Tommy mostly spoke in whispers. One of his high school teachers told his mother that whispering was due to a lack of confidence and more should be done to bolster him, especially at home.

"Dummy, Tommy, say hello, shake hands then he isn't a stranger anymore and besides I got my reasons."

"Sandy, no matter what anyone says, you're deep but *up*. We're all fucked-up as a matter of fact."

"Why?"

"Because, we're about to circle jerk with a total stranger."

The astronomer leaned a small telescope against a tree then watched it slide into weeds. Shoulders shrugged and right hand shot forward. "Hi, I'm Alex Zari."

Handshakes consummated over a small twiggy fire. Curious eyes focused on a forearm and face that was darker.

"You're not from around here?" A voice still irritated.

"No, from over there, a block away, Schuyler Avenue. We moved here last week."

"I meant New Jersey, maybe the whole east coast."

"Hey Cohen, try continent, you're so observant."

Sandy dropped to the ground, leaned into the fire, lighting another cigarette, mumbling, "Better throw newspaper into the fire, we need more light." A Playboy magazine appeared from underneath a tee shirt.

"I'm from Egypt, is that alright?"

Tommy still whispered, "Really?"

"An Egyptian Jew?"

"No, just Egyptian, but an American actually. My mother was born here, met my father in Egypt."

"You bet you're an American. If you live on Schuyler Avenue and go to Weequahic High, we're all Americans and that's what's important. I'm Elvin Stone."

They sized each other up, the two tallest boys, standing eye to eye. A simultaneous wink seemingly lasted as long as it took a beam of light to travel down from the sun and as Alex sensed, a special wink that would always be remembered.

"Hey Tommy, the Bamberger's bag, empty it."

Three pints of Gallo Muscatel wine sat on the log next to an ink stained wooden ruler. Sandy crunched the bag as Elvin connected fingers until the airborne bag bounced off his chin, through a make shift hoop, and yelling announcer like, "Two points for Weequahic! Do you think you'll make junior varsity, Sandy?"

"Nope. I don't give a shit but my father does, so the usual bribery, car, college down south. He knows coach Fein too. But I won't make the team. I'm out of shape."

"And the wine, who do we thank?"

Elvin seemed to worry about eavesdroppers hanging in branches overhead, looking up and around, finally confessing, "Joe Maddox. We bribed him with two pints, probably all gone by now. You can't talk to him anymore. His breath could kill or disinfect you."

Tommy finally raised his voice. "Go over the rules for the astronomer."

Wearing thick black plastic rectangular glasses, Marty spoke lawyerly, a vocal destiny for Rutgers Law School. "We draw lots to see who's first. Two swigs with or without Playboy help because it doesn't make a difference. When you're done, measure yourself and no sticking the ruler into stomach fat. Tommy would win hands down; he's probably got twelve inches of fat. The biggest wins whatever left over wine and a pack of Pall Mall."

"Looks like the new guy starts."

A perplexed look froze on Cohen's face before whining, "Shoot, you really can't be a Jew. I've never seen one like that. It's buried in there."

Elvin smiled, "And the new guy's real fast. Get's right down to business with no help from the magazine."

Two pairs of sneakers stomped on ashy remains of a bon fire that lit the way for Sandy to win a pack of cigarettes and a sip of Muscatel.

"Why do I have to clean up?"

"Well Alex, you started first. Now you're last. It's being fair and Sandy won so it's his choice. I felt like staying and helping you. How'd you like a bike tour around the Weequahic section?"

"When?"

"Go home, get a bike. Meet by the gas station in ten minutes."

"It's ten p.m."

"It's summer."

Elvin peddled faster, knowing where they were going, so handlebars weren't even but close.

"Do you know what it means when moving bike handlebars are almost even?"

"You're the astronomer, so tell me."

"Energy that propels us at the same speed, keeps us even, also makes us good friends for a long time. Actually TTE."

"TTE?"

"Not now." Alex motioned to dismount. "What about this store?"

"Marshall Banner's Hobby Shop. Millions of models. Tons of Testors' Glue. I made a battleship last year. My kid sister battled with it and won so no more making models until my sister is grown up. Come on, I want to show you something a block away. Wait, how do you know we'll be friends for a long time?"

"Don't think I'm weird or anything, but I see things. I know things. When I first heard you say we're all just Americans, something flashed in my head, like I've been hearing you for a thousand years and we've been friends for that long, you and me. It's just the way it is with me. I know it sounds strange. Everything we do was meant to be; my father meeting Sandy's father and then us."

"That's weird, because meeting you a while ago was the most natural thing. I felt it too. It's strange; when we winked, it was like we're old friends."

They crossed over and up Lyons Avenue- passed a drug store that Elvin loved walking into, smelling a hundred chemicals swooshed together, making you think good health was on shelves or behind the soda fountain- to a vastness protected by an iron picket fence that never ended. An outline of a building, far away, dark, looked like an imaginative old Victorian castle.

"What is it?"

Elvin described the scariest building in all of Newark, St. Michael's Orphanage; a place where they kept kids without parents and put a fence around like the kids did something wrong because they have no parents. Sometimes when he walked by, a few kids came up to the fence and put their faces near his. They were sad faces and he never knew what to say, so they ran away.

"Why do you think they fence them in; like they'd escape to where? They have no one. I hope….."

"Don't worry, you'll never be here. Me neither."

"How do you know that?" A right hand reached for Alex's shoulder to anchor a difficult answer.

"Because I look in my telescope all the time, at the sky and remember, I see things, sometimes even lying in bed in the dark. I walk at night by myself and look up and think about God and spirit and I see things."

"Tell me about seeing things."

"Things like my mother and father will be with me for a long time. They'll get old, gray and wrinkled. It's hard to explain. Don't you ever think about growing old and dying? Well I don't see myself dying, which means it'll happen a long time from now, beyond my vision, which means it won't happen soon. I see my parents getting old, but always with me, and bad stuff not happening for a long time. And now, my new old friend, I sense things with you, like me, with parents living for a long time and us being friends, TTE. Sometimes I can't sleep. Things inside my head get me up."

"Do you know who's going to win the World Series?" Eyes were squinting; comprehension battling cynicism.

"No, but I know there's something out there, calling me, waking me. I'm never alone even when I am alone. Now do you think I'm kind of weird?"

"No. I'm always looking for a place to be alone because there is an invisible someone out there for me to talk to. That was the second time you said TTE."

"I know."

A police car slowed then accelerated, siren on, fading quickly in humid night air.

"The guys asked you about being an Egyptian Jew before, but you said Egyptian, American."

"I'm half Muslim from my mother and Coptic Christian from my father. It's an unusual combination; one of the reasons my parents left Egypt. It's a bit easier to live in America. It is a scary building. I keep staring for signs of life, like a second floor light turning on because a kid without parents needs a bathroom."

"So what God do you believe in?"

"Just God and spirit."

"When you see things, did you ever see a UFO?"

"Not yet, but I will. That's why I keep my telescope lens clean."

"More biking tomorrow?"

"No more orphanages."

Two pairs of sneakers scraped the street. Schwinn bikes finished the descent of Shepard Avenue, stopping at the level corner of Osborne Terrace.

"That's Stein's, candy, soda and pinball. Tough Jews hang out there, right below that Coca Cola sign."

"You say Jews as if you're not one of them."

"I'm not tough. They'd kick the shit out of me if I walked in and forget what they'd do to you."

Turning around, staring at nasty steepness, they prepared to push. Two family houses lined both sides of the street. Elvin pointed to second floor porches, saying his mother thinks enclosed porches mean people are probably richer than the ones with flower pots on the open ledge ready to fall on someone's head.

"We used to take water balloons and try to knock those flower pots over, like on the boardwalk to win a prize- especially that house. An old lady lives there. She calls me a Bolshevik, whatever that is. When we get to my house follow my lead; my mother's got strange ideas about things."

"Prejudice?"

"Yeah."

Bikes rested several feet from a lone dying tomato plant in a small backyard with freshly turned soil and a large overhanging berry tree. Twenty years of berries staining their driveway, and Elvin's parents still had no idea what kind and if they were edible or worse.

A tall woman stood in the foyer, arms folded, hair under a kerchief, carpet sweeper off to the side. "I heard you stomping up stairs, and how often do I tell you, gently. You need to be in control of your body. Uncle George says you're going to be very tall. So, start practicing gentility."

"Mah, meet Alex. I told you about him. His father is a doctor at the Beth Israel Hospital; the kind that puts you to sleep during an operation."

"Elvin tells me you moved to Schuyler Avenue. You'll probably go to our synagogue. It's right there."

"My parents like to travel far to pray, Mrs. Stone. Tradition."

"Mah, we're going up to the attic to see the airport."

"I just cleaned the carpet in the living room so walk around to the front door."

Steps up to the attic creaked like a horror movie. They climbed out a window, onto the roof of the second story porch. Maple trees, one in front of each house, lined the street below, harboring a Buick, two Chevrolets and a station wagon with wood panel sides. A narration followed what house belonged to each car and if kids lived there. The station wagon was Irene's, with the biggest breasts in Weequahic and a new boyfriend every month, mostly from Barringer High School, where Italians went. Elvin never said a word to any of the boyfriends, mostly out of fear and not knowing how to talk *Newark Italian street*. His Spaulding ball once bounced across and a boyfriend picked it up, threw a middle finger and the ball back at Elvin, somehow managing to squeeze most of the air out.

"This is my sacred place. I'm here all the time. I stare at the *Fly Eastern Air Lines* building, catch a few take-offs, then lie down with hands behind my head. I love cumulous clouds and used to think they were part of heaven, faces of angels or recently departed relatives but I became more sophisticated. They're just clouds. Now, I'm with an astronomer and someone who sees things. Why did you guys move here? There are mostly Jews in the Weequahic section." Elvin shielded eyes from the sun as cumulous clouds coincidentally vanished after the praise statement.

"My father's job at the hospital, but really the high school. Weequahic can help me get into Princeton to study Astronomy."

Weequahic High School was solidifying a national reputation of producing more PhD degrees than anywhere else.

"The guys stared at your arm, face and other things. They could tell you're foreign, whatever the hell that means. Do you get that a lot?"

"Not in Egypt."

"Funny, how long....?"

"Been here? Actually I was born in Michigan. My parents came to America from Egypt because of religious differences."

"You sound like a pilgrim."

The scene suddenly darkened as a rogue cumulous cloud parked overhead. Alex began pinching his arm. "See this stuff. It gets us in trouble. In the grand design of things, we should've all been given the same skin; either, black, brown, red, yellow, or boring pink so no prejudice, crusades, concentration camps or men riding around with sheets over their heads. The less differences in people, less reasons for difference."

"I think the same thing all the time. I can't believe, we think so alike. Humans are a silly species. By the way, my mother is silly and so is my father. We argue about skin color all the time."

"My parents are silly too. I knew I liked you last night when you said we're all just Americans."

The cloud drifted, brightening a handshake.

"Hey, we're going down the shore to Belmar on Sunday, so you'll come with us."

"Sure, thanks. Say Elvin, look up in the sky, beyond the blue. Do you ever wonder about the universe? It goes on and on forever. My father makes me wonder about things, like what shape is the universe?"

"Shape?"

"Well, is it flat or does it come back to itself like the shape of a globe?"

"Why do you think about things like that? Why don't you try and figure a way for us to get into Stein's without getting our asses kicked so we could play the pinball."

"Let's make a deal with old man Stein. He gives us the keys to the store and we go play pinball at midnight. He can trust us. Everyone's sleeping but us."

"Funny."

Belmar beach was a throwback; bakery trucks canvassing each street, selling cup cakes and breadstuffs out of the rear and a boardwalk that smelled like telephone poles or do telephone poles smell like boardwalks? The odor never faded. Maybe they sprayed the wood with boardwalk cologne every year just after Memorial Day- Elvin almost believed. Jack Stone found an old picture of Belmar. Three brothers and unnamed women were laying on a wide beach. Elvin flipped the picture over, dated August 1937 in faded pencil.

"Where are you, Dad?"

"Taking. There's knocking."

"It's Alex."

A Nash-Rambler dropped Elvin's sister Judy, mother and a few beach chairs at Seventh Avenue beach while the men drove nearly back to the train station to park.

"When we get close to the beach, my father will point to an invisible hotel, *The Buena Vista*. They stayed in the attic when I was a kid. My father's voice gets wobbly every time we pass here. I asked my mom and she never said it directly, but I think it's where they did it for the first time. Maybe that's my beginning, a conception hotel."

"You may've begun near sand and me too, near the pyramids."

Tuna sandwiches were dealt out of a black bag like a deck of cards. A quart sized thermos dispensed overly sweet iced tea while the lifeguard's whistle was close enough to annoy and alarm. Martha Stone insisted on safe locations near whistles and warned about perils of swimming after eating in the same tone of voice that warned about poison ivy.

Elvin pointed to a fishing pier and beyond. "It's a private fishing club. They never let me on it, only under it, on my way to the Shark River, my favorite river in the world, let's go."

On both sides of the Shark River Inlet were boulders, defining the jetty. According to Elvin and geology books, it wasn't much of a river; just a mile or so long, connecting to a bay, where mostly party fishing boats docked, heading out to the Atlantic, returning either a half or full day later. Clouds were in a hurry, rapidly lightening, darkening the world, and agitating the ocean.

"My mother says white caps means a storm is coming."

"Yeah and she thinks eating, then swimming can kill you. It's funny; she's so much like my mother."

"Remember my attic roof? I feel close to heaven up there, well here too. It's weird, whenever I'm here, I find a lonely boulder and make sure no one's around, then I dream and talk out loud."

"Praying?"

"Kind of. I need to be a father; to teach and watch a child grow and take to a baseball game or ballet. Someday I'll bring them here and tell what I thought when I was a kid. Am I normal to think about kids, when I don't even have a rubber in my wallet yet?"

"It's a little messed up. As for me, when alone, I'm on a mountain, staring at the sky. I'd be afraid to take a child to a dark mountain."

"Why?"

"I'm afraid what's beyond the sky. Remember, I see things."

"Are we normal? We don't think like sixteen year olds? We're so alike. Friends forever, you know that?"

"I don't like that word."

"Forever? Why?"

"Not sure."

Elvin extended a hand, helping him down and reminding to keep everything secret.

As they approached, Martha asked, "Another tuna boys?"

"Hey Mah, are there peaches in the black bag?"

The boys moved away from the security of the blanket, facing each other, kicking at sand in back and forth motions and burying respective peach pits, thinking sand is infinitesimal. A shiny object appeared in the zone between their heels as they jumped forward, grabbing at a gold watch.

"It's a gold omen and must have something to do with our friendship. We'll switch off wearing it; six months you, then me and so forth."

"Agreed."

"Done. But my parents won't understand sharing; something about possession and law so stick it into your jock strap and keep it out of my mother's sight."

Clinton Place snaked around the Weequahic section. Watson's Bagels, with original wood floors, had large brown bags of plain and salted bagels along the back wall for delivery and a comfortable curb for dining.

"I can't believe you never had a bagel."

"And you never had babaganoush."

"The white stuff your mother made the other day? Sounds like someone's grandmother. How do you spell it?"

"Never mind."

"We've got time for a quick pinball game. Watch keeping good time? Five more months."

Decker's Candy Store had five swiveling fountain chairs and a pinball machine which lured kids that Stein's would never allow. Alex and Elvin could only dream about the pinball at Stein's. Sometimes they'd corner a marginal kid-someone who got beat up only occasionally-to find out about pinball challenges they were missing in life because they'd get beat up if they ever went in. Elvin sighed that poor Mr. Stein, if he actually existed, never knew how much business was lost by not finding a way to let them play his pinball game.

"Amazing how good you've become, Alex."

Bells and whistles, stainless steel balls elevating then descending, finally dropping from sight through a hole scarcely able to swallow it and flippers desperate to maintain the life of the ball was part of the *world*, just like taking a warm bottle of Coca Cola from wooden cases piled on the side when old man Decker wasn't looking. You pretended cold and refreshing, wiping lips, so Decker thought the bottle came from the bright red machine. Kids even pounded the side, simulating the noise of a bottle coming out. Elvin managed to save bottle caps; his mother thought anything saved might be valuable someday.

"You're a good pinball teacher. Now we're both going to summer jobs in different drug stores with me at Rubin Brothers and you at Kraft." Alex wiped his lips, complaining about not liking warm Coca Cola.

"Thank your Doctor father for your job and Sandy for watching over you."

"And you can thank your relatives for your job."

The machine died, lights went out. Alex almost never tilted it. "You jinxed me, not fair."

"Alls fair. Shoot, I better watch for the bus."

"Why do you take the bus to downtown Newark, then another to your relative's store when you can go up Chancellor Avenue instead and save hours?"

"I go through Newark, so I see how people are forced to live."

"Forced?"

"The skin thing again. Their skin is black and it's easy to see the difference. We blend in; well I blend in better." Elvin threw a playful punch to Alex's bicep.

"My mother said a colored family moved in eight blocks away. My father is ready to start looking at new houses in Maplewood. He won't live near them."

"Mine too."

"After high school, when eight blocks become one. It's so wrong, being afraid of people or not liking them because of the color of skin or not wanting to live near them. I yelled at my mother. She used the *F* word for the first time-sounded funny with her Mideast accent."

"There's my bus. Kraft Pharmacy awaits me. Sweeping basements and sidewalks. At fifty cent's an hour, I'm the best around. I never asked what you get."

"Don't."

Of all the Public Service buses in all the world especially those driving around Newark, New Jersey, I happen to be sitting by the only broken window that won't open on the hottest day of the year and people are standing to get my seat. Thanks Humphrey Bogart for the thought. Damn, I loved Casablanca.

Elvin pressed face to the window. It felt cooler. The bus stopped, jerked, started and sent exhaust fumes into a flattened nostril. Bus fumes were strangely appetizing. If he got to work early, then maybe an Italian hot dog from *Volpari's*; mustard, peppers, onions, potatoes, non-kosher meat all shoved into a bread pocket. Official hunger returned even after two dry bagels on a curb.

Summer heat brought out throngs of faceless people sitting on steps or looking out second story windows. He thought America the Beautiful and spacious skies but everything was so close together on Clinton Avenue. Elvin was a stickler for detail and it bothered. It's not necessarily a good thing to notice minute detail, so he thought, because it's burdensome, with responsibility to act, or feel or have something annoy your conscience so much, it messes with your sleep. Later in life, he'd realize it was sensitivity and humanity and something else, impacting life-long sleep.

Pervasive sadness in faceless faces made him think about his mother's pressure cooker; that gray steel pot with tight fitting cover, where meats or vegetables simmer forever. He never liked the taste of anything which came from that pot; there wasn't enough ketchup in the world. Newark outside his window was a pressure cooker without human tolerance, acceptance or understanding to ease or reduce.

Eyes filled with sadness seeing this world of mournful neglect. He took a sheet of notebook paper from a back pocket, folded it four times, leaned on knee, removed a yellow pencil poised between ear and temple and scribbled, "On a bus bound for market, I saw people leaning out of second floor windows; it was hot, no one had faces, except on shadows cast by brick and wood." For a brief moment, wonder about the words and would life's bus rides to wherever, lead him to a career bound Smith-Corona typewriter?

Elvin's parents thought about moving when one of the colored families outside his bus window decided to move close. How could he find a way to tell people outside the window, he was different than his parents? The bus at downtown Newark for the next leg was named *54 Devine Street* and reminded about a book his English teacher told him to read over the summer, *A Streetcar Named Desire*. If ever a writer- he smiled at the idea- maybe he'd write someday about a bus named *Devine*. The bus waited and spewed aimless exhaust on Broad Street, but perfect timing for that next leg, skirting the west side of Newark, meaning less sad, faceless faces and hopefully working bus windows.

Aunt Evelyn had a sixth sense or even a tenth sense if that existed. She was waiting outside Kraft's Pharmacy, arms folded as he crossed the street so therefore no Italian hot dog.

Evelyn Kraft was short, emaciated but well groomed and if a nonchalant passerby paid attention to her face, one might see a nose borrowed from the made-up face of Margaret Hamilton, that sweet wonderful actress, typecast for life, playing the wicked witch in *The Wizard of Oz*. When Elvin laid the observation on his mother, she covered his mouth, warning him to forget and never repeat, but not before Martha Stone laughed harder then ever, which sanctioned his telling the world that Aunt Evelyn really was a wicked witch.

"Why do you insist on that Devine Street bus? Do you know how much longer it takes?"

"I people watch Aunt Evelyn."

"Take a walk with me up the street. That girl keeps on coming into the store looking for you."

"Huh."

"The pretty one; our good customer's niece from Italy with a big cross around her neck. She's visiting for the summer. Unless you want me to tell your parents about the cross and the girl, make sure you discourage or disappear. We like disappear better, that way we don't risk losing a good customer."

"Disappear?"

"Basement. Do more sweeping down there if she comes in. We'll keep your broom handy or you can even take a nap on top of the *Modess* sanitary napkin boxes."

"Aunt Evelyn, I'm the only one who ever goes in the basement and my mother taught me to be clean and not messy. Does it really need all that sweeping?"

A new addition to my summer job duties, disappearance.

He smiled, thought about Dorothy and the ruby slippers, a real wicked witch in his life, *Modess* sanitary napkins and how every store wraps them in brown paper bags even before the kids or fathers that mothers send in, actually buy them. "Why bother going through all the trouble with pretty blue packaging if it gets covered up by the stores before it hits the shelves", he once whispered, taping the brown bag shut. Elvin was pretty sure what they're used for, but not entirely. Once he asked Martha, but she was too busy making gefilte fish in the kitchen sink.

TWO

There are certain times in life when air has unique aroma. Christmas Eve two years ago, visiting Aunt Evelyn and Uncle George, Elvin remembered a neighbor's fireplace shooting out puffs of smoke, aerating Kent Place in solemnity and holiness. He was Jewish, but there was a magic in the holiday. Frenetic energy, sights and smells, seasonal music like *Adeste Fideles*, all evoked childhood memories running around the neighborhood a few days after Christmas, finding a discarded tree, hiding it behind the coal bin in the cellar, so he could have a tree without mother evoking religious guilt that God would be very upset that a Jewish boy rescued a holiday tree.

Excusing himself from the dinner table, Elvin needed deep air inhalations. Deep pensive breaths in solitude soothed a restless mind. He walked by a slouching Uncle George, barely lifting heavy eyes, as if too tired for life. Standing on front steps, he dreamed that a sparkling celestial star would lead him to a special place and person; a girl somewhere in Vailsburg who could help him attain manhood. He'd fall madly in love, become a father, and take his child to the Shark River. Life was that simple; just find that special star.

Front steps were cold. Brutal cold made him think of Grandma Rebecca, recently deceased, lying in the ground, cold, lonely and missing Aunt Evelyn's special sweet carrot dish. Elvin wished Rebecca was still alive even though she took over his room, forcing him in with his sister Judy. Being a kid with a grandmother suffering ravages of diabetes, gangrene, and a leg amputation was hard. A commode in his old room generated smells he'd never forget and stolen glimpses of his mother crying, emptying foul liquid in the toilet. Mother knew about his surveillance, and told him, that seeing real life would make him a better person. Cold steps on Christmas Eve conjured up feelings that made him wonder where they came from and who put them there.

Two boys, wearing wooly hats- the kind a mother knits while watching the Arthur Godfrey show- ear muffs, gloves, stopped walking in the middle of a street lined with trees as tall as Redwoods, or so they imagined.

"Why do you suppose they're much taller compared to the ones by our houses?" Alex bent his head back, looking straight up, and grabbing tree bark for balance.

"Maybe the trees and houses came before ours, so they grew taller, had a head start."

"Good answer, Elvin. Makes sense. How much further to your temple?"

"Seven blocks."

"Your parents belonged there?"

"Just for a couple of years; mostly for my sister and Hebrew school. Rabbi Prinz is amazing. He fought Nazis, escaped, came here and fights for civil rights, human dignity and is good friends with Dr. King, like I told you. He thinks *silence* is one of mankind's main faults."

A white Chevy burned rubber, pulling out across the street. Friends sense things. It was quiet for a few minutes, no one talked, both leaning on opposite sides of a tree, until the lean slipped into cold concrete sitting.

Voices grew louder, needing strength to work their way around the tree. Alex talked about difficulties being Coptic Christian, living in Egypt while Elvin compared it to being Jewish in Jersey, both cases of minority living. They stared through motionless leaf-less branches at the starry sky.

"It's quite a sky, Elvin?"

"You want me to say scary?"

"Of course I do. Whenever you question spirit or God, remember how we're going to hear Dr. King speak tonight and we're sitting on a winter sidewalk staring at heaven. My father told me Albert Einstein knew the most incredible intelligence put the universe together and that it's so perfectly simple yet complicated, only God could've done it. Last night my father talked about some cat in the 1930's that was put in a box with poison and radiation but the cat was both alive and dead at the same time. So I laughed and he yelled at me."

"Why?"

"Because he wants me to think. So I yelled at him about wanting to move because a colored family is moving close to us. He said I was right. He never admitted, I was right about anything before and changed the subject pretty fast. Then he said to think about an atom and how they come together to form a molecule."

"What's that have to do with God?"

"Everything. If in the universe, the force between an atom and an electron is too strong, electrons aren't shared so molecules aren't formed and no life. Same thing, if the force is too weak, electrons can't go anywhere, so no molecules to form life. My father said life is so intricate, it has to be God."

"And here we are, on Earth, so perfect then, but we can't live next door to a colored person. That's the way we look at things, small, never a big picture; it's why we're a silly species."

"It takes pure friends to sit around a tree, freezing our asses off, talking about God and human prejudice."

"Pure."

Alex's voice preached, "We're really lucky to hear Dr. King talk. It's not every day that a civil rights leader known around the world comes to Temple B'nai Abraham in Newark in the middle of January."

Folded arms, eyes aimed at sky, Elvin was silent, distant, well into thought drifting and unresponsive.

"Elvin!"

"I was just remembering Christmas Eve a few years ago on my Aunt and Uncle's porch. It was cold like now. I thought about my grandmother and blacks and whites; so many real problems in the world and those two colors can't mix together because of prejudice and hate. What wasted energy. I'm getting tired of bus rides through Newark's injustice. I wish my father would sit down and talk to me like yours does. I can't remember really talking to my father. I'm not sure if he likes the Yankees or Dodgers."

"We're graduating high school in a few months. Maybe we'll go down south and take real bus rides, protest and sign up voters?" Alex walked around, reached down to Elvin.

"Maybe. How do we help?"

"We feel, just like we're doing now. We'll listen to Dr. King but I feel worry now."

"About him?"

"About people who don't like him."

"Are you seeing things?"

"Let's go."

Air was redolent with blossoms and warmth, churned together so memories would always serve up hope and life's promise. Maybe that's what moved Elgar when he composed *Pomp and Circumstance*. June graduation from Weequahic High School was a few weeks away.

A motherly sermon about falling in love and how it's just as easy with a rich Jewish girl as poor was delivered while Elvin stood on a kitchen chair during alterations on a first suit since Bar Mitzvah.

"Stop moving around. Do you want me to pin your ankle? Do you understand?"

"Sure, pins hurt."

"No, rich is easier. Look at Alex's father, a doctor. He got a car for graduation, because....."

"Money."

"Right."

"Wrong, Mah. It's the money *he* earned at the drug store. Finish already, we're going down the shore."

Shore season wasn't official until July Fourth. A few fishermen were overhead on the pier. Sand seemed fresher, virginal, like what Columbus saw, and no human footprints, only bird and animal. The sojourn to Shark River was actually part of their Independence Day; first time without parents a few beaches away. Their jetty side was barren except for a few gulls who relinquished territorial rights, making them cover heads. Facing the horizon, Elvin pointed to a distant ship.

"Medgar Evers."

"I know, it bothered me all week. I punched the wall above my pillow in anger, made a crack and moved Willie Mays to cover-up."

"Why'd they kill Evers?"

"I heard a sermon a few weeks ago. The Priest asked forgiveness because his sermon was old stuff, but relevant. He quoted Jesus. *Forgive them Father for they know not what they do.* Just like killing Medgar Evers."

Elvin stood, shielding eyes, thinking loudly that the distant ship was some kind of battleship, maybe on its way to the Middle East. The ship could've been the model his sister destroyed after a month of working on it.

"My luck, that's my model all grown up." A smile disappeared. "We still don't know what we're doing."

"Right."

Elvin's head shook back and forth emphatically. "Then when will we? You're the one who sees things?"

"Probably never or when it's too late. We're destined for things too late, never learning lessons. Why kill Medgar Evers? Do you think we're being given all these lessons of life for a reason?" Alex settled into *The Thinker* pose.

"It's always too late. We're a *too late* species, destined and stuck with it."

"Let's graduate. We can change things but first our California vacation awaits us."

The conversation shut off. Stubborn gulls returned, swooping close by, settling down on the other side of the inlet. A lone fishing excursion boat waited for a draw bridge to rise up. When the boat finally passed, a few forlorn fishermen waved at the boys from the rear, just above the scripted name of the boat, *Sedona*.

A Philco radio played *The Tymes* singing, "As we stroll along together," loud enough to carry from the kitchen into a small bathroom with cast iron tub. The door was ajar, so Elvin could hear while submerged, feet propped over faucet. It was a last bathtub day, ceremoniously honoring graduation from high school in a way to remember forever. Water swished in cyclonic fashion around the drain. Elvin stuck a finger into the drain trying to alter the course of history. The song would be remembered because lyrics suggested he'd be strolling in a few hours with classmates for the last time as they entered permanency of life. Martha yelled to get decent; she was coming to do her hair. A thick, slow flowing sperm-like liquid, sticking to palms, finally disappeared into sandy brown hair. Hard to use because of what it looked like, but Elvin's hair was frozen all day.

"Let me look at you. You'll be a parent one day and know how I feel. Where did the years go? My boy, my son."

"Mah, do you know where to meet Alex's parents?"

"For the tenth time, yes. Get dressed and go. They'll rehearse without you."

Untermann Field was crowded; over flow was relegated to aluminum bleachers opposite the security of concrete stands. A wire connecting a loud speaker system dangled between a second floor classroom at Chancellor Avenue School and the Weequahic Indians press box. The marching band lined up under the dangling wire; first chords of *Pomp and Circumstance* were practiced in late morning heat.

"It's a perfect time to finally meet. Our sons have been friends since we moved here. We're Adel and Sura Zari."

"Jack and Martha Stone."

Martha extended her hand, first securing a kerchief in the breeze.

"I have to say, when Elvin first spoke about you- he made it seem you'd be joining our synagogue. Today's youth under estimates parents. We did to our parents. Of course we welcome diversity and encourage Elvin to seek it out. He always talks about your special religious family."

"Thank you. In this mixed up world, special is a rewarding word. We're a multi-family; each with freedom to find God in our own way. Alex knows to find that comfort."

Adel, short, balding, round faced with moustache and darker skin and perhaps an only foreign look anywhere in the stands, shook hands with Jack.

Sura held Martha's hand, securing the beginning of a long friendship. "Alex hesitates and sometimes I think he waits to see where the better sermon is each week."

"My wife is the humorist. Anesthesia, blood and hospital wear me down."

"Climbing up ladders, showing women shoes who insist on three sizes smaller, then battling, shoving and twisting wears me down and my crotch. Five out of ten kick me there." Physically opposite Adel, Jack subconsciously ran fingers through thick gray wavy hair.

"Jack is our humorist."

"Here come the boys."

"It's the most perfect solemn music. Time to cry." Crumpled up napkins came out of Martha's pocket book.

Elvin waved then towards the end of the procession Alex waved. They knew where parents were; key was to sit close to the famous dangling wire. The boys carefully planned parents finally meeting.

An after party was tradition. The Tavern Restaurant had cheesecakes with candles lined up in the back waiting for the overflow Weequahic crowd.

Elvin stood up. "Let's toast with champagne. To Alex; at Princeton and me at Rutgers in good old downtown Newark and to this summer in California and Arizona, for our last fling of youth and innocence. I even took my last bath this morning."

A boy, walking ahead of two companions, pinched a forearm and then threw it in front, impeding forward motion.

"You might think I'm crazy now, walking Hollywood Boulevard as the sun sets. It's hot and there isn't a breeze, only a hint of car exhaust but you know what I really smell guys? Dreams. When I think of our time together and maybe someday, I'll be in Paris or London and smell something close to this, but I'll always think of now and you guys. This moment forever etched in the memories of my nostril."

"Crazy, Elvin, nope, screwed up, sure. But I'll confess and give you the benefit; there are dreams all over the place. Check out the eyes of people walking by; glassy, dilated, half closed, inebriated, needing sleep."

"Alex, reminder, that's my mother's nephew Steven, a junior at Stanford. He's a future doctor, so he uses medical terms in everyday life situations, so he can't say drunk, has to say inebriated."

"We're here guys, *Pando and Ernest*, Hollywood's famous restaurant. Try and act twenty-one."

Cousin Steven held the door open. He was older, taller, and with California swagger, knowing exactly where going, mostly from been there, done that.

Mahogany booths with high sides, red coated waiters, and sense of impending celebrity made the Jersey boys look around. A cautionary whisper about looking less touristy was ignored as Jersey necks rotated one hundred eighty degrees, back and forth, non-stop.

"Tourist, cousin Elvin, that word fits you so well. Check the menu then I'll suggest."

"Steven. Alex and me….."

"I know, you're going to be college freshman on budgets and can't afford real food here. Why don't we order six different potato sides? They're famous for that. Bread is free and you'll notch another vacation highlight."

"Seriously?"

"Sure.

"Alex?"

"Done."

"Done."

"Do you still smell dreams?"

Steven and Elvin's mothers provided tall genes which left Elvin nearly six feet three and him nearly six feet five. Mid eastern genes arrested Alex at six feet. Back on Hollywood Boulevard, after a boring starchy meal, Steven waved keys fixed on a pair of Vegas dice.

"Keys to what?"

"A friend's apartment at UCLA. He's in London for a month which means if we acquire the company of the opposite sex, there's a private place for us."

The Jersey boys stared at each other, knowing what each was thinking; morals, values and expectations. Living with virginity, they wanted it to continue for the immediate future. Eyes winked to notions of compromise and appeasement. Friendship took them to knowing what each other was thinking- perfect non-verbal communication. Finally, Elvin softly mouthed the words, *peace in our time*, but loud enough, on purpose.

"What the hell does *peace in our time* mean?"

"Remember I'm a history student. That British schmuck, Neville Chamberlain uttered those words of appeasement after he met with Hitler. He thought peace was guaranteed, so he gave Hitler the Sudetenland, thinking that's all he wanted."

"Stop, this is Hollywood. What the hell does that have to do with anything?"

"We're not ready for the big time. You're my cousin and I need your respect. When we winked, it wasn't to disappoint you completely."

"So, if I understand all this bullshit, you just want blow jobs. You're appeasing me. That's it!"

"See that Alex, my smart intuitive cousin."

"See this, boys? It's a fifty and your Uncle Marty figured things too. See this; it's Carol's phone number. She's a senior theater major at UCLA who likes fifty dollars and fellatio."

College apartments have distinctive ambience; cinder blocks, sweat socks strewn, paddles with Greek letters hanging near composite pictures of boys who look alike in a tonsorial way, and empty liquor bottles arranged on a mantle by a local interior design studio.

"Your friend cleaned up before London?"

"Cleanest I've ever seen it here." Steven's index finger covered about two hundred and forty degrees.

"Fooled me, but strange smell, can't place it." Dropping to all fours, performing a blood hound impersonation to a standing ovation, then Alex took a bow.

"Southern California just got out of wet season. It's dampness."

"No Steven, Jersey is damp but this has kind of a dungeon, light never shines smell." Alex picked up an ashtray from a coffee table top, missing all its legs. "Whatever, here it is!"

"Ground rules. Fridge filled with beer thanks to morning reconnaissance and once again, Uncle Marty. That door over there with masking tape in X design; that's X dimension; means one at a time and take all the time. There's plenty Peter Paul and Mary, Platters and Elvis records. Don't play too loud but no Bill Haley please- I'm tired of him. Carol is sweet, smart and talented. She'll be a real star one day. By the way Elvin, she loves old movies.

"An alley girl?"

"Huh."

"Right up my alley."

"Any questions? Treasure this first oral experience. I still remember mine and always will. It's poignant; another big word. Oh, I go first, and yeah, I went out with Carol in high school."

The Jersey boys watched a tiny blonde girl stand on her toes, jumping to reach Steven's lips.

"Can one of you take this bag from me and put it in the bathroom? Don't worry; it's just orange juice and mouthwash, my own gargling concoction."

Elvin was sleeping when Alex shook the startle reflex out of him with an esoteric wink. Alex held both Elvin's shoulders. "She's not a good religious conversationalist."

Crossing into X room, *Love Me Tender* was playing. After a few moments of silence, Carol sensed reinforcement as virgins need, faked a cough, throwing noise onto the scene while the record needle scratched back and forth.

Disbelievingly, Elvin shook his head, "You're so pretty, why?"

"Not another sermon. I'm in college, earning a couple of bucks because my parents are divorced and my father disappeared. It pays for acting classes, like a casting couch."

"What's your favorite movie?" Arms folded, standing, while she sat spread eagle at the edge of the bed.

"What is it with you Jersey boys, all you want to do is talk. Alex tried converting me to a life of no sex for money. My favorite movies; *Casablanca* and *From Here to Eternity*. The last scene when Deborah Kerr throws flowers into the ocean made my heart hurt all day and I cried black and white tears, but you'll have to see for yourself someday."

"*Casablanca*, me too! The last scene when Bogart and Claude Rains disappear into the foggy airport affected my heart too! This may sound crazy, but I have to go to Casablanca airport someday, maybe with a friend and it has to be foggy, just like the movie. I'll walk exactly where they did and breathe the same air Bogart did; air that passed through his lungs. Then I'll say something about the beginning of a beautiful friendship. Am I crazy?"

"No! Why aren't you out here in acting school with me? By the way, you don't have to go that far."

"Excuse."

"The movie airport, it's not Casablanca, but Van Nuys, just down the road from here."

Deep in thought, far away, maybe across the Atlantic on the northern African continent, Elvin asked, "Think it'll be foggy soon? Come with me to the airport."

"You're cute. I've got something better for you to do. There's a neat store on Melrose, mostly high brow antiques. For whatever reason, they've got old movie things. I saw *Casablanca* stuff there."

"Melrose? What's the store called?"

"Charles Blue, something or other."

A wallet with a loose lanyard string produced a sheet of three holed notebook paper. "Holy Shit! It's my uncle's store. I thought so. My father's brother Charles is also a movie writer, middle initial A for asshole. I have a cousin, but never met him. They're rich. We're poor. My mother wrote down all the information and lectured me on being noble, importance of family and even Gandhi, non-violence and all. I'll go there tomorrow. He'll never recognize me. Want to come?"

"Are we done?"

"Yeah, just don't tell Steven we didn't do anything, it's embarrassing."

"You're cute. Well, let me go gargle anyway. Sorry, busy tomorrow." She jumped up to kiss Elvin. "Tall family."

Three boys stood statuesque, heads cocked forty-five degrees, staring, deciphering the cryptic meaning of a Hollywood store with a strange name of an owner; one of the *Roy G. Biv* colors, Steven added. A white sign with blue lettering proclaimed *Charles A. Blue, Finery in Collectibles*. Were they trying to deter those that didn't understand the store name to keep moving along?

"We could be the youngest people to cross the threshold. A table in our den where my father keeps a pipe and ashtray came from here and our dining room table too."

"Do they only want *comprehendables*? Is that a word Steven?"

"Think it is; means customers who know what they're walking into. Nobody driving by on Melrose sees *Finery* and *Collectibles* thinks they ought to be shopping there."

"Lace curtains on the window mean no one will have enough cash for anything here." Alex held the door, role playing a butler, voice squeezing into a British accent.

"Why do you think the last name is Blue if he's a Stone like you and your Dad."

"Not a real Stone, but an asshole."

Antique tables, buffets, chairs and mirrors from eras and continents were presented elegantly, with a hint of incense wafting around. Lighting looked like the Broadway stage and credits on an index card acknowledged award winning lighting directors who lent services to Charles Blue. Looking at watches in unison, it was a long time to be browsing without signs of life.

"Sinking feeling guys. Wild goose chase. Carol screwed up, no *Casablanca* or movie stuff anywhere."

"Carol's smart. What's that in the back?"

A slow moving ceiling fan right out of *Rick's Café* from *Casablanca* circulated over a French Louis XV extension dining table-nineteenth century. Champagne glasses on a silver tray and a caviar jar hosted one side of the table and two full bottles of *Vichy Water, Eau Minerale*, on the other side.

Elvin ran to the fan. "Just like the movie. Wait! The fan is from the movie! Oh my God! Those Vichy Water bottles are from the movie too- extras and Humphrey Bogart signed them both. My God, Bogart, his autograph! Louis, Claude Rains threw the water in the garbage near the end of the movie. They kept a few extra bottles around just in case. Someone got Bogart to sign them. No price tag. I've got to have one."

A shaking, uncontrollable hand touched the bottle, carefully avoiding the signature. Suddenly a figure approached, unreal height, a Transylvanian like beard, shoulder length hair with the nerve of being gray, and open toe sandals. He came from inside or behind a huge armoire making the boys think, the wooden monstrosity was a coffin for daytime use.

"Most of our clientele understands the necessity of non-tactile behavior. Need I say more young man?"

"Pardon."

"Don't touch, not for sale. Who referred you to *Charles A. Blue*?"

"A girl who gave us a blow job last night. What else you want to know and my parents are good customers here." A couldn't resist smile erupted over Steven's face.

For the first time, tall Elvin felt insignificant, staring upwards at a scary man, maybe too skinny to have played a blood thirsty Dracula monster, and on closer examination, too effeminate to be scary anyway.

"Sir, I believe my uncle Charles Stone is the owner here. I'd love to buy one of the Vichy Water bottles. How much are they?"

"As I said, not for sale and presume it would be in the hundreds if it were."

"Would you please call my Uncle Charles for me?"

"Uncle how?"

"My father Jack's brother."

"One moment."

A long bony finger rotated around a phone dial, giving substance to the notion that life is proportional. How perfect the world Elvin thought, if he could walk out with that bottle. Long gray hair would never bother him again. Prayers and incantations were whispered pacing back and forth.

"Young man, the phone is for you."

In the theater of great reunions with so much to say and get caught up on, Elvin said several "thank you" and "of course I'll call you tomorrow."

"I would love to see you and Aunt Edith. Letting me buy the bottle makes this the best day of my life since my birth canal crossing!"

A quivering body couldn't find a place for itself, with more frantic pacing. An eternity passed watching a towering bearded man write a receipt.

"Twenty-five dollars young man. It thrills me that we're close to the birth canal experience, good day."

Four kisses were placed around the bottle neck before returning it to a bag. Hugs took place on the sidewalk while store linen curtains swayed.

"Your fucking Uncle still charged you."

"To be expected from Uncle asshole. This bottle will be with me the rest of my life. It never gets opened, not ever."

"There has to be one special occasion."

"Well, awful special, poignant, the word you used last night, Steven."

Four more kisses lipped the bottle neck.

"What about calling your Aunt and Uncle tomorrow and seeing them. I heard you promise."

"He's an asshole and I lie to assholes."

Heads rotated excitedly from side to side, front windows down, rear windows almost, but car manufacturers didn't make them to roll all the way down. The Stanford scholar theorized, it was logical, keeping infants and dogs from premature evacuation. Las Vegas was alive with electric desert energy.

"Guys, welcome to Vegas: Sin City. Gambling. Women. Lights. Action. Sinatra. Carl says Sinatra's friends helped Kennedy get elected."

"Hey Steven, tell us more about Carl. We'll be camping under Arizona stars with him for a week." Elvin's binoculars were adjusted at a traffic light and aimed up at the Stardust Hotel. "Holy shit! There's a nude woman in a window up there. Huge tits, I think. You lose perspective."

Alex's voice rose to frantic, "Let me see, Elvin. Hey Steven, pull over to the side before the light turns green."

Steven panicked, afraid of missing something. "Is she still there? Let me take a look."

"There are hands around them now."

Binoculars stayed with Elvin. "What a way to enter Vegas. Talk about living up to billing!"

Steven lost patience, "Carl is my fraternity brother, psych major, spiritual guy and eccentric."

"Eccentric means *putz* back in Jersey."

"Carl is far from it and you'll like him. He moved here a few years ago. His father was a real shrink; a medical doctor but he had enough of Hollywood shrinkage as he calls it. There's plenty of money and he wanted desert living while the mother is back in LA."

"Divorced?"

"Yeah. Carl knows a lot of shit and he's close with his father; that's why he's in Vegas. The father was a shrink to interesting people." Steven turned around, making sure they saw a wink. "He closed his practice and copies of medical records sit in an empty bedroom. Carl loves to read and he's good with deciphering medical handwriting. Get it guys?"

Blonde hair, blue eyes accentuated by tortoise plastic eyeglasses on a six foot frame threw a duffel bag into the trunk and jumped into the back seat with Alex, who immediately thought, but decided not to say anything, that a real beach boy was sitting next to him.

"Let's see what we've got; two Jews, an Egyptian and a Methodist, me, who's finishing a calendar year without the benefit of Sunday sermons. Carl Wyler here. You must be the Egyptian. Your forearm is a dead giveaway."

"Impressive work Steven."

"You mean the way I briefed Carl?"

"Briefing is a lubricant for human relations; need to know and that kind of stuff. I made Steven tell me everything, right down to your ill-fated blow jobs the other night." A shiny flask slid out of a jeans pocket. "I'd offer you boys but I don't mess with under age drinking."

The flask maintained perpendicularity for several seconds.

"Steven! How the hell did you know that?"

"Remember about Carol and me."

"Let's not dwell guys; next stop Grand Canyon." Another perpendicular event emptied Carl's flask, inducing sleep until the North Rim.

Four boys stood quietly at the precipice. Hands slid into pockets, not knowing what to do with moveable body parts. Reverence, awe and respect for nature mixed with cool summer air at several thousand feet. As far as eyes could see, vastness, depth, billions of years of muted earthy colors, and silence, not like silence in Jersey, but silence from deep outer space that found its way to earth. For Alex, everything was as he imagined all these years.

Steven watched Carl taking in Alex, breathing erratic.

"Elvin, you're the man of dreamy words, say something."

"Better sit down guys because I'm speechless, believe it. But….."

"But?"

"We're at the umbilicus of mother Earth, like God's planetary creation began here in front of our eyes. All things must have a beginning point and here it is, right?"

"As long as the word *beginning* is in the dictionary, then we really could be standing on that word. Steven asked me to plan stuff, so let's move on."

"Been here before?"

"A couple of times with my father. He likes to come here, smoke indigenous plants, pre-dried on the roof of the car-just teasing guys, so stop staring. Steven, show the Jersey boys the three sets of car keys I told you to bring."

"Why three?"

"No locksmith within a thousand miles of here; the brilliance of a long suffering paranoid condition."

"Funny."

"I know, let's hike."

"Does this trail have a name?"

"North Kaibab, I think. Watch out, we're sharing paths with mules that aren't toilet trained yet."

A large flat rock formation invited hikers. The Jersey boys removed sneakers to rub at circulation.

"At midnight, if there's no artificial light and real dark then you can see everything celestial." Alex's knap sack formed a pillow, hands slipping underneath. "Elvin, it's like your attic roof."

"Define celestial." Sunglasses replaced Carl's tortoise frames.

"UFO."

Six hours brought hiking into the canyon to a fatigued close. Snakes, high flying birds with large wingspans as well as humans and mules, constituted life form sightings and a visit to a real general store constituted supplies for outdoor dining.

"All we're missing is a Conestoga wagon, a tied-up horse and ten gallon hats."

"Do Yankee hats count?"

"Nope."

Carl was still wearing sunglasses. "Dark enough for you guys? Puts you in the mood? How's my cooking?"

"Mood for what?"

"Alex, pick a topic."

"The sky."

"I thought you'd pick that. Not so much here, but when we head south to a town called Sedona, there's plenty thoughts on UFO sightings. And we, meaning the good old USA are not the only ones who cock our heads to dark summer sky and look for shiny saucer like objects."

"You lost me."

"NATO. You know, across the Atlantic, protectors of freedom from big bad Russians and commies. Well NATO happens to think collectively there's a bunch of saucer pilots who watch us regularly down here, obviously smarter than us and if they wanted, could do whatever they wanted to us. There's actually a written report but you won't see it published in the Times of course."

"Oh come on Carl, stop feeding impressionable Alex with all that bullshit. He won't sleep."

"He's not going to sleep anyway. Your eyes peeled to the skies all night, right?"

"Right, but what about that NATO stuff."

"Believe every word of it."

"Your shrink father?"

"Of course. One other thing boys; my father's friend told me about me about a place in Bolivia called Puma Punku."

"Spell it?"

"Worry about this. It's a set of ruins on a plateau 13,000 feet high, going back 17,000 years ago. Blocks weigh 200 tons; one weighs 400 tons. How'd they get them up that high without a wheel, which probably wasn't invented yet, and the stones were cut so precisely, they could fit together? Do you ever wonder about pyramids appearing all over the world like they were directed by the same architect builder, maybe ancient space visitors, UFO guys or gals? Do you ever wonder why UFO talk thinks aliens are only guys and never girl aliens with tits, when artists draw pictures?"

Alex waved his hand, pretending sitting in the back of the class while a teacher ignored unbridled enthusiasm. "The Great Pyramid in Egypt is perfectly aligned to true north, south, east and west and how did they carry those bricks five hundred feet up?"

The two nights around north canyon were uneventful and cold. Carl apologized for lack of celestial UFO sightings. Alex absolved him in an improvisational hugging ceremony. Heading south, a large roadside boulder invited. Carl yelled to Alex while zipping up, that Sedona might very well bring celestial, spiritual memories. At the next rest stop, Elvin produced a bottle from the trunk, wrapped inside several towels. The bottle neck was kissed several times prompting Carl to offer the flask to the underage drinkers.

"What the hell, you need a shot more than me, so I'll break my under twenty-one rule."

"No thanks. This is Vichy Water, from Melrose Avenue and Casablanca. If we were stranded up here without water and dying of thirst, I'd never open it."

Red mountains suddenly appeared, like they shot up from underneath, at the flick of a magic switch. For the past hour, hills of dry grass and small trees were panorama and now blue sky and green forests blended perfectly with mountain red. No one spoke as they passed a sign, welcoming visitors to several thousand feet elevation and almost the same in population of Sedona, Arizona.

"I saw the name Sedona before but can't place it. Look at that mountain over there, all by itself. It looks like we're getting the finger."

"Bell Rock. It does look like a middle finger. Near there is home base tonight."

"Why there?"

Carl cleared his throat. "The buzz word in Southern California circles is that there's a magical energy around that rock and a few more spots around here. Iron is in the soil. Oxidation then rusting has been going on since the Cro-Magnon roamed. By the way, the *Cros* were my cousins. I've got papers at home to prove it. Anyway, iron yields electrical energy. You'll feel and sense it, especially you Jersey boys, coming here with all those dreams you keep talking about."

Heading into a supposed town, but there wasn't, just a scattering of southwestern ranch homes, clustered beneath the bosom of red craggy mountains and an occasional tourist store, western motif. A sign about eggs most of the time and the best coffee in the valley magnetized the steering wheel to a sharp right turn into a parking lot. Half the restaurant patrons wore cowboy hats, so Carl softly advised tolerance and acceptance of locals and leaving Jewish vestiges in the car.

Steven spoke softly, "When the waitress comes back, check out the red stain over her left breast. Hey Carl, Rorschach test approaching on the right."

"Five fingers of marinara. Probably a sloppy feel copped in kitchen but she's cute. Watch this." A wave brought her back. "Two Stanford juniors and a couple of Jersey freshman are admiring that unusual stain. What's the etiology? There's money riding on it."

"Etiology?"

"Who put it there?"

"My hand slipped into pizza, so it's self inflicted. What are you guys doing in Sedona?"

Timber Road was unpaved red soil and rocks. On the left was another street, even rockier, climbing higher and at that street's end was a log cabin. The builders of the cabin were in Phoenix for the week. Their daughter, waitress Maureen sat on the front porch in a rocking chair, drinking a Rolling Rock.

"Over there, she's waving like she can't wait for us. I like that."

A wallet produced a condom that slid into Carl's front pocket.

"Jersey boys, when it's our time to party....."

"We know. We'll hike to the top of the hill. You gave us plenty walking ammunition before, like stuff about President Kennedy not knowing a lot about civil rights when he started his political career. We're both Kennedy and civil rights fans."

"He needed to learn like everybody. The campaign probably sent observers when he was running for President, to even take notes on lunch counter sit-ins down south. Don't say a word; just think about it as you hike. Remember what my father did and where he did it. We'll talk later at Bell Rock."

"Now be sociable and say hello to Maureen. You could change your mind guys and join us. In a little while, she'll say yes to anything."

"Thanks, but remember Neville Chamberlain."

Silence around Bell Rock was deafening in a curious way. No aircraft, autos, barking dogs, bats hitting balls or mother's yelling *lunchtime.* The group talked about silence all around and being far away from home.

"Feel something, Elvin?"

"I do. A tingling, something."

"You're at peace?"

"How do you know?"

"I've been here. By the way, no regrets about Maureen? We did a first, your cousin and me. We double teamed her. She would've done anything."

"Why?"

"Chemistry. Loneliness. Imagine living here in the hustle and bustle of obscurity. Try and get some sleep."

The moon slid over while they watched.

"Everybody still up? Let's go to a better view, higher up and closer to the sky for you, Alex. We might get lucky, lost and wind up *there*."

"*There?*"

"We're not supposed to be *there*. It's someplace. They don't want tourists, imagine that! What are they hiding? We've got a perfect excuse if we find *there*. It's two a.m. and we're pretend lost, so they won't kill or erase us." Carl's shiny flask was refilled.

Elvin comically stuttered the word, *erase*.

"Piss off the government. They get a pencil and erase you. All is gone and forgotten including all my work at Stanford, like term papers and most importantly, my lost virginities list. All knowledge of Carl is gone."

Wiping whiskey off his lips with the back of his hand, Steven scolded, "Shit Carl, stop scaring the Jersey boys."

The overlook summit was a three hundred sixty degree panorama of mountains and a sprinkling of houses. Far below, a headlight crept along dark winding roads under a clear sky. Cold night air had them wearing college sweat shirts in sleeping bags. Silence strangely forced communication in whispers, no one wanting to upset the natural balance of things. This world was special for Alex, too restless, unable to sleep, talking about having imagined everything long before they got there and sensing what was going to happen.

"Up there on the right! What the hell is that?"

"A shooting star. Alex!"

"It's fast. The trajectory is parallel."

"Meaning what?"

Alex yelled, "Not necessarily falling!"

"See that, a half-hour and pay dirt. So is it a UFO Alex? Keep passing the flask around, it's freaking cold."

"I don't know. The view is amazing but it scares me because there's too much sky." Circling to the timing of a second hand, they watched Alex closely.

"Be scared about UFOs. A couple of years ago, those well known think folks in a tank reported that people, especially religious ones, would panic and send the world into chaos if they told us everything about UFOs. We're like children. Government protects children." Carl's salute to the sky went un-noticed.

Steven added, "Sounds to me like government is afraid those visitors are smarter and might hurt us? Shit like that."

Starting his own counter clockwise circling, Elvin met Alex at midnight. They looked into eyes, hands slipped into each other, attempting to squeeze fear away and whispering out of range of Carl and Steven. They were sharing elements of friendship that would last a lifetime and both knew that no one could ever understand. Feeling shivers at Bell Rock before and now at Airport Road, something happened but they weren't sure and couldn't tell anyone. Hands slipped apart after a last hard squeeze.

Steven's voice turned comedic, mocking, "Positive thought. We're not alone. Maybe they'll come down and give us technology, cures for cancer and the sense to eradicate prejudice and hate."

"All right, Steven!"

"I knew you liberal Jersey boys would like that thought, devoted to civil rights as you are."

"By the way Carl, what's in the flask you keep refilling and I keep drinking?"

"Alex, you're a Jack man."

THREE

An Intro to Sociology class at Rutgers Newark tackled post Kennedy assassination, murders of four young girls at the Sixteenth Street Baptist Church in Birmingham and everything relevant outside their Washington Street window during Friday open discussion.

Newark sat on the other side of a couple of rivers from New York. Decades back, the city peaked with immigration and in water quality, which suited a number of breweries. The skyline filled Elvin's municipal sense of pride that if they kept building, Newark would become just like New York, with plenty room along the Passaic River waterfront. Contentment was being at Rutgers Newark, absorbing real life not just from the back of a bus, through a window.

A city was going through changes, like his mother described recently, what was happening to her, explaining mood swings, tantrums and lack of toleration for people of color. Two years ago, he yelled back too loud, that it was bullshit; she was never tolerant of people and to stop making excuses. A wildly swinging broom handle forced him into the bathroom, fortunately with a supply of comics stored behind the cast iron tub- enough reading material, running water and the only toilet in case of a long siege.

The class discussed Newark's infra-structure being pulled apart like warm Bonomo's taffy. Patience and tolerance were thrown into a beaker of indifference and heated up in a chemistry lab at the renovated old Ballantine brewery. Migration and exodus were dramatically changing the color of faces leaning on Newark's bus windows. Thoughts of changing worlds echoed constantly in the classroom.

Elbow patches on corduroy sport coats helped define college professors. Elvin had a defined professor, who never appreciated his raw enthusiasm. Professorial resignation set in, Elvin told Alex, that no matter what, the class is a *D* or *F* and nothing could change it. The professor probably was anti-Semitic too.

"Good work class. Stone, stop waving, it's annoying. Alright go ahead, you're recognized."

Elvin jumped up. "In a few years I hope to be standing where you are Professor. I'll let you know about waving hands and enthusiastic students. I've been taking a Newark bus all my life and still do. Everything is changing. Miss Cronin is right. I'm not sure what the right word is. It's polarizing, negative and anti-human sociological behavior. People run away from people because of skin color and carry enough hate around to kill those sweet innocent girls in Birmingham. I wish, when we were designed, color blindness was standard issue. I've got this idea that there are more important problems facing the world and so does my best friend. Skin color or religious differences shouldn't be the real future world problem. Go ask the Brookings Institute people and hook them up to a lie detector if they go for it. That's if you really care to know."

"How long has that been percolating Mr. Stone?"

"A long time. I can't climb enough Arizona Mountains, walk on deserted Jersey beaches or travel on Newark buses to understand, find peace, toleration or something spiritually ecumenical."

"First of all Mr. Stone, stop rocking back and forth in your seat and pick up the note that Miss Cronin just threw on your desk. We're adults, Rutgers is progressive and you need good college boards to be here which means we're smart and hopefully mature. Class dismissed. There's a quiz next week. Stone go outside, walk around and take deep breaths. Maybe find a mountain or tall building nearby."

"Meaning what Professor Swill?"

"Meaning you need to soften a bit, take that energy and release it through meditation where the air is thinner."

For the first time in his academic life, Elvin let an under the breath *fuck you* out too loudly. There was a brief stare, before Elvin quickly ran out of the classroom to meet Miss Cronin.

The student lounge across from Washington Park on a late Friday afternoon was as deserted as an Arizona mountain at two a.m. The description made Caye Cronin laugh.

"Were you embarrassed when I threw the note on your desk?"

"Absolutely not. Actually I plan to put it in plastic and wear it to class on Monday. Do you have an extra safety pin?"

"You're funny. Are you bothered to be seen alone with a colored girl?"

"Nah!"

"You're different. Confession, I've been staring at you and listening to what you say, waiting for the right time to talk to you. I think you like being here with me."

"I do. There's something about you too. Now my confession; I hoped you'd find a right time to break some kind of ice. I'm really shy. Your note kind of rescued me. I was heading down the road to calling Swill, a *mother fucker* in front of the class with an inevitable invitation to summer school, so thanks, Caye."

"I know you were treading water. Are we going to get to know each other better? Don't answer that! I have to go now; church stuff with my family tonight."

"That's funny, I'll be in church tonight in Princeton with my best friend; we're going to a lecture about Kennedy."

Seconds seemed eternity. Hands ventured half-way, met and did their thing. Elvin squeezed harder, carefully looking for a reaction. Caye had a radiant face; black, illuminated, soft and animated. Large brown eyes, smiling blinks told Elvin she liked the squeeze intensity.

A white painted church with steeple in the heart of Princeton had a certain transporting drifting value. Drifting was an extension of dreaming and a favorite Elvin pastime. If you dull visual and auditory senses, you were back in Revolutionary times. General George Washington was addressing the congregation. Troops and horses were out back near a camp fire. A musket leaned against the pulpit. Elvin startled himself back to December, 1963 with the help of Alex's gentle left elbow into his rib cage.

"Not living up to expectations, is it?"

"Another semi-sermon conjecture lecture on Kennedy's assassination. The past few weeks have been inundating, but at least I get a chance to come to Princeton and spend time with you. Thank your elbow for keeping me awake."

"I've been hanging out with a couple of guys who the eating clubs restrictively avoid. You know the routine, like Stein's; nobody wants us because we don't fit the Aryan image."

"You're all minorities with un-blond hair?"

"More or less. There's a Princeton alum who lives nearby in a big house with a fancy library and St. Bernard dog. We spend time together in a discussion group. Interested in coming along tonight?"

"Sure."

It was dark but one could sense wealthy expansiveness. Elvin grabbed Alex, wanting a few digestive seconds before the doorbell and servant scene. There was a little known theory, which he explained, that the slower a door opened, the more money on the other side of the door.

"Back in Newark, ring the bell or knock, doors opened right away like a whip ride in an amusement park."

Without sound effects the door opened.

"Nolan. We thought a servant would be opening the door. Elvin was certain. He's impressed with your lawn and house."

"You always bring a smile. And Elvin, I heard a lot about you, come in."

"Pleasure to meet you Mr. Morris. Appreciate the invitation."

"A Rutgers man, so Alex tells me. There's wonderful intellectuality at Old Queens including an aging mathematician, a long time friend of mine. He hides in the back of the Military Science building."

"Pardon?"

"A lot of brain power at Rutgers. Thanks for joining us."

The subject had been changed quickly.

Elvin thought about being transported again. Walking up, the house looked like a medium sized Scottish castle; all the owner had to do was find water, build a moat and enter pictures of the house in Scottish Castle Times.

Nolan Morris led them to a library, equipped with moveable ladder rivaling movie depictions in size. Burgundy sofas faced each other under a chandelier. Six Princeton undergraduates sat with tea cups or long neck beer bottles.

"The Rutgers refugee has arrived. Jump right in." A voice got trapped in the mouth of a beer bottle.

"We're told you were fond of Jack."

Elvin was quick, "My father, Jack?" He wasn't sure which of the six needed the answer, looking around for a moveable mouth.

"He's got a sense of humor?"

"I know so you deal with it."

"We're arguing Jack Kennedy may've made his own bed."

"Interesting people helped Papa Joe with the Union vote then Jack lets Bobby go after them. He snubs Sinatra, like all of a sudden he's too good for him. And of course Lyndon hated Kennedy, who never appreciated his Texas college degree. It wasn't Harvard. Sam Sethi here."

Barely a handshake was felt, but at least some effort was made by a lofty Princeton undergrad to a visiting Rutgers man, although it was more like two palms passing in the night, amusing Elvin.

A tea drinker stood up as the room quieted. Nolan Morris whispered, "Listen carefully if you can?"

"Comrades....."

The room burst into laughter, all eyes watching the unsuspecting Rutgers man. Russian language blurted out with correct inflection and tones. For dramatic effect, Ted Severance marched goose-step until the only bald head reminded, that he was imitating Nazi's not Russians.

"Translation gentlemen. The military and industrial profiteering partners didn't like Jack either. They wanted to party in Southeast Asia and he didn't."

"Ted is our resident foreign language major. How many Ted?"

"Five and counting, Nolan. It's a hobby. I don't take it seriously. Nice to meet you, Elvin."

Maybe because of long blond hair and new world charm, but a solid handshake caught him off guard. Ted seemed mainstream, not minority, making him think that he could've gained acceptance at Stein's or at Princeton eating clubs but then why was he here on a burgundy sofa with minorities?

Another tea drinker stood up.

Nolan coached again. "Calvin Graham's a Brit and hard to follow. He might ignore you. Rather arrogant, so smile and shake your head affirmatively even if you're a non-believer; less confrontation that way."

"Who said Cuban's before? They'd never get involved murdering the President, a ticket for invasion, U.S. reprisals. Nope, they'd never do it but maybe Florida's Cubans who lost relatives at the Bay of Pigs. I don't think Ted's Russian motherland did either."

"Fuck you, Calvin. I was born in Des Moines."

Despite Calvin's aristocratic arrogance, there was something about the Brit that Elvin warmed to. It was an instant mutual chemical electrical bonding future friendship.

"Hey Rutgers, what do you think?"

"Calvin, my sentiments exactly- never the Cubans."

"I like our guest. You can invite him back."

Across a sofa divide, they shook hands. The sound of Elvin and Calvin together by the shank of the evening might twist a few tongues. Someone was practicing in the background, two rungs up on the ladder. "Calvin, Elvin, Elvin, Calvin."

Elizabeth Avenue parallels Newark's Weequahic Park. Near the intersection with Chancellor Avenue there's a car entrance and off to the left was one of Elvin's favorite structures. When asked to describe it, he called it a structure, looking Greek or Roman, maybe marble, probably not, but open on all sides with a roof, with built in *transporting* potential as a place to think, dream of antiquity and eating grapes from the fingers of a nubile virgin. Too unseasonal for grapes, spot traces of snow were scattered. Elvin sat on a ledge, holding an invitation. Nolan Morris was hosting a small informal party for the group where he was now an artificial member. Calvin Graham loved to refer to him as that; artificial, even embellishing by calling Elvin, *Art*, life's first nickname.

The party for celebrating the last 111 days meant Halloween through Christmas, New Years 1964, recent Valentines Day and anything else significant. A post script added dates could be invited. RSVP didn't appear on the invitation because Nolan knew they'd all come.

A rear end was cold numb sitting on the ledge, trying to scrounge up courage to ask Caye Cronin for a date, but should he, would she? *Hell* was the last word of a decision phrase; it revolved around Alex, their talks about life, courage, digging deep into one's soul, looking for glimpses of a place in the universe, and being true to self. Heaven forbid your place in the universe if you're not true. They were close, always needing and loving their time for joint introspection, always looking forward. Caye Cronin was truth. Alex reinforced truth.

A few weeks back, Alex showed up in Newark late on a Friday. They walked around the periphery of Washington Park until the sun had long set. A few Rutgers students passed, acknowledged Elvin, and deposited two quarts of locally brewed beer with the pair. Prudent behavior with underage beer in downtown Newark meant chugging, disposing of empties and settling down at George Washington's horse because their knees wobbled like Jack's voice did, passing the ghost of a hotel, where Elvin might've been conceived.

"Do you still get those feelings of having been someplace, because I do all the time? It's weird. I could be taking a bus home, passing a store as the sun leaves a strange shadow on the front window and think I've already seen the same shadow and been there before. It's a warm, comforting feeling, nothing scary or supernatural. I think if someone waved at me from the front door, I'd pull *the next stop string* and jump off the bus."

"Same with me. Princeton trees on campus cast shadows and the way a building looks early in the morning and you're right, I've been there before too. I like the feeling; it's warm and inviting, telling me we're not alone. Maybe it's a spirit somewhere like a woman with a piece of red fruit seducing us. As we both seem to feel, it's a remnant from Sedona. We're not the same since."

Elvin stood up and looked down at his friend getting comfortable leaning on George Washington's horse. "The beer made us oblivious and you're right, we're not the same."

"Oblivious to what?"

"Birds claimed this statue a long time ago. Like our gull friends from the Shark River, they've left white indelible reminders and you're well entrenched."

"Oh well. Do you have any more friends with beer?"

Strong northwestern wind cracked branches laden with ice, producing whirring sound effects, like you'd expect to hear on deserted Alaskan tundra or in a black and white horror film. Bitingly cold air made a bundled-up couple break into a half jog to the front door, skipping same steps together.

Elvin asked, "Are you sure you don't feel you're in the arctic. Do you hear a wolf's mating call?"

"It's the door bell silly. I'll bet a servant lets us in."

"Maybe."

Elvin and Caye's entrance into Nolan's library was greeted by a visibly slight hesitation before effusive greetings. To his moderate surprise everyone was paired up.

"Attention everyone, I'm taking Caye over to the ladder, to fill her in on all of you, before formal introductions."

Turning around, she smiled, trying to absorb as much as she could in this new world.

"Art, it's why we like you, honesty. Go ahead; take her to the ladder without introducing."

"Thanks, Calvin."

"Doesn't he know you, he called you Art?"

"It's our little joke. Over there Caye, the bald guy, Michael Lauzone, a physics major. His father went bald at twenty-five. He wants to cheat genetics so he started shaving his head last year. Our group has him on a suicide watch; his father died at forty-five and we figure he might want to cheat again." A right arm rested on Caye's shoulder, prompting more narrative.

"Let me wing it the rest of the night."

"Sure, but you must see the garden."

Almost on cue, the wind lessened, leaving it silently night cold. Elvin led her around enthralling and endless property. "It's not a Newark or Montclair backyard; such a different world here."

"What does he do, to deserve all this?"

Shoulders shrugged. "Don't know but I'm glad you're here."

"I know you are. Me too."

Their hands touched. She squeezed harder. Done the proper way, hands touching, could have more impact than a hug or kiss. Squeezing was a serious step in formative moments of a relationship.

A visual appeared of Aunt Evelyn and the Italian girl with the big cross around her neck. If only the wicked witch could see him now. Maria was beautiful, right out of a movie and kept coming around the drug store to see him and the first girl ever actively dreamt about. Maria would smile and stare at him until he was ushered to the cellar and sanitary napkin boxes, eventually showing the wear and tear of Elvin's napping, as in crushed contents. It was easier putting a man on the moon, then asking her for a date, Elvin consolingly thought. Aunt Evelyn was omnipresent, flying around the store on her special broom. Childhood memories linger a long time. He knew that about himself. Wouldn't life get a jolt, if you could pick three people and be able to find them and see what they look like in forty years and if you made the right decisions. Maria made the short list. A friend from Pharmacy school reminded him to check a date's medicine cabinet and also never go on a first date unless you met the mother, crystal ball or acorn. Stall as long as you could, pretend you're dizzy but wait for the mother to come home unless she lived in Italy, like Maria's.

"Are you alright?"

"Sorry Caye, bad habit. My mother calls it day-dreaming. I call it drifting."

"Hey Elvin, come back. Alex's got an announcement."

"What did he say first, it sounded Russian?"

"Everyone's waking me up. That's Ted Severance; speaks lots of languages so we call him the Bolshevik. I finally found out what a Bolshevik is. An old lady used to call me that when I was young and bad, throwing water balloons at her house. Ted starts everything in Russian then translates."

"Throwing water balloons is bad?"

"Breaking flower pots with them was."

Alex was pacing circles around the room with a date comically following a few steps behind. Calvin yelled out, "There goes Groucho!"

"The Ludwig Land Observatory discovered asteroid #2444 the other day. My father's medical connections worked for me. The observatory founder, Dr. Land was a physician and....."

"You get so emotional and serious. When are you going there? That's what this is about?"

"Three weeks this summer in Indiana, my second dream. The first of course is being here at Princeton. Speaking of dreams, Elvin's got one in a bag.

Nolan interrupted, "Remember the party's theme, *celebration*. Michael is celebrating Halloween and *Goldfinger* with a face partially painted gold. The Bolshevik celebrated Edith Piaf before by singing *La Vie en Rose* in Russian, with a pretty decent voice. Maybe he should change careers to crooning? Elvin, go celebrate now."

The Vichy Water bottle was held up. "In celebration of the best movie, *Casablanca* and a signature from the hand of Bogart."

Smirking at the bottle of water in the hands of a Rutgers man, Calvin chimed, "What have we sunken to; kindergarten show and tell? Just kidding, Art."

"If you're celebrating Vichy France, then be careful? Vichy government was a touchy subject when they made that movie. We didn't want to piss off the French in that scene when the Vichy Water hits the garbage. It caused our government paranoid agony with the symbolism." Frank, usually the quietest group member spoke after an hour of silent reclusiveness.

"Frank is our World War II expert." Nolan was surprised by his verbosity.

"Don't forget I'm a Princeton tennis player, more important than anything right now."

"Maybe it's a good time for a toast but not with my Vichy Water. It needs to age. Here's looking at you folks." Elvin liked the line from the movie, feeling a spiritual Bogart connection and wishing a forties vintage hat for mood effect.

The other day he found old pictures of Yankee Stadium with stands packed with white men, dressed in ties, wearing hats.

"Dad, when did hat wearing disappear? Maybe it's like a vestigial tail."

"The day you were born."

It was too early to see activity at the airport from an attic perch. Elvin preferred jets leaving to far away places for adventure rather than boring landings. Taking off was more exciting; an imminent dreamy fulfillment of tropical palm trees, azure waters or red mountains. Landing was boring, depressing with nothing to look forward to unless you missed your bed or refrigerator.

Looking down at the quiet street, Elvin saw Joe the milk man next door, doing a street last delivery. He'd miss rotund Joe and the big block of ice in his Diversey milk truck with strange doors that open and fold like Superman's telephone booth on television. Grocery stores were becoming supermarkets and no one burned coal anymore.

He wasn't in the mood to lie down, stare at clouds, talk to God and departed, but he needed it now. "Grandma Rebecca, I think I see you in a cloud. It's pinkish because early morning. Now that Joe's truck pulled away, it's quiet. He never shuts it off. No one gets milk delivery any more. You do remember him? I know you'll see me down the shore later with a girl who isn't Jewish or white. Here's my thought: self-determination and being true to self. I can't change the way I feel. People are just people. My Princeton and Rutgers friends tell me all the time to pursue, dream, live and feel. I want to feel nineteen, free and true. Please understand Grandma, I like her a lot and we're all just people on Earth. Besides, there is no catering hall in my near future, so Alex tells me all the time."

This May Saturday was in the careful planning stage for a while. Elvin spent the past month talking to Caye about Belmar and why it's important in his life. Belmar beach would be deserted for the most part. The real season was weeks away, so a colored girl and white boy together would only be noticed by gulls and crabs. She'd never been to the Jersey shore and wanted to be part of Elvin's world by exploring, picnicking and sharing dreams.

The clandestine operation to sneak down the shore spoke military precision and Humphrey Bogart wearing a trench coat, following a suspect or Sidney Greenstreet in the *Maltese Falcon*. Elvin wanted to wear a trench coat when he picked her up in Bloomfield at a complicit girlfriend's house but it was too dangerous to smuggle both a blanket and coat.

Two honks, drive around the block, return for the third honk and Caye would be there with picnic basket. Did she like Muscatel because that's the only kind of wine he really knew?

She wore a Rutgers sweatshirt and beige Bermuda shorts, and like his mother, a kerchief.

"We did it. I keep turning around to see if we're being followed. Were you careful last night when your girlfriend picked you up? Did you keep checking and slide low in the seat until you were out of Montclair?" Elvin pretended serious.

"You're funny. I got cheese, bread and the grapes you asked for."

"Muscatel wine is on the back seat- a few bottles."

"A few!"

"Maybe a long day."

A perfect weather day was defined as not much of anything; clouds, sun, warmth or cold. If it was sunny and warm, Elvin conjectured the beach might be crowded. He thought of everything, like Bogart would, but mostly about their being racially invisible. For several minutes, they were too quiet; perhaps holding breath would help their get-away. Hands managed to touch at the small space between. Was space for hands touching good or bad?

"Where are we?"

"That's my structure over there."

"What?"

"Welcome to Weequahic Park, a little detour. Bring the grapes. Remember Nolan's celebration party? I found the courage to ask you, sitting right here on this ledge. Can you do me a silly favor, feed me a few. It's a dream of mine like you are."

She whispered, "Can you tell?"

"Huh."

"I'm blushing."

The Garden State Parkway lifted the Pontiac Catalina over the Raritan River. Elvin pointed to river banks below that inspired Rutgers alma mater. The landmark Carborundum factory below on the right meant the Atlantic Ocean was nearby.

"What do they make there?"

"Probably carborundum."

The river separated worlds of dreams; north from south Jersey and was a point of no return. Once over the river, how would the day go? Stomach queasiness arrived from nowhere and did it have something to do with a beautiful girl sitting next to him, moving closer to fill in the space?

"We're in Asbury Park, open your eyes. That's an old merry-go-round, quiet, not moving, waiting and the horses were probably just painted for the new season. When the horses come to life, they open the sides so everybody can hear organ music. There's the boardwalk and our ocean."

"Is this our beach?"

"Not yet."

They drove passed Loch Arbour, a block long beach where ironically a lot of the Stein's gang hung out. Elvin decided he was too cool for them now. The car slowed to a crawl through Deal, a white, Jewish, mostly summer town that looked like F. Scott Fitzgerald and Gatsby may've taken up residence at one time. Sprawling homes, Victorian atmosphere, and ostentatious opulence induced a slide to the window for a closer look.

"Only Jews are here?"

"Mostly white Jews."

"Are there black ones that I don't know about?"

"Somewhere, it's a big world."

"Open eyes, Belmar. Seventh Avenue and home for the day."

Clouds, cold ocean breezes were friendly by keeping the beach deserted. The smuggled blanket, still pungent and musty from the cellar's moth balls, was spread over sand. Easy to open Muscatel in paper cups toasted horizon, dreams and a future time when freedom would cease to be a word because everybody had it. Two cups swallowed in rapid fire helped Elvin's confidence to let the *poet* out as Caye moved closer. A distant ship skirting a previous toast was going to Africa and Kilimanjaro. Hemingway's ghost was aboard. Hemingway and Fitzgerald were friends and maybe they hung out in Deal together. More wine moved behavior from poet to silly. Running barefoot to white ocean foam- like the head of a hastily poured beer left over by waves- they signed names in the sand, watching how long it lasted before another wave.

Recently seeing the movie, *From Here to Eternity*, Elvin described a scene with Burt Lancaster and Deborah Kerr on a beach just like Belmar; famous and steamy for those days. Ocean waves rolled over the couple, still locked in each other's arm. His movie passion made her laugh.

"Beyond that pier is the Shark River and my world of hopes and dreams. I can't wait for you to see it."

Before walking and holding hands, he made sure no one was around. Gull friends saw them coming so it was smart to even cover her kerchief. How would she explain gull droppings to a mother if she was supposed to be in urban Bloomfield all day? Of course how would her mother know they were gull droppings anyway?

"This is my place, Shark River Inlet. Only Alex knows, not my parents or sister and now you. As a little kid, I came here to dream, sometimes about being a father. Imagine a little kid dreaming about being someone's father. Now I dream about a world without war or hate, so mankind can save all that wasted money and build better pathways to understanding spirit and God, and making earth life better for everyone. I ask Alex all the time, if it's normal to think these things. Now I'll have you to dream about whenever I come here."

"It's more than normal. Do you come here a lot?"

"Whenever I need to, but its better when deserted, like now. Once it was snowing and I stood right here. Even gulls were gone. Tell me all your dreams."

"It's amazing; yours and mine are the same. I wouldn't change a thing."

Hands slipped into each other's with the same squeeze intensity while they stared at the horizon. Caye turned to kiss him. It was so sudden that he had to quickly open his mouth. The kiss lasted long enough for a boat in the inlet, waiting for the open drawbridge, to sound its horn. Lips retreated with noise.

"Was that for us?"

"Nah, it was to let the bridge people know they're waiting. I need to catch my breath."

"That was our first and....."

"Last kiss, I know."

"The road is too hard with parents and people around who don't understand. It's a wrong time for us."

"Someday Caye; an easier road, better time."

"Do you really believe that?"

"Yeah, sort of."

"Thank you for today, showing me your world."

While the bridge lifted up and the boat passed, they still held hands. Suddenly, he remembered, it was the *Sedona* again. Maybe fisherman remembered and honked. The coincidence of the boat, life's first real kiss and beautiful Caye Cronin would transport him back to Shark River with swelling certainty, he'd never run out of dreams.

There's always a first night in August when temperature drops, making air smell like September and back to school. More than dying of light, it's relinquishing of a season's hold, part of life's cycle. A myriad of notions surface: aging and change, hope and turmoil, birth and death, passing of carefree times. If you're a teacher as Elvin aspired, then you're not going to like a first smell of autumn, no matter how much you love inspiring and teaching youth. The day of change and doom called Labor Day is inexorable.

Sneakers lay on a beach towel, socks protruding. Rolling up jeans over knees meant wading in the Atlantic. Ocean was wavy rough. Somewhere beyond the scary darkness were remnants of a tropical storm. Remnants were failures; couldn't hold themselves together long enough to make landfall, hurricane status and folklore. That was Alex's take.

"Glad to see you've moved away from Muscatel. You've grown up while I was in Indiana. What is it?"

"Chardonnay."

"Eleven p.m. Belmar Beach. Shivering and soaking wet from that bastard wave you said would never get us and you've got wine. This whole scene is probably from a movie, meaning you had a bad day."

"Bad!"

"That bad?"

"I know you got back from Indiana late last night and slept all day. They found the bodies today."

Friends leaned into a long hug and another swig; cups blew into the inhospitable ocean.

When civil rights workers, Goodman, Schwerner and Cheney disappeared in Philadelphia, Mississippi, the boys began their own personal vigil, talking about making a difference and going down south to help register voters. Alex's Indiana observatory summer work changed plans. Yet they also knew from that first news story, those brave boys were gone forever.

"Pass the bottle, everything hurts. We need to empty it. Something else is bothering you."

"This morning in Washington Park, by our statue, I said goodbye to Caye."

"What!"

"Her father changed jobs and they're moving to Atlanta. Caye's transferring to Spelman. She called my house, wanting to see me for a last time."

"And?"

"And, I kissed her goodbye in front of all downtown Newark. She cried. I stopped her and said we'll always have Belmar. She teary smiled then disappeared. You'd better tell me about the Ludwig Land Observatory before I'm too drunk to appreciate what you did."

"I'm sorry about Caye, but you guys knew it could never go anywhere. Maybe in a hundred years if the planet holds up and you live that long. Anyway, it was a nirvana summer. I worked with a ten inch astrograph- Egyptian-American, Alex Zari."

"What the hell is an astrograph?"

"It's used to recover asteroids whose orbits were sort of lost during the War; not that they were really lost, the war changed astronomical priorities. Guess what? Me, Alex Zari discovered an asteroid and helped name it!"

Leaning together for another hug, Elvin sensed his joy. The Chardonnay bottle went back and forth with little time spent in the sand.

"In keeping with the spirit of the day and creeping inebriation....."

"What?"

"My parents started looking at houses in Maplewood; it's moving time."

"Mine too."

"Maybe we'll get to be neighbors."

"We might get to know each other."

"We just might!"

They laughed at funny absurd, before sobering; living next to a Newark black family wasn't in their future.

FOUR

arnivorous smoke billowed from a brick barbecue. Overly cooked hot dogs were served on bone china. Collegians roamed Nolan Morris's manicured grounds on a mid September Sunday for welcoming back old discussion group friends, mixing them with coeds from local colleges. A bouquet of orange and black Princeton tiger balloons escaped, chasing the barbecue smoke.

"Hey Alex, did you catch that new TV show, Star Trek? Right up your alley." Senior year made Michael Lauzone waver on baldness versus genetics, so he wore a Yankees cap and re-assured all his friends not to worry anymore; he passed over the cheating fate and genetics stage of life.

"Well, lot's of hype. They say it's the hottest new fall show of 1966. The crew's integrated. I like that more." A lone hot dog was held up high, over head, slowly descending towards Alex's oral cavity.

"Hey, no more moustache, Alex!"

"Morning restlessness. I got rid of it this morning."

A pretty girl, dipping a stalk of celery into white wine, caught the astronomer's keen eye, because it wasn't being chewed but licked.

Nearly as tall as Alex, sandy hair, piercing blue eyes, that held or repelled, depending, smiled at him. "I saw you watching my celery. Just curious, but are you preparing a question for me? It looks like there's deep analytical thought going on."

"Actually preparing three questions if that's alright, so are you ready?"

"Fire at will."

"May I paraphrase?"

"If you like."

"The distinct taste, habit or just something to talk about?"

"It's the last. I'm Christine Winthrop. Rider College junior. Hi." Celery was left in the glass for the handshake.

"Alex Zari, Princeton senior, may I?" He reached for his own celery stick but used her glass.

"Well?"

"To impress you, I should rave review dipping celery in wine for the Princeton Epicurean Review."

"There really is a review?"

"Should be, maybe, sounds good, but celery in wine does nothing for me."

"Me neither but we're talking."

Winds kicked up, sky darkened and doors to the house remained closed. They were an intuitive group; deductive reasoning meant it was time to thank Nolan goodbye. Alex walked Christine to the street, wanting to hold her hand if only there was a moat filled with evil South American fish that she needed protection from, which is actually how he expressed himself to a giggling new friend.

"My dorm is Kroner room 111. Not too presumptuous of me, is it?"

"Industrious and cute. You knew I was going to ask anyway." For as long as it took the classic Volkswagen to completely disappear down a straight and narrow tree lined road, Alex stood frozen, in a dreamy, longing state. Something happened and he knew it.

"Alex, over here." Nolan was sitting on a marble bench on the front patio. "Sit a minute. The party was obviously a success for you. Where's she from so I know to keep inviting the school?"

"Rider College."

"I have a favor to ask. A friend is flying in this weekend. Why don't you come by Friday at 9:17 p.m. Just you."

The human voice is an amazing tool; rising and lowering of tone, passing of a whisper mixed with precise timing and specific choice of words delivered and received. Nolan's invitation was so not meant for anyone else; it almost moved him to ask *why*.

Nolan's front door bell morphed into the wall, replaced by a giant squid's tentacle designed by Jules Verne, reaching out for Alex's right arm. He kept backing up; a tentacle can stretch so far. Nolan's lawn was safe harbor. Sky was poised for total darkness, and if it were a month ago, he'd be staring at dusk and the sun's pastel artistry. March of earthly time, he thought, never stops, leaving just a little left before the doorbell depression. Depression was a powerful word. If you accentuate the *ion*, saying it out loud, maybe it could reduce the severity of the condition by lessening the impact of the complete word. You just need to say *depress shun* a few times. Alex drifted comfortably; Elvin was an accomplished drifting instructor.

The past few nights were the same; dark sky, whispers for divine intervention and hope for celestial sightings. A dread existed, yet paradoxically, anticipation of meeting Nolan's friend. Alex saw this night coming. A deep sigh on the lawn meant wanting more time to be an undergraduate of life. God would listen to him for a few more moments until 9:17 p.m. Tentacles retracted. A servant was waiting at the door; moments later disappearing into a room on the right that Alex had never been in.

The library chandelier was dim. Even a few floor lamps strategically distanced, strained to adequately illuminate the room. At the rear, by the ladder, a small table hosted a single burning candle on a silver tray. Without entering, Alex surveyed the scene, finally hearing vocal familiarity urging him to get comfortable. The burgundy sofa was a favorite sitting place since freshman year. Hands behind head, thoughts of Princeton senior year induced a nervous smile.

Nolan walked in.

"Sit. Glass of wine?"

"Sure. I've never seen a candle in here. Your lighting director has done wonders with surrealism."

"You never let me down; always observant, passionate, expressive and intense."

"Was the candle a test?"

"Perhaps, but first a toast. Alex, to the mysteries and exigencies of life. Surely goodness shall follow you always."

"Wow," followed by a faint push of air through puffed cheeks was the best he could expel. Glasses clicked.

The library door opened to a tall figure standing just as Alex did a few minutes earlier, surveying room and occupants. A silent, impeccable presence loomed. What a dramatic theatrical entrance but actually not, just a life freeze frame.

Acknowledging forward motion, they stood to receive. A middle age face with a disproportionately long forehead- almost alien looking and scary if you thought for more than a few seconds- approached. Alex tried not to think for more than a few seconds, not really wanting to being scared. A journey he'd visualized for years was about to begin and there was the journeyman, sticking a long right hand out at him, covered by a white shirt, rolled to the elbow.

"Meet Stuart Grafton, from Utah, California, New York, Kansas, Winnipeg and Washington. Did I leave anything out?"

"Technically, Hudson's Bay too."

A perceived sense of humor makes scary foreheads less scary.

"I'll take leave now that you're both comfortable." Nolan vanished.

"Tell me about yourself." The voice contradicted the forehead; gentle and soft spoken.

An hour later Nolan produced a sterling silver tray with coffee, tea and cookies then vanished again.

"We're patriotic and dedicated. There's a love for what we do. You'll feel it. We're taken care of, no expiration date. We have responsibility to live life normally. Never want or need. Materialism is fine. We're at peace with the world but there's powerful responsibility to think, plan and strategize. I'll say *love* again because it's partly a metaphysical, spiritual state. Love is also an ability. Nothing in your life will change. It's your life; unique and unto itself but always think with us and for us. Take your family to a football game or to church or to a supermarket. It's American. We're all Americans."

Alex wasn't counting, but it must've been his tenth deep breath across the sofa divide. Each exhale made Stuart smile. Bonding was happening with an emerging additional father figure, which meant comfort, trust and no lingering thoughts of strange foreheads as impediments. He kept thinking about the phrase, "Think with us and for us." It reverberated and pounded, beginning to feel like a judge's gavel beating on his temples, bringing on a headache.

At midnight, Nolan made a third appearance at the library door, exiting just as quickly.

"Thinking about Harvard or MIT and a PhD?"

"Everyday."

"Then do it and of course we'll take care of everything."

"I figured that."

"Do whatever you feel in life."

"Is there a name for all this? What about a brick building with or without windows and a lounge in a basement with a soda machine, sofa, television and a non-descript person, maybe even without a face, sitting in a room the size of a closet, with a pair of scissors and large garbage can, cutting up sensitive papers?"

"You're thinking palpable, with a sense of humor too!"

"Maybe."

"Sleep late tomorrow. Good luck with senior year."

"That's it? My decision? Timetable?"

"Not now, be comfortable, secure. You'll know, we'll know. Good night and God Bless."

Without saying goodbye to Nolan who was probably sleeping, he left. A gold watch with faded face pointed 1:11 a.m. Making sure twice, Alex closed the front door without assistance from a missing servant.

Was he really a servant or someone who disappeared into a basement filled with all kinds of recording devices?

Stuart Grafton, shirt sleeves now buttoned, walked to the candle, passing a right palm over the flame apex. Nolan appeared. They shook hands, then simultaneously bending down, blew out the candle.

"Happy almost Birthday, Gabriel!"

Taking out Maplewood garbage late at night and seeing a first snow flake meant seasons were officially changing. Who needs official winter solstice hoopla, Elvin pondered. If air was cold enough to support ice and snow in upper levels of the atmosphere, then get shovels and boots ready, as reported at six p.m. by a New York weatherman. How much was hype and filler? Filler was a great word. If you need to kill time on the evening news, fill it with something or interview people on the street. Thanksgiving was near, therefore, a favorite food, stuffing. Stuffing is filler too. Innards of a basted bird are filled with heavily seasoned stuff. Stuffing is the ultimate stuff and the only kind of stuff you're supposed to eat. Drifting deeply, sitting on a garbage can lid, snow flurry activity increased. For a brief moment, Elvin looked up to the street light nearly overhead, and felt certain, he'd seen the same snowflakes, artistically caressing that same street light. Everything he was doing was a repeat performance. Sedona energy was everywhere. Something lunged for his hand. He reached out, pretending to shake hands with the personification of deja vu.

It was time to anoint Maplewood snow flakes by running under the street light with a projectile tongue, trying to catch as many flakes as possible in a sixty second period. Records need breaking, remembering the forty-four lingual flakes back in Newark while Alex watched, and since no one was around for legal verification, his tongue retracted walking back to the lid. What's the use if there's no one around to verify and to socially interact with? What if he was stuck on a remote island or planet, with all the modern conveniences of life; television, music, movies, food, everything but human beings? No, solitude wouldn't work for him.

Just that morning he decided to go for a Master's Degree at Rutgers and become an official History teacher. A car turned into the street, provoking reposition, not wanting anyone to see the face of a poor soul sitting on a garbage can at midnight.

Deep breath sucked as much air as he could stuff into his lungs, thinking his vital lung capacity had to be right up there with Gertrude Ederle, the first woman to swim the English Channel and about whom he wrote a grammar school report. He'd always regard her as one of life's role models, remembering how she lost all her hearing by 1940 and taught swimming to the deaf. And of course she had a lousy manager who should've done more for her. Thanksgiving air was precious, filled with memories of departed family, parades and football. A vision of a Pilgrim appeared.

A man with a funny triangular hat, sitting pensively on a recently chopped log, was wondering if there'd be enough food and wood for winter. Would militia come in time if needed? What could be done for a toothache? How'd they survive without the stuff that Alex's father uses in the hospital to numb pain? Nature is remarkable; it conceives people who can best handle their time.

God I love Thanksgiving. Alex and his parents are coming for the first time. Screw you Aunt Evelyn, Margaret Hamilton, or wicked witch, whatever the hell you are. I'm not sweeping for you any more, because I'm all grown up and if I want to go out with a girl with a cross around her neck, I will. I miss you Uncle George. Why did you have to die so young? It's the first time I watch March of the Wooden Soldiers in Maplewood. God I love Thanksgiving. Shit, another car. What the hell is happening to Elberta Road?

"Ever since, you spend Thanksgiving mornings watching *March of the Wooden Soldiers*, so I can never see the whole parade. Well, Mom wants you to go buy Apple Cider now! So there." Sister Judy annoyingly tapped feet on the linoleum floor waiting for a response, just like Martha does to Elvin.

The belligerency of a sister, nine years younger and a generation removed, manifested itself at the den door, hands folded under sprouting chest, mouth in need of braces, and making obnoxious bubble gum sound effects.

"Judy."

"What?"

"Absolutely nothing. I needed to say your name. Tell Mom, that Stan and Ollie are in the warehouse about to start the soldiers up. In another twenty minutes, you can see Santa arrive on his float."

Fourteen holiday guests stood around a festive table, observing a moment of silence for late Uncle George. Martha Stone ran into the kitchen for a long spoon to dig the stuffing out of the largest bird the Stone's could remember. The Zari's sat across from Elvin's parents purposefully, so they could face off comfortably, talking, bonding and bringing cultural backgrounds towards an artificial synchronicity, which according to Alex, meant general awkwardness and presumption of their first social engagement.

After picking out the apples from fresh baked pie, the boys excused themselves from the table. Adults were doing coffee. Both boys hated the symbolism of coffee; liquid reasons for after dinner small talk, holding a cup in your hands, intellectualizing about the latest United Nations session. Whispers went back and forth between them, how well parents got along, birthing a new holiday tradition. Jack and Adel were almost non-stop obnoxious, each trying to out-perform the other with growing up stories, depression, war and falling in love. At their father's romantic juncture, they decided to leave. Going to a ballroom to dance to Glenn Miller was not their thing. Both sets of parents sarcastically waved goodbye. Jack called out before they disappeared. "Wise guys. You never heard, *In the Mood*. Go find a record store. I'll buy."

"Where to Elvin, upstairs, basement?"

"Basement! There's only boxes of old Life Magazines down there. Martha swears one day they'll be worth a fortune."

"So?"

"Grab your coat for a surprise."

Erie Lackawanna trains connected North Jersey suburban towns, ultimately with New York City. The Maplewood train station was painted by Norman Rockwell, both on canvas and actual waiting room. That was Elvin's thinking the first time he discovered its quaintness and timelessness. He wanted desperately to believe Rockwell had a hand, but not.

The Stone's had been living in Maplewood a few weeks when his mother and father had a fight over money. Selling shoes wasn't enough to support a family any more. Jack broke down. Highway stores were replacing him. Martha wasn't supportive but denigrated and that upset Elvin. He never knew this side of his father. It was a strange feeling, a father figure, like a small Sedona mountain, old, wise, intractable, not quite human, but really like a rock, now too human, teary, voice fading to resignation. Elvin snuck out the side door and drove around until a train whistle beckoned. If only the train was heading up to the sky, he'd jump on and never come back. Fear was going home any time soon because his imagined mountain of security was gone forever. He knew there wasn't much to his father and their relationship, but it was still a father, the man who did the sperm thing. Sperm does count. A train whistle fading away was a sad sound, just like the whole notion of train travel was fading as was the vision of some sense of fatherhood. Probably there'd be no more train whistles that night; it was so late.

A tunnel went under the tracks. Walking back and forth, he settled on the south side. Old wooden benches invited. A small wooden sign, *To New York*, was blowing squeaky in night wind. It was three a.m. before he left the station. The only positive thing all night was a discovered new place for him and Alex to ponder their universe close to home.

"It's not the Shark River. Do you have a preference? The track to New York side or we can walk through a tunnel, bounce voices off graffiti walls and sit on the North Jersey side."

"A dark tunnel near midnight? Let's pull up a bench right here. Any trains coming?"

"Nope. I think they stop around eleven. It's a neat place for us."

They sat for a few minutes, quietly absorbing and digesting, as food and thoughts entered the blood stream. Almost a contest, they waited to see who breaks silence first; tension meeting eagerness half-way. They knew each other's limitations and breaking point.

"You first." Both bellowed, both laughed simultaneously.

Alex blew into his hands. "It's almost too cold. So that's Aunt Evelyn, the intense lady who didn't want you to mess around with a girl because she had a cross around her neck and made you nap on sanitary napkin boxes and sweep till concrete faded."

"Yeah, exactly. When my uncle died a few months back, I pretended to be sleeping on a living room sofa. A few people were talking. Aunt Evelyn worked him to death. The newspaper said he died from a short illness but they said depression and overdose. Since there was no way out, he was life tired; pleasant thoughts for a sleeping nephew to hear. So what's on your mind? I can tell there's something?"

Alex got up, walked around, pushing the *To New York* sign, making a rusty squeak. "I love that sound, because it's so real. You know, we're past describing ourselves as *like brothers*. We're better than that and getting closer."

Elvin copied sign pushing. "I know."

"Will you always trust me? Sometimes I might not seem to be myself, distant, evasive, secretive or nasty. I don't know. Please, always trust me, *forever*. There's the word I don't like, so you know this is serious. I'm going to slide into a secret thing at Princeton. I made the decision; been thinking for months. It's deep, heavy and personal, but good stuff, so don't worry. My parents won't even know. I love you, Elvin."

Both stared at the track and those special railroad rocks, thinking the same thing, that the word *love* was used for a first time.

FIVE

Venetian blinds helped somewhat in blocking morning light, prolonging sleep. Light still trickled in through parts that refused to flush up against windows. Elvin pleaded with Martha for an opaque window shade or anything esthetically pleasing to her as long as it kept morning light out of his face. First a pillow covered his head, then covers, finally jumping out of bed, pulling the blinds all the way up in frustrated defeat. Standing half nude at the window, surveying landscape and realizing it never snowed, he played with blinds, dropping then lifting.

This is the day of the blind. Blinds failure to do their job and a blind date tonight.

Saturday morning meant rifling kitchen cabinets looking for that detestable pressure cooker pot. Martha moved it around, maybe spitefully. Wheat flakes, three bananas and most of the family's remaining milk came together in the pot. A large breakfast pot and teaspoon was for prolonged contemplation, giving ample time to think about Merrie Freed, a Columbia History Major and Calvin Graham's first attempt at fixing him up. He perseverated for a month why Elvin should go out with this girl and being a social scientist and a Brit, which had nothing to do with anything but make Elvin laugh, he felt sure of success. Calvin believed it was potential long term relationship material, perhaps getting him to the promised land of manhood and loss of virginity.

Three Merrie phone conversations took place during the week. A first call dealt with History which they both studied; a second dealt with Judaism which they both shared and third with the Vietnam War which they both hated.

Calvin's *AF* girl friend, Bethany, a Columbia English Lit major and her college room mate, Merrie were taking the train in from the city to Princeton. Alex's steady, Christine from Rider College made dinner arrangements. Hyperventilating Nolan was excited; he invited the six for wine and cheese before dinner. Elvin especially liked the idea, maybe impressing Merrie right from the outset, that he had a friend with a castle.

Burgundy sofas in the library were filled by gender; boys stared at girls across the great divide while Nolan hung around the ladder.

"Third time, Calvin you've referred to Bethany as *AF*."

"Acronyms are fun. Bethany, a fellow Brit, is officially my *almost fiancé* as of last weekend. Key word is *almost* so no congratulations yet."

Eyes fixed on Bethany, smiling, sipping and shaking her head. Elvin took to absorbing Merrie's face who stole the same smiling glances right back from Elvin.

"February 15th 1967, last week, thirteen US helicopters shot down in one day, a New Vietnam record. It's horrific."

Merrie was re-tying a blonde pony tail; all traces of a smile that captivated Elvin, were gone.

"It's hard carrying around a penis!" Bethany's heavy British accent delayed an expected reaction response.

"What was that, Bethany?"

"I wouldn't want to be a young American man these days with war, jungles and dying. Remember men have penises."

Nolan agreed. "She's got a valid genital point. Johnson is going to announce in the next few weeks something called a draft lottery which means more penises to Southeast Asia, right Bethany?"

"Exactly."

"How do you know that about Johnson?"

Alex moved to the ladder's first step, looking back around at Nolan who replaced him on the sofa. Nolan was silent, waiting for the sophistication of his guests to change the topic.

"Hey Alex, Robert Oppenheimer died recently. You always wanted to meet him."

"Elvin, you're so smooth changing subjects. You're right about my wanting to meet him. Oppenheimer thought about old stars, with enough mass, collapsing, becoming this thing which sucks everything into it."

"Wasn't he the atomic bomb guy too?"

"Yup, that too."

Fidgeting, knowing his discussion group needed to convene soon because a cat just got out, Nolan also needed to reassure Alex, that Lyndon Johnson could do whatever with a draft, but their discussion group members would be geographically situated far from jungles, rice and chemical herbicides for as long as they wanted. There was nothing ever to worry about; friends of Nolan's could keep the boys far away from bullets.

Another graduation was shared. Rutgers and Princeton had the esteemed honor to have faculty approve, confer rights, privileges and immunities on Elvin Stone and Alex Zari. At a Claremont diner brunch, with health salad, cheese cake, parents and no sister Judy, who was greeted by a monthly cycle first calling that morning, Elvin toasted their college graduation with plain seltzer. The boys were separating over the summer. Alex would visit observatories while Elvin stayed home to work in a Newark industrial bakery.

Later Alex drove down to Nolan and his new garden fountain; an artistic rendering of four cherubs, oval mouths spewing water onto an unrecognizable object. Mesmerized by constant water flow, Nolan sat with a tall glass of alcoholic something.

"Interesting fountain. I like it." For whatever reason, Alex wore a shirt and tie, sensing a formality of the visit and always the man. In all their years, he couldn't remember Nolan not wearing a tie.

"So Mister graduate, you're about to ask me the object of the fountain's oral discharge of water? I see it in your face. Why didn't you take off the tie and come casual? I should've reminded you."

It was so incongruous for Nolan to be wearing shorts, Alex was having a hard time adjusting, looking away from eye contact as if he caught Nolan in an indecent state.

"I was going to ask you about the fountain but I'm clueless. Is it an interpretative exercise, ink blot test or final exam?"

"You've passed finals a long time ago; just stages of growth from now on, so interpret for me. What's the object of water flow? Look carefully." Nolan struggled to get up, Alex lent a hand.

Folded arms and intense concentration brought out an Alex wide smile. "Lyndon Johnson's profile. His prominent obsequious nose getting all wet. I really do see something facial and olfactory now. If I'm correct, then maybe the flowing water from the mouth should've been discharged anatomically further down. It makes sense."

Nolan stumbled, laughing to the point of breathlessness. "Funniest thing I've heard in a long time. Priceless. Anatomically further down, so piss on Johnson. Is that what you're saying?"

"Interpretative. I meant no disrespect. You know that. On the other hand, Elvin and I say it all the time, speed doesn't really kill, Johnson does. I guess you can't blame him, not wanting a legacy of being the first president to lose a war. Elvin always says we'll be selling North Vietnam hamburgers and cola right after the war. Thank God for cola, America's greatest export; not Hemingway but colored sugar water."

"Let's walk. You've impressed a lot of people with your sensitivity and grasp. Having your parents take care of Harvard graduate school finances is commendable. It's the right thing to do for now, not imposing on our little group."

"My father is a comfortable doctor." The tie was stuffed into a back pocket.

"Of course, but it's your whole mature attitude. Here's a graduation gift. You've asked so many questions; most still going unanswered because we believe in stages of growth but here's your gift, a little basic knowledge. We're called Gabriel; simple isn't it? No nickname or code."

"And?"

"Gabriel is vaporous, amorphous, old and born at World War II."

Nolan's right arm was around his protégé, looking cautiously before clearing a patch of trees. Everything was carefully orchestrated; a waiting marble bench, a tray with bottled soda, two glasses with ice cubes, solid, not close to melting. Someone must've just put them there and vanished, amusing Alex.

"Sit. A little history lesson. The attack on Pearl Harbor. A man named John G. Barton, middle name Gabriel. Barton lost someone close on the Arizona. Barton was a Washington insider; deeply, invisibly inside. Mysterious reports got to him that Roosevelt knew long before about the Japanese invasion fleet. A secret decision was made to finally get us into the war because there were still too many powerful isolationists in Washington and Britain desperately needed active help rather than Lend-Lease bullshit. Roosevelt and Churchill became friends, meeting secretly a few times. Very few knew about the Japanese fleet. A spy deep inside Japan found a way to get a coded message out about their fleet sailing to Pearl. The pilots, who saw them, disappeared, never seen again after December 7th. Japan invades and we're at war the next day, but a problem existed with letting the invasion take place; a major underestimation of Japanese fleet strength and amount of damage to be inflicted and lives lost. Our military underestimates things all the time. General Westmoreland keeps saying we're winning in Vietnam. Son of a bitch, watch, he'll ask Johnson for more troops soon."

Color drained from Alex's face.

"Barton swore this would never happen again. Checks and balances not covered by the constitution were now essential. Gabriel was born."

Twice he felt knees buckling and once he leaned on Nolan for support.

"No more knowledge today. Your face looks ashen. You'll forget everything of course. Happy graduation. Have some Club soda."

Alex managed to internalize a sarcastic laugh. Hours ago he was toasting graduation with seltzer at the Claremont diner and now in Princeton, it was called club soda; the same fucking carbonated water. Growing up in the middle of the Polio epidemic with children being paralyzed, he felt frozen like those children but still felt Nolan's arm leading him back to the house. Not knowing for whom or why, a tear was poised.

June breezes rattled Venetian blinds through an open bedroom window as bright sun invaded. Double annoyance ended Elvin's morning sleep.

So much hatred for Venetian blinds. I'll never marry a girl who likes them.

A Rutgers tee-shirt and boxer shorts walked in the kitchen. Wheat flakes filled a small bowl and sprinkled raisins added ambience because it was cheaper than raisin bran. Breakfast took place on a backyard lounge chair. The Stone's had a small backyard for a trendy upscale suburban Jersey town. Thoughts flashed to Nolan's endless rolling lawns and the fact he never saw a fence around the property. An old fence leaned precariously close to falling down just over his right shoulder so a safe distance was measured, with stretched arms, in case it collapsed while he was eating cereal.

The newspaper mentioned a race riot in the Roxbury section of Boston, making him think about Alex at Harvard in the fall. Race riots last a few days then TV news trucks roll to the next story. Societal issues at the root of riots simmer for long periods, like Martha's pressure cooker, now on the stove, doing its thing to apple sauce for the past four hours.

No one ever riots against astronomers, like who cares.

Watching floating wheat flakes in a bowl made him think about Merrie yesterday, and their walking, holding hands on South Orange Avenue.

Merrie exhorted, "Let's go on the Staten Island Ferry. There's a snack bar on board. Rumor has it that maritime tuna salad has sweet pickles chopped up."

Back and forth for two trips on choppy water, there was time for kissing on the upper ferry deck with tuna breath, and several times, with inspiring Manhattan buildings in the background, he got close to the amorous pronouncement of a lifetime, but all he could do was proclaim joint love for tuna salad and their quest, like a surfer's looking for a perfect wave.

Merrie was liked a lot; the first real anything since Caye. They were *passionate* together which was a euphemism for verbal jousting on everything, but always after confrontation and agreeing to disagree, came the kissing, hugging, shrugging shoulders and making up; a real tempest of a relationship according to Martha, who wasn't buying Elvin's glib usage of *passionate*. Twenty years into a relationship, maybe you find points of difference, not in twenty dates. Little patience existed for motherly lectures on relationships because Martha once yelled at his father, cursed him and brought himself to tears at the train station. He wished never hearing parents fight. It may've screwed up the lining of his stomach or worse.

Back in April, he wondered about experiencing that painful legendary boy thing. Would Merrie finally be the one to inspire physical pleasure pain? Several times he asked Alex, reasoning astronomy and boy's biology must have a link of commonality. Hanging out with the discussion group once, the subject came up, partly orchestrated by Alex, who thought peer support would help his anguished best friend. The group told Elvin not to worry, that it happens to everyone and you'll know when it's time. You won't be able to stand-up or breathe hence turning blue.

Calvin was the most explicit. Sitting on the burgundy sofas, with beer and tea, expounding the joys of Friday night, Calvin preached. "The pain is obscenely pleasurable. I spent wonderful hours not knowing what to do. Stand-up. Lie down. Take a shower. Cold versus hot. Forget oral analgesics. You want it to last. It's like wearing a combat medal to a first run picture show. You want the pain originator to come back in a Florence Nightingale costume. Don't ever do anything yourself unless last resort. It's the responsibility of the other pair of hands."

Wheat flakes were finally soggy. Did thinking of blue balls have any connection to his Uncle Charles Blue, now called *blue balls* who charged him $25.00 for a bottle of water? Virginity was getting burdensome and he liked his Uncle's new nickname.

"Is everything alright?" Martha was dusting blinds on the screen porch, with hair wrapped in a multi-color cloth, resembling gear from another continent where Kilimanjaro, Elvin's favorite mountain, resides.

"Things would be, Mah, if I had opaque shades in my room. Don't you have a friend who wanted to buy my Venetian blinds?"

"When are you going to work at your summer job and stop with the shades and blind. You're such a nudge sometimes."

"Night shift starts today. Take a good look at your son. See you in September."

The industrial bakery was near Weequahic Park and Newark Airport, on a street named for a former early New Jersey colonist hero, Frelinghysen. Rutgers Newark's school physician recommended Elvin for the position, which paid obscene amounts of money to smell aroma of baked goods, wear a white uniform, but work close to hot ovens. That job description couldn't be turned down. Ellen Davis Bakeries were part of the national food chain E&D. A fabricated name, it was designed to make shoppers feel comfortable that Ellen was personally measuring sugar and pulling trays of baked goods from ovens with flowery patterned asbestos gloves. Actually it was Elvin's job description to be pulling things out of ovens, reporting to the hard roll department at eight p.m.

Uniform buttons kept on coming undone in the fly, so he was preoccupied when someone cleared a throat.

"Sorry, the buttons aren't working. I was told to look for a man with the tallest hat, like an old fashioned chef's hat. I assume you….."

"Ever been in the army young man? Never assume anything. I got friends who assumed and visit them once every five years. Do you know where?"

"Assume a cemetery."

They both laughed in unison.

Roosevelt Dix wore a tall white supervisor hat and was short, black and soft-spoken. Instant like of the man was important because of the height of Roosevelt's hat and the industrial bakery power it wielded.

Elvin marveled how fast he bonded with strangers. By the end of the first night at the ovens, he offered Roosevelt Dix a ride home and his new friend accepted. He couldn't tell how old Roosevelt was, but assumed older than his father. Eyes had glassy, cataract opaqueness with brows matching a hat.

It was six a.m., punching out time. In Elvin's book of life experiences, it had been a memorable night, spending a few dawn hours on a bakery roof located about a mile or so from one of his favorite dreamy places in the world, Newark Airport.

Job was to empty trays of cooled hard rolls into huge baskets for bagging. Rolls were dough formed, oven baked then traveled into a huge multi-level cooler. The process took an hour and half with an hour down time until the next batch.

With so much in between time, Elvin explored. Railroad car sized vats of cherry and apple pie filling were at the back of the second floor. Quick walk-bys meant bare hand, messy scoops. Chocolate chip cookies made an appearance at one a.m. on a front, second floor conveyor belt. The third floor freezer housed ingredients for creative beverage experimentation. A heavy metal door next to the freezer signed, *To Roof* and *Keep door closed*. Of course there wasn't a sign prohibiting opening the door and exploring the roof.

Slowly, he pushed the door, stopping briefly to fix buttons in case anything popped out with a roof full of people. Newark Airport was shrouded in early morning smog. No one was on the roof, making it feel like a new Shark River or Maplewood train station. Pure ecstatic solitude made him run around the circumference, going airborne, almost tripping on cherry stained whites, attempting to click heels- all because it's a new place to dream, think, snack, get paid and still be at work. Grandma Rebecca was informed about Merrie's Judaism with fifteen minutes still left.

Fifteen minutes could become a sort of lifetime, sitting on an industrial roof, looking at nearby buildings, smog, filtered street lights looking exhausted, and a sleeping airport. Why feel like he's seen the roof a hundred times or that someone was holding his hand, whispering in faint breezes, that he needed to think about the world and that he was really home? "Sedona" was whispered. Then, he said "what do you want?" The breeze answered, "Think."

Suddenly there were a billion cars all driving to the closest ocean. Everybody wanted to go swimming or fishing. Every car was puffing exhaust into the air. Why was the world created so that exhaust is a bad thing? Why couldn't breathing all those exhaust chemicals do wonderful things for a person instead of killing cells? Why are there always side effects when you take medicine? Why can't a package advertise, *if you take this medicine for your heart, it'll probably kill all your cancer cells too.* Another voice, seeing the billion cars, whispered, "It all has to end."

While sitting, pondering the joys of roof-top solitude, something struck him, as if wind driven snow flurries were slapping his face even though it was probably still eighty humid degrees. Early that afternoon, he walked to the side of the garage for no particular reason, looked up at the old decaying roof then down at a semi-corroded piece of two by four. He kicked at it; there was a worm, dried out from the hot sun, on top of the wood. Why think about that worm now? He felt sorry for it, alone on top of the wood. How did the worm get on top and why try in the first place? What was the lure? Why think worm now? Why continually conjure up random things? What does it all mean?

How would he get Alex up on the roof to spend introspective time together? Maybe Roosevelt could help? A few dozen men gathered at the time clock. Clean white uniforms disappeared by morning and you could tell what each man was doing for the past eight hours. Elvin was new to this world, but the Asian with strange glasses probably hung around cherry pie filling while the guy, right in front, had chocolate stains all over his rear. He'd love to know the etiology, remembering Carl Wyler once used that word on a waitress. The guy looked too mean and German to even jokingly ask about the stain.

"Where do you live, Roosevelt?"

"Do you know Newark?"

"Born, raised and love it."

A lingering pungent cherry smell made him keep a distance from Roosevelt in case of a good sense of smell. No one had to know about his dipping into the vat of cherries although he didn't play baseball at three a.m. with the hard roll boys, who used raw dough for a baseball.

"Fairmount Avenue."

"My mother was born there."

Henry Fonda, no Mr. Roberts, one of Elvin's favorite movie characters stood by the railing of a cargo ship, watching a convoy heading in the opposite direction towards the Pacific war which was slowly ending, dying. How frustrating when one is powerless to change things. Stomach muscles tighten, fists clench and maybe a tear appears. To be on a battleship in the war and not on a measly supply ship was important to Mr. Roberts. It was part of his dream, to actively fight for freedom, justice and America. Fulminator mercury can really do that explosive thing to a ship's laundry room? Recently seeing *Mr. Roberts,* Fonda's image was sealed in Elvin's memory. Curiously, you can't shake off a visual thing, like it stubbornly covers the retina.

Standing by the bakery roof railing, empathy sprayed him in the form of drizzle. Elvin felt for Mr. Roberts who wanted to be part of a bigger thing and fulfill a sense of self and purpose. He briefly thought that father Jack and Mr. Roberts were similar characters. He'd never stand by water's edge and watch an unfulfilled life sail away empty over the horizon. Whatever life dished, served, threw, he'd never think, ponder, waver, but jump in, because it was life, and something was now leading him down a road and he had to trust. What if something was a spirit, then decisions or choices could never be wrong. Spirits are never wrong. Was this life just a training base? Was time something or nothing?

Maybe I'd been better off if I never saw the movie in the first place. My father makes me sad like Mr. Roberts makes me sad. They are both yearning; my father for respect and Doug Roberts to be in the war. But there's something else. Maybe you have to be forty to begin to understand.

Drizzle stopped at three a.m. Elvin looked down at the bakery parking lot; dough boys, roll makers, smoking and passing brown bags back and forth. Thoughts danced while drifting; being forty years old, providing for your family, sharing brown bag moments of relief and it bothered him like the swarm of mosquitoes and one solitary lightning bug invading his roof. Alex phoned earlier. He wished being on Cape Cod with Alex, instead of on a drizzly, pebbly roof in Newark.

"Where are you exactly?"

"Nantucket. Any chance leaving your hard rolls and coming up here for a few days? Shark River has nothing on this. We could hike and beach comb on virginal beaches right near where John Kennedy breathed life."

"Don't tempt me, but I've got Rutgers Masters tuition to come up with. I work a lot of overtime. Roosevelt Dix, I told you about him, well he likes me. I drive him home every morning and he gets me overtime."

"I figured it'd be hard. I've been at the Maria Mitchell Observatory and from here to Harvard then home end of June. Meanwhile, the Six Day War is finally over, so you must feel better?" Alex was yelling over annoying background noise.

"It still hurts. People in the Mideast hate Jews who survived death camps. When does hatred end and acceptance begin?"

"For me too, hurt. Too much hate, indifference, injustice. Nobody understands Earth life like us. We get it."

"Let's stay positive, Alex. Thurgood Marshall, a Supreme Court Justice; how wonderful is that. We're heading in the right direction, but why does it seem to take a lifetime to move an inch."

All the time I spend on the roof every night to think about the world, dream and there's always fifteen minutes left.

Dear Heaven, when am I ever? How is it going to happen? I mean it has to happen. It happens to everybody. People are born but it's such a hard thing to conceive of; doing it and putting it there and finding a girl willing to have it put there. The energy involved in just getting there. How will I ever find the place? I'm going to mess up. I know it. I love this roof and Merrie. I think.

Sitting, legs crossed, arms folded, eyes closed, roof pebbles left indentations in the epithelial layer of Elvin's ass. Distant sirens wailed, bringing him to run around the roof. Views were smoggy, sleepy and quiet. Three a.m. July summer mornings do that. A cherry, apple, lemon, freezer-made concoctive drink in a leaky container was chugged, container tossed over the side, provoking the roll dough boys to yell *fuck off*. An only summer regret was that E&D bagels were farmed out, probably to Watson's on Clinton Place so he couldn't sneak them up to the roof in oversized uniform pockets and satisfy never ending hunger pangs brought on by the constant smell of baking goods wafting in the air.

Wonder how many people are overweight who live downwind from an industrial bakery?

Roosevelt waited by the time clock at six a.m.; it was part of their routine, as were all the probing questions Elvin could come up with. Driving Mr. Roosevelt home every morning was like research on a term Sociology paper. His life was hard. Roosevelt felt powerless, pushed aside. People always stared at his color, not character. This morning there were memories of down South, always in the back of everything and being thirsty because they didn't even have colored water fountains yet. Progress was that first *colored* fountain, all by itself around the side of a building.

"I remember it well. My mother was excited. It was always hot in Mississippi and now I could take a drink; how little things in life get you excited."

Turning the corner onto Broad Street, Newark's aorta, brakes were suddenly jammed as Elvin threw his arm across Roosevelt's chest. Eyes filled with surrealism of military personnel carriers, soldiers with rifles and burning buildings. Soldiers, just to the right on foot patrol waved them on. Other cities had riots, now Newark. Roosevelt lived nearby in the central ward, but didn't know where he belonged. Covering his face, tears slid underneath shaking hands; he asked Elvin to take him home. A tightened stomach felt just like when his father cried to his mother. Back then, he ran away to the train station and felt he was running away the same way now.

"Come home with me, Roosevelt. You'll stay with us a few days. My parents would love to finally meet you. I talk about you all the time. Please. It's safer. It's too scary."

"Thanks. You're a good friend, Elvin. Young and idealistic. Always stay that way, no matter what, but please take me home for all the reasons you sense."

Elvin drove around for hours. Fires, sirens and soldiers were everywhere.

No people were out so why call it a riot? Why am I allowed to be here? Why the hell am I here in the first place, a white boy in a black Chevy.

Far from ground zero was the Weequahic section. To know memories weren't burning, Elvin needed to see his old house. No fires or soldiers-just painted signs on store windows, *Soul Brother*, a message for obvious reasons.

Later Elvin and Alex drove back into Newark as a responsibility to feel what was going on first hand. No sense of fear or danger but empathy with people suffering through violent expression. They had to do something, even if it meant seeing first hand and putting themselves at risk.

"Is the old neighborhood alright? Any damage?"

"Nah, just funny signs on windows."

"My father told me about those funny signs."

"Bet they're busy at the Beth emergency room?"

"Schmuck! Where you told me you were this morning, right about that time too, people were shot and killed. My father saw them cover a body with a sheet."

"You said schmuck real Jewish like." The car swerved sharply to the side. "I know that girl running over there!"

"What!"

"She was in a Rutgers class with me. Hey Tasha. It's me, Elvin Stone. Rutgers American history class. Do you need help?"

A girl with a gashed far-head, some blood, stopped. "Stone?"

"Yeah. Come in. What happened?"

"Cops chasing looters on foot. I ran opposite and tripped."

"Let's get you to a hospital."

"You guys shouldn't be here, being white and all. You won't be able to get out. There's martial law or something like that."

They looked at each other and instead of showing fear, they smiled. Alex calmly spoke, "What a revolting development."

"Life of Riley, Bill Bendix."

"What are you guys saying?"

"It's from an old television show. When times were innocent, people didn't lock doors or riot."

"Like now, burning buildings and fighting for freedom?"

"That's why we're both here. We feel."

"You always did, Elvin. Funny how a sister can tell."

At a phone booth, Alex paged Dr. Zari and met him at the Beth emergency room entrance. The boys delivered Tasha. Dr. Zari delivered a nurse.

"Meet Nurse Casey. She's been working eighteen hours straight since the riots began. When you get to the police barricade and they won't let you out, introduce them to Nurse Casey. She shows ID. Medical personnel move about at will. Then get both your asses home and don't come back."

"Thanks Dad."

"Hey Stone, thanks. By the way I got a letter a while back from Caye Cronin, we're friendly. She liked you."

"Do you think it's a record; almost two hours and only one slice of pizza apiece completely masticated? Good thing it's almost Christmas. Maplewood is deserted or we couldn't tie up a table for so long."

A wet napkin attacked Elvin's fresh red marinara stain. "It's good for business, people walk by, see a couple of college kids eating in the window."

"College kids, we're graduates!"

A water glass was finally emptied directly onto the stain's resiliency.

"Look at our sweatshirts. Rutgers, with a red stain and Princeton, unstained and you're still a virgin."

"Don't be such a big shot. It was barely a month ago for your ascension to manhood with Christine and I'm impressed how thoroughly modern you guys are."

"To help your modern quest, Elvin my boy, there won't be anyone down the shore at Sandy's mother's summer house, so just bring you know what."

"Bedding."

"Exactly, as per Sandy. His mother is sensitive and he doesn't want her to think sex happened in the house but said to tell you, "lose it for God sakes already." So did Calvin, before he left for London. Here's the house key. Maybe make an extra one? Remember Carl and the three sets of Grand Canyon keys? Do you have a plan how you're going to get Merrie upstairs in the dead of winter and be nonchalant about it?"

"*The Graduate* just opened in Millburn, then once we get over the Raritan River to Bradley Beach, we'll walk on the boardwalk followed by wine around the fireplace and get really romantic and a little drunk."

"A fireplace in a beach house? I don't think so."

"By the way."

"Yeah."

"When does a Harvard sweatshirt replace Princeton's? Don't you think it's about time you acknowledge going to graduate school there?"

"Good point. How about right after your official ascendancy to manhood?"

"Why don't you just say, after getting laid?"

"Ascendancy mixes love and caring, doing it with a girl you care about. Getting laid is really basic no-frills vaginal penetration without feeling."

"Thanks."

Heavy snow flurries excited Elvin because you're on a winter boardwalk for privacy and falling snow keeps winter strollers away. Brisk wind also meant snuggling, which is all pre-cursor stuff to ascension.

Sandy's mother's house on La Reine Avenue was dark, deserted, and reminded of the hilltop house that Mrs. Bates, Norman's psycho mother lived in. A porch went clear around the back. Maybe all the rocking chairs weren't packed away. If Merrie loved the Staten Island ferry, imagine sitting on a snowy porch before Christmas, rocking in his arms. After fumbling for an eternity, he found one of the three keys made by that foreign speaking locksmith from Maplewood Center, who was insightful enough to ask him why he was so nervous.

A threshold was crossed without drama or carrying. A steep staircase with ornate wood railings welcomed them. Martin Balsam from *Psycho*, head stabbed, tumbling down a full flight, crashing at his feet, sending shivers, greeted him in the hallway. A voice was raised, "Martin, I always liked your acting until you were stupid enough to walk up those stairs without the National Guard. Actually it was Hitchcock's fault."

Meanwhile Merrie was exploring, looking for light and heat switches; one of the things he really liked about her, self reliance and a pink tool chest in her trunk.

"Heat, action, and kiss me." Merrie held wine glasses and a cork screw. "Let's toast, to tonight, waking up together in this deserted place after convincing our parents we're a hundred miles apart at friend's houses."

Winter protective sheets on the living room sofa were tossed.

"Elvin, do you think Dustin Hoffman as Benjamin Braddock could become the torch bearer for our generation? I think he spoke to us. Don't you feel he was having the same hard time relating to his parents? *Scarborough Fair* ripped me apart with a sad, lonely feeling. *Remember me to one who lives there.* True love is fleeting?" She lifted his hands to her breasts.

According to texts on foreplay, they started and things were happening much easier than expected.

"Benjamin Braddock our torchbearer, never! There wasn't a word about Vietnam or Civil Rights and I don't think he knew how to treat women right. Where is your activism, feminism? He pulled off one of the great rescues of all time but sat in the back of the bus with Elaine and not a word to say, just smiling like a schmuck. He isn't bearing my torches and Ben had no clue what do with his life- well maybe plastics. I would've been all over you in that bus, close to ripping your wedding dress off, kissing your breath away."

Hands still rested on her breasts, after all he thought, she put it there and she should take it away.

"We'll finish this later and you're wrong. In the meantime, why don't you rip my clothes off now? Wine did what it's supposed to do. Get what you have to from the car and meet me upstairs."

Candles fit into pocketbooks and he never knew they'd been brought until seeing shadows in the most perfect place in the world, an upstairs bedroom, hopefully not Sandy's mother's. Her blonde hair was free flowing, nude body shivering sitting up in bed.

"Throw me the covers, stop gawking. Didn't you ever see a nude girl? Sorry, I did your clothes removal job for you."

"Nope, never saw a nude girl before and you did good."

Expectation was always being nervous at the juncture of nonchalance and virginity loss, so he undressed slowly, methodically.

"Elvin!" was shouted, so removal speed picked up.

Merrie held the covers off to the side, letting him drop on top. They kissed. Elvin rubbed and moved, trying to line things up as in dry run, not sure where certain anatomical things were situated and how much penetrating force if and when he got there.

"I love you, Merrie."

"I love you too, from that first time I saw you."

"Me too. I kept staring all night."

"I stared right back at you on that burgundy sofa."

A jig-saw puzzle image appeared all of a sudden. Body puzzle pieces tried to fit together and then quietly, he whispered ever so softly, an improvisational prayer for help and not being embarrassed by the end of the night. Elvin wasn't lining up, instead jabbing over a wide section of her thigh, like the up and down motion of an ice chopper. Merrie grabbed, stroked, helped with the alignment and then came wholly ascension and climax of a lifetime. It happened too fast to permanently record lifetime memories.

"My God, that was incredible. Experience will make it last longer the more we do it. I have a confession, I prayed."

"Thought I heard."

"For you to help get me inside."

"So I did."

"And I love you."

Later, when back to analyzing *The Graduate*, he wondered what he'd remember most; ascendancy, jig-saw puzzles or Ben Braddock.

Christmas Eve Day and the boy's were having pizza again. Dramatically thrusting his chest out, Alex proudly displayed a Harvard sweatshirt.

"Christmas Eve, Midnight Mass tonight. Are you comfortable coming with us, Elvin?"

"Sure, I love sharing our spirituality. I've been looking forward. What about a dress code?"

"St. Leo's is an old un-pretentious church, so come as you are. Christine's family has been going there for years. I'll pick you up around seven p.m. We'll hang out with her family; egg nog around the tree and Lionel trains in the basement."

"The thought just occurred to me, this is your third pathway."

"Islam is peace, contentment and soulful. Something is so hauntingly beautiful about the call of the Azaan at the break of dawn and fall of dusk. The Coptic Church has been the same for me all these years; peaceful, fulfilling and purposeful. The Catholic Church with Christine has warmth, love and forgiveness. Look at Yankee Stadium. There are dozens of highways, streets, trains, airports and a river; all different ways for people to get there. Everyone sits together, watches, cheers their beloved Yankees. For me now, it's same thing. I have three roads to find God and spirit and besides I've got another sermon choice. Why, do you think maybe I should take Bar Mitzvah lessons?"

Solemnity was everywhere. Someone near St. Leo's had a fireplace. From years ago, he remembered Christmas Eve and Aunt Wicked Witch and Uncle George's house. Air had that same mystique, so he shoved as much into lungs before walking up steps. People dressed just like Alex said, as they were, somehow making it seem, the only important thing going on, was the holiday, Christmas and having a fashion show with people wearing new finery in a bragging way, just wasn't important.

Sitting mid church, Elvin did everything except kneel and cross. Christine's father took care of the plate. An image of Jesus on the cross, behind the pulpit held him tightly, hauntingly. *Adeste Fideles* transported him to a clearing in a valley, with people gathering. On top of a boulder, a bearded man talked about God, love, forgiveness and mercy; things so forgotten. A voice was soft, filled with an eternity of love and understanding. Elvin squinted, closed eyes, wanting to be there, listening with all the others gathered, wrapped in a penitent sheet.

A visual of Jesus, a Rabbi, carrying the cross appeared. What could've been done if he'd been there? If he was living back then, he'd surely have a lot of friends in Jerusalem. Wearing masks, they could've overpowered and outnumbered the Romans. All of a sudden women and children were being led to gas chambers at Auschwitz. Elvin's mind was firing again. He'd been in St. Leo's before; he was certain or was it Sedona's deja-vu. If people outnumber bad guys, and sense evil about to happen, why don't they fight back? Maybe it's the same thing as looking the other way when you're one of the bad guys. No one really cares except about living out their life's time and maybe getting a shot at heaven. Apathy must be part of human chromosomal makeup. Eyes were still half closed, wrapped in thoughts.

"Hey, you're drifting, wake up, come on back."

For the next hour, Elvin absorbed everything about the service and spirit. Music made him remember looking for Christmas trees and hiding one in the cellar. He wondered about liking Christmas so much and observing Hanukah, thinking someday, if he had all kinds of disposable income, he'd find someone like Carl's shrink father and explore the mysteries of mind and connecting heart, why he was so spiritual. Something indeed happened in Sedona.

Being back out in cold aromatic air felt good; so did wishing everyone *Merry Christmas* and so did Alex's hug, thanking him for their friendship.

SIX

"The sun is hot, perfect weather. Thanks for getting me out of my Harvard environs. Look at that billboard- Welcome Alex, Christine, Merrie, and Elvin." Alex managed to clasp hands together prayerfully, as in exclamation mark.

Christine played along with the fake billboard notion. "Where?"

"Great idea doing this weekend in Cape Cod. Check out that restaurant with the curtains and flower pots. Probably means diner food, so I'm a happy guy."

"Hey happy Elvin, don't forget Bobby winning the California primary yesterday."

"And look where we are, right in the heart of Kennedy country."

"Hyannisport, between the Kennedy atrium and ventricle."

"Is the Kennedy compound near?" Merrie was running fingers through Elvin's hair, longer now than ever. Once in a while, he expressed disappointment in not going through the hippie, long hair stage of life, exploring inner worlds, but instead opting for short hair, and a Masters at Rutgers to teach. But how can you teach young adults, if he missed part of a generation's tumultuous time? Alex came to the rescue. Look at him, worldly, communicative, in touch with world and inner self, and that's what's important, not length of hair, but knowing yourself. Rescue and enlightenment often took place at the Maplewood train station at midnight when Alex came down on weekends.

Christine's Dodge Dart performed its namesake, darting over streets of Hyannisport. Kennedy was an elusive compound to find. No matter how much bad press over the years surfaced about the Kennedy mystique, the boys settled into a lifetime of devotion and reverential respect. Deep within a soul, Elvin Stone had a biological, psychological need to be close to where hero's stood tall, walked on earthly ground and breathed the same air. Part of spirituality existed in that, especially inhaling a molecule of air linking him to Kennedy's Camelot. The world is spirit, waiting for people to discover. Alex shared similar notions. Kennedy was the first president they related to. Eisenhower was a vague image of a bald man whose head looked liked the capital rotunda building. Cape Cod was mystique; Kennedy loved it, sailed on its waters and played touch football on its grass. For years, Elvin felt pulled to the Cape's desolate beaches. Merrie thought it was recovering innocence lost while Elvin asked if it was just paradise that was lost.

In front of the car, a non official looking uniform was giving directions to a car, hands moving up, sideways, so they drove around, never looking in the rear view mirror, at frantic waving hands in *X* formation. Down a hill to the right was an impressive group of houses, with tennis court and ocean view. Christine imagined rich and famous living there. Another uniform stood in the middle of a street as they approached.

"Excuse sir, where's the Kennedy compound? We're tourists from Jersey."

"You just drove out."

Dining in Provincetown could be sublime. They chose ridiculously expensive. *Inn at the Mews* swung on an overhead sign. *Mews* was British, meaning stables- Calvin Graham once explained. A walk down a courtyard behind a building helped the restaurant check feel worth it, because the ambience was as clandestine as a roaring twenties speak easy. The wine list was kept from the Muscatel kid; Jersey palates discovered Coquille St. Jacques as put on earth to be tasted, Cape Cod style.

Commercial and Mechanic Street crowds were mostly tourists. Small quaint shops with candy, beach apparel and post cards dominated. The subtle clash, between old English, Pilgrims and 1968 merchandisers, made Elvin think about running to the old town hall to yell about preserving antiquity, but asked to be restrained before he got into trouble. Artisans and craftsmen spread out on narrow sidewalks; some working with metal sculptures, while others blew pastel dust off easels of caricatures or full head drawings.

"Merrie, I'd love a pastel of you, to hang in my room and look at when we're not together, at least till we're married in November. Excuse me sir, how much for a real pastel not cartoon?"

"Twenty-five."

"You'll always have me Elvin, but I can't pose and see myself on canvas. I really don't want anyone else to see me."

"For real?"

"Really."

"But it's for me. I'll hide it so no one sees, not even my parents. I'll take it down every morning."

"Come on honey, let's go."

Merrie ran to catch up with Alex and Christine but Elvin turned the opposite way, distraught over rejection and stubbornness.

Clouds shot across the moon like a fast frame horror picture, with expectations of a hollering wolf but wolves don't hang around New England beaches. Elvin sat on a driftwood log close to waves that looked like a wake after a canoe speeds by. Despite small waves, tidal changes were dramatic. Every half hour, the driftwood was moved further from water's edge- like sitting by the Bay of Fundy. All this time, he battled with Merrie over philosophical things, not sex, or money, or forgetting a birthday card. Issues were more suited for a psychologist's couch, not for two young people in love. After eavesdropping once from the porch, that was Martha's take- get help.

Swinging a bottle of wine, cork protruding as in a recent opening, Alex found him on the wood, by the beach.

"Thought I'd find you here. Take a swig. Chardonnay in your honor."

"Sorry, hope I didn't ruin your weekend. I felt crushed and confused before. Maybe you need to live with a different girl every month for a year, and then start dating. We're such passionate opposites."

Alex raised his voice, "You always passionately disagree. Martha once pulled me aside, walked me in the backyard, and pleaded with me to talk to you about Merrie. It wasn't natural arguing all the time. Of course I defended you, saying its better ironing all the differences out now before you guys hitch up."

"Do you believe the ironing stuff?"

"I think Martha did."

"Well thanks, I owe you. I always owe you. When Merrie wouldn't pose, I lost it and all over a freaking pastel portrait; big fucking deal."

"But a big fucking deal for her not to pose. It's all in orientation, what side you're looking at. We've been with her. She's really insecure, right down to her face. A father that breaks her down and mother involved in her own vanity- too busy to care or nurture an only daughter. Do you think our parent's generation didn't know how to be involved because their parents were probably first time Americans- immigrants more concerned with food on the table, oil in the lamp?"

"Astronomer you say? Did you switch doctoral studies to psychology without telling me? You nailed it. Our parents never got much from their parents. I think they were more concerned with material things to pass down. We'll be better, modern, caring, involved. Maybe I should go to her now?"

"A few more items before you fix things."

"Sure."

"Bobby Kennedy was shot before and it's not good."

"What! First Dr. King a few months ago."

"No details yet about Bobby. A few words about the draft. Remember when I told you about my sliding into something at Princeton and you'll never have to go to Vietnam. Johnson won't ever get his hands on you."

"Yeah, but I'm OK. I'm going to teach at Weequahic in September. Just found out this morning. I wanted to tell you in person. Teachers in special zones get army deferments." They hugged. "Now Bobby's shot. Ever since Dr. King died, the sun doesn't even seem bright anymore. It's so weird; the whole world has been an empty, dull place, like someone using pastels and rubs things with erasers to tone down. I'm so glad we heard him speak."

"You have no idea how relieved, that you're safe from the draft. Our group is safe too. I've been staring at the ocean all day, thinking, that we've been here before and right now, talking like this. Do you see all the fishing boats?"

"Sure."

"Elvin, we're running out of fish. Too many boats, people, appetites and dependent countries. Fish can't reproduce fast enough. It's a sick feeling- had it all day. Remember walking on the beach last night? I was quiet for a long time because I saw the world without tuna, our favorite food and no one cared, thought or believed it could happen. Can you imagine a few countries fighting a small localized war over the last remaining tuna boat filled with the last catch? Wars are going to break out one day over food. Shoot, you've got more problems right now on the social front. You said *pastels* a minute ago. Maybe you better go to Merrie now."

Merrie was lying nude in bed, a candle glowing on the night table, like the scene from their first time sex. Elvin's lips found her toes. Upward motion was met with uneasiness and squirming by the left knee cap.

"Not that honey, I'm not ready."

Motion continued, legs crossed tightly, knocking a front tooth with a soft thud.

"It's perfect timing, our first oral thing. We love each other and we're making up so uncross. It's to please you and learn."

"Remember the pastel portrait? I'm shy about pictures and embarrassed where you are so just come inside me-you're so good at it now." Arms reached out for him.

"There's no one here but me; nothing to be embarrassed about." Suddenly, jumping out of bed, he ran around the room turning furniture around, looking under things. "There's no one here, promise."

Squirming and rigidity lingered, legs still were crossed.

Looking at the ceiling and a spider in the corner, getting comfortable, ready to watch what happens next before finishing a web, Elvin stopped forward progress. "It's part of love making, exploring and learning. I've got to find out where it is, what it looks like, how to get to it and how or when am I ever going to learn?"

"It embarrasses me. It's ugly down there."

"Watch this!"

Elvin rummaged through a duffel bag, finding a medical text book and a flashlight, sensing back in Jersey, these prop items might come in handy if resistance was encountered for what was on his mind. Covers went over head, like a boy scout tent on overnight.

"There's nothing to be embarrassed about now because you can't see me and by the way, it's not even close to ugly. Natural pink and beige tones like a pastel portrait. Relax, pick up the book you were reading when I came in and I'll see you in 15 minutes."

Voice was muffled and pages stopped turning at a color picture of intricate female anatomy. The flashlight rested on her stomach, angling downwards.

"Think I found it!"

Professional rewarding experiences for a teacher mean standing in front of two dozen teens, talking about the world, managing to hold attention. Elvin was realistic; how do you get high school kids-he's almost one himself, not that far removed-to understand that forgetting history means being condemned to relive it?   Glenn Ford played a high school teacher back in the fifties movie *Blackboard Jungle*. Ford's character inspired but fostered a little paranoia, once randomly calling Merrie at school to make sure she was alright and that a blonde incorrigible student with rolled up tee-shirt and cigarette dangling wasn't following her around. "Are you sure?"

Whenever his class was tested and the room was quiet, he allowed himself drifting time. Sidney Poitier transitioned to *To Sir with Love* years later, as a teacher and became an American acting treasure so maybe he could chase that dream of getting discovered by Hollywood. Sometimes he wondered about his belly and if that acting spark was buried deep inside, after all, some life experiences, learned things, came from powerful movie scenes. Was there something holding him back from digging into his belly? Is digging what separates those who rise up from those who stay put-an unknown element like a chromosome which regulates belly/gut excavation? Even the blow job girl, Carol saw something and thought he should be in acting school with her.

Wonder if Carol ever made it into movies. She would've changed her name, so it's hard to know. I ought to call Cousin Steven anyway.

Teachers lecture, look at student eyes, watch body language and are perceptive, knowing who's paying attention and not. Rutgers taught him how to open doorways of a young mind by embracing, empathizing, and caring. A couple of times during his few month career, he questioned life, second guessed fulfillment; twice at Belmar and once at the train station at midnight. Reality was *teaching* but there were hints of something else, but he couldn't sense what it was. It haunted, taunted, made him uneasy. Something was out there, just waiting. Was teaching just a station or period in his life? Was the real reason for being, existing, still coming attractions? Recently sitting at his desk, in front of the class, he drifted deeply. It was early 1942. Several students said good-bye to him after class to enlist in the Army to fight Germans. He tried to stop them. War was all wrong. They wouldn't listen. Did glamorous movies make the kids enlist? He wondered about the power of antiquated media.

A student yelled, "Hey Mr. Stone, come back."

His head shook sideways, embarrassed that a student had to get him up.

"All right Weequahic freshman history students of mine. We have a new President today, Mr. Nixon. Who knows when and how it becomes official?"

Class seating policy was there is no policy. Students sat in a different seat each time, so they could see a different view of the classroom and when they were gazing out the window, a different perspective there too. Hopefully minds would be stretched to view history differently as well.

"Rolinda."

Her hand always seemed to be waving in front of his face.

"Mr. Stone, Nixon gets something by January."

"Gets what, Rolinda?"

"In something."

"Inauguration means officially becoming President. Right now Johnson is considered a lame duck. It means he's still President, but we know whatever happens for the next few weeks doesn't count. It's almost not fair, if he does something lasting, because we all know he's done."

A student in the last row, always slouching so low, Elvin wasn't sure what he looked like, jumped up.

"He should be done. That man drafted too many kids and got my brother killed."

"I'm sorry, Charles. I thought we'd devote a whole week to Vietnam before Christmas. I think we all have a lot to say."

"Ain't that when you're getting married, Mr. Stone?"

Rolinda smiled too much. Just that morning Merrie stared, said she saw a tinge of aging and that he was getting strikingly handsome. He'd better watch out for those high school girls, being just a tad of a generation away himself.

The nice thing about both their teaching and getting home around the same time was by six p.m. they were having wine in their Maplewood duplex apartment, sitting on the sofa, reviewing day done, and stealing a few kisses. Back in mid September, it was silly for them not to be living together. Parents would have to understand changing modern times.

"Toast. To November 27th and our marriage."

"Does it bother you that there's no honeymoon until Christmas?"

"Nah, bothers me we're not upstairs now."

"It's the craziest thing; two glasses of wine on an empty stomach."

"And?"

"Why don't we go upstairs? You can go under the covers for awhile. I'll start reading *Gone with the Wind*."

Pre Thanksgiving warm stagnant air was met by a windy cold front. Nature was catching up, especially getting rid of lingering leaves. Elvin and Alex strolled around desolate Maplewood center. Store window decorations were in a state of flux; brown themes coming down, replaced by red, green and white, appearing like window dressers just punched the time clock; a mesh of colors were still unorganized behind glass.

"Day after tomorrow, you're finally a married man. Are you nervous?"

Elvin stopped abruptly. "Look at that brown paper bag, blowing around the windy street. It's the loneliest empty bag in the world right now. You're a scientist. Plot out with dots on a graph where it's been and what it's saying. I'll bet there's a message. Look at its free form movement. When the wind lets up, it'll fall to the street and wait for more wind. Should I rescue it?"

"You are nervous."

"You and Christine are getting married in a month too. At least we're each other's best men. We calm the other by listening to narratives about brown bags blowing in the wind."

"What about the Vichy Water?"

"And?"

"The occasion you've been waiting for- your wedding night, romance, poignancy. You're going to open that damn bottle already?"

"Nah."

Laughs echoed on the empty street. A right and left turn down a path brought them to the tunnel entrance under the train station.

Late Tuesday before Wednesday before Thanksgiving, Elvin was puttering around outside the garage. How strange, he thought a few moments earlier, that the two by four was still on the side of the garage, with what looked like a stain from where that worm had passed away. Why still thinking of that worm on wood, still one of God's creatures, or was it? Merrie pulled up in front, accidentally sounding the horn. When you get out of a car quickly, with something on your mind, there's always a body part that confronts the horn.

They went to Martha's kitchen. Elvin tagged first floor rooms with a personal name. It was Jack's porch and Judy's den. Since he was getting married tomorrow, he relinquished all rights to room possession. Hands on hips, she yelled while bringing out an accusatory finger for drama.

General George Armstrong Custer, one of his favorite historical figures with long red hair, almost Beatle like, a handlebar moustache and a sword in a right hand, reminded his troops that the Indians surrounding them were probably friendly. What happened to Merrie? Did his troops need reminding? Elvin readied more onslaughts with a deep breath but knew because of a life promise, he wouldn't reciprocate the high decibel level, but only react in a soft modulated voice. After seeing his mother yell at his father, he swore never to be on either side of raised voices but he'd never give up using *fuck* as an adjective. He knew for sure-it was too valuable a word, irreplaceable and everlasting.

"It's your fucking family. The whole wedding is mostly for your side. Merrie, you pissed my parents off because my mother's close cousins weren't invited and now you're pissed at me because we didn't have lunch together today or dinner last night. I was with Alex but you moved back home two nights ago because the white wedding gown is purer if you're virginal for two nights. We've been fucking, no excuse me, making love; no excuse me, sleeping and eating together and each other for months. I don't get it; you're yelling and screaming about nothing. It's your Mad Freed family magazine that's behind all this and I know it."

"Enough sarcasm. You just called my parents Mad Magazine! Don't say *fuck* to what we do. Stop denigrating. Stop! Stop!"

Merrie ran into the small bathroom off Martha's kitchen. A few minutes later came the emergence with red crying eyes, now slits. She slammed the bathroom door with such force, causing old tiles to evacuate older walls leading to a tile crash like the stock market did. Merrie ran out the front door without closing it. Elvin stood stoically alone, frozen. The only thought which crossed his mind was that Mom, Dad and Judy were sleeping soundly and hopefully, no one heard. Nothing mattered; just family sleeping peacefully.

Life is never simple. Martha Stone walked in from the dining room. Elvin fixed on two tears journeying down cheeks, finally evaporating under the chin line. Tears tied- both moved at the same speed with obviously the same mass. Alex would be proud of his physics comprehension.

Martha took two deep breaths. Suddenly he knew where his deep breath taking came from.

"I'm a mother and we know things. I'm not sure what's appropriate to say. I know you can't marry this girl tomorrow; stop it, call it off. It's not meant to be and there's nothing wrong with stopping it. You fight, argue and sure you do other things too."

"Did you hear everything, Mah?"

"Why, you're living together and your father and I don't think you do those things- well maybe not all of them."

"Mah!"

"It's not a big deal. Get out your phone book, call the Freeds, Merrie and our guests and return the engagement gifts. Most of them are still boxed. Stop this madness. It's not meant to be. Be a man; be true to yourself. You always tell me you need to be true."

Mother almost sounded plausible. Key word was *almost*. Two deep breaths were returned in kind, calmly ready to address a curiously calm mother. "We are getting married tomorrow. Let me tell you something about my generation. Magazine articles say it all the time. My generation is getting divorced all over the place. There's a dramatic rate increase- almost can't avoid it. It's a cold statistic. It doesn't matter who I marry tomorrow, I'm going to get divorced. It's like a gun to my head, so I might as well get a head start and get things statistically out of the way like that first marriage so I can get on with the rest of my life. I can't explain it now, but I know there's something else out there waiting for me. Merrie isn't the final resting place. Do you understand now, Mah?"

"No."

SEVEN

A fireplace, logs nearly consumed, showcased a den. Several mid-eastern artifacts lined the mantle. A family favorite was a bronze reproduction of King Tut, gifted last year when cousins from Cairo visited. Sura thought it one of her happiest times; Alex and Christine settling into marriage, Adel winding down anesthesiology, and dear cousins spending two weeks. The reclining occupants in easy chairs, leg rests horizontal, wore slippers and bathrobes- glasses of red wine, also nearly consumed.

"Christine and mother went to bed. It's been a long day, especially for you and that long drive down from Cambridge."

"Distance seems less each time we come down. Familiarity breeds diminution of mileage. Didn't you ever hear that?"

Wine swished around the glass, passing close to nostrils. Alex smacked lips, thinking about joys of red wine and straying from Elvin's long obsession with whites and muscatel.

"Even with a doctorate, your sense of humor is alive and well. Christine was able to steal away from tax season without upsetting her bosses?"

"She took a course at Rider on flexible life accounting. They love her. I love her. It's OK."

"And you Alex, happy, fulfilled?"

"Hey Dad, why so bittersweet and introspective?"

"I'm a couple glasses ahead of you. Mom and I miss you, so does Elvin. He's here all the time."

"I know, but be careful, he doesn't drag you to the train station at midnight; it's a bad habit."

They had a good laugh- one of those delayed reaction laughs; each knew the other had things on their mind.

"In a few more years your mother and I might do the ornithological thing."

"You and Mom flying to Florida?"

"Maybe. Maybe even stay here in Jersey? One other thing; your mother went for some tests but don't worry, there's no symptoms, it's just a little precaution."

"Dad, don't glib me with the precaution word."

"No glib, no symptoms, just being careful so kiss your father goodnight. I'll close my eyes when I feel your lips on my forehead. You're eleven now and the world is innocent. Tender is the night. Goodnight, Alex."

There was a lack of bounce and vitality out of Adel's exit from the den. Slippers shuffled on shag carpeting; maybe thick pile or extra wine slowed him, but probably not. Aging was detestable in the eyes of a loving son. An evil invisible force was stealing the essence of vitality, youth and memory from his father, but he was still grateful having a father. He always knew spirit would allow both his parents and Elvin's to live a long earth life. Those visions from early teen years, in part just walked out of the den, comforting him that visions were accurate, but confounding him, why people age in the first place. Mother Earth has been around for three billion years and time means nothing- no definition in universal politics. Seventy two point three years meant nothing to Einstein or the universe, unless there's another explanation for life span. Notions of trial runs, extra chances to get things right suddenly popped into mind, perhaps part of a great intelligence. Like Elvin, he experienced moments of strange random thoughts. A temptation to throw the empty glass into the fireplace passed; not wanting to clean broken glass when he'd be meeting Elvin soon.

"Happy anniversary, Elvin!"

"Huh."

"It's 1970, almost ten years ago to the month we met in that vacant lot and here we are- the only semi-downtrodden souls at Maplewood train station."

Alex got up from their bench. The *To New York* sign was rustier and squeakier than normal. "I still love that sound."

"What's the matter?"

"My Dad, aging is dramatic especially since I'm not around much. He's slow motion; thinking, verbal, walking. They're thinking about retiring one of these days. Do you see your parents like that?"

"Sure I do. It bothers me just like you. Whenever I visit, my dad is napping, breathing heavy, chest rising and falling, almost like a last breath scene from a movie. I walk away angry, hating aging. It makes me think about Michael Lauzone. Do you remember our suicide watch for him?"

Track rocks between ties were objects of aimless stares until focus switched to a leaf being pushed around, sideways, resting, and starting all over, thanks to a stiff breeze that smacked them in the face. Alex remembered a vision almost ten years to the day; parents being around until old and wrinkled.

"Did you see the numbers coming in from Nigeria?"

Alex got up again to push the sign.

"A million people died from disease and starvation in just three years."

"Igbos peoples, right?"

"Yeah. I used to think the world only hated and didn't care about Jews. I lost relatives in Europe because of the Nazis. But you know what, the world hates and cares nothing about people who are different colors, poor and have nothing to trade with like oil."

"I know. It hurts to see so much death and suffering and the conscience of the world does nothing. We'll never learn. Bob Dylan's song, *Blowing in the Wind;* think I can listen to it for hours on end. I let it play over and over."

They paced in opposite directions. The sign started squeaking under its own power, in a stronger wind. Their track leaf disappeared into the unknown and both noticed but didn't say anything. Friends knew and didn't have to say. Someone should've rescued it; both thought the same random curiosity. Five minutes passed. Another leaf briefly flew across their field of vision but they were still silent.

"Say Elvin, did you ever think about newspapers and bottles, oil and drinking water; we keep using and taking. It's a small planet. If we were like planet Jupiter and habitable, then we'd almost never have a problem of running out of things. But we are going to run out. No one gives a shit because they know they'll be dead. Live for today and fuck the future."

"We are fucking the future."

"We are. I see it. Hey good news about Jupiter. My father told me just before over a glass of red wine, not your muscatel shit, that in the grand design of things, like the universe, it was a pretty smart thing to put Jupiter where it is because it's so big, it blocks a lot of bad stuff that could hit us."

"So Jupiter is like a secret service agent watching the President and taking a bullet."

"Exactly."

"Tomorrow while wives and mothers go shopping together, we'll see that new Altman movie, *MASH*. Funny thing, Merrie was reading that book recently."

"What's funny about reading a book?"

A single 40 watt light bulb tried to illuminate the tunnel.

Weequahic was yelled, echoes bounced.

The Friday night movie line circled around the block away from the center of town. Why long movie lines? More movie going population, Hollywood doing better marketing, fewer theaters, the world is a boring place with nothing to do on weekends, nobody wants to read or go to lectures anymore.

A recent lecture was held at Rutgers Newark with a presidential historian. Several hours the night before were spent at Maplewood library, so that Elvin could ask an intelligent question. Martha Stone preached about never knowing who's sitting around you. Perhaps an administrator from Rutgers was looking for a bright, talented outspoken History graduate to fill a vacated position. Elvin stood by his seat looking for the administrator. Way in the back was a black girl. His heart raced as adrenaline kicked in. Could it be Caye back from Georgia? Elvin ran up the aisle, tripping on a step. When he got up, the girl was gone.

"One popcorn and two sodas. Alex, Milk Duds?"

"Of course."

Front row seats were all that was left. No one was in front of them so their annoying conversation back and forth trying to figure which one of them was closest to Donald Sutherland and Elliot Gould, *Hawk-Eye* and *Trapper John* didn't offend too many. On screen personalities were uncannily similar to them. Good friends on screen, good friends sitting in the front row, annoying people behind. Forever etched in some kind of stone, Hawk-Eye was Alex and Trapper was Elvin. Before the movie ended, they decided to see it again, same time, next night. Somehow they'd convince Merrie and Christine that people were just too noisy for them to appreciate it.

In a meandering walk near the train station, back to the car, they were too absorbed to notice an elderly woman being mugged by the entrance to the tunnel. She died at Saint Catherine Hospital the next day. Consciences would take time to heal. Elvin thought about a gun. Alex lectured on Dr. King and Gandhi resulting in no more weapon think.

"So, Alex, what did you do this weekend back home in Jersey? Well Harvard colleagues, I went to see *MASH* the whole weekend."

"Don't you feel Vietnam all over instead of Korea?"

"It's just war all over, plain and simple."

Later at Gary's Diner, finishing California burgers, Christine and Merrie finally caught up to their men who didn't stop talking about the movie. In typical humoresque, they ordered apple pie- hold the crust.

"Alex, what's your favorite scene."

"You know me."

"Either when they inject the player at the football game or the dentist scene with *Painless*. John Schuck played the dentist who wanted suicide. That's it- the pretend suicide!"

"The dentist's suicide. Good job Elvin and yours must be the *Hot Lips* bet scene?"

"Yup."

"When are you boys seeing it again?"

"How'd you know that?"

"For the same reason I knew you'd say something about my licking celery dipped in wine."

EIGHT

A wading pool almost filled the area in a small backyard composed of half grass and tired soil- perhaps a conscious refusal of grass to grow on the other half for unknown reasons. Four metal seats showcased flower pots. The plastic liner disappeared years ago on a journey from Michigan to New Jersey. Since Alex grew up fast, the Zari's never replaced the liner.

"I can't believe you found a use for that pool, Mom. It's brilliant."

"Thank your Father, the sentimentalist. He never wanted to part with it; such memories of you splashing, laughing and being a happy boy."

"I'm still that way. Wait, I'll be right back." Alex ran into the house. "Happy Birthday. May 20, 1971. You're sixty. This is something for you now; we'll party tonight."

Sura stood into a hug; the kind that you didn't want to end, with swaying back and forth, no one letting go.

"Sit Mom, open it."

Hands trembled making him think plausible reasons why; medical, situational or aging.

A few motherly tears drifted and hands steadied.

"*The Pieta*, it's beautiful. Thank you my beautiful kind son."

"You up for a walk?"

"And I thought you were going to drag me to the train station! How is your career."

"Every dream, vision come true. I loved Princeton, Harvard and astronomy but miss you and Dad."

"Christine is a miracle in your life; Elvin is another miracle. They were meant to be. Qadr, in my Islamic teaching, means pre-destiny, like your father at the Beth. God works. My age, sixty, brings with it perspective and dreams."

"Life begins at sixty."

"Forty and sixty. Can I ask my son about someday becoming a grandmother and what it means for you to hear that?"

"It means a lot. We think and dream about it, especially holding."

"Holding?"

"You and Dad, Christine's parents, holding a grandchild."

Alex leaned left, kissing Christine goodbye. The new Dodge in their life came by way of spending wedding gifts. Christine's father had a car connection, so four more Dodge years because of a perceived discount and relative in the business of selling cars.

"All these years hanging out with Elvin at this train station and now I'm actually going to take a train."

"Go over your schedule again."

"Maplewood train to Newark, Washington for three days of meetings and back to Boston. Maybe we'll do the Cape next weekend and drag you off to Provincetown to get a pastel portrait."

"Go lick some celery, husband of mine."

A round light in the middle of the engine body told approaching train. Below on the train rocks was a lone Maple leaf, dry, brown, ready to break up into a hundred pieces once the train bore down. Why did he suddenly want to jump down and save it before it was too late?

Something made Alex remember about train tuna salad; specifically about sweet pickles being mixed and crushed. Tuna was on the dining car menu so two sandwiches were ordered, feeling lucky and not wanting to ask a steward if the recipe called for pickles.

Sura was her old self last night- spry, happy and laughing. Elvin called it *blinking well*. If you blinked your eyes long enough in a certain way, everything felt and sounded like ten years ago. Elvin was a big time blinking man, joking about a whole new form of communication. He'd write the first blinking book, and get Calvin Graham, to blinking publish it.

By the time Trenton was announced by a conductor in an art deco hat, he thought serious things, sensing what lay ahead the next three days.

Are there really art deco hats?

Instructions were to find a man wearing a Georgetown sweatshirt and Phillies cap by the taxi stand at the Washington train station. The station was crowded. Thirsty from tuna and pickles but the only visible water fountain was being expectorated into by a man in a trench coat.

"Zari?"

"Yes."

A PhD from Harvard and I don't even get Doctor. On the other hand, who needs to hear it?

"Throw your suitcase in the back seat."

"Alexandria. Is that where?"

"Exactly where we're going. Compton, David. I answer to both."

A front seat handshake was hard to orchestrate and show excitement but Alex didn't think excitement was high priority.

"Alexandria. I was conceived there and named after it."

"I know. Follow baseball?"

"No to that."

Near the Washington Zoo, they pulled over. Thoughts surfaced about taxi cabs in New York and passengers being taken for excessive rides to pump up fares. A foreigner from Kennedy Airport gets on the local news once a year with a horror story of being driven around Manhattan for an hour when he wanted the Bronx. Orchestration came to mind in Nolan's backyard when a tray with soda and un-melted ice cubes waited patiently.

"Say Zari would you mind? Glove compartment. A little box."

"Sure. Compton, David."

A young couple, perhaps in their twenties, approached jogging. Both wore head bands, shorts and plain gray tee shirts. The woman kept pace even with muscular legs and a heaving chest. Alex watched a few sidewalk denizens watching her; watching them watching was actually more entertaining.

By the car, the woman jogged in place while the man came around and bent down at Compton's window. The box was passed.

"See you. Thanks."

"Nice looking running partner."

"Yeah."

Alex turned, watching jogging continue. The box was tossed and caught a few times.

"Breakable contents?" He was still able to catch side views of the heaving chest, watched by people lined up on the sidewalk, like they were at Macy's Thanksgiving Day Parade.

"Packed in newspaper. It's only a vial of Digoxin. Your father would know. Too much brings on a heart attack. Say Zari, are you hungry, because there's a great deli near here with the best tuna around, if you're in the mood for more tuna?"

"More?"

"Two tuna sandwiches on the train."

Alex smiled nonchalantly.

Late Saturday morning. An Alexandria eye doctor's waiting room was full. Magazines were neatly arranged on a table. The arranger probably suffered from an obsessive compulsive disorder. Every title and date was evident. It amused how magazines were returned exactly in place. Eyes that were being examined as the last patient, closed for a few minutes. He couldn't get last night out of mind, obviously back in yet another castle, with endless gardens and an extensive library minus the ladder.

What is it with these people all living in a castle?

Walter Losk showed off the estate with no mention about Gabriel or World War II. Not in the mood for pounding headaches or dizzy spells, he didn't care about getting extra information. Career issues did come up when they approached an ornate fountain, although there were no cherubs pissing on Johnson, so Alex was relieved.

"Alex, we'd like you to think about political astronomy; opportunities that are waiting for you, with your credentials and successes in life. You come highly touted; our group looked forward to meeting you." Losk could've been a distant cousin to the alien forehead, Stuart Grafton; soft spoken with vestiges of a scary, elongated forehead, except his was covered by glued down hair, reaching almost to eyebrows creating a Julius Caesar look and no trace of any gray either, which bothered him.

"Political astronomy, Walter?"

"It means activism in your profession by getting involved with select committees, research arms, Washington itself and slowly gravitating; all which brings you to the world of security clearance and leadership. Remember to think with us and for us. There are benefits to activism. You're a scientist. You'll be able to look down from high up, participate and be involved. When a general is in a helicopter, looking down on the battle field, he sees enemy troop formations, and is able to make adjustments. Generals in helicopters also see a storm approaching over a distant mountain. It's your brave new world so think about it. Before they launch rockets and satellites, hardware sits on the pad getting fueled up; all life support systems checked and re-checked. Let me know if we should continue with launch preparation."

"Do so by all means, Walter."

"Good. You're a quick thinking analytical man."

Walter's arm found Alex's shoulder in a first gesture of warmth.

"Dr. Zari, Dr. Jones will see you now." The waiting room was empty. Three pole lamps were turned off, office keys dangled from the door lock.

"Miss Addonizio, call the service, let yourself out, see you Tuesday."

"Dr. Alan Jones at your service. Let's refract you, check your eyes and we'll chat. A small gift for you; Walter mentioned your enthusiasm and quick decision making. We appreciate self assurance."

"May I?"

"Please."

The gift was gold foil wrapped, about the size of a legal pad, a little thicker. A 1972 Calendar Book was opened- blank pages were rifled.

"I was never much of a long range planner to get a calendar seven months ahead of time. Thank you."

"Why don't you open it to July?"

Two weeks in July 1972 were artificially blacked out and smelled from fresh ink.

"You'll be out west, enjoying security clearance, position and science. Now I've got to put in a couple of drops. Hold this tissue while I dilate your eyes. Remind me, I've got sunglasses for you."

Chateaubriand sat at noon, two round boiled potatoes rolled into each other at six p.m. and three strands of asparagus, tied together with what looked like an umbilical cord linked the two food groups down the middle of the plate. Alex marveled at the precision of the servers. Each of the eight plates honored meat at noon. Four wine glasses, varying sizes, surrounded the plates in a semi-circular pattern. If this was to become part of a new world, there could be a serious withdrawal from the joys of California burgers and tuna with or without crushed pickles.

Toasts followed, one quietly mentioning Gabriel. Earlier that morning, during another garden constitutional, Walter Losk prepped Alex about dinner and afterwards in a direct fashion with no metaphors, generals in helicopters or rockets about to be launched.

"You'll need to listen and absorb. Remember growing up and parents reminding about age, that you should be seen and not heard. Well, you're growing up here so just listen, no contributions or comments and after the meeting, disappear out the glass doors and walk in the garden. We'll have some brandy later, understood?"

"Understood."

The scariest man stood up as they finished dinner.

"We're looking at the publishing of the Pentagon Papers in June, not everything but enough."

Giggles mingled with cigar smoke. All eight men smoked Cuban cigars except Alex and boasted about the banned Communist country of origin and their ability to smoke whatever they wanted.

"Stratton, take a bow."

Another scary man bowed right from his seat; eyes piercing everything in its visual path, making Alex look the other away. Stratton was scary but the subject matter was scarier.

A scary man had a certain look. Guys at Stein's were scary; most of them probably never threw a punch, but stared their prey away. Intimidation was an art form. Stratton was an artist. What the hell are Pentagon Papers?

"Stratton, any comments?"

"Gabriel knew about my proximity to Defense Secretary McNamara and to Gerber. A top secret study got commissioned about US and Vietnam relations from 1945 to 1967 and discusses deliberate military expansion with air raids and other offensive actions. Of course things are kept quiet but Gabriel wasn't happy, so at the beginning of the year, a newspaper was given the information. A few of you smiled for days about First Amendment issues and coming attractions. Gabriel feels people need to know and Stiles is willing and able."

"Stiles?" Losk acted like he didn't know him, but actually wanted the group to know more.

"He's an old fashioned reporter. Gabriel also watches Ellenstein."

Stratton shook his head at Losk, acknowledging the ploy.

"The report won't be kind to Lyndon; looks like he made up his mind to send combat troops long before he had to. I know some think Lyndon's involvement in Vietnam was to preserve a legacy of not being the first President to lose a war. We know it killed that legacy in spite of great work with civil rights and social legislation and maybe our greatest President with social legislation. Thousands of young lives sacrificed mess up legacies."

"And who here gives a damn about Lyndon's legacy? Good old Lyndon, quite a character. I remember having a drink with him at his ranch. We finished, he got up and damn washed his paper cup out in the kitchen sink."

"Any other pending business gentlemen?"

"Astronomer, Dr. Alex Zari, acknowledge yourself."

Sitting in his seat, he bowed.

Three cheers for intestinal fortitude. No smiling, standing and no facial evidence of disbelief. I never wanted to be on a train heading north so much.

Two weeks before Christmas and all through the town there wasn't an empty parking spot. Because Maplewood was like walking in a Currier and Ives painting, it always seemed busier at holiday time. People showed up who didn't belong. The town was slowly coming out of a restrictive phase, although an area country club still kept out Blacks, Catholics and Jews while flying the American flag on a prominent pole in front of the main building. Elvin dreamed of the day when they'd be forced into catering Bar-Mitzvahs because Jews were the only demographic left in town. Imagine Jewish dances and Hebrew National kosher cocktail franks near their flag pole. A phone booth let Christine know she was on call to drive him back to the station.

Perfect timing got Alex on a New York train without a bench wait. Visiting his parents regularly was a blanket of security in an ever changing, cold world. Harvard academia and scientific pursuits would understand extra time with family at Christmas; just get a capable assistant to cover your classes. Asteroids about to

---

be discovered would wait a little longer for their name and number in lights. Tired eyes closed, helped by old-fashioned swaying of the Erie-Lackawanna train. Just before eyes closed, approaching East Orange, he whispered *Erie-Lackawanna* three times, like Dorothy did in *The Wizard of Oz*, except she said, "There's no place like home." Alex knew he was home a long time ago, even in Michigan as a kid. Home was comfort, security, and fulfilling visions of destiny.

Arrival at Penn Station was easy to figure even if you were foreign. Contents of each car jumped out of their seats, grabbed belongings, and condensed themselves at exit doors as the train slowly pulled in. Alex did what Elvin would've done; sat in his seat, pretending there was another stop, closed eyes, and become that leaf waiting to float with windy impetus. Now he was all alone beneath the street, in a strange inhospitable place, with funny smelling air. Too bad there are no blowing leaves in subway tunnels, he thought, as an emerging smile connected ear lobes.

Being a scientist helped with wind direction, adjusting walking accordingly. Northwest wind meant avoiding cross streets, so Fifth Avenue was reached quickly. Window decorations slowed him down; larger stores had a long line of onlookers waiting to see holiday animation displays. Eventually reaching Central Park, near a special Fifth Avenue apartment that was hosting a luncheon, a wallet note confirmed the exact building with doorman in art deco hat, just across the street.

The Metropolitan Museum of Art was decked in flags and banners. Chestnuts roasting were irresistible; museum steps slowly climbed. Another wallet note produced a list of what to see, prepared by Mr. American History. Elvin had him spending time with American Paintings and Sculpture. Parentheses and asterisks advised him to sit, absorb and be prepared for a quiz over pizza later that night.

Double asterisks and parentheses led Alex to *George Washington* by Wertmuller from 1795; unremarkable but yet a hauntingly real portrait. The more he stared, eerily, the more attraction. Elvin loved George Washington; a man way ahead of his time. Washington was the only president, maybe ever, who had feelings about people that mirrored their own; a man of all the people. A Charleston, South Carolina synagogue got a warm letter of congratulations from Washington just after they formed. Roosevelt never sent letters like that- just a ship filled with German Jewish refugees back to Nazi concentration camps to eventually die. Washington, with the help of John Jay, bravely and quietly worked out another treaty with England well after the Revolutionary War. Despite popular opinion and calls for his removal, it was done to keep young America safe from another war with England that could've been lost.

When Alex shook his head, laughing loudly, thinking about Elvin's notes and a future quiz, an old woman, perhaps staring at self in one of the paintings, turned, frowned and silenced him with a finger over lip. Fortunately, it was lunch time and not confrontation time.

"May I help you?"

Sure, I'd love to buy your art deco hat.

"Dr. Zari. For Cunningham."

"Yes. 502. This way please."

I hate mendacity. I can press the elevator button myself and should've never used Doctor, so it's my fault.

A servant with funny patterned socks- maybe pants were too short-opened the door just after the bell, like he was lurking. "Dr. Zari, I presume."

No schmuck, I'm Dr. Livingston.

A library room overlooking Central Park was filled with smoke, bookcases and half-dozen bespectacled men. At this stage, he couldn't help but think strange requirements of assembly at these meetings; scary foreheads, castles, cigars and now round wire eyeglasses, some without rims.

"Gentlemen, Dr. Alex Zari."

"Thank you Stade. Alex, pleased to meet you. I'm Morten Cunningham. We've been waiting, holding off lunch."

Adjacent was a dining room, with same view of the park. Alex gazed across the street, realizing when you can't hear city noise, the park takes on a surreal quality. Heavy wind was still blowing but trees looked stationary and people strolling seemed statuesque, like the view was a borrowed museum painting. Handshakes revealed two generals, two doctors and two plain first names including Morten.

Small triangular sandwiches on three plates were placed perfectly equidistant. A silky frilly table cloth was rubbed between fingers out of visual range; part Alex nerves, part feels expensive.

Stade announced contents as Tuna, Egg, and Caviar. Food sociology is fascinating; doctors opted for black, generals and first names passed beige and yellow. Morten passed tuna directly to Alex without prompting.

Go directly to jail, don't stop anywhere or collect anything. Morten knew about my tuna thing just like Compton, David did.

"Believe you're partial."

Wouldn't honest human relationships receive a real shot in the arm if I just simply yell out, "Stop with the damn tuna already?" I know you all know. You probably put a bug up my ass when I fell asleep on the train. Last time I fall asleep in East Orange, New Jersey.

A dark blue bottle refilled water glasses. When a napkin slipped off, *Eau Minerale* was exposed to a flash back of Elvin's Vichy Water and if that's what this was, or something close, Elvin could be setting himself up for an anti-climatic, uneventful taste experience someday.

"No thank you Stade, perhaps plain seltzer-something with a bubbly kick for the cilia in my nostrils."

"Club soda, I presume?"

Can you imagine a whole day with this guy and his presumptions? Wonder why I'm so contentious. Wonder if he understood the cilia joke?

Sandwiches were consumed before Alex realized that no uniforms were anywhere in sight including suits and ties, except his.

"A brief tour of the apartment. Interesting dining episode before. You noticed we're rather sophisticated with likes and dislikes- part of our job description. The Germans call it *grundlich*, being thorough."

"Impressive Morten. I suppose it's a process for me to acclimate to."

Wonder why a German word was referenced?

"And you will acclimate. General Schmidt will continue the tour in the library."

"Dr. Zari."

"General."

"Please, call me Bill. I'm not in uniform."

"Then, Alex. But I am in uniform."

"The gift from Dr. Jones, the 1972 Calendar book."

"Yes?"

"Two weeks next July, blacked out, but there's a bit more involved, so we need you here first for a briefing on California, then time in California for briefing on Arizona. Why don't you black out an additional week?"

"They ran out of black ink before they gift wrapped it?"

"Amusing."

December sunset light in Manhattan seemed artificial. Alex knew that seasonal adjusting of clocks change illumination by lessening effects of a burning star ninety three million miles away. The Great White Way is always so lit up, one hardly notices when one luminescence sets behind the Jersey skyline, while the other gets flicked on by switches.

Broadway and 42nd Street at Christmas time is a perfect place to meet, even though people were crammed sidewalk to wall. Thoughts about being aching tired, walking around the city, then relaxing muscles and rigidity, so crowds move you along without expenditure of energy was brilliant Alex thinking; a new form of human movement, name borrowed from a new planet or asteroid. Taurus energy was conceived, like bull, not all relevant or truthful, but fun and chargeable with horns. A tired smile surfaced.

A Rutgers cap waved high in the air from one-quarter block away.

"Just get in?"

"I did. Parked at Port Authority. Drove around a few times, figuring probability was high someone had to get back to Jersey then an Arizona plate pulled out."

"Should we walk or cab it?"

"It's cold."

"Cab."

Greenwich Village at Christmas was unlike Times Square with its melding intellectuality, freedom, protestation, diversity, and folk everything, jewelry to music. On Bleecker Street, Elvin stopped to inhale holiday city air.

"I'm hungry Mr. Deep Breath."

"What was your Fifth Avenue lunch like?"

"Triangular thin sandwiches with no crust, tuna barely self evident."

"Harvard alumni's perception of lunch; tuna barely self evident?"

Much like an asthmatic gasping on an inhaler to survive, Elvin needed another deep breath.

"There's Ray's Pizza. By the way I liked that George Washington portrait."

"Knew you would. Here's your quiz."

"Screw you."

Across from a spit of a playground which hosted the best pick up basketball in the city was the Waverly Theatre. *Film Festival* and *Casablanca* lit up the marquis. Elvin blinked, looking at Emerald City for the first time, with a not so eager Tin Man by his side. The lion would've been game for anything Bogart related. Teasing back, Alex said he was an astronomer on loan for the night, but really felt like he was stuffed with hay.

Elvin's hand gesticulated enthusiastically, wildly. "Pretend its World War II. Sometimes I wish being around during the 1940s. Men wore hats as a matter of routine. Imagine owning the first hat supermarket. This may sound crazy, but it was a great war to fight because evil was all over the world and had to be stopped. Evil touched everybody with no safe haven anywhere. The only safe earth people were Aryan blonde, blue eyed and uncircumcised. They would've found me eventually, even you, unless you bleached everything."

"You're just a graphically funny guy. Is it two thousand years of pain and suffering?"

"Of course it is. Alright, back to the scene. It's 1942, and I still wish for a brimmed hat. Look across the street. Humphrey Bogart starring in a new movie, *Casablanca* with Ingrid Bergman and Claude Rains who reminds me of Uncle Charles blue balls. Let's go see it, then Horn and Hardart with tuna stuck behind glass doors and all for thirty cents."

The low voice hole at the ticket booth made him bend down. "Excuse me, but does your theatre give discounts for us sailors about to ship out to Europe?"

"Ship out? Sailors? What do you mean?"

"Never mind."

Casablanca was a serious endeavor so there were no distractions of popcorn, Milk Duds or soda; nothing oral or manual, just concentrating, rocking back and forth. Whispers of impending lines made it to Alex with a three second advance time; accuracy was confounding and annoying by mid-film.

"*Of all the gin joints in all the towns in all the world.* Do you feel his pain?"

"Think I feel your pain more."

"Good thing theatre is empty. Maybe everyone shipped out? *Play it for me, Sam. Play As Time Goes By. You know what I want to hear. You played it for her.* How's that?"

"Verbatim and annoying. Favor old buddy, let me and the old lady with the umbrella, sitting right behind you, watch the movie as God intended, minus parrot impersonations."

Rocking reached crescendo when Major Strasser took a bullet to the abdomen with usual suspects being rounded up. Elvin threw his arm across Alex's chest. "It's my bottle of Vichy Water! I've got goose bumps. Rick and Louis walking into the fog shrouded Casablanca airport but it's really Van Nuys. The beginning of a beautiful friendship; it's me and you, Alex."

"Thanks Rick. Can we go now?"

"Wait for the credits if they come on. Joy Page, the pretty young wife whose husband was losing money at Rick's roulette wheel, was Jack Warner's daughter-in-law. She barely got paid for being in the movie."

"Weren't you at her wedding?"

"Funny."

The old lady hoped for credits too. "Excuse me young man, I almost used this umbrella. Merry Christmas."

In the light of the after movie, the old woman looked like the lady from the museum.

Could they be recruiting that old or was it great make-up or my over zealous imagination after a long day?

A jeep was sputtering. Three uniforms and a civilian walked near an overlook of the Pacific Ocean with the Point Arguello Lighthouse just off to the right. Wind forced securing hats. One hat was removed and slapped against a right leg.

"It used to look like a small church with a pitched roof and lured sailors to find religion a long time ago, then came a disaster when the Lighthouse failed to help a bunch of sailors back in the twenties and they all died. In the sixties that tower was built. There were barracks here, a little community now gone. Everything is part of Vandenberg today."

"I'm disappointed gentlemen. I would've loved to stay in barracks being partial to ocean views." Alex inhaled. Salt air was invigorating; little effort was needed to fill lungs, just face the wind and open wide.

A uniform with the most decorations led Alex back to the jeep while the rest remained far behind. "Yesterday, American History was made at a special event."

"Did I miss something?"

"July 12, 1972, George McGovern wins Democratic nomination and if you're in the party, hibernate and wait four years."

"That bad?"

"Affirmative and that other business, Watergate. Gabriel is watching closely. So is J. Edgar."

"Your take sir?"

Wrinkles formed on Alex's forehead; a dead give-a-way of concern. The past few years, Elvin tried getting him to lose the wrinkling, keeping deeper thoughts to himself. "Pretend you're Steve McQueen, playing cards against Edward G. Robinson in the *Cincinnati Kid*. Show no emotion, never tip your hand."

"I have no take on the situation. Have a nice flight, Dr. Zari. Your suit for temperature variation- just in case- is on the way and sunglasses are not for use on New Jersey beaches."

At the airport, hours before Phoenix take-off, Alex wondered if the old lady from New York was anywhere around and why high ranking military officials are so bland and emotionless. There wasn't a doubt in Alex's mind, that plenty was already known about Watergate, just like so much was known about Kennedy's assassination but as imagined, for the welfare and health of America over the long haul, it was better to let it be. Perhaps at some precipice of doom, when it doesn't matter any longer, those truths could be self evident and promulgated for the curious Kennedy fans like Elvin. Imagine that writer's windfall profits, getting the scoop on all the crimes and secrets we'd like to know about.

Leaning on the window while the plane boarded, he glanced a few times at the next seat, an antithesis of the old woman with a short skirt, perfect knees and meniscus. Smiles were exchanged. Smiling at a random person was a form of mendacity because there's no reason. If the woman weighed three hundred pounds or if it was another man would they be smiling at each other? Sex made them smile at each other. He loved Christine dearly, so he was always conscious about meaningless smiles going nowhere.

Was the pretty meniscus really a passenger or there to see if I eat tuna for lunch?

An arrow pointed to baggage claim. "Just be a regular passenger and follow signs." Those were the last instructions from a man with multiple stars on his shoulder. Were there three or four stars? He couldn't remember. Several planes neared departure as a constant stream of people passed on the left. An LA Dodger cap broke formation, crossing over to parallel Alex at the same time a refugee from a men's room exited with hand drying motions, dramatizing why you don't shake hands with a man leaving a restroom. The stranger lined with Alex on the right.

"Dr. Zari, we're your escorts, welcome to Arizona. I'm Jack, he's Dave; hands are still wet so don't shake yet."

Keeping pace was a struggle. After luggage retrieval, a black Chevrolet, defying airport parking rules, waited half on the curb. After a brief detour to glimpse the license plate, Alex hit the back seat.

"Dr. Zari, General Motors presents a Chevy, specially fitted and serviced for comfort and quick acceleration out of this fucking airport. You don't mind colorful language? Let me know."

"Feel free."

An only thought those first quiet miles was luck to be riding in a special black Chevy, absorbing July hot desert sun for the next few days. The *moist hands* fellow suggested relaxing. If there was no compliance, he thought maybe a blindfold materializes from the specially fitted glove compartment. Small talk segued to prep for barrack, trailer living in mountainous terrain. In between dozing, there was a sign, Route 17 North. That was the only highway sign he noticed. Two hours after arrival at camp, there was an early bedtime.

The next morning, back in the Chevy for a winding drive, they eventually parked by another trailer outpost. A middle trailer was designated chuck wagon; air smelled bacon and eggs. Jack and Dave played monkey in the middle with Alex wherever he went, which required serious getting used to. Intellectually, Alex was coming to terms that he was not put on this good Earth for matters of security details and cloak and dagger intrigue.

Scenery was almost beautiful compared to back home; some trees looked undernourished with stunted growth. Grass was arid brown even though it wasn't desert, but moist mountainous terrain. Several meetings during the day and a few people including him, moved from trailer to trailer, occasionally fake saluting those that might salute back but with no real conversing. Most were ushered along by their own monkey in the middle team.

Back at the ranch at night, in their own set of trailers, there was a briefing ordering comfortable boots for the following morning. Tossing and turning on an uncomfortable bed, near three a.m., Alex moved to the front steps outside then walked out back, found a boulder, looking like it was on loan from the Shark River.

Head was cocked to the sky, whispering, "Why am I here? Is it necessary?"

One-half of the monkey team retrieved him, nearly tucking him back in bed.

Hiking time was designated for after breakfast but first they drove in a caravan of black cars for thirty minutes. Fifteen people were lead down a path by a pony-tailed dark skinned guide. Red mountains, forests, and local botany around the trail were highlighted. It struck Alex's scientific inquiring mind that the guide called all the sights by an own self derived name. A voice was raspy, and hoarse, sounding like fifteen years of nicotine addiction.

"Check that red mountain over on the left, by itself with a flat summit where you could land a fleet of helicopters and don't be fooled, it's vast. The side view looks like a red headed angry woman. *RHAW* if you're into letters. Look for her distinct face. You'll remember always that its *RHAW* mountain, but you won't find it on a map."

Several hundred feet were descended into noticeably warmer temperatures and suddenly, without impunity, Sack, their guide pulled a gun from where socks met pants and shot a snake dead to a stunned gathering.

"A Rattler and pretty common around here. There are a lot of us, so someone was going to get bit and I wasn't in the mood to start sucking or injecting anti-venom. Sorry if I shook you up."

Dinners were meager and the last one was followed by a trip into extreme darkness. Alex missed Massachusetts city lights and basic human needs. Skies were always clear, abundantly filled with stars. He thought about talks with Elvin about fearing the sky and how he'd be afraid to show his young child. Being here reinforced notions that a Zari child would never know that fear. Maybe Elvin had the right idea by just wanting to show his child the Shark River and the horizon. Strange trucks followed them everywhere.

Knowing it's still July but it still felt like a month had gone by even though it was the third night. Their next group drive was into major darkness to a new grouping of trailers and more meetings. This time all fifteen observers were together. Down time, which was like recreational time, didn't provide much opportunity for dialogue and communication. Everyone was fixed in listening mode; every moment accounted for, every step taken, right into the john, with one or two of the monkeys close by.

The fourth night was different. It was eleven p.m. Instructions were to put on special suits delivered from California. A caravan of jeeps arrived, loading them into the cool open air. Sunglasses were secured even though it was unnaturally dark. After thirty four minutes, the caravan ended. Walking seemingly forever, it felt like they were a herd of elephants in a circus, some reaching out to touch the one in front, out of a fear and not seeing where they were going. Arrival was at an open area overlooking something or nothing. Artificial light sources were scattered, some bright, beacon like, aiming high. For Alex there was that sensation of having been before, but this time not out of spirituality but actual. Sensual feelings and emotions played with eyes, mind and heart rate. Alex suspected most of what was happening for the past year, even longer, but especially since opening the calendar book.

After an hour, suddenly came the anticipated arrival of indescribable fear brought on with special effects of incredible white brightness and strange noises challenging a stranger silence. Lights flashed in pretend Morse Code. He appreciated sunglasses but eyes still squinted, mostly in reflex. Air was filled with sprayed adrenaline particulates; that thought crossed Alex's mind, trying to reason elevated heart rates, pounding chests, arrhythmias, and knees wanting to give way. Repeated deep breathing through all the head gear was more than physiologically necessary to fill lungs. Getting dressed earlier, Alex saw a few observers being wired for cardiac and other medical tests. The group stared at eternity for what seemed like an eternity until forces of entropy returned, becoming dark and noticeably cooler again, and back to extreme silence.

By sunrise they were back at base trailers. Along the way, they stopped at a trailer for depositing uniforms into steel cans with lids. Not in decades of life on Earth, had he been so tired and spent, emotionally and intellectually drained. Through it all, he thought of Elvin, and scenarios of explanations, and things his best friend would be able to psychologically handle comfortably. Sura preached, "Better left un-said" and "You're the master of the un-spoken word." Friendship was intense-everything could be shared. What wasn't shared was temporary, inconvenient or protective but never for lack of trust. Their friendship was a beautiful thing in modern times.

When Alex awoke, other observers were gone. Almost amusingly everybody had quietly disappeared into their trailers afterwards. Nothing was spoken as if too beaten, worn down or frightened. The monkeys were even missing last night.

Dave, Jack and the driver without a face, all returned by late morning. Heading back to Phoenix, they stopped for another de-briefing and medical exam a mile off the highway, on a deserted road right out of a John Wayne western. His monkeys decided to fly back to Massachusetts with him. Being close to God at 33,000 feet was looked forward to. Alex needed God, playfully guessing how many, *Dear God* would be whispered by the time they were over the Mississippi and how many before seeing Christine, who'd surely sense something different about him. Of course he'd say there was nothing to talk about, just mundane boring meetings in trailers. Christine was a miracle of insight and companionship, going back to celery days. What was special was the way she knew her man and accepted changing of subjects and waited patiently for inevitable revelations, which always arrived, because Alex quipped all the time, they were both so full of trust.

A taxi pulled away. Dave yelled to have a great Labor Day weekend from the open window and Jack just waved. Still July and do they really care about a holiday months away, so Alex was forced to mouth the *F* word to the accelerating cab. Christine missed a step running down, but he was there to catch her.

"I missed you."

"Me too."

"Let me look at you. Pale. Face looks sunk. You didn't eat much, probably chuck wagon dining. Love is wonderful, a super power with x-ray vision, so are you alright? I can tell there's something."

"I love you. Tell me the bed spread is turned down. It was a long flight." Alex decided that was enough of a subject change.

Nearly three hours on top of a bedspread and a sleeping astronomer slowly awakened to a nude Christine, with a flower paper clipped to pubic hair, holding two long stem glasses of white wine. After a few blinks of comprehension, he slid up in bed. Both now nude, the bed spread and flower were tossed on the carpet.

"That was wonderful. Maybe there's something to be said about three hours rejuvenating down time before. Have more wine; I want to ask you a medical thing."

Broadly smiling, Alex was quick. "Medical is a euphemism for birth control."

"You're too smart, sensitive, intuitive and a wonderful lover; yes birth control." She curled up close. An index finger drew figure eights on his chest, pushing tufts of dark copious hair aside.

"Remember that concerned look with x-ray vision you saw before. I know things are hard to hide, but hours at 33,000 feet, close to God, I prayed and knew we'd have to talk. It's a long way to Tiperarry."

"That's what Elvin says all the time. What are you saying?"

"We need more time. There are fears of being so unsure because I never felt this before. I wonder about bringing a child into this world."

"Something up there or in Arizona made you feel that?"

"Something. I like that word all of a sudden. We'll pray, think, wonder, talk, and love each other and figure things out together."

"Wait, I almost forgot, there's cut up celery in the kitchen."

NINE

"Say the date out loud." Elvin's right hand waved in a prompting motion.

"May 12th 1973." Alex's palms nearly touched the car roof. "Why the strange question?"

Two deep breaths preceded Elvin's impending soliloquy. "You're an astronomer. Time is fleeting. But in the scheme of the universe, earth time is a grain of sand, near where we buried those peach pits a long time ago. Forty earth years means a few generations have roamed. It's long for us, but minor league compared to the Yankees of earth history, and doesn't amount to a hill of beans in this crazy mixed up world. It's still an earth life of knowledge and experience, love and hate, procreation. Do we realize how much we accomplish in that time? But for time, the measurable thing or whatever Einstein thought it was, forty years is nothing but an amoeba crawling around on the bottom of the Pacific Ocean. Mountains in Sedona have been red and around for billions of years and they're just warming up."

"Aptly put History teacher. Do you want to pull over to the side of the road, so we can properly chat about that for the next eleven weeks? We'll find a food store with a working bathroom and talk the weeks away. Of course we won't be able to shower, just wash our hands."

The first laugh, since they left Maplewood for Princeton Hospital arrived like a scene of a vaginal birthing of an infant; a lot of celebratory loud laughter, forced, joyous, painful but therapeutic. Alex and Christine drove half the night from Cambridge which left enough time for a short nap on top of the bedspread. Simeon Morris had called them both; Nolan was passing but there was still soulful flickering, enough to warrant a last trip. He asked for them.

Route One traffic inspired a detour through New Brunswick. Windshield wipers and dark sky kept mood somber.

"I don't know if there's ever a time that windshield wiper sound is happy or mood elevating, unless you're a farmer in Iowa and it hasn't rained in two months."

"Elvin, lighten up."

"I can't, it bothers me- I like Nolan. He needs twenty more earth years, and I wouldn't be so upset. Look over there, beyond the main gate of Rutgers. That building on the left is way more than a hundred years old. Real men-there were no women brick layers in those days- cemented those bricks together. I'd love to research and find information on just one of the workers on that building, like where he's buried, visit his grave, thank him for helping to build posterity. What about his family, descendants, where they are now? The brick at the front entrance of Geology Hall; the third one up on the left was cemented in place by a human man who was here on earth a long time ago and I recognize his accomplishment. It's sanctified; a living and dying." Playing with thumb cuticles, peeling skin to redness, Elvin rubbed his left eye. A *Band-Aid* was opened, to the observation that the *Band-Aid* maker was headquartered nearby.

"Why do that to your cuticles?"

"My father, an uncle and sister Judy do. It's a genetic cuticle gun, drawn from the holsters of nerves."

"You need Carl Wyler's flask right about now!"

"We need levity and the best we could come up with is a brick on Geology Hall and an irritated cuticle. Should we bring something to the hospital room?"

"No, but I'm looking for a carry out liquor store for you and watch the road."

A pale green hallway passed open rooms; oxygen and EKG monitors hissed and bleeped but nothing seemed extraordinarily intensive about the floor. Alex whispered about making patients comfortable. Simeon Morris waved from down the hall.

"Alex, Elvin, Dad will be so happy to see you."

The discussion group used to comment on the power of genetics, when it wanted to be powerful, as in the case of Simeon Morris, so much his father's son. Both stood erect at the same height with identical receding hairlines and round impish faces. Graying temples just over ear lobes completed the genetic mystique and made Elvin think of the actor, Alistair Sim as Scrooge, a perfect look-alike for both the Morris men. Simeon was close to Nolan in thought process as well, so logically he'd go into the family business. Of course, no one knew what that was.

"Can we see him now?"

"Perfect timing. Do you remember that Rutgers math professor and lawyer son? Dad always wanted you to meet them."

"Sure, the invisible man, who hides behind the Military Science Building on College Avenue. I heard it a few times, never questioning and won't now. They're inside?"

Alex opened the door. Nolan turned and smiled. Weakened voice and snaked oxygen tubes didn't deter proper introductions. "Josef, Peter Simmons, finally meet, Alex Zari and Elvin Stone." Breathing was labored. "See the synchronicity here, Josef and Peter teach at Rutgers and went to Harvard."

Alex and Elvin surrounded Nolan, palming gray sunken cheeks.

"Pleasure finally to meet you both. I think you know where my office is. Nolan, we'll be back next week. Bless you." The mysterious mathematician had wildly flowing, disarranged white hair; at first glance an Einstein tousled look. Josef seemed as frail as Nolan. Peter shouldered him out.

A breath was struggled with, and held for a long moment. "No reason to talk about anything other than how you both are. I'm fine with everything, no pain and at peace. When you get to a certain age there's life reconciliation. Boys, I'm fine. Can I still call you boys?" His voice seemed stronger as if saving up and breath holding was working.

"We'll always be boys, Nolan; with a youthful mind and heart even though integument ages, stretches, sags and spots."

"Only you can describe things like that. By the way, I still read the Times. An article this morning said charges were dismissed against Dr. Ellenstein by Judge Barnes." A wink was aimed at Alex.

Intensive care hospital rooms were stumbling blocks for meaningful conversation. Visitors worried certain words or phrases were linked to a future, which was in doubt. The boys sensed it was time. Kisses found each Nolan cheek simultaneously. The boys looked at each other, then Nolan's smiling face; all these years knowing Nolan Morris and respecting, fearing and admiring him, they never envisioned this show of affection. Death bed farewells evoke.

"Why do you suppose he winked and talked about Dr. Ellenstein?"

"You saw that?"

"Never mind. I forgot you slid into something at Princeton. I'm alright. Let's go to Endicott's for a hamburger, hunk of lettuce and a beer."

"Did you feel being with Nolan that he's accepting of his condition, not worried or fearful and he almost looked forward to the next stage or place and was so confident about getting there?"

"Like he knew something we didn't."

"But that something we're closing in on. Maybe we need another dose, Elvin?"

"Sedona?"

"Love you, Elvin. I felt like saying that- my friend forever who thinks so much like me."

"Love you back."

A light mist, almost invisible except for the feeling of moisture on your nose, covered their train station. Elvin lightened the conversation, thinking they were in the land of Dracula, or Baron Frankenstein, waiting for Lon Chaney to show up in costume. It was a dreary night- even too somber for Hollywood visual images.

"Love you, Elvin. How many friends indulge a friend at midnight on a train station bench? I couldn't take it any more. I love my family but there's too much mourning. Nobody goes home. I'll miss her every day for the rest of my life. I tried napping but every time eyes closed, my mother was there. We were walking hand in hand around the block. I used to tease her about coming here at midnight. She'd laugh and said only you could appreciate a hard wooden bench. She loved you and said you and Christine were miracles in my life. And you know, it all fit with what I've sensed years ago, having her around this long. God, I'll miss her."

Walking to the end of cement platform, pretending to stretch, Elvin allowed for a tear. First Nolan, now Sura and soon his marriage would pass on. A Maplewood train station and a mother's afternoon burial were not appropriate backdrops to tell a best friend about finally becoming a divorce statistic. Alex expected it sooner, making comments all the time about his tenacity, like a cling peach in heavy syrup on fly paper.

"Hey come back, you're almost out of sight. You could've right here you know."

"Could've what?"

"That tear."

"Forgot about your intuition. You up for current events?"

"Sure teacher."

"Tom Bradley is the now the new mayor of LA. We're getting there Alex, slowly. June 22nd, yesterday, Skylab dropped back to earth after twenty-eight days up. Would you ever go up in space?"

"Maybe, if they asked. Walk with me to the North Jersey side, we're never there and I need indulging."

"Done."

"Done."

Apartment lights were on. It was two a.m. Merrie was packing, ready to return to parents. Why postpone or try working out inevitability going back to the night before they got married and even before? A sarcastic chuckle waited to be expelled like a piece of meat stuck between teeth or trapped gas in a coal mine, deep beneath the earth. This whole misadventure of marriage to Merrie was pre-destined, right out of Sura's world of Islamic Qadr; so not meant to be. But why did it take so long? Merrie never stopped tightening or wanting to cross her legs when he messed around. It was all now plausible, making sense after the fact. Drifting on the lawn was avoidance, plain and simple and useless energy at this point in his life. "Gurnicht helfen," Martha yelled the other day as he was leaving after dinner. It was Yiddish or German meaning nothing was going to help at this point. What positively amazed him, was at least up to the present moment, there wasn't even a whispered hint of "I told you so."

She's ready to leave, it's early or late, depending, and she orchestrated everything perfectly. There can't be verbal exchanges, no risking waking neighbors. If she could climb back into the womb she probably would. She'd do anything to get close to her mother, who still doesn't give a shit about her. That's a nasty thing to think. But these are going to be nasty times especially when we get down to possession of the Simon and Garfunkel albums.

Merrie was a practical woman. Perhaps he'll always love her in some fashion, his first girl in a few ways. Sentimentality has to count. Then again, *always* loving her was probably bullshit, not a real world. Standing on a patch of grass, staring at the red brick apartment facade, an overwhelming sadness overcame. His stomach really hurt so it was physical too. Whatever, it was over. A relationship breathes and smiles like a person then ends and breathing tubes are un-snaked. Searching for a fragment of redemption, he amused himself; who else would've let him go under the covers with a flashlight and explore all these years? On the other hand, she did a lot of reading.

Three sets of keys in hand. Door was opened. Merrie was sitting on the sofa-a gift from Martha and Jack- so at least, he'll inherit a sofa in good condition after settlement.

"Hi, how's Alex doing?"

"Numb, like me for lots of reasons."

"Don't go there. We've been going there for the past year so please let it be. I'm all packed. After school tomorrow, we'll do money and property housekeeping. Good news, we've got no real property. Maybe it pays to be poor. We've discussed everything the past month."

"No matter what you say and argue, the *Bridge Over Troubled Water* album is mine. I bought it at Two Guys on sale last year. Why can't you remember?"

She wasn't amused and he was visibly pissed at lowering himself with strained humor.

"I'll sleep on your parent's sofa, good night."

Bones, heart and mind ached. Emotionally drained and stomach still hurt. There wasn't any food consumption so it wasn't anything he ate. Shoes were kicked off and tie thrown on a bench. Bedroom door was gently closed. With head on the pillow, which was moved to the middle of the bed- a symbol she wouldn't be back- eyes staring at dark abandon, he whispered, "Fuck you, Merrie," helping him find deep sleep. He'd have to remember about the pillow in the middle of the bed and to think he promised God, the family Rabbi and one hundred fifty guests that he'd always love, cherish and honor.

$$\bigcup \bigcap \bigcap$$

The Garden State Parkway southbound on Saturday August mornings defined car bumpers being close. A dashboard was pounded with a closed fist. A car on the right, keeping sadistic pace and watching pounding, rolled down a window, motioning him to do the same.

"Hey pal. I know how you feel, no escape. We're trapped like animals. So what beach you heading to? " Crossing the dotted line, the yell was loud and clear.

"You know what pal, fuck you! I had to say it. Have a nice weekend though!" Leaning across where Merrie used to sit, sometimes rubbing his crotch or stroking hair, Elvin rolled up the window. The other window was still down; a middle finger pumped angst. Shoulders shrugged, palms rotated upward with laughter at the other car, but no middle finger reciprocity, surprising himself with so much restraint.

All morning a refrigerator door opened and closed for milk, orange juice and beer. The pantry, near bare, was also violated. An early morning nap-sometimes the best kind- searching for deep sleep didn't work. Pacing and television failed to ease a restless mind. Lonely weeks weighed heavy on spirit. Elvin was beaten, confused and lonely. Earth was not a place for him to be alone. We're social beings, needing nurturing, sex, someone to make tuna noodle casseroles, love, companionship, hope and future think. It was all gone. No love was left and perhaps it was too late in life to learn how to make tuna noodle casseroles. Welcoming her back for that alone would work. Carl's shrink father might've kept him on the couch for hours on the tuna noodle thought-kind of a misbegotten form of prostitution since the marriage was really over. Perhaps the worst, his main support system, Alex, was in Massachusetts. How can you miss a friend so much?

Nolan, Sura and a marriage all succumbed so close to each other. A few nights ago, air smelled like September and back to school. History teaching at Weequahic wasn't doing it for him anymore. Challenges faded away. A chest felt heavy, physically hurting.

A new loneliness surfaced because of so much down time to think. Merrie was somewhere at that exact moment. She was at least with parents but maybe with some guy she convinced to go under the covers for fifteen minutes. Mourning dearly departed that morning was now complicated by jealousy which is a miserable emotion, eating away intestines like some flesh eating bacterium.

I need Belmar and the Shark River. Wish it was last December when Sura and Nolan were still here. It was a better state of the world. Maybe there won't be any Parkway traffic.

Something to finally rejoice about- the middle lane bogged down, so that annoying persistent middle finger was lost forever. Empty boulders were all gone when he got to the river after driving four hours. Grandma Rebecca's spiritual shoulder would have to wait until midnight at the train station. Everything was nightmarish; no sanctuary anywhere; just obscene trials and trails of life and a strange pain in his left abdomen.

No one to listen or care, just abject loneliness filled Elvin. Alex was on the Cape, probably having a pastel done of Christine or on a blanket in the hot sun with the Bay of Fundy lapping at his feet. Alex called at the beginning of the week, pleading with him to spend time, take in a Red Sox game or hang in Dennisport with a promise to stay far away from Provincetown memories.

Wine, his parent's sofa and deep sleep took him to Sunday morning. A Maple tree outside the living room window supported a family of sparrows and chirping meant time to get up. A perfect summer morning if you appreciate the ability to wake up, was out the door, but the world was still dull and empty; a feeling hanging over like a bad aura since Dr. King died. Brightness in the world was diminished. The sun was using less wattage.

What a gentle peaceful man. Dr. King dreamed of tolerance, acceptance and peace which was so little to ask for in this crazy world and so much to hope for. He couldn't even find that. God, I cried watching his funeral procession. I really cried. I wish I could've traded places with Dr. King. I'm a grown up and I cried. So, what's going to happen to me now? Do I care? I hate. I'm angry. There's no place, no one. The left side of my stomach hurts so much. My God, I can control the pain. I'm making it worse right now. The fucking pain is listening to me, actually listening. It's getting worse. It wants me to feel sorry for myself. It wants me to drink. It wants me. It should have me. It's an amazing pain. Maybe it's not pain. It's like an obscene narcotic or nude woman on a Zebra, seducing me. Why? There is no hope. I feel like I'm on my knees, at the base of Mount Everest and all I can do is crawl like that worm from my garage- that poor worm. I'm looking all the way up. It's a long way up. I don't want to or do I? This is a hard thing to think of. Maybe that's why so few people follow through. It's hard. My side hurts so much. Forgive me. Anyone.

Hyperventilation squeezed a few tears, trailing away naturally. The television was still on. He slept a few ticks away from afternoon. More tears drained while the rest of last night's wine was too. Television volume was turned up.

He was nude. The bathtub was filling. Merrie's bubble bath was emptied, another bottle of white wine was opened and a box cutter taken from the kitchen drawer that Merrie forgot to empty. More tears wiped and a few *Dear Gods*. Elvin slipped into the sudsy bath; one hand holding wine, the other, a box cutter. The sharp metal blade touched his left wrist; just before, more wine was chugged- almost half the bottle. A left abdomen hurt worse than ever.

Suddenly there was Humphrey Bogart's unmistakable voice then Lauren Bacall. Water splashed explosively during tub evacuation. A black and white movie was on with no recollection of having ever seen it. A new old Bogart film. Bogart and Bacall were standing on a dock near a hotel with dark, ominous, choppy water all around. Lionel Barrymore was in a wheel chair nearby. Elvin froze. A gangster film, *Key Largo*, Edward G Robinson as Johnny Rocco, a hurricane, Indians, all held captive the soul and life of Elvin Stone. For him, it was the blackest and whitest movie ever. Almost frozen standing, he swayed after the last swig. An hour passed, still standing, watching. A curious erection came and went. The hurricane was gone and Bogart, Frank McCloud was going back to Nora Temple on the *Santana*, the same boat name he used in real life.

Suddenly life was real too. An image flashed of standing at the base of Mount Everest, looking up.

Bogart mysteriously came into his life, got him out of a dangerous bathtub and the nadir of life, and gave him a reason to live, if for nothing else other than a promise to stand on that same dock that Bogart and Bacall were on, breathe the same air, look at the same Florida Key waters and to thank God for being.

A lonely apartment wasn't anymore.   Something Bogart was there. Was Bogart symbolic of a spirit in the universe that looked out for him? Elvin smiled, mopping the bathroom. Merrie forgot her mop. He couldn't wait to see the movie again and for the rest of his life, it would be a tech noir reminder of a special energy around his soul. It's really there. You can call it whatever you want, but it's there. Sedona and Bogart were joined in his bachelor apartment, bringing life and hope to a wayward soul. For the rest of his life, and then some, there'd be restlessness, searching and voices only he could hear. A spirit was alive and well, inside and around. He knew about needing time to find this spirit and soul. It's all there for the taking; you just have to be in a position to receive. Elvin thought bathtub and how to go about telling Alex about being in that receiving place, close to eternity.

TEN

Tray tables and seats were back to normal for landing. Alex passed a newspaper to the stewardess. Earlier in the flight, the paper was on the opposite side of the aisle. It was read, folded and stuffed behind a seat until a seatmate politely asked for it- all that before the Mississippi River. The seatmate read for a while then fell asleep. Finally turbulence woke him, letting Alex go to the restroom, retrieving the Times as he squeezed back. Reading passed time over Pennsylvania. The date caught a lazy eye. May 21ˢᵗ 1975, two days old, a fact not realized.

"By the way, Ellen, you've got an old Times floating around the fuselage."

"That's not our paper; ours is floating around first class, so blame it on your fellow passengers." An expressive wink of a beautiful green eye mellowed him.

On the approach to Newark Airport a small, probably inconsequential epiphany arrived. Everything out the window was old, tired, brown, gray and basic dull. The approach into Arizona a few days ago was bright, vital and sharply alive. Was this an unwritten comedy routine? Clouds over Newark seemed dirty old, maybe tired or polluted. Arizona's clouds were virginal wedding dress white. It wasn't Newark's fault that the Pilgrims landed on the east coast first, giving the east a hundred year head start at looking haggard and worn.

A suitcase traveled around baggage claim twice while Alex and Christine hugged. Bedspread naps after long trips were tradition as were train station benches at midnight. After a two hour nap, a nude Christine waited with wine and a fresh flower. Meanwhile, Adel was still anesthetizing patients at the hospital. Visiting Adel in Maplewood more frequently since Sura passed also gave Alex time with Elvin as well.

For the first time at the train station there was another soul, comically downtrodden, head slumped, a NY Mets cap facing backwards, just sitting and looking near death, maybe dead, with no discernible sign of life. Concern about vital signs made them stare at the body, waiting for movement; when satisfied, they took the tunnel to the other side and benched it.

"Midnight and no trains are coming so why is someone just sitting over there, barely alive? What do you think?"

"Why are we?"

"Good point. How'd you like Kitt Peak Observatory?"

"Everything was first rate. What could be bad, Arizona, learning, absorbing, doing my homework. You're going to ask me about the name Kitt Peak- the historian in you. Kitt is actually someone sister's name. Just like Sedona was Mr. Schnebly's wife's name. Remember Schnebly settled Sedona and named it after her."

"I remember that waitress lived near Schnebly Road. We made a mistake."

"How?"

"Maybe we should've joined the fun with her- well maybe me and not you- because I'm single now and I can think those things. By the way, as of this morning my career is over at Weequahic High School. Time to change life patterns and surroundings but I'll miss it tremendously, a very special place. Our molecules are still there though. I check before inhaling. I need change in my life. You've been listening to me talk about it for months. I'm also going to Club Med in July, a singles resort in the Caribbean."

"Do you have another teaching job lined up or are you being rash and impetuous? You have that history." The *To North Jersey* sign was pushed without a rusty squeak, bothering Alex. "Do you believe someone oiled my sign?"

"I'll be at Cranford High School in September, eleventh grade history."

They hugged with the news, while the soul across the tracks took it all in, now sitting upright, Mets cap facing forward.

"Do you think he thinks that.....?"

"Nah!"

"I spent time in Sedona and climbed a mountain barefoot to absorb spirit and energy through soles into my soul. It was our same mountain, certain of it. The sky was perfectly blue. I closed my eyes and sat for hours. Strange, but I think it helped me with seeing things, understanding. You know how we worry about the environment- how into Earth Day we've been. Planet Earth is really heating up. Existence is a race between forces and I'm not sure yet what the finish line is."

Suddenly, Alex walked onto the tracks, avoiding metal, bending down, picking up a Maple leaf, stem intact. "We've been thinking of doing this for years, so now it's ours."

Two hands reached for Alex, holding a leaf tightly. "Finish line? Define. It's too cryptic for me at one eleven a.m."

"Not now. Later. Actually it's late."

"Tunnel time?"

"Done."

Elvin yelled, "Cranford High" right in front of a dim light bulb. Laughter echoed off newly painted walls without local graffiti.

Motion was slow around Rutgers, New Brunswick. The few students around meandered. School year finished. Spring heightened horticultural awareness; everything indigenous to central Jersey bloomed, including weeds and grasses of sneezing variety. Alex sneezed right into a parking space on College Avenue near Rutgers-Old Queens main entrance. A distant doorway in a building was scoped out; the same one Elvin talked about on the day they visited Nolan.

The lawn was traversed to Geology Hall, where he rubbed the third brick up on the left and similarly thought, a long time ago a mason worked on the doorway, had a family and a small house with chimney. Was he a happy mason? He got old, maybe sick then passed. Great grandchildren were somewhere. Leaves swaying in breezes made a soft swishing sound like angels whispering. Maybe he wasn't alone, so he smiled and thought about a best friend.

Before leaving, there was a final palpation of the brick. Rubbing made him think about the train station the other night, sliding into something at Princeton and how they'd always trust each other no matter what. Elvin understood completely; not knowing everything wasn't important, only their friendship. Nothing ever needed to be said, but if ever, then that would be alright too.

Brower Commons dining hall with rectangular pillars was a landmark; a few hundred feet passed on the right was the Military ROTC Building-more like a refurbished house with innocent rear entrance and small shingle, *Dr. Josef Simmons, Mathematics.*

This day was fulfillment of a promise to Nolan Morris after sliding into Gabriel, that he'd find time to meet and get to know Professor Simmons if for no other reason then to learn about the universe. There were ulterior motives. Nolan never elaborated, but Alex always sensed something beneath the obvious things. How thankful Alex was every day on Earth, for the gift of vision and sensing.

"Good afternoon, is Dr. Simmons in?"

"Please have a seat. He'll be right with you."

Immediately an office door opened, as if the opener had an ear to the door, waiting for an arrival.

"Dr. Zari, come in. A long overdue pleasure."

"Just Alex. I'm comfortable leaving the Dr. in the top drawer of my desk back in Massachusetts."

Another man stared out a window, almost appearing like an ornate coat rack, one arm raised and the other half as high.

"Alex, meet my brother John Simmons."

Alex was a noticeable second or two off in timing, words not forming properly, bordering on stuttering.

"Of course your scientific mind must be racing around logic-explains the response delay- how I have a brother who's black, after all, I'm a Jewish immigrant from Russia."

"Actually a quanta of racing around, just like Einstein wanting to ride next to a beam of light and it rather intrigues. I like black and white togetherness."

"We know; proper explanations some other time. Meanwhile we're all sad and miss Nolan- there's a terrible void."

Gray hair clinging to temples, balding palate resembling the symbol for infinity and a paper thin nose made one think Einstein but there wasn't physical similarity, a moustache or even sandals. For shooting star moments, Alex saw many older men in his life looking like Einstein.

"I think about Nolan the same way, repeatedly."

"Did you notice that barn like building with botanical visitors creeping up the side?"

"Ivy, across the street." Alex was fast to reply.

"My real office, the Rutgers gym."

"Meantime, I'm off to the library and a slow descent into the stacks; the deeper into world, lower floors, less life forms, more solitude. Nice meeting you, Alex." John Simmons reached out, both shook especially exuberantly.

Alex would've liked a few more hours with John Simmons and wondered why Nolan never mentioned him. Maybe in wisdom, he knew the thrill of discovery, so typically Nolan. Words were needed to remember this soft spoken man, quickly settling on *infinitely wise.* When the door closed, the back draft shoved air in his face; air then inhaled into circulation and comprehension. A wonderful mysterious presence just left in the person of John Simmons. Alex was John Simmons at times in his life, somewhere, maybe a long time ago or maybe in a hundred years. What this man was, and he wasn't sure yet, but maybe they came from the same helix. A strange deja vu overcame. A universal force brought them together, and would do it again. Josef smiled at Alex's silent contemplative gazing.

The College Avenue Gym was built back in 1938. A small lobby presented glass showcases for trophies. Josef pointed to an up staircase. The gym below was almost empty; a lone student running back and forth while a basketball rested at mid-court. Windows on the second floor were open, waiting for a breeze.

"When the kid starts bouncing the ball, the echo will sound proof us. Nolan thought you as a visionary and perfect liaison. We're different worlds but similar goals in a complicated existence. You just need to shake your head either way- a simple yes or no. Nolan said your intuition was celestial."

"Understood."

There was a brief, once up and down head shake. "I do have one question at this advanced stage of our relationship."

"Hydrocarbons. Oil. That's what we do, Alex."

"I didn't even ask the question yet."

One on one basketball raised noise levels in the old gym.

"Home brewed tea back in the office?"

"Green?"

"Only kind I have."

Two tea cups clicked over a desk; steam drifted straight up.

"To our time together and to universes."

"And to you, Dr. Simmons."

"Just Josef. Dr. is in the top drawer of my desk also. Do you know about Everett's Princeton mathematical doctoral thesis?"

"No."

"You're a spiritual astronomer so you'll understand basic thought."

Two men, in synchronized comic timing, took deep breaths, leaving a vacuum over a cluttered desk.

"What do you think about John?"

"A haunting presence that still fills the room." Alex leaned as close to Josef as the wooden desk allowed.

"John's mother died the day after she gave birth to him under a Maple tree in our backyard. She was a housekeeper next door in Plainfield and had no family, husband, no one anywhere. John became my brother and as you sensed, has unusual gifts as you do. Perhaps we can delve into parallel worlds and quantum thought, perhaps not. John sees as you do. Visions. Ideas. Feelings. You've talked about how you and Elvin sense having been but never were."

Josef walked to the window to lift the shade up. The draw string acted like a silent metronome. Both watched quietly until motion ceased. Alex was tempted to ask why the shade had to be up. Both sensed each one was thinking about the shade, but it wasn't important. Suddenly, Alex thought about a Maple leaf rescued from the railroad track. It was back in Massachusetts, lying under glass on his desk.

"Alex, the doctoral paper thinks about universal wave function which is how particles move around and which may mean everything that is possible happens-mathematically proven!"

"Everything that is possible happens. Do you know what that means to me?" Alex jumped up and started pacing, taking a deep breath, "It's another way to understand God. Infinite wisdom brings quantum mechanics and spirit together. Josef, that alone could explain the Red Sea parting."

After giggling, Josef continued. "There are two worlds, macro and microscopic. Our world is classical macroscopic. Things obey physical laws easily. Macroscopic is composed of microscopic particles acting in unison but indeterminable, because we'll never know what's going on." Josef reached across the table and patted Alex's backhand. "Take a gram of any element. It contains trillions of atoms that are quantum; small mechanical objects all interacting with one another, so we can't even comprehend how many configurations an elemental gram could be in."

"God and spirit?"

"Alex, watch. That one gram of an element with trillions of atoms that are in different positions but we don't see all those positions. We just see one, the gram of any element. Some say wave function collapses into one. So, it's the universe we actually see. If it doesn't collapse, then maybe things melt and become like jelly with no form and if no human consciousness, the universe wouldn't exist."

Alex's voice quivered excitedly, "Accordingly, human consciousness, you and I, collapse the wave function. Our consciousness collapses wave function and without it this desk where you keep patting my hands for reassurance, becomes jelly. Fascinating idea."

"Precisely. It's our consciousness. Now watch parallel worlds come into being. Let's take a gram of iron. Before you or I look, it's in millions, or trillions of possible states with atoms making it up, and after you look at the gram of iron, it's in one state. What happens in between, remembering the gram is made of trillions of positions? Does a person split into copies of himself, for each position, to see each state?"

"Is there contact between the copies of one self?"

"No, each self goes off into separate universes. Do you ever wonder about whether you should've done something or not? Well, maybe you actually did it, because everything that is possible happens. And Alex, there's God for all of us. God is everything possible."

"Strange, I just remembered my father talking about a cat in the 1930's that was both dead and alive at the same time inside a box. Other than provoking thought, I wondered why he talked about that cat."

Josef was standing, looking out the window, flicking the shade draw string, setting it in motion again, "Schrodinger's cat. Your father is wise."

Alex joined him, putting an arm on his shoulder. "But if everything is possible, what happens to probability?"

"No more today, we'll save that until next time, but ponder this, Alex. You asked me about deja vu and why you experience it. What if there are millions of universes? What if there's a leak somewhere into our universe and energy escapes. What if that energy is quantum and has a lock and key mechanism?"

They watched a small group of students tossing a Frisbee back and forth. It sailed onto College Avenue. A lumbering Rutgers bus flattened the Frisbee, crossing the solid white line to do so.

"Lock and key?"

"You take an aspirin. How does it know it's supposed to relieve headache pain?"

"Molecular."

"Of course. Lock and key. Molecular. The brain has a receptor, a lock. A molecule of aspirin comes along and a key finds that specific molecular lock to relieve headache pain- same thing with spiritual energy. From another universe, energy escapes into ours and finds us through lock and key, and makes us feel we've been before, deja vu. But what if we really have been before? What if there are certain places where this energy escapes? When you and Elvin visited Sedona years ago, your souls were opened to receive this energy. Remember, everything possible happens. Energy of thought and feeling is quantum- God's infinite wisdom in creating a very complicated universe."

Alex dispensed a classic exhalation, whispering, "Next week Josef, maybe John could join us."

"You'd like more time with him?"

"Indeed."

"But he might use multiple universes and turn it into being able to fill your car with gasoline for the next fifty years."

"I'd like to hear that."

"Perhaps you've heard it a million times before."

"Perhaps."

They laughed, still staring out the window, watching a student administering first aid to a Frisbee.

Sunday after July Fourth, sitting on an Air France charter to Club Med Guadeloupe with mostly women, probably teachers ready to kick off after school ended. Want to kick off myself after that packing session with Martha last night. Somewhere a seatmate existed, briefly meeting at take-off. She was elementary education, maybe kindergarten and lack of voice modulation filled her MO perfectly. In retrospect, let her roam the aisles for a thousand air miles.

Mirrors never show the same thing to different people. Every so often Merrie complimented Elvin for a certain rugged look, penetrating eyes and becoming more seductive as he aged. Elvin didn't see it, but women passengers passing and smiling did, bolstering a fragile ego and making him briefly believe in wisdom of an ex-wife.

A tall red-headed woman asked permission to sit down.

"Please. Somewhere in the congestion of the aisle I have a seat mate, but then again she might've gotten off at the last station."

"That's a train."

"I know, but still think that's what happened. Elvin Stone, 11th grade history."

Her hands were rough enough to make him humorously think, construction worker, no matter whatever she said.

"Dawn Carter, fifth grade. You from Jersey?"

"Maplewood."

"West Orange. Close."

Elvin never thought they were that close and why didn't he pretend to be sleeping in the first place when her shadow fell on him. The *no chemistry between us* rescue came when seats and trays returned to upright state. A mendacious "see you at bar later" and Dawn Carter vanished down the aisle. Chemistry is a wonderful word but a pain in the ass to teach and not to have when someone sits down next to you for a thousand air miles.

Arrival was festive; scantily clad buxom girls were all over, some handing out native fruity drinks in shot glasses, others dancing. The women got the same treatment from native men. Elvin needed bed after the 1000 miles of Dawn.

For the slightest moment, Elvin thought Robert Redford was sharing a room with him. But why would he be here?

"Ari Weiss, nice to meet you, room mate. First floor is premium at La Caravelle, no schlepping, easy access for quickies when they materialize."

"Elvin Stone, pleasure. You've been here before?"

"Third trip and maybe that charm. You must be a rookie?"

"RRD."

"Rookie, recently divorced."

"You know your letters, but almost divorced. How about showing me the ropes?"

"Throw on some bathing gear, but the kind you part with quickly and screw the orientation meeting. I'll tell all you need to know on the nude beach; sunburned testicles await us."

Being cool means controlling genital excitement and hopefully control comes quickly when you're sitting nude on a towel, gazing at rampant nonchalant nudity, trying to project thoughts beyond pastel water, sagging breasts or pubic variations to hamburgers with holes, grilling at a White Castle in Jersey.

Just think ridiculous things. Erections hate that.

The nude beach was uneventful, but the bar scene amazed. Beautiful people were everywhere- all wanting to get laid before the end of week and most were forthright and open about it. The disco bragged about being open until five a.m. A few hours before that, Elvin nursed a native beer on a ledge just outside. It was a ledge like the structure back in Newark. Ari strolled by, flashing open palms twice, needing twenty private minutes back at the room with a much taller Dawn Carter. Her extreme height made him think of the expression, *acres and acres*, uttered by Sinatra in *From Here to Eternity* from the second floor of the New Congress Club. Elvin loved anything Sinatra who was right up there with Bogart in the cool mystique department. Donna Reed could also be a second mother anytime.

A morning beach calisthenics class woke him with no recollection of passing out on a plastic contoured beach chair the night before. Leaving for a day of scuba, Ari managed to remind him about a Club Med bus trip and not to worry about La Soufriere, a volcano that was going to erupt one day. Nearly out of range, Ari turned to yell a metaphor about Dawn; something about not needing twenty minutes last night because of Arctic Circle temperatures.

Palm trees and azure waters drifted Elvin back to his attic roof. Not long ago, he was in a bathtub, with a sharp instrument. Now he was gulping tropical air, feeling better about life. What if he never turned the television on and no Bogart's voice? Ocean water felt like the bathtub.

"Thank you God, spirit and Alex's universe." No one was around to eavesdrop.

Green, lush tropical views were everywhere out the bus window. When mountains weren't visually holding, panoramic sea views did. Two dozen bus riders bounced side to side at every turn. At a rest stop, a large pot and ladle came out of the belly of the bus. Back in Jersey the same pot was used for pre-soaking clothes. In Guadeloupe, a native, tropical Vodka Rum punch replaced detergent and bleach. Inebriation was as close as an overhanging palm tree frond.

A blonde guide, probably a native Southern Californian, led the group down a path. Every few steps took you closer to a cascading thrashing noise. Bringing up the rear, busy inhaling, touching leaves, Elvin was drifting. From nowhere, a clearing produced a towering waterfall emptying into a dark water lagoon surrounded by thick woods and foliage- dense enough to prevent air reconnaissance. The native punch did what was intended by the Club Med staff- getting everyone nude and in the water.

Sunburned testicles, maybe more irritated than burned, made him decide to explore and not do nude water carousing. Boulders were smooth and slimy, not like the Shark River. There was a way to get under the waterfall; to the left of the falls was a good vantage point. Another bus arrived, adding to nude bather's numbers.

"Excuse, can you help?" A hand reached up just below his perch.

Bending down to hear better, he answered, "Sure, what?"

"How about taking my waving hand and pull on it- called can't get out of the water. Boulders are slimy. I can't grip anything."

Elvin reached and pulled. A full torso nude woman emerged but slipped back.

"Keep pulling, you're losing me."

Ideas about heaviness and gravity were needed to explain her slipping back, but nudity messed him up. She was beautiful; the tug of war continued, still trying to get her out but she didn't think so; her face contorted in obvious frustration.

"By the way, I'm really trying for selfish reasons, maybe a dozen reasons, like wanting to see the real you out of the protection of dark opaque water. In Australia, they'd say you're in a billabong."

"What?" A voice projected more annoyance.

"Never mind. How many times does a Jersey guy get a chance like this? It never happens in Belmar."

"I go to Belmar, what beach?"

"Seventh Avenue."

"My God, me too!"

Elvin was in synchronistic love, maybe.

They walked together until Evie Harris from Manhattan and Westfield found the bushes where a bikini was tossed. An Elvin confession came out about memory failing in hot sun and hoping said condition was applicable to right now. The prospects of never finding that bikini made him smile.

"I like your honesty, hoping I forgot where my bikini was. You must be enjoying yourself; it's not everyday you pull a nude woman out of a tropical lagoon and walk around with her."

"Not everyday."

It was a difficult time for him; avoidance of meaningful staring. Pubic stuff is all right there. It could take months or years back in Jersey to get views like that but he couldn't or shouldn't and didn't look. Maybe there's a universal reward, earned for restraint and keeping eyes straight forward?

"You're cute and you owe me." Evie's face exploded into a Cheshire smile that wasn't going away any time soon.

Her amazing bikini was back on, but there was no need for imagination, he'd seen all of her. Thoughts all of a sudden about thanking the travel agent seemed absurd, but he would.

"Owe you, how?"

"Well in the words of Ms. Evie Harris's fourth grade teaching mentality, you've seen me but I haven't seen you."

Primal arousal traveled all over his body, centralizing at genitalia with throbbing. This elementary school teacher, in less than a hundred words uttered since pulling her out of dark bottomless water, wiped him out.

Elvin rubbed his chin in thought, "My silence is I'm avoiding stuttering by digesting, trying to comprehend intent and stuff like that."

"Enough said, pick me up tonight about. . . ." She looked him up and down. "Two hours before dinner. Room 211. I don't have a roommate. You can pay your debt if you're a debt payer."

"I am."

Tropical climates are perfect for quick disrobing, without much to vacate. Shorts and a Rutgers tee-shirt knocked on 211.

The same smiling bikini greeted him. "From the moment the bus dropped us off, I've been thinking about how much I want you and it's not palm trees, pastel ocean or even native wine doing thinking. Remember we've got Belmar between us and that's reality. I can't get you out of my mind and it's all right if this is all one sided because I'm sure you won't mind at very least fucking me for the rest of the week but if you feel just a little of what I feel then you were standing on the right boulder before and God is doing the rest."

Life's biggest exhale took place. "We've got a decision to make right now!" He held her to a kiss. "The decision will last a lifetime."

"What?"

"Where's our first time place going to be?"

Elvin released her.

"In the shower. I need one badly."

Shorts were pulled down as her knees dropped to the hard floor.

"My goodness. You're all sunburned down there, how come?"

"Long story."

ELEVEN

"Second anniversaries have a symbol- silver is twenty five years. Don't worry, there's lots of time before that. It's a long way to Tipperary." Elvin's razor aligned across a foamy sideburn. Depression of the blade downward took care of a lingering sixties look, bringing him to February 1978.

Evie wrapped arms around her groom, loosening his towel.

"Hey, it's cold."

"Not for long, let me look at my man." Her palm rubbed a shaved face then stroked around. "Not sure about second anniversaries, whether its paper, glass, definitely not gold but pretend its red ribbon."

"Huh?"

"Come with me."

Evie led him by his pointing genital, careful not to walk too fast.

"Get into bed. Spread your arms and legs."

A brown bag on the night table produced a roll of satin red ribbon.

"Don't move to get free, cause you can. No chains or hand cuffs needed for this second anniversary red ribbon treat. Pretend you can't move. I'll do the rest. You're mine and I love you. It's perfectly perpendicular now, so I'm climbing on top for a pretend rodeo."

A few wiggles got her into position, straddling, symbolically and physically in control of the act, something which she liked doing.

"What if I was in that waterfall pool with everybody else, I could've never pulled you out and. . . ."

"Pay attention, here goes."

She reached for a cowboy hat, hidden inside a plastic garbage bag, lying next to the bed.

Glasses clicked, two waiters in old fashioned white aprons approached and when Elvin nodded, a chorus of *Santa Lucia* was belted out while everyone at nearby tables applauded.

"Asti's perfect-feels like we're in Italy. Happy Anniversary." A little box found his crotch. "It has nothing to do with where I put it, just a tease."

"Lovers think alike." A similar little box found her crotch.

Tiramisu with a candle arrived as he got up from one knee, sparking another round of applause.

"You're sweet. It's funny but I'm not embarrassed by you on your knees in the middle of a busy restaurant."

"Now a little housekeeping, I've been thinking that you're right. Maybe this summer we should look around for a house with extra bedrooms."

"There's housekeeping for you too, darling, but actually a confession. I thought for sure you'd pull the Vichy Water bottle out of storage after our rodeo this morning and open it for our anniversary."

"Nah."

A fully carpeted basement seemed like a world without end, or a Great Wall of rarity. Rooms along a hallway had the audacity to be numbered. The hallway finally spilled into a great room with a wet bar at the far end, pool table on left, ping pong on right and rows of sofa seating, like bleachers. Walls were adorned with autographed Philadelphia Eagles paraphernalia. Both sides of the bar caught Alex's eye; on the right was an old fashioned pin ball machine and left was a door with the word *talk*. He couldn't wait for a few things- playing the pin ball if it worked and opening the *talk* door, strangely signed in small case letters. A few casually dressed men milled about like they were in a museum, staring at art treasures while others took to venues.

"Misspent youth, Alex?"

"I had a wonderful pinball teacher back in Newark. Well here goes, my first test at Bryn Mawr." A Gottlieb machine, a favorite brand, was given healthy shakes, knocking lights out, allowing a silver ball to roll silently away.

"Is that a tilt?"

"Sure is. You've got a sensitive machine, Randolph."

Randolph Parker was purveyor of basement and Bryn Mawr estate. Not quite six foot, long thick gray hair was held back tightly by some form of mucilage. Glued back hair made him look taller. When they met earlier, first impression was the portrait of George Washington from the Metropolitan museum. This George Washington was wearing a jeans outfit-western style. Billing called for a casual meeting at the Bryn Mawr estate, but when you're meeting a living portrait of antiquity in jeans, you need fortitude from biting lips. He could hear Elvin yelling, "Schmuck."

"Have you met everyone?"

"Yes, first names only and of course Simeon."

"Good. Before we adjourn to the *talk* room why don't you and I and Simeon meet in room three? Meantime, go play another pin ball game but don't shake so hard."

The largest, most muscular man in the basement put an arm around Randolph, leading him over to the pool table. Alex stared at Victor, meeting him earlier and being an astute first impression man, decided he was a Provincetown caricature; massive broad shoulders tapering to a non-existent waist, so a strong wind might tip him over. Question of the day for Alex was Victor's utilization; physical or intellectual. He hoped the former or there was terrible injustice being perpetrated in the world of Bryn Mawr.

Numbered rooms. I'm in anal retentive heaven.

Scotch and water on a couple rocks arrived with Randolph and Simeon.

"Scotch?"

"No thanks."

"Alex, you've had a chance to think. Does teaching at Princeton interest you? You'll also work on a Washington committee which doles out Federal grant monies and do all the research you want, wherever and whenever." Randolph brushed back hair- the mucilage might've been losing grip.

"Very interested and I'll be near my father. Christine would love to be back in New Jersey too."

"Good, then we've got a done deal in September. You can start to look for a house, whatever you want, Gabriel will. . . ."

"Simeon, can you help with the real estate end. Imagine that, we'll be neighbors. Of course, I won't need a medium sized castle, or even a small one."

"Is that what you think I live in, a castle?"

"Elvin's thinking. He always hoped Nolan would build a real moat-felt it would add a certain ambience."

"Grab a club soda and let's go talk in the big room."

There goes the neighborhood again. Club soda. The privileged class just can't reconcile calling that liquid seltzer, like they do in most places in Brooklyn or Fairfax, Los Angeles.

The *talk* room was an expansive room of bookcases with conference table and eighteen chairs on wheels but actually might've been a recent after thought or addition; no books on shelves, just a fresh paint smell.

"Gentlemen, our Dr. Alex Zari is going to meter out Federal monies for astronomical research and move to Princeton to teach."

A few hands managed a muffled clapping sound while a brand new face appeared with a pile of papers pressed against chest. Packets dropped next to each beverage glass, maybe doubling for an oversized coaster.

"Read silently gentlemen and when done, raise hands, we'll collect."

Strange intestinal twinges shot around his belt line, while a make believe gavel started his pounding headache.

Somebody out there outlined the first year of Ronald Reagan's presidency but Reagan has to be at least a year or more away from even considering or announcing he was going to run. Life is strange. Gabriel is strange but I'm actually accepting all the testicles around or should I call them just what they are to most souls, 'balls'. Plain and simple balls and these men have all the different sizes; some droop more than others. Some droop so much they get wet when they sit. It's so frustrating, because I know so little. What the hell does it all mean? Oh hell, I don't give a shit. I'm going back to Princeton and Adel, Christine and Elvin, so I'm happy. I'll just forget about balls and headaches.

An hour or so after thinking about balls and reading a strange report, the meeting adjourned and Alex decided on being the last to leave the room at the same time Randolph decided the same thing.

The George Washington almost look-alike put an arm around his shoulder, practically yelling, "Happy? Princeton is a good move. You'll be all over the country, writing whatever tickets you want. Were you bothered by that report?

You seemed nonchalant. That powerful looking man you've been admiring. . . ." Randolph raised a hand, covering his mouth, lowering the decibel level.

"I was admiring his physique. You don't miss much, Randolph. I'm impressed."

"He'll be watching over President Reagan one day."

Of everything that transpired the past few days, the comment about Reagan and Victor bothered Alex the most. Too much Gabriel, too much order in the universe, little left to chance. A lingering gavel headache gave way to soothing notions of rushing home now to tell Christine about their moving back to New Jersey.

The day after Memorial Day, 1979 and a spent body feels like it's in slow motion. A three day weekend, summer dreaming made Elvin's morning drive to Cranford High School difficult. Thoughts of vacations, beaches, reading on a blanket under a hot sun, and Kohr's frozen vanilla custard on the boardwalk battled with images of standing in front of twenty-five eleventh grade students, trying to get them excited about Warren Harding and Teapot Dome. No one living in the Continental United States could ever get excited about Warren Harding. If Houdini taught American History, he'd even be having a *hard time* with Warren. Elvin was busy internalizing. Mood for teaching wasn't there today. The last few years, this same mood has been floating around, but he wasn't sure what it meant. Some experts on mood, contributing editors somewhere, said Elvin was burning out. Life wasn't at mid point yet. Without enough life experiences, it's hard to understand etiology of mood or if you're really at mid-life, since you don't know how long you're going to live.

When a rocket is finally launched after sitting around for a week, it's painstakingly slow to lift off the pad because of the enormous expenditure of energy just to move a few feet. He felt like a rocket. Maybe calling in sick was better advised. It was seven-thirty a.m. During the whole school year, his morning meditative time was spent with coffee, a plain bagel at *Clara and Ike Breakfast and Lunch Eatery* near the high school. Tradition was what defined Elvin; an attic, Shark River, bakery roof, Maplewood train station, and now *Clara and Ike.*

School day mornings began with solitude; small table, single chair because he was early enough to slide other chairs away. A water color painting of a beach scene, wispy grass clinging to sand dunes by a leaning retaining fence was near his table. After four months, he once asked Clara about buying the painting for sentimental reasons but was refused for same.

Evie's teaching home, Wilson Avenue Elementary School in Westfield was geographically close enough for her to be with him every morning but the timing was a little off and Evie right backed him, that he should come to the Westfield diner. The subject was never brought up again after that first bilateral rejection.

Coffee spilled on an article about an American Airlines plane crash in Chicago last week. A panicked bare hand blotted and sprayed while a foreign chair approached the table.

"I see you here all the time and on the second floor. I'm Marilyn Winder, English."

She jumped into the seat, trying to win at musical chairs.

"I've seen you too. Elvin Stone, History."

"I know. I asked about you. Meteoric rise on the kids' popularity charts. Congratulations. Cranford can be a tough audience."

Marilyn was older, massively chesty and dressed for accentuation not camouflage.

Barely making eye contact he replied, "I appreciate that. We put a lot into it, but you know that."

"Well, I'm sliding this chair back now, because, but you're an interesting man Elvin Stone. See you on the second floor."

Her moist hand hung around for a few seconds, but was disappointed. An intentionally shaky rear departed. At least the brief interlude helped dry the newspaper. Cranford's first proposition was finished and he still had fifteen minutes left.

Tepid water shot into a narrow space between two backsides. Both body fronts were lathered- Evie's with the benefit of a washcloth. Turning around and helping each other's lathered state, they kissed. A rubber mat with suction bubbles on one side was draped over the stall shower door and plopped near the drain, to rest Elvin's knees.

"Perfect time and place if you're into Pasteur's work with antimicrobials."

"What the hell does Pasteur have to do with where you're at? Bring your face back here."

"It means there isn't a microbe anywhere within five feet of us. We wiped out two bars of soap. It's a perfect time and place."

Water eventually turned cold. Evie wrapped around him, his strong hands supporting her buttocks while lips approached her ear.

In a teacher's scolding voice she blurted, "You're not going to attack my ear now, I hate that. You men think blowing in an ear seduces but it panics me, like I'm in a hurricane and the wind is so strong, it even invaded my auditory canal."

"No hurricane; it's just a whisper to tell you this day began in a special way. An interesting feeling to be down there, like working out in a rain storm because it's hard to see clearly with water in my face. I do hope I got to all the right parts. Seeing my childhood world with me and glimpses of its heart and soul is center stage today and it's deeply personal- all because love means needing to share."

"Sounds like *Love Story*, almost"

"I know, Jennie, I wanted it to."

For the duration of the car trip, Elvin noticed there was no space on the seat between them- a purist sign of love and need. Evie kept hands to herself after their almost accident on the Parkway last winter and a guaranteed summons for Elvin, being exposed and stiffly erect in a moving, swerving vehicle.

"This is my structure, Greek or Roman, not sure. Weequahic Park was magical growing up and just beyond is Newark airport, where dreams begin. This ledge is for thinking. Someday this park will make a remarkable comeback; a shining caring knight on a charging horse just needs to light a fire."

They positioned themselves on the ledge, getting comfortable for a history lesson.

"Can I ask you something?"

They were facing each other, knees near chins.

"Sure."

"Was Merrie ever at these places?"

"Never."

"Why?"

"Because I knew that it would never last? So why bother opening my heart and soul."

"Did she know they existed and how important they were and that you're so spiritual and tender?"

"It never really came up. It was a short marriage, confrontational and unimaginative. We were old before our time."

"Where to now?"

"The birthplace."

Lehigh Avenue bordered the Beth Israel Hospital; a group of buildings with red roof and an old tall smoke stack just as erect as he was once in the car.

"What do they burn there?"

"I'd rather not know because I lived a block away. I could ask Adel to find out."

"Did your mother breast feed you?" Evie mussed hair before glancing by his crotch.

"What the hell does that have to do with anything?"

"Just being silly, romantic and thinking."

Elvin pointed and gyrated, pretending entrance to an amusement park with the world's fastest roller coaster. "That's my house. The fire hydrant let us play stoop ball whenever. Mrs. Dunlop lives on the second floor. I had her son Quincy for senior history and gave him an *A*; maybe subliminal because I knew where he lived. I called a week ago and asked to see their attic and they were thrilled."

Twenty brick steps led up to the porch. The front yard down on the left could've been measured in inches, defining the descriptive word patch.

"Martha tried growing grass every year, but it never happened. Maybe the soil had a built in herbicide."

A tall slender woman, reminding him of tennis great and life-long role model Althea Gibson, who lived a few miles away, opened the door.

"Mr. Stone, welcome."

"Oh, please call me Elvin. I'm too young for Mister. I can't thank you enough. Much of my life is in this house; molecules, atoms, and the air I breathed and of course my dreams. The steps still creak the same way. I love that sound and that some things never change."

Elvin climbed out the attic window. Face rendering cumulous clouds filled the sky. He lay down with hands behind head. Teary at the tender sight, Evie wondered how many people go through all this trouble to find peace, dreams and is able to bring a strange black woman to tears. When he got up, eyes shielded for a glimpse of the airport. After climbing back inside, Mrs. Dunlop and Elvin stared at each another; tears welled before a long silent hug.

Elvin referenced the Raritan River below and the Carborundum factory and how close the ocean was. Ten minutes of silence filled the car. Evie sensed space and time and moved further away. Eyes were intense, perhaps focused on the road, but really not. Elvin was in a drifting state but managed to stay between the dotted lines.

"Sorry."

"How far away were you?"

"Far. You're so much a part of me. This trip, I've done a hundred times. But it's real now, with only one dream left. You're that next to last dream, part puzzle, part life's quest, purpose and where I fit into the scheme of the universe. I'm sharing my eyes, heart, brain waves and soul with you. This day happened many life times ago and now, most importantly with you. This is the only life time that counts, well for now anyway, and an answer to a prayer- a dream and a hope. Am I making sense or are you hearing rambling? I'm so happy taking you around today."

Reaching to muss his hair, with minute pieces of shingle from the roof, Evie's voice wobbled. "There's a spot somewhere in the Pacific Ocean that's so deep, no one knows. But honey, you're deeper. Always stay like this. I think if you do, you're not going to age much. A heart and mind busy searching for something is too busy to age."

Hands squeezed tightly in the middle of the seat.

Sneakers swayed in hands, walking under the fishing pier. Belmar beach was crowded for late spring. A fisherman was casting off just to the left near the end of the jetty. Jumping up in the air triumphantly, dramatically highlighting jetty arrival, his voice strained, "Spirit, hope and the mighty Shark River, really not mighty, maybe just a fancy stream or brook if you're in Montana. It's hard to believe you've never seen it, coming to Belmar for years. I bet you probably expected something with girth like the Mississippi or the Hudson, but it's simple, poignant, filled with memories. I should've etched my name on this boulder and dated it each time, so you'd believe that I was here in rain, snow, heat and wind. I couldn't wait to sit here with you, point at the horizon, watch ships disappear, heading to Africa or the Caribbean. I'd love our child to know about dreaming all this and how it represents hope and that's my last dream. Do I make sense?"

She looked three hundred and sixty degrees in segments before speaking. "That's why I asked you about breast feeding before. I want to help that dream in a practical way."

A long kiss was followed by a boat horn. Elvin was quick to look at the name. No Sedona. During the next hour, she walked away twice, giving him space. Dorothy and Oz and dreams beginning and coming true were part of his drifting pattern. If he had written *The Wizard of Oz*, the ending would've been different. Dorothy would be wearing the red ruby slippers at the black and white ending, back in Kansas. When she finally woke up, *Huck* and *Auntie Em* asked where the ruby slippers came from. Where did they come from?

TWELVE

A shovel pushed light snow down a sloped driveway, exposing black top in four trips. Elvin waved at Evie at the den window. Bad weather meant leaving their East Brunswick home earlier to be on time for teaching. The last four years, being home owners added forty minutes to drive time. Time complaints were few, even when it snowed and the commute became an extra hour or two, because it was part of fulfilling a last dream, painting a bedroom pink, blue or white. Neutral white meant they couldn't wait to see what gender crossed the birth canal.

"Follow me and stay in my tire tracks although it's really not bad, just a little icy."

"You're so good to me."

"Well, I need you perfectly safe because we're winding down on all this basal thermometer shit and right times of the month."

Gloved hands met on the driver's window.

Clara and Ike was empty. Because traffic never materialized, Elvin was early. A favorite gang, the media, splashed news reports for the past two days of the coming snowstorm. Milk and bread in supermarkets were speculated off the shelves. A foot of snow was coming with certainty, now called ninety percent probability. East Brunswick looked like a ghost town when the first flurry arrived. By morning, only two inches had fallen, no traffic on the roads, and the media stuck their tales between, embarrassed for five minutes. One local New York channel featured a bodega robbery story, hoping no one remembered or noticed there was basically no snow.

The Jersey Star Ledger's front page date, January 14th 1985, was circled with a pen and doodled with strange flagella like projections radiating. Why flagella, he wasn't sure. Clara dropped off a pumpernickel bagel and coffee.

At page ten, the front door opened, and Elvin looked up briefly at the pretty blonde woman who sits alone near him and also pushes extra chairs away, does a bagel, coffee and newspaper with no socialization. When Elvin first saw her a year ago, there was an initial smile and a return of same but basically nothing else since, except a few stray looks and smiles that get lost in respective coffee cups.

It was like the game he plays with Alex; who speaks first and abdicates self control. Perhaps even a minutia of high school is mixed in, by having a beautiful girl so accessible but really inaccessible; the girl who never gets asked out because of presumption and spends a lonely four years in high school; if guys only knew.

Mirror image, spirituality and something else, perhaps the way they coolly reacted or didn't react to each was confounding. What a game of cat and partially smiling mouse. Glancing at one another was accomplished by pretending to be inside a coffee cup. Pretend reading material like a newspaper, a Time or Newsweek was always close by. Was it active imagination that he was being subtly checked out? If so, she was smooth.

Page twelve had a story about a robbery in a drug store just up the road in Roselle where once, out of desperation, he stopped off for prophylactics, which the druggist had hidden in the back room. A chair's metal legs squeaking on Clara's hard floor, stopping at his table, made him look up. She was about to sit down, motioning Clara for bagel and coffee.

Before Elvin could react or reject the advancement, she spoke. "A year spent making believe we're not looking at each other but we were. We've passed the test of time and since I'm a European, I moved to you first. We're a bolder continent." A fresh Italian accent sounded like it just flew on Alitalia or came off a boat at Ellis Island.

"You're right. I've been looking at you, especially behind newspapers and magazines. Someone should write a book and call it *Restraint and Stealing Glances American Style* and you're right again, we're not as bold a continent. We've been letting you Europeans set styling trends ever since George Washington kicked your continent out. I'm Elvin Stone. Glad you slid first."

"Sofia Zahl."

"You have a wonderful Italian accent. We should go outside and talk. Your accent could melt the ice instead of all that crunchy salt."

"Thank you." She blushed, giving color contrast with bright green eyes.

"Teachers mostly hang out here, but something tells me you're not a teacher."

"Something is smart then. Since you'll never guess; my father owns an eyeglass and sunglass company nearby."

"I'd play hooky all day just to listen to your accent."

"Hooky? What does it mean?"

"It means, I'd call Cranford High School and tell them I'm sick and can't teach today."

"Are you?"

"Enamored but not sick."

"Enamored?" Sofia look confused, in need of an interpreter.

"It means I like being around you because of your accent."

"Should we sit together, after all, we both do bagels, coffee light and no sugar?"

"If you've gone to all the trouble to notice light and no sugar, then we should sit together."

$$\bigcap \bigcap \bigcap$$

January weather along the Jersey shore is variable. Sometimes a thaw arrives, jerking temperatures up to the sixties or seventies. Most people leave Long Beach Island right after Labor Day and by January, it's nearly deserted. Municipal workers even shut off traffic lights, letting them blink harmlessly until Easter. Speed limits increase by ten miles per hour. Walking a mile for a Camel cigarette is real. Few stores on the long skinny island stay open all year. Snow drifts, absorbing abundant salt air, were shrinking fast.

The island separated bay and Atlantic. Homes closest to water seemed larger with porches, long driveways, and backyards. Several cars were parked by a house on Tenth Street in Beach Haven, near the ocean. Two more arrived just after noon. Four men, dressed winter appropriate walked to the front door.

"Victor. Alex. Smith-Stein. Peter. Welcome, come in. Victor, while you're still dressed, how about a walk on the beach?"

"Sure, Stuart."

Waves seemed tranquilized with small breakers, muffled sounds. Birds with razor thin legs ran near the water line. Victor bent down, scraping up enough snow to ball, then threw it as far as he could. Stuart's eye followed the flight. "Ever pitch, pretty good arm?" He attempted a snow ball throw, except it traveled a few dozen feet, imploding into pieces.

"The art is in packing snow tight."

"No Victor, it's in the massive strength of your arms. I know you've got some time off and spending it on Beach Haven isn't what you had in mind, sorry for the inconvenience."

"There is no wife to lay guilt, so therefore, no inconvenience. I was here a long time ago. My parents used to come from Pennsylvania on daytrips, packing lunches in shoeboxes. Locals took to calling us *shoe-bees* accordingly. It wasn't an endearing term, so I still have a chip on my shoulder only there's no one around right now to try and knock it off."

Another Victor snowball scattered a bird family.

"How's Mr. Reagan? Ready for the second term?"

"He's a good man; just what everyone sees. He loves America. He'll pass Nancy in the hall. They stop and kiss- real love. When we travel to England, sometimes we tell him to stay close because of their ridiculous gun laws, but he slaps his chest and tells us he's packing and that no one would ever think to search him. He's a real all-around man. A little slower lately, but that's alright."

"Reports outlining assigned progress? You've read them?"

"All on target."

"We're pleased."

"I like Gabriel's placement service so to speak. It gives justice to the play on *world* words, brave, new, changing and scary." A last snow ball came apart. "See that Stuart, snow balls break up for me too."

Lunch on a deserted island was imported deli sandwiches from the mainland. Grafton was meeting chairman and official bus boy, clearing the table, pouring coffee.

"Peter, report on that congressman. All we need to know is that everything that can be done was done, that every effort……"

"Every effort, a year's worth."

Peter sat with a furry hat, flaps down over his ears, accentuating a Galveston man dealing with Jersey cold.

"Then arrange what you have to."

"Also gentleman, notes to be passed out and collected about several companies and you may proceed accordingly, exercising policy limits on investment amounts."

Grafton stared down at notes with no guest eye contact.

"Real inside traders. We make it look easy."

"Ted Severance signed on as an interpreter. Good for us and for you, Alex. He graduated with you from Princeton and is in your class so to speak."

"We called him the Bolshevik back then, spoke Russian better than. . . ."

"Is your discussion group proceeding along, Alex?"

"Yes. I'm also going to Europe in May and Hudson's Bay in July."

Pacing around the table, mostly because things were on his mind, the group accepted Alex's way of releasing nervous energy, and let him pace away.

Grafton mumbled, "Hudson's Bay is as close to leaving Earth without really leaving. Anybody else want to go? Victor you can't. Reagan would miss you too much."

"April in Jersey. Isn't that a Gershwin tune?"

Elvin carried Evie's school bag, papers jutting out in different directions like flowers in a vase, until she was comfortably in the car.

"Stop hovering. I can close the door myself, perfectly capable."

"Do you think the next nine months can be hovering free? It's April sixteenth and with the call last night, I have to hover. It's my new job as an expectant father."

Annoyingly following the car down the driveway, Elvin provoked tires screeching; Evie's delivered message about laissez-faire.

Clara and Ike was busy. Hovering allowed two nervy strangers to capture his table. It was a rape and violation of sanctity.

"Excuse me, it's crowded." Elvin's hands clasped together prayerfully.

Sofia's eyes lifted, a yellow pencil behind a right ear almost perfectly blended with blonde hair. "Sure."

For the past few months sitting together was also role playing - each morning appeared to be a first chance meeting, just in case anyone from school or office had crazy notions.

"I was getting worried, you're never late. There's a glowing look about you; tell me good news."

When Sofia Zahl got excited or emotional, green eyes exploded, taking up twice the area on her face, with a small wrinkle just over the brows, like an informal boundary line.

"Last night, the call came, we're having a baby."

A quick glance at people at the next table made Sofia's hand reach for a perfunctory shake.

"Congratulations. I owe you a real hug. When's Evie due?"

"January, and it's so scary. I've waited most of my conscious life to be a father."

"I'm so happy for you. Did anyone ever tell you that when you walk into a room, you bring energy and spirit? You can almost touch it. There's something about you; a warmth, caring and sincerity. I've felt it for a long time and yes, there's something about us too, of course nothing romantic. It's hard for an Italian girl to express with the right words."

"And there's something magical about you too and forget how beautiful you are or any romantic stuff, but you're right, something about us, a friendship and I'm never at a loss for words, except now. We'll figure it out someday."

Legs brushed briefly under the table, like one or both was probing on purpose.

"This may be the craziest thought since my coming to America." Sofia's eyes exploded again.

"Go ahead."

"My father's starting another division in the fall and we're going to need sales reps- there's good money selling eyeglasses. Why don't you think about it?"

Leaning against a Maple tree, Elvin watched student party guests rotate around a smoky barbecue like spokes on a wheel. Orange and black balloons, some with the Princeton Tiger, were tied to table weights. Blinks were recollections of Nolan's backyard parties and life's full circle with Alex now doing the same. Blinking is remembering that a few short years ago, he was in a different world, that's not coming back and why after every blink, was it a better, more innocent, bittersweet time back then. He wondered if in human history, present time is ever viewed as all the things past was supposed to be, meaning, live for the *now* moment. He read about two North Jersey murders yesterday and thought back to childhood days in Newark; there was never a time walking home from Maple Avenue School, when house doors were locked. A piece of tree bark was squeezed tightly in his right hand, meaning he wanted back those innocent days of separate music and art teachers and having to wait patiently most summer nights for the *Good Humor* man to find his *Toasted Almond* bar buried under a hunk of dry ice. Sometimes the ice cream man gave him a piece of dry ice which was quickly dumped into a pail of water to watch the smoke boil over the side, giving Elvin special inhalation memories.

Wish it was 1955 and the Dodgers were about to win the pennant and World Series.

Alex approached with an Asian student. "I've been looking for you. Figured you'd be supporting a tree. Meet Fai Lee, junior, computer engineering and star of my discussion group. He reminds me of another passionate Calvin Graham."

"I don't know how much Alex has told you, but I was an artificial discussion group member way back."

"Artificial?"

Fai managed a slight bow in the midst of their handshake, leaving Elvin doubled up in case reciprocity was protocol.

"Artificial meant I was Rutgers not Princeton."

"And now?"

"I teach history with an asterisk."

"Asterisk?"

"I've been teaching high school since my Masters degree. Alex knows that I decided to do a geometric thing and. . . ."

"Geometric?"

"One hundred eighty degree turn-around in September to selling eyeglasses."

"I moved here when ten and still learning American expressions like mid-life so is that what one hundred eighty degree means?"

"The expression always bothered me. What happens if you're forty, change careers but you live to a hundred, then it's not mid anything, theoretically."

Evie and Christine beached chaired themselves away from the smoke. They had become good friends almost like starting grammar school together. Both men lightheartedly thought that they'd wind up at their own Princeton train station at midnight one day. After Evie's announced pregnancy, Christine made a point to reassure her not to be uncomfortable because she wasn't pregnant. They were secure in decisions to take different life paths.

"Hi Dr. Zari."

"Miss Zelin."

A cool, slight nod of acknowledgement caught Elvin's eye.

"Wasn't much of a greeting?"

"Correct. She doesn't need encouragement. Would you believe she propositioned me a few months ago after class? Came right out and said "I'll get right to point Dr. Zari. You're amazing and if ever, you know." She walked away, turned around and waved at me. I think it was the turn around wave that bothered me the most. Too cocky, self assured and arrogant."

Christine pantomimed a watch to Alex.

"Attention everybody. Christine thought to share upcoming trip information with everyone instead of a dozen individual performances. I'll pretend conductor on a train calling stops out. Madrid and Barcelona for a few days. Then to Calar Alto Observatory on a mountain in Andalusia, a joint venture by Germany and Spain and part of the Max Planck society. This new site was picked because of better weather. Astronomers don't like rain clouds, now do I? Their telescope is one of the last and most advanced of its kind. Then I'll check out the Isaac Newton Telescope which was moved to Spain's Canary Islands and then to Hudson's Bay in July and somewhere in between all of this, the Yankees in the Bronx. So as the song goes, see you all in September."

"Question, Dr. Zari!"

"Sure, Miss Zelin."

"That Senator from Utah."

"Jake Garn."

Having been frequently asked about Garn since April, Alex knew what was coming.

"He was the first senator to fly in a space shuttle. Would you be Princeton's first professor?"

"I might; one never says never." Alex thought about asking if she wanted to be the first student to go up.

"Space shuttle reminds me that the European Space Agency recently launched their probe and didn't you meet with them?"

"You remember everything. The probe was called Giotto, looking at Haley's Comet which gets close next year."

Continuing to bond with a Maple tree, Elvin watched guests leave and Alex lead Fai around to the front. In a few weeks, a friend of Alex's was flying in for the weekend and Fai would be asked to stop by on a Friday night at 9:17 p.m.

⋂⋂⋂

Princeton in late August was quiet compared to intellectual hustle and bustle of autumn. Tourists and summer foreign students still crowded Nassau Street. A specialty sweater store window displayed a winter offering with a slogan of *Woolen portent of things to come.* A British themed book store had part of a window decorated for international winter vacation guidance. A picture of a downhill skier confused summer strollers. Alex suggested the store might not be presumptuous but actually behind the times, by not taking the display down since last winter.

"Why do you suppose the emphasis on winter in August?" Evie outlined the growing globe of second trimester. "I felt something. It's gone."

"Everybody's too busy in September to pay attention to wintry pursuits. Get them while they're summer hot and not preoccupied. Brilliant merchandising and creating a mindset."

"Girls, why don't you continue down Nassau Street around Palmer Square? We'll head down Witherspoon, to Hulfish Street, where we'll look for a fallen Maple leaf and finally boys meet girls for dinner at the *Botanist and Jurist.*"

"Alex, that Maple leaf reference- do you want to tell us girls, what that means?"

"Actually, I'm not sure us guys understand either; perhaps symbolism in a mundane life. Leaves swirled around us in a windy desolate town before Christmas. Another renegade leaf beckons us to a rescue from a train bearing down. Leaves bloom, turn vibrant colors and clog up drains after they fall."

Christine thought a few moments. "Turning vibrant colors before falling is like one of your stars turning brightest before dying?"

"A leaf is part of life's cycle. Good thinking, Christine."

The genders separated.

When the girls were far enough away, Elvin brought up Hudson's Bay. Alex was quick to answer, waiting to talk about a remote world. "Churchill, Manitoba is a small town on the shore of Hudson's Bay. Its geology fascinates; almost on a borderline between forest and tundra. We stayed in a quaint house that belongs to a friend but no amenities."

"Did Christine like no amenities?"

"I think she liked everything more than me. Churchill is famous for Polar Bears. Tourists come up there in autumn when the bears are poised for icing over and winter hunting for seal. Churchill is a big seaport because it links to the Arctic Ocean. We did Beluga whale watching. I felt close to God there. It was quiet, majestic and cool. You think and meditate a lot, like Walden Pond, but a really big pond. We rediscovered ourselves in a good love making climate."

Alex dropped his palm, Elvin slapped it. "Are we too old for palm slapping?"

"Remember what we told Nolan before he died?"

"We'll always be boys."

"Fountain of youth."

"Tomorrow night, Alex. Full moon. I checked. It's easier to walk on jetty boulders at night if there's a celestial extra bright light."

"Pick you up at eight."

They turned on Hulfish Street, passing the girls, barely nodding as if they were strangers. Elvin twirled a leaf by the stem, making sure both girls saw.

The restaurant got its name from a biologist and an attorney deciding to go into the prepared food business. Walking down a side alley towards a crowded patio, Evie patted her stomach indicating a new international symbol for pregnancy, needing air conditioning and not sitting outside.

"Evie. Wine? Mineral water?"

"That reminds me, Elvin, and there are witnesses here; if it's a baby boy and there's a bris, you'll open the Vichy Water?"

"Nah."

Route Eighteen was one of New Jersey Department of Transportation's best kept secrets. A regular highway cutting through densely populated Middlesex and Monmouth counties, it didn't serve a hell of a lot of purpose, taking a select group of people from New Brunswick, East Brunswick, Old Bridge and

Marlboro, down the shore. If you didn't live close to the road, you never bothered using it, and if you did, you were basically a lone traveler, like a pioneer, looking for the Northwest Passage. Elvin figured a very powerful politician lived near access and lobbied for the highway. New Jersey was a wonderfully respectful state, respecting their powerful politicians. By eight thirty p.m., whatever traffic disappeared, except for Alex's Mercedes. Six months earlier, the Zari's departed from a life long commitment of buying American cars. They stayed loyal as long as they could. American cars were designed for obsolescence with too many choices and costs and arrogant, uncaring customer service. Give the people what they want. Every customer counts. Those basic rules were lost. Alex was walking out of his last domestic car dealership, turned around and yelled back to the sales manager, "You've got a few decades left, enjoy it, because the way you people in Detroit do business, you'll be out of it. And if you've got some time, go read the fable, *The Tortoise and the Hare.* Did you know the Japanese eat turtle soup and rabbit?"

The Mercedes was following signs to Bradley Beach on Elvin's prompting. The overhead car lamp was flicked on. "Say Elvin, I noticed the logo on your polo shirt when you first got in. I've been thinking about that logo-a brown saguaro cactus on a bright red shirt. Can I see it again?"

Elvin half turned and pulled the shirt closer to him. "So, what's up?"

"Cactus. Why not an athlete on a horse playing an elitist game?"

"Because the whole designer process is sick. European Jews were led into cattle cars. Americans are led to cash registers where most designer money winds up in Europe anyway and they hate us like the Germans hated the Jews, but they take our money."

"LaReine Avenue. There's the house."

"Pull over a minute." Elvin rolled his window down. An old man was rocking in a chair on the porch that went clear around. Pungent pipe smoke aroma made it to the car.

"Sandy's dad."

"I know. I'd love to jump out now, run up the stairs, hug him, and thank him for letting me use his house to get laid for the first time."

"Now that Merrie's gone from your life, you said getting laid, but when you were here back then, it was making love; funny how words change over time."

The boardwalk at Belmar was still crowded. Parking a half block from the fishing pier, they scoped out the Shark River jetty and could see it was fairly deserted. Elvin noticed Alex was wearing a blue polo shirt with an elitist logo. "So that's why you brought up my cactus!"

"Actually, it's synchronistic. We ought to get back to Sedona and desert cactus for another dose."

"Maybe I'm afraid of another dose. Heavy responsibility." Elvin sat on the last boulder, facing the horizon. Ocean waves were calm, so spray wasn't moisturizing. "Christine made Evie really comfortable about our baby coming, and you guys heading down different roads. It made Evie feel good. But you've known all along, even from the first time we met, that you'd never have a child. I talked about bringing my child right here to the jetty. You were afraid of the sky and saw something back then and still see it."

"Remember not too long ago, I talked about a race between two entities and uncertainty at a finish line but left it at that? You're right. I've never seen a child in my life. I worry too much about the sky, what we can't see. We both worry about the Earth and people away from coastlines becoming first time ocean front property owners because we can't stop what we're doing. Life style is a powerful incurable addiction and an environmental murderer."

Faint lights near the horizon probably meant a ship was heading to romantic places. They talked about the few people who survived a Japan Air Lines crash the other day but over five hundred still died. Those that survived, was it science or spirit involved? Friends couldn't find an answer sitting on the jetty.

"Do you see me selling eyeglasses in a month?"

"Hard to explain but I've seen your existence for a long time. Remember, I never know who's winning the World Series. I worry a little though."

"About what? Do you see something else?"

"Social complications, not seen, but known about since the early Egyptians."

"Feel like pizza?"

"Done."

"Done."

An infant's cry drifted downstairs to a living room filled with ritual anticipation. Dress code varied; suits, jeans, dresses and Rutgers sweat shirts. The dining room dispensed aromas of tuna, lox, onion and Bobka to those who braved light snow and were about to brave the circumcision of a little Jewish penis.

"Come upstairs everybody, Rabbi Mazur is ready."

Family tradition going back to Russia made Martha Stone wear an apron to a bris, complete with large pockets and room to store an extra bagel.

The Rabbi was the Mohel, an ordained man with cutting knife and brother of comedian Jackie Mason, so there were jokes while the penis was officially made Jewish. Heavy red wine was rubbed on the infant's lips for anesthetic purposes. Alex had the honor of holding infant Nelson, so there was no movement and slipping of the knife. Elvin slipped away to a window.

"It's snowing again everybody."

"Get back here."

"Nah."

Martha yanked him.

The first cut was fast. Evie's parents secured Elvin for the final cut. Adel was reassuring, the baby felt nothing.

"Mazel-Tov" was yelled. A first Elvin thought was that an East Brunswick fire code was probably violated with so many people cramped into a small space. Bris papers were signed, dated January 12, 1986.

"Penis is officially kosher now, so eat everybody." After twenty-four hours in delivery, Evie's words came out inaudibly. Elvin re-yelled penis status and bagel options and what spreads were available, like whitefish or chopped herring.

Something was bothering Alex. "It seems a bit incongruous, eating like this after watching genital reduction surgery."

"I totally agree but it's thousands of years of tradition. Do you still want to take Bar Mitzvah lessons?"

At 4:44 in the morning Elvin held a sleeping Nelson, gently rubbing his back and bottom.

"Out that window is a wonderful world. I've started counting all measures of time until we hold hands and walk together, near the ocean by the Shark River, boulders under our feet. I want to look at the world through your eyes but I'm not rushing a thing because it's been a lifetime waiting for this moment and all the moments to come. Daddy loves you Nelson, my last dream."

THIRTEEN

Seven men, spaced around a library, some with cigars courting ash trays, watched a woman slowly descend a ladder, hand waving a retrieved book, like balancing on a high wire.

"*The Fountainhead*, thanks Simeon. I'm impressed you knew exactly where it was."

"You know the exercise, Catherine. My father started me at an early age. I had to read everything. There was an unspoken compromise, growing older, as long as I at least knew what was here."

An overdue cigar ash was tapped down. "Maybe we should get her up there again, rather pleasant rear."

"How many years until you're seventy, Wilton?"

"Five, so there's five more years to notice those things."

Wilton chuckled merrily. Varner said Wilton was beginning to sound like Santa, after sliding down a chimney, and finding fresh baked cookies and bourbon waiting for him on a little table. Wilton said Varner talks like a writer. Varner reminded aging Wilton, his third book was published last year.

"Alright gentlemen. I'll have this book read again by the morning, so tomorrow we can discuss Ayn Rand's philosophy of selfishness and selflessness. One other thing; Howard Roark is my ideal of the perfect man just as he was Ayn's. Part of defining perfect does not include finding more reasons for me to climb the ladder again while my ass gets visually assaulted. And yes, Wilton, you can say it's a rather pleasant rear, because it is and soft to the touch." Catherine Rhode pressed the book to her chest as the library erupted into locker room laughter.

"Well done. If you're taking the book back to the Nassau Inn, sign off on the date in the back- an old Nolan tradition." Simeon Morris motioned everyone down.

Ayn's book had a sheet of paper in the back with several names going back to the late fifties; last name and date borrowed was R. Rose, November 22, 1963. Catherine scribbled illegibly- January 11, 1992. Initial pre-med training at UCLA and a sudden switch to political science helped screw up last traces of normalcy. Georgetown Law left her hopelessly illegible, curiously misunderstood with unlimited life energy, as stated in one of those East Coast *city* magazines. Fierce competitiveness, trial law mastery and social sophistication brought her to Gabriel; but mostly a genius IQ.

Still holding the book to chest, Catherine sat next to Alex who whispered, "Amazing how you work an audience."

"I appreciate you, especially since you're the only who didn't stare at my African-American back side."

"How do you know that?"

"Women's intuition."

"Say, Varner. . . ."

"Simeon, by springtime, we'll have final details for malfunctioning of an engine. One less. . . ."

"Enough." Simeon pointed to a thin, aging man, wrinkled face and jowls. "Dan."

Dan fumbled through a briefcase. A single sheet was passed around and collected back as Simeon watched a hundred twenty seconds elapse.

"Memorize and observe guidelines and begin after May 12th. Now, let's do dinner and watch those smiles on your greedy faces. Another quick item, our friend and colleague Victor has been assigned to hang around the next President, including upcoming primaries and campaign."

"From what state. Remind us?"

"Arkansas."

A hand came down on Alex's shoulder at the library door.

"How's security clearance life been, Alex? Are you adjusting without inconvenience or infringements on your real work?"

"I get to the see the world, Varner. I feel like a sailor sometimes but its observatories, not ports I keep frequenting. We've got a security meeting at Fort Monmouth soon. I remember what Harry Truman said about the kitchen, if you can't stand the heat. . . ."

"And?"

"I love heat, remember my parents are Egyptian."

"Christine, where's my blue striped shirt and red tie? I looked everywhere."

"Alex, where's my St. Laurent beige suit?"

"Sorry."

"Look on the refrigerator. The cleaning ticket is under a magnet. February 10th ticket. The other one is my dress."

Running around the second floor, in and out of rooms, passing each other in narrow hallways, they stopped often to kiss, just like President Reagan and Nancy did all the time. Alex reminded her about his security clearance. Christine settled into part time accounting work and Princeton societal endeavors, dressing now for a women's political tea.

"The Paul Tsongas tea is for fund raising?" Alex's starchy white shirt was buttoned and reserve red tie modeled for Christine.

"What about the tea?"

"Keep the donation to a minimum."

"You're telling me something? I know you. Remember the celery?"

"How's this look?"

"Better than the one in the cleaner. That pizza marinara stain will still be there on Monday when you pick it up. I almost want to say, you're getting as sloppy as Elvin, but I won't, but I just did. What time are you coming back from Fort Monmouth? Should I call Evie and Elvin?" Rubbing her chin, Christine contemplated, "Wait, how do you know Tsongas will lose? The New Hampshire Primary is first coming up. Do you want to bet?"

"Only bet I'll do is in November and call them, dinner's good. We haven't seen them in a month."

"I ought to write a memoir, *I Married a Smug Astronomer.*"

Alex paced around the living room, then in the library, which Christine insists was a replica of Nolan's, right down to the ladder, which was vestigial, performing no real function except for resting a few plants.

Library curtains parted at the right time; a Chevrolet was puffing into cold windless air and judging by exhaust elevation, probably just arrived. Horns were not allowed as a Zari retrieval agent.

"Good to see you, Dr. Zari. Here's a badge. Nice tie." A decorated military man handed credentials.

"Colonel."

Fort Monmouth slept in Eastern Monmouth County, about an hour from Princeton. It was near Freehold, an old Revolutionary War town which hosted General Washington according to historian Elvin, now selling eyeglasses. Passion for George Washington never subsided and knowing about Alex's Fort Monmouth meeting, he sent notes on Monmouth Battlefield State Park, where the longest Revolutionary War battle was held, starring Washington, James Monroe, and Alexander Hamilton with footnotes that modern currency was well represented by battlefield participants.

The fort was locally referred to as sleepy but if you wanted bigger Jersey military adventures, head down to nearby Dix or McGuire or hop a barbed-wire fence at Earle. Elvin teased listeners about Earle and what a perfect place to store nuclear things, rockets, firecrackers and the like. After all, the ocean was ten minutes away, giving rockets a head start on their way to Moscow. Earle reminded Elvin of the scene in *Strangelove*; funny but nightmarish when Slim Pickens is screaming on top of an atomic bomb dropping into Russia. A few weeks were needed to get over that scene. The more brought up, probably meant, he never got over the insanity of nuclear anything.

The car passed through a red brick gate, stopped by a guard house and was directed towards the fort rear and a two story building. Barracks reminded casual visitors of World War II scenes, like Schofield barracks on Oahu, with the Atlantic Ocean just a few miles away instead of the Pacific.

The small entourage was met by two military guard types right outside the building entrance. Credentials were inspected.

Alex liked being in a room with six decorated uniforms and his back up red tie.

"Gentlemen, primary season off and running."

"Meaningless, it's just another Commander-in-Chief and for you too, Alex." General Dixon sat next to him, so the last comment was whispered, for his ears only.

"There are several reports for you to read after or during lunch." A man with the least decorations spoke.

"Alex, with your world travels visiting observatories, any particular comments for us now?"

Alex cleared his throat, "General Dixon, these past years I've studied installations, capabilities and state of technology and I'm heading to South Africa soon for the same."

"Has your work at Princeton and Harvard opened special international doors for you?" Colonel Sautten winked an eye.

"Yes sir."

"Well, we've got a reward for your good work. You're moving up the security clearance ladder. Congratulations, Alex. Now that you've moved on up, we've got a Pentagon meeting to plan."

"Meantime Dr. Zari, draw up a two year plan for returning to those international astronomical installations. Objectives. Analysis. You know the routine."

"Same format as I've been using, General?"

"Affirmative."

"How's April in Washington everybody for our little Pentagon get together?"

"General, can we throw in some Cherry Blossoms?"

"We're a bunch of accommodating guys."

"The military or Gabriel in us?"

"Both."

Clara and Ike on Friday mornings always seemed busier; maybe a subliminal weekend beginning effect. Being in eyewear sales and on the road, those innocent by gone days of lazily eating a bagel with coffee and reading was over. A new world of corporate pressures, writing orders and units, answering to European owners and bosses, and having to justify every hour spent, took over his life.

Sofia Zahl stood over Elvin, smiling, "I'm glad you mentioned having appointments in the area. I liked it better seeing you every morning, now it's a special occasion or an appointment close to *Clara and Ike*. But I see it on your face; you love what you're doing now."

"I do love selling. What's strange about everything in my life, is for many years, I knew there was something more out there. Maybe that's why I drift all the time; I feel something tugging at my restless soul, an unfulfilled part of life's destiny. I used to think teaching was a newsreel before the main attraction. Maybe you and Solchiali are the main attraction, a reason for my being."

"What's a newsreel?"

"When I was a kid, they showed news about the world in black and white before two movies and cartoons. Gosh I miss *Mighty Mouse*. Funny, I don't know what happened to newsreels and the mouse."

"What's a special occasion?" Elbows supported Sofia's large green eyes, carefully watching Elvin.

"Special occasion is coming to Solchiali. I drop in, scrounge up posters, order pads, pass your office and see my boss mostly always on the phone."

"My father's your boss. I'm just an admiring recruiter."

"It's amazing how good your English is. Better every day."

"It's amazing how well you sell eyeglasses and now number one in the country."

Coffee cups touched with the news of being number one but voice decibel levels dropped at the sight of company phone operators doing bagels and coffee a couple of tables away. Going back to when they first sat together, being distant and not too familiar was prudent in the crazy mixed up world of company office personnel or teachers assuming things if you smile at someone the right or wrong way. Office workers were part time sex novelists or journalists.

Elvin leaned close, "It's hard to express, we're always hinting at something but it's nothing. The word, *something* is always around us and something about you, Sofia, that makes me a successful sales rep. Does that make sense? You bring something to my personality." He reached to gently pat her hand making sure no one around was paying attention.

"Something is a beautiful word and you say beautiful things. I'm going to the office now. There's a computer virus called *Michelangelo* that's spreading world wide. Funny, that it's an Italian name. If you have time, stop by the office on your way home. You can pick up posters that just came in. I'll be there until eight."

Solchiali was decades old; started in Germany by Adolfo Zahl and invisible investors as a small regional German sunglass company; hence the names *sol* and *ochialli*, Italian for sun and eyes. Adolfo was mostly German, Italian and even some fashionable French genes. Small regional things grow, sometimes in spite of themselves. A few German retailers appeared one day, on their way to the Alps for holiday. They liked Adolfo's company. Shortly thereafter, Adolfo moved the factory to Italy where many eyeglass factories were setting up shop and started making ophthalmic eyeglasses for European distribution. More growth followed in the late seventies. Adolfo first discovered New Jersey and then, the rest of the American market. A small office eventually moved to a larger facility in Cranford as distribution approached national. Solchiali's timely styling and price points interacted with a hungry American eyeglass market. Sofia was his only child, arriving in the Garden State in 1981 on her twenty-first birthday.

Selling and cold calling made for a long day. Driving around Passaic earlier, around four p.m., on a hilly side street, with the setting sun in his eyes, there was something in the sky. It moved fast and then it was gone. Elvin pulled to the side, rubbed eyes, opened the window and took in a chest full of air. Everything happened so fast. Strange emotions and stomach queasiness had a direct line to optic nerve and imagination pathways. The sky thing was probably nothing, but Sofia was becoming something. The universe was a confusing place. Why think a vision in the sky was tied to Sofia? Why think he's been through this day before. Going to the office after six p.m. was something meant to be? He's done it many times. It was Sedona deja vu. A two family house on the right had a strange shadow across the front, like he was being waved at. Was it a shadowy hand? He'd seen the house and shadow before, maybe a hundred times, so he was comforted, but he never saw the house since this was his first time in Passaic. The universe was confounding and comforting.

After six p.m. meant using a front door bell to alert the night crew someone was cold, shivering, needing access to Solchiali's office. Sofia and Nathan Knight came to rescue.

"Nathan, it's good to see you."

"You too, Mr. Number one in the country. Figures came out yesterday. We're all proud on your rise to the top of the company. Are you here for posters?"

Elvin never found a way to lock into Nathan's eye contact, plastic warmth, or anything resembling bonding. Sofia's theory was Nathan's persona may've resulted from early childhood development difficulty, fucked-up siblings or lack of breast milk; all contributing to adult bastardry, if that was a legitimate word. Nathan was a tonsorial throwback to the sixties, still sporting an afro hair style. His preference for bow ties provoked whispers of Black Muslim sympathizer despite obvious white Jewish party affiliation.

"Lock me out, Sofia. Elvin, keep up with the merchandising. Posters are great silent salesman."

"Our national sales manager has left the building. He wanted me to test the waters with you and ask about becoming a regional sales manager since we're going to be expanding lines."

"You caught me off guard. I never thought of managing which means travel and less Nelson and Evie."

"Less of me too. Just teasing." Sofia sat behind a sprawling desk, elbows back to supporting green seductive eyes.

"What's the decision time frame on the manager position?"

"A few months, so think about it and one other thing, I noticed your call schedule next week. You're in Atlantic City for a few days."

"Good business for me there."

"I'm there next week too; taking some time off. My father bought a beach house in Longport, so next Wednesday night, how about dinner?"

"Well, I planned on Atlantic City boardwalk pizza though." Proposing going out with the boss's rich fancy daughter for plain, simple pizza should be enough to discourage. Elvin confidently smiled.

The bluff was called. "I'm Italian, pizza works, seven p.m., Tropicana boardwalk."

Seagulls on fly by, rough surf back dropped the boardwalk. A few tourists braved cold. Businesses closed early on weekday nights, leaving a semi-deserted atmosphere. Elvin and Sofia walked north, near the old Steel Pier, freely swinging hands nearly touching.

"You're the expert Sofia, rate the pizza." A tie was yanked and stuffed into a suit pocket.

"Do you want me to say unbelievable and worth the trip but its not Venetian pizza." She pulled the tie out of his pocket and held it up. "It's so long."

"Venetian?"

"Venice pizza is paper thin crust, eaten with knife and fork. Atlantic City's crust, well should I be honest with you?"

"Be."

"Doughy, chewy but our walk is wonderful. What's a Steel Pier?"

"Over there, built in the late 1800's. Famous people performed on it then someone got the idea to jump off a high platform on a horse into a pool and that became famous. But now it's shopping mostly. Are you cold? Do you want to keep walking?"

"Let's keep. You're like a tour guide."

Resorts Hotel was just ahead. "We're near the end and it's too cold. Would you like my coat?"

"I'm fine. I feel a little dreamy."

They retraced their steps until briefly holding hands, standing in front of a late model black Mercedes.

Free flowing blonde hair was tied in a pony tail. "Our favorite word is *something*. Tonight was special. Words are still hard for me and I'm confused but I feel something about you. It has nothing to do with kissing or romance but would you like to spend the night with me. It's not about work or anything else and I had to ask, otherwise I'd think for the rest of a life, wondering about decisions and things not said or done that should've been. I know all your personal life things so I'll understand whatever you say. I don't know why I'm saying all this. It's not me. But since the first time I saw you at *Clara and Ike*, I knew about tonight."

The first thing that ran through Elvin's confused mind was the hope that this beautiful blonde Italian woman has no power to see things like Alex. "Something I don't understand tells me to say yes and I'm not going to grab or kiss you either. It is something else. What's your address, I'll meet you there."

After a half hour heading in the general direction of Sofia, Elvin found a dead end street with beach entrance. Sand was bitter cold, sitting near waves. Foamy spray slapped him, and it was cold enough to freeze on skin and what if it did, and he appeared at Sofia's looking like Dr. Zhivago standing at Lara's door? Was he, Dr. Zhivago and Sofia, Lara? Was this a Freudian trick planted in conscious thought? Twenty minutes later, the angry ocean convinced him, that he was just Elvin and to get into his car.

Longport is a special Jersey place that could wholly, comfortably be transplanted to Palm Beach, Malibu or the Hamptons. Rapid blinking in a driveway was an attempt to diminish the expansiveness and splendor of the beach house, more an estate and like nothing he'd ever seen. Three garage doors simultaneously opened.

A white silken bathrobe highlighted long blonde hair, hazel eyes. A pony tail was gone. Sofia was holding two glasses of wine, looking beautiful. Color co-ordination seemed borrowed from Michelangelo or DaVinci and made perfect sense as she was involved with choosing colors of eyeglasses, ordered from the factory in Italy.

"No sipping, just gulp. You look like you need it."

"A toast?"

"Sure."

"Here's to something. Someday, we'll understand. Salud."

"Salud. Another?"

"Please."

Stainless decor highlighted a kitchen. A picture window looked onto a dark beach, waves barely visible, crashing in the background. A bathrobe opened without provocation; visions of artistry, pink skin and a patch of blonde hair conjured up notions of delicate, soft and wispy. She turned, he followed. A flick of a light switch darkened the kitchen.

Dizzy, he leaned on the wall to steady himself. Was dizziness because of two glasses of wine or guilty fear? Looking up at a tall staircase, made him think about the Empire State Building and *An Affair to Remember*. Should he stay on the ground floor and avoid heights, emotions, experiences and internalizations of guilt, capable of lasting a lifetime? That first step up meant never going back.

"That room over there is always locked. It's the master bedroom, really master, my father's. He insists on keeping it locked but he's never here. This is my room. View of the ocean makes breathing difficult. Get comfortable."

Clothing was folded neatly on a long bathroom counter. Cold water splashed, a towel dried. A small lamp on a night table glowed like a candle, leaving the bedroom moody dark. Sofia's open arms induced hours of intensity and release. Hours were strangely quiet without pronouncements, each drifting into an own world of discovery, meaning and relevance. When backsides touched and eyes closed, he thought about classic literature, themes of loveless passion, trying to remember the first time they saw each other and if there were ever clues that this night could happen. Being in Passaic the other day, he sensed this was going to happen; maybe it was the shadow hand waving at him. One senses an event will take place, and no matter what, can't stop it from happening. No power can let you change destiny. If every sense tells you not to get on an airplane, you still do because it's just a sense, not practical to miss a flight. How would it appear to people waiting for you? Would you ever live it down? Can you stop living, being human, and asking forgiveness for transgressions? It's what we do, our chemical makeup and frailty.

Dark curtains forbade sunrise over the Atlantic. A dressed Sofia stood with a glass of orange juice. "Good morning. It's still dark. I'm leaving for Philadelphia for the day. Towels in the bathroom. What time's your first appointment?"

Thoughts of a cucumber and a calculating business woman intertwined.

Whatever happened to adjectives about the night? How good it was. Then again that's what this was, a night without adjectives or pronouncements.

"Ten."

"I can't find anything to say that's appropriate. All this is hard for me but what I can say is please come back tonight. Here's the house number, call me."

At the bedroom door, allowing time for congealing thoughts, she turned around and waved.

"Chinese food?"

"Sure, ciao."

Two brown bags with top handles and bottom grease stains rested in a kitchen sink, chopsticks poking out of each bag.

Excitedly, like a kid, he spoke, "Not sure what you like except pizza and bagels so I got a variety."

A white button down shirt, tucked into jeans, walked over to his tie and slid it off. "The oven's on low, keeps everything warm for a while. I have to show you something." A light switch flick darkened the kitchen again. "You couldn't see anything this morning or last night, too dark and curtains, so look at the sunset on the Atlantic. It takes my breath away. I could stay like this forever."

"Funny, me too. I've spent chunks of my life looking out on this same ocean but that's a long story."

She helped him off with a suit coat.

"The bed faces all this. Do you know what I'd like to do right now that I've never done the right way and I can still see the ocean at the same time? Remember I'm a rich man's daughter with worldly experience."

Sheepishly, hoping he had the right answer, "Think I know."

"How fast can you be ready?"

"Basically I am."

Pillows were propped, hands behind head. Elvin thought about cumulous clouds and an attic roof. Sofia climbed opposite on top.

"Confession, I dreamed of this years ago in *Clara and Ike*, the first time you smiled and every time I'm here, I wondered what this would be like; relax, be still, dream."

"Would you like to be alerted?"

Sofia giggled. "Not really."

Elvin giggled.

"What's funny?"

"Everything is so amazingly improbable; the sunset on the Atlantic and this particular astronomical position you're in. I don't know if I can lay still."

"Astronomical?"

"A heavenly body so close to me."

"Do you think the food is edible? It's been warming for hours."

"Chinese food is the most resilient of all food groups."

"How about topless dining? Do you mind?" She un-straddled in a single bound.

"Sure. Topless works."

"Can we lose the chopsticks? I don't pretend to be something I'm not."

"I just noticed something in the bright light, you're very chesty."

"Big tits, that's what you American boys call them."

"How long have you been divorced?" Elvin sailed chopsticks into the sink.

"I married a rich Italian playboy at twenty-one who spoke no English and played with everything, but my father said that he came from a fine family and told me to be more understanding and forgiving. When our business was taking off, my father sent me back and forth to America to learn. Ricardo said he'd never come here. The son of a bitch wanted to stay married, with me in America working and him in Italy not working. All kinds of legal things went on. The same thing happened to my father when he divorced my mother. By the way your food selection is *bellissimo!*"

"I saw a picture of your father in the office. He's really tall like you and he doesn't come to America very often."

"He doesn't like America. He really doesn't like America; actually he hates all Americans. I could never marry an American, only another German or Italian, preferably from the homeland."

"Why?"

"I need five hours to answer and it would take time away from upstairs, but someday, *promiso*. There are movies upstairs too. Do you like to watch movies?"

"Five hours to answer that!"

In 1912 the city of Tokyo donated three thousand cherry trees to the people of Washington, D.C. and in April 1992, an eightieth celebration festival was taking place. Two military uniforms and two business suits strolled together. Late morning sun warmed aromatic air while expressions in pink and white created a Disney fairyland effect.

"Have you ever seen anything like this, Alex?

"Well Colonel, it's perfectly sunny today and not to rain on a parade but I'm a Newark man and Branch Brook Park comes pretty close to this."

"Smythe, what do you think?"

A coat sleeve slid over the hump of an obtrusive watch face. "We ought to pick up Thomas now and head over."

Sitting in the back of a car weaving around Washington, nearly running red lights and being non-observant to other motor vehicle regulations, Alex humored himself. Why are government cars painted drab, mundane colors? Was it budgetary concerns or simple genius being so far ahead of their time, style and color wise? Mundane and drab would have to eventually make a comeback, after all, it hadn't been in style since colonists traded trinkets for land.

The car semi-circled around a drive. An art deco hat opened passenger doors. "Say Alex, could you retrieve General Lewkins? Room *444*."

Strange thoughts surface in empty elevators.

When was the last time I knocked on a hotel door- maybe never. Who really does? Maybe a hotel phone was better? How do I approach the situation; with several loud knocks or gentle, yelling through the door?

After several loud knocks, a young woman opened. A tee-shirt hinted college age. All Alex saw were breasts bursting at seams.

"Hi, you must be here to pick up Tommy? We're running a little late. He's still in the bathroom. I'm actually leaving, good timing sir."

Not being a big fan of *sir* terminology, a stern face took over while looking around the disheveled room-closed curtains evaded sunlight.

"My name is Susi, here's my number, spread it around if you want." She went over to knock on the bathroom door, "Tommy, your ride's here. I'm leaving. It was fun."

Soon a full bedecked military uniform emerged with a strong hint of freshly splashed Aqua Velva. "Dr. Zari, sorry for the delay. I got dressed in the bathroom; my guest didn't need to see my uniform. Of course you met Susi, a college kid earning tuition. I love American ingenuity; met her last night in a Georgetown bar. It was a civilian night, if you get my drift. Grab that suitcase if you don't mind. Are you excited about your first Pentagon experience?"

"Thrilled."

"There are sixteen parking lots here, like a baseball stadium."

"Reminds me, General. Camden Yards just opened the other day. Can you get us tickets?"

"I can get you anything Smith-Stein."

Five men cleared security, winding up on an escalator. The deeper into the building, less employees milled about. When Alex broke formation to a water fountain, General Lewkins whispered, "Almost a thousand more fountains all over."

An outer office, then another hallway was marched through. Two civilians and four military men already waited in a drab beige room with a flag at the far end. A picture of a grinning President hid behind the flag. Alex would never get used to military design and color schemes; the room decor reminded him of their government car.

A decorated military chest spoke. "I think everyone is familiar with one another. The President wants us to begin a think project but not conventional nuclear think, rather other approaches to deal with a piece of a rock falling down on us from space. We know the Pentagon is already thinking about a weapon that launches, stays close and fires missiles. Enough said."

Alex quickly added. "I'm sure everyone knows that shooting missiles and breaking an intruder up into a million pieces is not desirable either; you get a million things to consider instead of one."

"Don't worry Dr. Zari." General Lewkins slowly sat down, taking long seconds of hesitation to finally bottom out.

And this is the man who hung out with Susi in a college tee-shirt. Shoot, how did he ever get it up if he can't get down?

Colonel Graves stood up. "A big question floating around the Pentagon is can they actually hit a moving target up there. We'll begin to think together these next few days. Break off into splinter groups and a few more will join us for feasibility studies lasting right into the next presidential administration or two. That's how long term this all is. Anybody ever work with plastic model making?"

Thoughts just took him back to Newark, the hobby model store, an orphanage that imprisoned kids. But he was the one who was imprisoned now. For the first time since meeting Stuart Grafton, he was uneasy and unsure. Eyes blinked in long intervals allowing some to think he was dozing or in pain.

"Are you alright, Dr. Zari?"

"Just fine. I'm visualizing a little corner of outer space."

"Graves, you mentioned cost analysis. There's not much budget money for us or anyone else around here."

"Testors' glue actually fits into our budget nicely." Alex tried to force laughter in the bland room. Maybe it would make them forget he drifted away in thought. No one should know he's prone to drifting like that. It doesn't look good. It might worry captors. He also found out who was winning the election in November so he could've won that bet with Christine. Paul Tsongas dropped out of the race. Another vision appeared, like an aura before a seizure and it left him sweaty wet.

There's always a scary man hanging around meetings. He just stood up. The only man in the room I don't know; he's starting to speak.

"Project code name is *Ahab* to make you think harpoon and white whale."

A new administration and Ahab to think about. Bill Clinton, I'll be seeing you around.

Four beach chairs on a deck encircled a small boy playing with blocks, a Hess truck and yellow school bus with soft inflatable black wheels. Sandy brown hair climbed on top asking, "Can this take me to school?"

"Nelson, a real yellow bus takes you, but in September it'll be a different bus."

"Why?"

"Because it will say Marlboro Township. Remember we're moving to a new house in July?"

Christine raised her hand, role playing with Evie. "Why Marlboro?"

Evie said Marlboro is an up and coming new community with nearly hundred percent immigrants. Alex refrained, "From where are they all immigrating?"

Elvin's chair slipped to one hundred eighty degrees, but he still managed a response. "They're all from Brooklyn. Well, a few by way of Staten Island but not one from North Jersey. I think there's a Jersey emigrating tax if you're north of the Raritan River."

Elvin's prompting whisper to Nelson inspired a walk over to Alex.

"How was your trip, Uncle Alex? Did you look at stars?"

"Do you know where South Africa is? Bring me the globe Aunt Christine and I bought."

"How was South Africa?" Elvin's chair maintained parallelism.

"Interesting, fascinating and beautiful and so different than anywhere else. Since 1972, the South African Astronomical Observatory has had the advantage of dark, unpolluted skies; conditions perfect for star gazing. They do good work with stars, life cycles, galaxies and black holes with pretty sophisticated technology. You wouldn't think, but they're able to pierce our galaxy dust clouds with infrared cameras and detectors. I've been working with Ian Fielding who studies stars whose size and light varies. Wish I had more time with him, but I'll get back there. We've become good friends."

Evie put down a wine glass. "Do you ever do naked eye astronomy things?"

"Funny you ask. Early one morning, actually it was still night, we drove hours away, mostly for sightseeing, but we met up with some men who were there for the star Canopus. It's an old South African tradition. Men gather in tall mountains around camp fires and look for Canopus in the South sky. First man to see it means he'll have a prosperous year. We spent two days there camping, hiking and praying. You know me."

"Are we watching movies, Daddy?"

"After lunch. You'll love this movie called *MASH*. Daddy and Uncle Alex love it."

"Mash potatoes, Daddy?" Nelson sat in his father's lap. By the *MASH* football game, Nelson slept and by movie credits he awoke.

"Tell Aunt and Uncle what you watched with Dad on Thanksgiving morning before the parade."

"*March of the Wooden Soldiers* with Ollie and Stan, but Daddy slept most of the time."

"Girls, what's my favorite *MASH* scene? Quick quiz time."

"Knowing my husband, it's the suicide scene with the dentist."

"Mine?"

"The *hot lips* bet and silly men you both are, asking the same question every time."

"Elvin, take orders for Chinese and don't forget hot mustard."

"Can you use black plastic plates for dinner? Paul Henreid just died. He played Victor Laszlo in *Casablanca*. I'm still upset that Ilsa flew away with Henreid and not Bogart. She stared, with those glistening eyes at Rick and that said it all. She knew he was lying and that they loved each other but they were sacrificing love for the war effort. The good old right thing to do."

"So serious he takes that movie."

"So Elvin."

An Italian marble table filled a conference room. When meeting participants needed American Standard fixtures, a careful squeeze between padded walls and backs of chairs was the only way out. A sarcastic observer called out that during a three day meeting, a half day was lost in the squeezing process and holding both stomach and bladder muscles until finally out the door. Faces coming back into the room had a slight smile of relief.

Solchiali managers and executives were treated to the rarified presence of Adolfo Zahl, in from Italy to personally thank the team for successfully launching a new eyewear line. Severely broken English and hand gestures thanked everybody. A few smiles managed to escape. Adolfo was neither a smiling German- Italian, nor an American admirer either. Once you knew him, just being in America was an effort. Sitting around a table with Americans who were making him a lot of money, he nervously fidgeted, looked at his watch, stared a few managers down, asked a few irrelevant questions via an interpreter but couldn't wait to leave.

Finally it was time. Sofia opened the conference door and got fatherly kisses on both cheeks. An executive bathroom door was unlocked temporarily. After finishing, several men escorted Adolfo out of the building to a waiting limo and first class Alitalia back to Rome. Nathan Knight whispered out of Sofia's range, that the executive washroom toilet gets flushed twice a year when he's here and they routinely bring in a plumber to make sure the toilet functions despite minimal usage. The plumber has to wear gloves. A voice asked if it was the Howard Hughes *fear of germs syndrome*, keeping a locked bathroom. Another voice confirmed.

Once Adolfo was gone, the group officially welcomed Elvin Stone to management. They kept Elvin a secret while the boss was around. Adolfo didn't have to know Solchiali was paying a new American Jew manager more of his money. For Elvin, it was a management so perfectly constructed, it was hard to refuse. New Jersey and Pennsylvania needed watching over. Elvin would be mostly doing local sales, rarely leaving Jersey except for a few managerial trips to Pittsburgh or Harrisburg, so there was never denying Evie or Nelson precious time. Perfect construction was Sofia's lobbying behind the scenes.

Later that night, the Manor Restaurant in West Orange hosted the annual manager's banquet. Champagne toasts segued to buffet lines. An ornate radish display caught Elvin's eye. Radishes were ignored in salads, rare in supermarkets and maybe cast off from a vegetable orphanage. Radish depth on his plate was measurable.

"Hey radish man, can I call you that?" She brushed up close to his ear.

"Feel free, Sofia."

"Next week, Atlantic City, you're selling down there so would you?"

"Seven p.m. Boardwalk. Wednesday night pizza. We'll try a different place, maybe with a better crust recipe."

"Same everything?"

"Not necessarily I'll play hooky Friday. Do you remember that word?"

"Phone Cranford High School to say you're sick when you're not."

"You're so smart. Favor, can you buy or rent a black and white World War II movie? Surprise me. We'll watch it Friday when I'm playing hooky, but it has to be black and white."

"Why?"

"Long story."

"Elvin, try the cutting station over there, the roast beef is wonderful." Sofia was on top of all situations, sharp, aware and meticulous. She saw Nathan Knight's bowtie approaching, and winked to Elvin, as a voice faded to a whisper, changing subject to roast beef.

"Welcome again to our management team. Must love radishes?"

"Nathan, for some reason the farmers in central Jersey don't produce enough radishes. I think it has something to do with lack of government subsidies."

"Amusing."

Three garage doors simultaneously lifted, reminding Elvin of a Broadway theatre when a curtain rises slowly, dramatically, while audience, Sofia, is poised.

"Why do all the doors go up?"

"I can't figure out which button and door." A long delicate index finger pointed at the kitchen picture window, then towards the staircase upstairs. The kitchen went dark as they left.

Quietly they watched sun and ocean, changing shadows, perspectives. The beach outside was still sprinkled with sun people and bathers. Re-positioning herself into a straddle, Sofia pushed breasts together, leaning forward. "We've got two long days together. I bought you a black and white war movie and not easy to find but no guilt intended. Do you see my two small dark projections? If you give them a lot attention, they'll get especially sensitive and make me feel good."

"What movie did you get?"

"I'll spell it. G-u-a-d-a-l-canal Diary."

"I heard of it. Thank you. I'll talk to you later but now pay back time for getting the movie. I've got projections to work on. By the way managers do projections all the time."

"What?"

"Regional budget projections."

"You're right."

Closing of curtains means night time or the end of the Broadway show. Elvin watched intently, wondering why people on second floors or higher up feel the need to prevent the ocean from looking into an upper window. He drifted to a medieval castle on top of a mountain with a deep moat. Did a beautiful princess, beckoning from a high tower in a locked castle room ever push curtains out of the way before calling for help?

"Can you leave the curtains open?"

"You're funny. Guess what hurts me which means you've been doing a wonderful job."

"They look even bigger now. Did I do that?"

"Maybe. Maybe hormones. Let's go downstairs. I bought you a gift. It's in the fridge."

"Fridge? I can't imagine."

"I bought two corned beef sandwiches from a deli in Clark with a sign on the window, *Kosher,* and a Jewish star."

"You make me smile."

Sofia led the way downstairs. Staircases were steep and imposing but he was getting used to them. Her naked rear made following easy- like a search light in the sky heralding a movie premiere. But how would he ever be able to eat corned beef looking at a nude beautiful woman? Never in the history of the world was a kosher corned beef sandwich eaten with a nude Italian blonde woman watching.

"Last week, seeing your father at the office, he's scary in person with all that wild bushy brown hair. Doesn't he own a hair brush?"

"Try scary all the time and he doesn't care how he looks. He wears suits off the racks, never tailored."

"You don't like him. I suppose if we weren't the way we are, I'd never sense it."

"He hates you because you're American. Maybe I hated him for what he did to my mother but I sort of accept him now. Maybe it's part of a culture thing, not sure. A week after my parents married, he walked across the street and fucked a young woman whose husband was away in the German army. My mother actually saw them in an upstairs window together. Maybe that's why I close the upstairs curtains all the time."

"That's a terrible story."

"My mother cried and told me everything when I was older, mostly to teach me so it wouldn't happen to me but of course it did."

"Was he ever violent?"

"No, just unfaithful to the point of destroying my mother and me. I knew everything as I got older. He once brought home a woman from a nearby town. I was in high school. The woman actually waited in our kitchen while he packed an overnight bag. He said they were going to buy raw materials in Zurich and she was his driver but in all fairness, she did carry his suitcase out to the car."

"Why does he hate Americans?"

"Good question, not sure. A cousin told me that my grandmother was raped by an American soldier and there was a child. My grandmother was kind of poor and another mouth to feed didn't help."

"Is that true?"

"Who knows? You're all spoiled and don't know real work ethic. He'd love to fly a plane load of Americans, one plane at a time and make them work in his eye glass factory and teach every American what real work is and how to sweat. You're all lazy, spoiled and arrogant. He told that me years ago. It gave me chills. Money lets him kiss me but I secretly put a lot away in Swiss banks, just in case one day I get tired of kissing him back. When he first started making sunglasses in Germany, mysterious money arrived."

"Mysterious?"

"German money. When he expanded into eyeglasses there were more German investors and that's no secret, everybody knows. He's always been surrounded by people who don't like Americans."

"How's your mother?"

"Well taken care of and comfortable. She lives near Rome. I miss her a lot because she's never here. Alright Elvin, Adolfo class is over. Take me upstairs."

"Sure teacher." He jumped in front, flicking the kitchen lights off.

"I have something to say right now in this hallway before we go anywhere. Hearing how I feel about my unfaithful father and knowing you're married, deeply in love with your wife and son, it pulls me apart and I know it does you, but you know what I feel, that this is different. We're smart but we can't pinpoint.

We never say *love* because we're not. You once told me, this was all meant to be and keeps repeating. I don't understand."

"When international awards are given out for sensitivity and beauty, it's you. You say things well, tenderly with passion and honesty. We are something. In times of sleeping together, I think about us and feel guilty. Guilt doesn't consume me because we aren't in love. It's something we don't understand. Maybe it's just a mechanical thing. I'd like that. It's almost absolving to think mechanical."

A radio plug met a wall socket while a hand was moving counter clock wise over a foggy bathroom mirror. A round viewing area appeared. Mariah Carey was singing *I'll be there.* Elvin dabbed shaving cream; fog was contumacious so he wiped again.

A flowery bathtub curtain moved and steam spilled out. A soapy arm waved, with inquiring voice, "Aren't you the least bit curious to see what's behind this? Didn't you wonder where I was when you woke up?"

"It's Friday morning and I figured projections could use a rest. My lips are tired too."

"Come on top of me. The water's nice and warm."

"Pulling this shower curtain reminds me of Mrs. Bates or whatever the hell she was at the time of interrupting poor Janet Leigh's shower. What the hell was her name? Marion Crane! And to this day, I never forgave Anthony Perkins for doing that to Janet Leigh."

"What are you rambling about? Did anybody ever say that you ramble a lot?"

"Sorry, it's black and white Alfred Hitchcock movie talk."

His hand swished around the tub, accidentally rubbing sensitive female anatomy. "Some of us like hot water."

Morning beach sun was warm. A few dogs with walkers hugged the water line, dispersing stubborn birds. Elvin and Sofia counted streets as they walked; at a mile they turned around.

Sofia was topless and Elvin made sure there was no chance of telltale sunburn sitting under Sofia's favorite private backyard tree. When thickening clouds spit drizzle, Elvin announced, "*Guadalcanal Diary* time."

"Why a black and white war movie?"

"Black and white is realism and a magic carpet ride back to the glory days of movie making, like *Casablanca* in 1942. Going back in time is important, especially when you see them fight a black and white war, defeat tyranny and hate, watch lovers say goodbye at rainy train stations. Did you know black and white rain is sadder than colored rain? If there's a special magic in this movie over the next few hours, I'll have to go to Guadalcanal one day. There has to be a mystique, something that winds up in my heart and soul while I'm watching with you, like a message about life, death, tomorrow. That's why I'd go back, to relive, discover or remember you."

"You really would go all the way to the Pacific?"

"Let's watch and let go of me, I can't concentrate."

Elvin slid out of arms way, establishing an independent corner of the bed where erections are not permitted. Boundaries and restrictions were not respected, evidenced by a sarcastic laugh and meandering left hand.

"I love Lloyd Nolan, a wonderful, real actor. Hook Malone is such a great name."

"You're so into this."

Music was at a climactic point. Elvin jumped out of bed as his voice cracked. "The veterans, tired of war, but always brave and patriotic, watched the new troops march to replace them, and fight and maybe die. What a scene; do you feel how real it is? Our soldiers died on Guadalcanal, buried, resting there, away from families. Lives were sacrificed for freedom and America and for Germany and Italy too if you think about it. Such a lonely place to die. New troops arrived and some of them knew they'd never get home. It rips me apart. So sad. So much bravery. You picked a wonderful movie. I'm really going there."

"Why?"

"To thank them, to feel human, to breathe the same air they fought for. Also, it's probably destiny. I don't know why I feel this. Maybe I need a shrink once and for all, but it's also one of the reasons I'm holding a nude Sofia in my arms right now because of what's inside me."

"I'll go with you to Guadalcanal if you want."

"Let's go for pizza instead and thanks for offering. Maybe someday."

After pizza and when the sun was long gone, they walked on the beach again.

Life is fulfilling, accumulating and a journey to reckoning, reconciling and arrival. Holding a son's hand, walking to a dream was as good an example of the word, *poignant* as Elvin knew. Maybe he'd write dictionary people and ask them to add to the definition of poignant. How strange this day of fulfillment; there was only one solitary cumulous cloud overhead, following them, changing shape to different faces. There could've been an entire sky of clouds but only one was there. Why only one there? Where did it come from? Was it special condensation from the breath of an angel?

"A few more blocks Nelson; are you alright?"

"A little tired. What's that, Dad?"

"It's called a fishing pier. People catch fish with those long rods."

"But they can get fish from a can like Mom does."

"Good point but some people don't like fish from cans."

"You do."

They sat near breaking waves. The Shark River was two blocks away and a six year old boy, filled with expectations of a father's dream, was tired from sand trudging. Elvin's foot uncovered a sea shell. He held it to Nelson's ear. "Listen, it's magic, you can hear the ocean. Where are we going now?"

"Shark River."

"Why?"

"Because you always dreamed about bringing me there."

He hoisted Nelson up to a boulder then sat for an emotional time out, occasionally stroking his hair. An entire lifetime flashed around- like being at a railroad crossing with an approaching train-slow to arrive and gone before a chance to blink. Elvin's teary state was hidden from a nearby fisherman by turning away. He was with his son at the river of dreams and horizon. Life was special. What about the odds of existence? A father's sperm and mother's egg get together exclusively, which made existence a billion to one shot and for him, it probably happened at the old *Buena Vista Hotel,* a few blocks away. Nelson was billions to one and these moments together at the river, off statistical charts because of a solitary sperm and egg. Would he ever be able to thank that particular sperm for starting Nelson by being a good, fast upstream swimmer and penetrating the egg wall?

"Dad, why did you say, *Thank you, God?*"

Boats lined up in the inlet. A loud horn made Nelson cover his ears. The draw bridge started up and Elvin just knew one of the boats would have ties to the past. The *Sedona II* was there. How strange and unreal the day. Their cloud had company now.

"Look how the street goes up in the air so boats fit underneath?"

"Did that happen because we're here?"

"I think it did. Look way over there, it's called the horizon and you can't see anything past it. Horizon means future, tomorrow, hope and good things. Daddy loves you a lot."

Alex, Christine, and Evie were tanning in mid July sun, back at Seventh Avenue.

Nelson yelled as he got close, "Hey everybody, we're back. I saw the Shark River. It's my favorite river in the world."

Alex and Elvin deep looked each other, remembering those same words from a long time ago.

FOURTEEN

Pittsburgh Post Gazette pages kept turning despite a dimly lit motel room. Elbows pressed into Elvin's breastplate. "Do you read every page, even want ads for January 14, 1999. Cars for sale. Look at this one, Gladys Falltrap, from Monroeville, is selling a 1966 Mustang." Sofia started a slide further down, giving up on elbows into breastplate.

"Not every page but I try to absorb everything. Don't you want an informed manager working for you?"

Taking a deep breath she reminded, "You work for my father, remember?"

"You're a visionary genius."

"Why?"

"We're in Pittsburgh. I'm here to manage a sales rep while you're at the *Eye-FYve* office for meetings. Your father has finally vertically integrated, starting up local *Eye-FYve* eye glass stores and the office just happens to be in Pittsburgh and conveniently, you lobbied, cajoled, lured me with your body, finally convincing me to manage, and we're together in a dark motel room, discussing Gladys Falltrap's Mustang for sale, and having sex, which gets better all the time. Practice makes better, not perfection and now you're poised to totally wipe me out for the next few days although rejuvenation gets harder the older you get."

Sofia used a hotel towel for fanning. "Do we shower now or lay in sweat?"

"Maybe lay. They do change sheets or we can switch to the other bed."

Elvin's reclining head hit the wall hard. She followed with a less intensive hit, laughing and fishing off the bed for underpants.

"Morning wine?"

"Blonde or red?"

"Red."

"Let's toast Solchiali's success in the retail eyeglass business and *Eye-FYve* stores?"

"We can. Remember this was all meant to be. My father's partners in Germany." Sofia was trying to find Elvin's shorts on the floor off his bedside. "We can also toast *Shade-FYve*."

"*Shade-FYve*? What the hell is that?"

"Adolfo's going to open up a few retail sunglass stores soon as an experiment. Remember original German partners came from retailing. From day one, when my father started out manufacturing, they knew eventually about doing retail eyewear as well."

"Where does all the money come from? Germans?"

"Maybe Italians this time. Get it?"

She helped an erect penis gently find the front hole of boxers, careful sliding them, not getting anatomy caught. "It's staring at me. Do you think its upset?"

"Hardly. You've been a draining best friend all morning. You're an only child, on Solchiali's board of directors. Secret meetings must go on in Germany and Italy?"

"Yes. Half of you wants to play- the half still peeking at me; the other is all business, with so many questions."

"Give it time. The peeking half is going to disappear real soon like the reverse movement of a groundhog at the beginning of February. How many meetings do you go to? If I'm out of line, tell me."

"We just had sex, now dripping sweaty wet, drinking wine, so ask anything. I go to some, not all. Germans and Italians are funny. They're not big fans of a vagina attending secret business meetings. I have one you know, so things are limited for me, but I know enough."

Elvin leaned closer, dramatically lowering his voice. "Better whisper, because the room may be bugged as in industrial espionage."

"My father, my blood. I spent a week in Germany a year ago and heard about plans to create unique consumer demand by concentrating on special eyewear products and re-classifying wholesale optical accounts to determine who to help and who to put out of business. Third class is lowest- poor optical business people. They're too old to change thinking, barely hanging on; you know the type. New products with European fancy names and made-up rules, like who's allowed to sell- means third class won't be involved and maybe go out of business faster. When there are fewer retailers and demand increases, Americans will have to pay more, according to Adolfo. Less retail accounts, the better chance for customers to go to *Eye-FYve*. My father hates Americans and you too, especially if he knew you've been fucking his daughter. He likes some American companies because they know how to maintain profit by screwing their own citizens, even allowing people to die or get sick from products, right in front of law makers, on television for everyone to see. Adolfo thinks product recalls are a waste. Companies should compute keeping a bad product on the market versus how much legal fallout costs. Elvin, I'll teach you all the things he taught me." Sofia was standing on top of the bed, modeling a lacey bra and panties, which came from a seedy sex store near downtown. "I've never walked into any store like that before, so part, no most of the blame, falls on you, regional sales manager."

"That's funny. I walked by a store yesterday too. They sold tee-shirts, magic supplies and buttons. One button said *live guilt free*. I bought it."

Underwear had a smooth feel, gently helping her off the bed.

Downtown Pittsburgh made you think about an American shrine to urban progress. The skyline was a bunch of plastic models from the old hobby store in Newark. Elvin was drifting. Glass buildings glistened in the sun. Three rivers came together near steep hills and a quaint Italian restaurant. An optometrist told him about taking a romantic cable car up the incline. Elvin had no qualms about dining in public; Pittsburgh was a long way from Jersey and besides he was with his boss on business. Sofia ordered cavatelli and broccoli in garlic because it was her favorite pasta and interestingly, she mentioned that the vegetable was brought from Italy by James Bond's movie producer, Albert Broccoli's family.

Sofia was a public magnet. Rare beauty and brains, blonde hair and accent attracted owners of Italian restaurants. Elvin bragged, "She's a real, real Italian and loves your food." Complimentary tiramisu arrived for dessert.

Near midnight, driving around the outskirts of town, they pulled into a vacant lot attached to a lone building. There were no windows on the first floor, just a foil wrapped glass door which led into a dark maze-like hallway. Music was coming from somewhere.

"Are you ready?" Elvin covered Sofia's eyes.

"For what?"

They walked into a nightclub. She stopped short and squeezed Elvin's hand. The only two whites briefly halted the music. Bar stools spun back around facing the tender, a cue to restart the music.

"Elvin!"

"George!"

Two men hugged. "George, meet Sofia, the friend I told you about."

"Welcome to *George's*. I have a special table in the corner for you. Linda Geen comes on soon, best blues singer around."

Sofia kept turning around, absorbing, smiling and squeezing his hand, excited to be around so much underground electricity. "How'd you meet George, he's wonderful."

"Sylvester, my rep took me here once and since that time, we've become friends; been to his house, mostly talk about civil rights, American history and blonde Italian women."

"You're an amazing man, Elvin Stone."

"Nah."

St. Catherine Hospital in Livingston, N.J. used to live in Newark then sociologically, two words figured prominently in its future; migration and exodus. Blacks were migrating into Newark, whites in exodus west to suburban Essex and Morris counties. Changing times began in earnest during the mid 1960's. Residents who left before Newark's riots in 1967 were called visionary; so was St. Catherine Hospital administrators, for undertaking the sacrifice of moving, with weighty, new responsibility of providing medical care for a growing white, middle class suburban community.

The hospital lobby was subdued on a Saturday night. Patients were tired from the week long barrage of visitors, flowers and boxed chocolate candy that was tinged white when you opened it. Visitors dropped off passes on their way to a front parking lot. A lone security man was engrossed in the sports pages for March 13[th,] 1999. Horse racing results were meticulously circled with a pencil; a raspy voice softly *fucked* each circle under his breath, meaning yet another race lost to a bookie. Two suited men walked by, slipping into a stairwell off the lobby.

"Next flight up, we'll switch to the elevator."

"Good evening, Doctors."

"Nurse."

Cardiac intensive care kicked out last lingering visitors. The two *doctors* walked into several rooms, checked a few charts then walked in opposite directions down the corridor. A last room on the right, overlooking Old Buckingham Hill Road had a lone patient. The chart was checked, forehead felt for warmth. Temperature check turned into a gentle cheek rub. A syringe, rubber banded to a small vial, was pulled out of a suit pocket, liquid withdrawn and injected into the IV. The *doctors* met again by the elevator, pushed *down* and said goodnight to the same nurse. Security was still verbally *fucking* race results.

"Two burgers medium, diet Cokes and can I steal a sliced onion from the salad bar?"

The waitress spent most of the order taking time smiling at the man on the right and obvious enough for the man on the left to want to reduce the tip.

"I'll bring you fresh; the bar's been open all day."

"Thanks, it's why we keep coming back, for fresh onion and thoughtful waitresses."

The two men stared at a foot of teased, sprayed, almost artificial looking hair, waiting for her exit.

"How does a mother let a young daughter look like that?"

"It's a mother who wants her out of the fucking house by attracting someone like you."

"Fuck you."

"How did it feel being a doctor today?"

"We missed our calling."

"Second thoughts?"

"About tonight?"

"No, about not going to medical school."

"Funny. What time tomorrow?"

"Eleven a.m. Woodbridge or Iselin. One of those Jewish cemeteries. There's a map in the car."

"How long before expiration?"

"Soon."

"I always liked him."

"Pass the ketchup."

Gray sky over the Beth Israel Cemetery in Woodbridge created somber mood and special deathly effects. Narrow streets separated burial areas by house of worship or family group affiliation. Seven men gathered around a grave marker: *Richard Rose. Son. Husband. Father. November 26th 1969.*

"Richard was a Gabriel catalyst, making things happen in a lifetime of energy and devotion. Nolan insisted every few years that we pay respect." Simeon Morris reached into an overcoat pocket, handing out skullcaps or yarmulkes. "Lets look the part of Jewish mourners. Alex, we wanted you here, your baptism if you will." Simeon smiled after mentioning baptism. "Your first matter of consequence; a death and passing of a life."

"It's macabre for us to be here." Edward, towering over the group, continued talking, "Tomorrow Weingast is laid to rest over there somewhere, but purely coincidental that we're here now. Do you have a question?" Bothered by cool temperatures, Edward wore scarf and gloves.

Whispering almost inaudibly, Alex asked, "Absolutely essential what was done?"

"Gabriel is essential, nothing ever without extreme reason. Weingast lost control, had a mental breakdown- deterioration with outbursts. We can't afford leaks. He threatened us. This is standard operating procedure and fortunately he had a heart condition too. You understand our position Alex, we exist on trust."

A hand rubbed over a mouth softening a thought. "How was it done?"

One of the men who played doctor tossed an empty vial.

"Catch. Rather pleasant way to pass."

"I've seen it before in Washington near the zoo."

"Elvin, ready for God today?"

"Absolutely."

A tentative Christine was massaging a chess piece while Evie did the same stroking to a timer in a room with mirrors, chandelier and floor length curtains. The two chess playing women converted the Zari dining room to a Vienna palace at a grand masters event. The men failed to break the door plane because of the perceived event tension.

Alex yelled, "Continue play, we're going to pray. Nelson is in my office on the computer."

Both women stopped massaging and waved. Evie called out as they about faced, "Leave him a guilty Jew please."

Thirty minutes in the car and two gregarious friends became lost in thought, trapped in silence and staring at meaningless scenery and abundant shadows.

"We're here."

The Mosque was on a slight hill with scattered trees including a prominent weeping willow. The depth of the low hanging branches, almost all enveloping, nearly touching earth and yet reaching majestically to the sky was quietly absorbed.

"Heaven and Earth," Elvin stated.

"Take a walk with me first. Aarif al Hakim has been a close friend for years. He knows about our friendship and history since 1960 and about your searching heaven from an attic roof, sojourns to the Shark River and about your spirituality. This is a quiet time; no one really around, just us. There's a Muslim feast of meat and sacrifice next week, March 27th."

"Elvin welcome."

"May I call you Aarif?"

"Please."

"Aarif, your hospitality means a lot to me; being here is a fulfillment."

"Fulfillment?"

"Of a promised journey. Friends on earth need to understand and feel one another. It's our journey together of pathways to God. These last few years I've felt things, as if I'm not alone. There's a presence inside and around me but it's hard to explain. Much of my recent past, I'm not alone. Something is there. It makes me notice things in the sky or a shadow on a building or leads me to the ocean to look at the horizon or makes me look at the clock at 4:44 or 1:11 in the morning."

They were standing in a carpeted room with rows of pillars.

Aarif looked like Omar Sharif. Tempted to comment, Elvin caught himself, as in not appropriate.

"Perhaps an angel is with you. These are real signs. You are very special to be feeling this. Angels are important in the Islamic faith. Malak is Arabic for angel-means messenger. I think the word in Hebrew is almost the same."

Standing in the middle, Alex's eyes glassed over as friendship tears battled restraint. A best friend was absorbed and it deeply touched all inner chords of bonding, trust and love.

"Aarif, tell Elvin about destiny and Islam."

"Islam believes in predestination, called Qadr. God knows and controls everything going on. That's why you're here, but predested. You can follow me."

Aarif kneeled.

"Salah, Elvin, ritual prayer. We face Mecca."

"Focus your mind, heart on God, feeling and thinking, all consuming spirit."

The room was quiet. Occasionally Elvin fidgeted not from anything other than having Jewish knees out of shape for this kind of prayer. The explanation brought laughter later. A half hour passed but Elvin refused to move, wanting more time absorbing, reflecting. "This has been wonderful and moving for me."

"Then Elvin, I shall extend an open invitation to continue sharing, searching and know that you're welcome here anytime especially for a fellow history teacher."

For Elvin, a farewell hug was one of mankind's great communicative sharing experiences. Hugs said so much about seizing a moment, treasuring time spent, hoping there'd be more but just in case hold each other tight for several seconds and pat a back for emphatic sincerity. Elvin and Aarif hugged while Alex beamed, fighting back a tear.

"How was prayer?"

Two coffee cups, a glass of milk, and empty wine glass on a stark black table cloth could've been from a still-life composition entitled, *Beverage variations at kitchen table*. Evie and Christine got up to hug them.

"Warm, enlightening?"

"All of the above."

"Say, Dad."

"Yes, Nelson?"

"Aunt Christine wanted me to ask and I thought it was a good idea too."

"Conspiratorial thinking and planning while I was gone?"

"Silly dad."

"Permission to ask granted."

"At my bar mitzvah back in January, I became a man in Jewish tradition; an important milestone in the life of a Jewish boy and his father."

"Yes, it really is very important."

"Don't you think it would've been the perfect occasion to crack open the bottle of Vichy Water that has been crying out, sweating all these years in Mom's armoire?"

"Nah."

FIFTEEN

❝ Memorial Day weekend at the Jersey shore, summer's first debut, ocean aroma and Coppertone, memories of chugging wine at midnight sitting on the sand; it all brings an energy, something like a horny, hungry bear finally waking up after hibernation." Alex leaned back, laughing.

"My fifty seventh summer at the shore. I can't believe its summer 2002 already. Look at the size of these pizza slices; obscenely large and America is becoming more obese, so it's kind of like a graph, pizza slices getting bigger at the same time as American waists. I don't think we needed a whole pie."

"We're fans of Ralph Kramden's big mouth. So we did."

"Who asked you?"

Even though it was Friday of the holiday weekend, but early crowds still made them park near Main Street, making for that hike to the jetty, passing a long gone Buena Vista Hotel's ghost, where Elvin thought he was conceived. A boulder at the far end, covered with strands of sea weed with foamy sea water gushing up through small spaces was ambience they looked forward to.

Horizon and bright sun brought Alex's hands to shielding eyes. Elvin flipped a pair of sunglasses over, "Wear it. I'm in the business you know."

Uncharacteristic silence and gazing lasted through a rising and falling of the drawbridge. Elvin finally yielded and spoke first. "You're not yourself, far away, with those worry lines on your forehead."

"There's a lot going on."

"Does it have to do with your being away the past few months? I figured something wasn't right if you're in Hawaii for two weeks and didn't take Christine. How was Hawaii? Where were you?"

Sea weed was pulled apart and tossed into the river. "W. M. Keck Observatory, on the summit of dormant Mauna Kea volcano and other high spots."

"Why there?"

"It's among the world's largest optical and infrared telescopes. For the picky astronomer like me- a nearly perfect place to gaze. The ocean is pretty stable, heat wise. There are no other mountains around to interfere with the atmosphere and no big city lights either."

"That's why New York City doesn't have a telescope."

"Exactly."

"Great Britain, California, New Mexico, Arizona, South Africa and Puerto Rico this year. Did I leave anything out? You have been busy. Is it your Princeton slide, security clearance or are you still giving out research money?"

Elvin slid closer, almost automatically, sensing something, after asking the question. Both heads rotated around the jetty, making sure they were alone, out of earshot range.

"Do you remember a long time ago, we talked about having children and I told you about a serious race with two contestants and a finish line that was unclear, which explains certain things in my life, if you get the drift?"

"Drift away."

"Two wrinkle contributors. The Princeton slide brought me in contact with someone not too long ago, quite deep in the government; as deep as you can get. It's been advised for those sitting at special desks in geometric offices, to pretend green and positive, go through appropriate motions, pass a few environmental laws, don't cause any undo panic- no point to it- but scales have tipped, and there is no reversal. Things are accelerating faster than thought. Do you remember Carl Wyler in Sedona, scaring us with things the *think tanks* and NATO said about UFOs and not letting people know for their general welfare? You and I laughed at that but that shooting star made us squeeze each other's hand tight."

"Sometimes I love the way you express things as a major indirection. But that's you."

"The other wrinkle." Alex was always uncanny precision, now pointing directly overhead at the sun, "There's something up there."

"The sun is turning off?"

"Not for billions of years. I found something but don't quite understand. Maybe I'm wrong and fortunately pencils still have erasers, so I've been running around to see who else knows and re-looking at things, end of story. Basically, it's not a big deal yet. We're quite the arrogant, conceited profession. We don't like to miss things and speaking about missing things, I didn't miss you saying Sofia's name out loud back at the pizza place."

"Yet is a scary word; maybe it's one of the scariest words in the English language, if you think about it that way. You're the only earthling that knows about Sofia. It means nothing, a loveless entity. I don't know if that's rationalization or denial. Have I broken something? Evie and I are wonderfully, imaginatively in love. I don't know, Alex. I just don't know. I come here enough, looking for answers and questions. It's strange, but women sense things, but there's nothing for Evie to sense. Sofia is part of Qadr; pre-destiny and learning about life; what Aarif told me. As a matter of fact, you're Qadr too."

Pretending to push an imaginary *To New York* sign, Elvin walked around their little corner of the jetty until Alex waved him back.

"It's hard for me to know so much."

"I know. Am I imposing too much on you? She teaches me things. Last month she told me that Solchiali and many other optical companies have been moving a lot of production to China. One day China will be the eyeglass capital of the world and just about every other consumer product. Kind of like ten Japans rolled into one. Her father hates America. God only knows what happens to the prices of eyeglasses coming from China and how much he raises them above and beyond to screw Americans, even though he's paying much less now to manufacture. And God help the Chinese people working for that man."

"Why so much hatred of us? You've been telling me for years."

"German partners and Sofia thinks Nazi sympathizers and children of the Third Reich. He's an evil man. Why does the world hate us? Maybe it's jealousy. Americans all originally immigrated here and look what we've accomplished since Washington was President. America's concept works better than anyplace on Earth and we're still like the new kids on the block compared to Europe. People do anything to come here. Sure, we're a little conceited, but we earned it." Elvin got up and walked to the end of the jetty, pointing at the horizon. "Everything is out there, waiting for us. Spirit. Tomorrow. Maybe some answers. Better, hope."

"Good news, hate is all around, an equal opportunity. Everybody hates. A South African scientist recently tried to sell biological weapons to flat out kill. Fighting is still going on in Nepal. Hindus and Muslims riot against each other in India. An uprising in the Congo and a couple hundred dead there. A regular hateful day at the office. There's still good news to report. I feel like the lead into World News Tonight."

"Go ahead, Peter Jennings."

"They just convicted that bastard Bobby Cherry for murdering those four girls at the Sixteenth Street Baptist Church back in 1963 in Birmingham."

"I remember talking about that in Sociology class at Rutgers. I was typically rather outspoken about that, then I remember Caye threw that note on my desk."

"Ever?"

"Hear? No. Think about her? All the time."

Meteorological reputations have a way of being lived up to. Washington extreme heat and unbearable humidity for late June 2002 was expected, anticipated but not looked forward to. Four men, over-dressed in slacks and polo shirts walked near the zoo elephant house.

"Asian elephants, a remarkable species, unfortunately hunted. One day we'll wake up and only have pictures and video's to remind us of what we made extinct." A camera snapped.

"Every year we lose more of Earth's family to extinction and if we keep things up on the global warming front, we'll lose ourselves. A friend whispered in my ear while we were in a long line to buy popcorn at the movies last week; it's basically all over. Global warming has won. Animals become extinct. Coast lines disappear. More tropical disease ravages. Weather messes up food supply. It's pretty ugly. The think tank gang says leave it alone. Nothing we can do anymore. The scale tipped. Future Presidents will be advised to go through motions and pass a few green laws. Everything is pretend. Don't panic the people. It wouldn't accomplish anything positive. Say Alex, back up a little, let's get you in the picture. It means more with a human not yet extinct to be in a picture instead of still or animal life." A General in civilian clothes was having a hard time depressing the shutter, looking like he was about ready to punch it.

Perhaps the biggest gavel headache arrived with the quickest onset. Alex was speechless. Everything he secretly heard about the environment was just regurgitated by a General removed from his sources. So, therefore, more of secretive, clandestine Washington now knew things which he thought just a few select people knew. If a lot of people tell you it's raining, one day you'll get wet. "Thanks, General. Your overview makes me want to rush home and do things I haven't considered yet like going on shopping spree."

"I'm Martin today. Lose the General title."

Alex posed, whispering reluctantly, "Martin." He had a hard time not respecting rank. Nick and Tim laughed; their uniforms were home too.

"Say Nick, you're quite versed with security issues and it's the craziest thing, but there's a dark skinned woman who's been following us since reptiles, but far enough behind. Maybe because she's strange looking that I noticed and I'll feel bad if it's the heat of the day playing tricks on optic nerve processing." As Alex began to sense a vague familiarity, he stared brazenly.

"Well done. Actually we've got a small security entourage hanging around. You've seen her before; name is Sack, your young guide in Arizona a long time ago. She whispered to me before that she shot a rattle snake right near you. I'm impressed that you remembered. She will be too."

"She was pretty good with a gun; just one shot killed it." Alex threw a half salute in Sack's direction, getting a cautious smile back.

Bald Tim Damper always looked angry and scary. Occasionally, zoo tourists made eye contact with him then looked away, fearing for their lives. Alex categorized Tim as being in the same league with scary alien foreheads. When *plastics* and *Benjamin Braddock* was slipped into the conversation at the Gorilla exhibit, recalling *The Graduate*, Damper was clueless what it all meant. That ploy was learned from Elvin. If someone doesn't know about that movie, then they're too young to hang around with, so don't waste your time.

"Gentlemen, it's meeting time." Tim was programmed for getting fast compliance.

Half dozen people, obviously security, were relatively close, some drinking soda, others pretending to take more pictures. Sack walked by, taking the lead from Tim. She looked somewhat prettier up close, key word being, *somewhat*.

After a ten minute brisk walk, they arrived at a civilian residence hosting the meeting. It looked like a New York brownstone with a couple of brick steps, minuscule porch and heavy wooden door with ornate metal knocker. A man in a gray flannel suit pointed down the hallway leading to a dining room. A curious painting of the President and First Lady hung over a fire place mantle, showing them standing in front of a wire fence with an open Jeep and one lonely tree in the background, all the grass around tinged yellow, instead of green. Analytical Alex studied it.

What a brilliant protestation. Grass tinged yellow behind the President. Yellow is the color of cowardice, his record on the environment.

"I bought it at a motel parking lot sale. It was next to an Emmett Kelly type clown and a Churchill Downs portrait."

"Seriously?"

"Well. . . ."

"Gentlemen, Dr. Zari needs your attention."

Air was consumed without a trace of an exhale. "I spend time in New Mexico as you all know and help to secure grants for MIT Lincoln Lab. Air Force and NASA helps too. We excel at discovering asteroids, better than anyone. It's part of the field of asteroid radar astronomy."

"Why are we better?"

"Our telescopes have one meter apertures. Big advantage. I also travel to Spacewatch at University of Arizona, and to Hawaii, Jet Propulsion and play around so to speak; spend time at Arecibo Observatory in Puerto Rico and Goldstone in California. I found something which I need to look into more. The Earth's atmosphere protects us from most things that fall down. Bad things hitting Earth happen once every million years. Spaceguard survey tells us what's actually coming down."

Seven men squirmed to the right and left, while two played with collars and the General in civilian clothes, took to biting a thumb nail. Alex thought about the General's civilian clothes, and wondered why civilian motif.

"If something big comes down, what can happen?"

Two fruit plates adorned the table. Alex picked up a pitted prune and spoke. "If this prune, traveling less than the speed of light for a long time, hits the Earth, it puts a crater a few miles wide; this one single prune, which I need to eat now, because I touched it. My mother, Sura taught me well." Laughter was brief. Silence followed and he figured more information was needed. "Big things hitting Earth can do all kinds of nasty things from *impact winter* which doesn't help crops and food to the *E* word."

Standing in place for the past few minutes, they were looking up at him, almost like children waiting to be excused for play period. Alex sensed an audience about to be lost for a variety of reasons.

"*E*?"

"Means unpleasant."

"Zari, does anyone else have a clue what you've been looking at?"

"Not really. There's only a few people world wide, mostly here in the states even remotely capable and. . . ."

"And you need do a lot more homework." Bald oblong faced Tim Damper glared at him as if this whole day wasn't necessary, taking time away from water polo, tennis or polishing his head.

Martin felt the glare too, almost speaking to Tim alone. "All very necessary and protocol. It's what we get paid the bucks and hold onto security clearance for. Alex, why don't you spend the next several months doing what you have to with extreme caution? If you've got gut feelings about our European friends, get over there and lead them astray. I think we need security containment beginning now."

"How does late September sound everybody for round two?"

A few prunes were scooped up. Nick did two at a time. "Good stuff. I never thought they were that dangerous!"

"It's hot walking around Center City at the end of July, especially when I have a beach house on the cool breezy ocean and we could be lying there right now; me mostly nude and you mostly not, because you can't get sunburned and go home." Reaching for Elvin's hand, suddenly Sofia remembered, and recoiled.

"One smart woman is walking next to me."

Elvin, always the aspiring actor, played the role of salesman, walking around with his boss, rolling up sleeves, loosening a tie, pretending to be at work, just in case. Hand holding in public was something that still needed avoidance.

Philadelphia was crowded. Anything close to July Fourth and the city of Independence can be overrun by tourists. Elvin began a three day stint selling eyeglasses in the morning in Atlantic City until Sofia suggested one of her favorite American slang expressions, *playing hooky*. She coaxed him into teaching American history. Given any opportunity with a favorite subject, George Washington, Elvin responded positively. Walking around Philadelphia with an Italian woman, who knew little about American history, might transport Elvin back to teaching days and a sweet innocent time, standing in front of kids, trying to penetrate minds.

Just in front, a young couple took pictures by a gate leading into something that needed protection, eventually enlisting Elvin to snap their picture. The woman said, "Pictures mean more if there's people in it" and asked if Elvin wanted one with his wife.

"I called this morning to make arrangements for us to get into this cemetery at three-thirty."

"Elvin Stone?"

"Yes."

"Sam Levy, nice to meet you."

"Meet Sofia Zahl, a student of American history."

"How do you know about the Mikveh Israel Cemetery?"

"Masters Degree from Rutgers in history and taught about it for years."

"Then you know our history here?"

"Sure, fascinating."

"Would you like some quiet introspective time?"

"Sam, you read me well."

The cemetery was too small to be an urban breath of fresh air with just a few grave markers inside cement walls. A tree stood in the middle. Hands were held exploring.

"This is the oldest Jewish cemetery in Philadelphia. I think it goes back to 1730's then during the Revolutionary War, the Israel Mikveh Synagogue was given this land. Believe it or not this synagogue was the only Jewish place to pray in all the colonies during the war. A Jewish man named Haym Salomon helped finance the American Revolution. They still needed money in those days. Salomon is buried here in an unmarked grave. I would love him to feel us. I'm thanking him as we walk."

"You're a sweet, sensitive, caring, soulful man. It's one of the things that attract me."

A forehead kiss landed.

Wine glasses clicked at a rear table. Vetri's on Spruce Street served the best Italian food anywhere. Sofia insisted they share a chocolate polenta soufflé. Right after snatching the check away, she asserted, "You'll be doing me for the next few days, it's the least I could do."

"Does that make me some fancy gigolo word from a dictionary, accepting a $200 dinner for services?"

"Cute."

"I was wondering about your father's beach house mansion; is it company owned?"

"No, it's strictly my father's investment."

"If it was a company house or converted to that, it's so beautiful, they could use it for entertaining, especially since they moved *Eye-FYve* and *Shade-FYve* retail operation offices to Cranford from Pittsburgh."

Sofia responded to Elvin's *what's so funny?* "There are a dozen women in Union County as we speak who have swing sets in their backyards for their kids, paid for by *Eye-FYve* and *Shade-FYve* discretionary funds."

"Huh?"

"When they bring retail people from Italy and Germany to Jersey to live, my father likes to play pimp. He wants them to find local mistresses, get settled into routines, so he tells the company to use discretionary funds for whatever comforts. They won't need the beach house if they have mistress's houses because it's better, cheaper and he doesn't worry about laundry bills in Longport. One other thing; you asked me a few weeks ago why my father overcharges for glasses so much at *Eye-FYve* stores. Father reminded me last week when he was visiting, that being expensive makes stupid Americans think the quality in his stores is superior and people are glad to pay for quality. I know the retail world of *Eye-FYve* is so far removed from our wholesale world, but you can't help but be curious."

"And to think last Christmas, the company sent my yearly holiday gift, a tin of biscotti. A week later another arrived. It was a computer glitch. The office called me to send the extra one back. Were they losing a dollar?"

"Not quite a dollar. Adolfo's partners actually bought half the biscotti company, so he could save thirty cents a tin. I didn't know about them asking you to send one back."

A bare right foot briefly probed Elvin's crotch.

"Time?"

"Time."

About to open the door, leaving the restaurant, Elvin deferred to a couple walking in. He held it open. The man, like a suntanned albino, smiled at him and stopped moving and so did the woman. Everything froze. Sofia actually pulled gently forward, not knowing an impending spiritual log jam. The man was wearing a round button near a sport coat lapel, with only the number *444* in burgundy, tan background. Elvin's eyes fixed, the man smiled, because he knew and Elvin knew. They almost shook hands, but Sofia tugged at him again.

"Goodnight." That was all Elvin had time for, as the couple passed.

The man put both his hands together, fingers touched mirror image, but it was an illuminated smile back to Elvin that would be remembered.

With the key in the ignition, Elvin said, "Be right back." He jumped out, walked into the restaurant, pretending, but needed to confirm where the man was sitting.

"Something happened with that man back there."

"One smart woman is sitting next to me."

Sofia left Elvin in the driveway idling. A few minutes later, three garage doors opened. Elvin pulled into the middle. She palmed both his cheeks. "It was a special time for me in that cemetery. I felt what you wanted me to; history and brave people fighting for freedom a long time ago. We were alone there, like an oasis in the middle of a concrete desert. Do you remember the far corner, grave markers giving more privacy and no one around?"

"Sure."

"I wanted you right there. Do you think people fantasize about doing it in a cemetery?"

"You should've asked. You're not shy and people do fantasize that."

"Would you've done it there, just a quickie? You're a spiritual guy. Don't you think cemetery fucking gives all the spirits hanging around a rare cheap thrill by helping them remember good times? Don't you think they'd be glad to see that human mechanisms haven't changed?"

"Sofia, you're growing a sense of humor. But no, I draw a line and besides I was trying to send a spiritual telegram to Haym Salomon. How'd you think he'd take to our fornication near him? The others might've liked to see us, not him. By the way, that's what they called it in those bygone days, fornication, not fucking."

"You're right, come upstairs, I have a present."

"For me?"

"No for me."

Sofia went to shut the kitchen light. Elvin held her arm. "For once, leave the lights on."

"Why?"

"Be different."

A package, about the size of a medium television, wrapped in pink with bow was on the bed, card attached.

Surveying the scene, he smiled, trying to imagine. "To Sofia from Sofia, enjoy." Elvin laughed.

"Open it for me."

One downward swipe of the wrapping paper revealed a crescent shaped pink pillow.

"Meaning of this?"

Sofia got undressed, positioning herself on the pillow. "Watch, my bottom goes here. It lifts me all the way up in the air. You enter and then I move my legs like I'm riding a bike, one leg at a time. The sensation is supposed to be amazing and everything needed to be exposed and felt is."

"Where'd you get the idea from?"

"My friend Antonia, she lives for the letter."

"Letter?"

"*G.*"

Morning coffee and juice was a dimmer experience in the kitchen which lost a bulb during the long night.

"No more leaving lights on."

"No more, promiso."

"Funny man, go to work, make my father richer."

"How rich is he?"

"Bye, Elvin."

A fourth floor hotel window, at four a.m. on November fourth. Breathing was shallow as if in a trance-like state. Washington was sleeping. Moments before, a starchy white shirt took on a red tie. Body indentations outlined a hotel bedspread. A Gideon bible at the head indent was opened to the Twenty-Third Psalm. A dozen piles of paper on the other bed were organized like hourly points on a clock. On top of the noon pile was a hotel glass with a trace of red liquid.

After snapping out of it, the *six* pile was flipped through, notes scribbled on margins. The next pile had the words *blind spot* circled in red ink on the side page and a facsimile crucifix drawn on the top. The sun was near up; eastern exposure helped position a bath towel- knees dropped in prayer, long enough for the sun to make a brightness impact.

One prayer was answered quickly- getting to the Pentagon at nine a.m. without excessive traffic delay. Two strange men accompanied Alex once the building threshold was crossed. One wore an Elvin hat, defined as something Bogart might've worn back in a forties tech noir movie. Analytical Alex wondered about a civilian hat in the Pentagon, perhaps allowing for extra surveillance equipment to be safely tucked underneath. An escalator, water fountain and an outer office arranged like a maze highlighted the inner journey. The escorts disappeared before the maze.

Six uniforms and Alex's civilian suit with red tie sat around a table. He thought it was the same room as a recent meeting but maybe not; last time he couldn't take his eyes off another curious portrait of the President but today there was just a flag.

"Dr. Zari."

Alex sat alone at the far end of the table. Someone mumbled, "Civilian section." The bed arrangement of twelve piles was recreated.

Eyes around the table focused on his deep breath. Alex wanted to use the *F* word to describe nervousness as he spoke. "There are probably less than thirty people in the world that could discover what these twelve piles may indicate. In the world of security, which concerns this room, we're operating in a vacuum so to speak."

An aging General William Safton, slumping shoulders, perhaps as Alex conjectured, because of heavy responsibility, asked, "What you're saying Dr. Zari is at this time and place, you remain the only person with this indication."

Palpable tension was everywhere. It smelled sweaty or perhaps it was heat being turned on for the first seasonal time, leaving a pungent smell. Preliminary document briefings two days earlier produced the same concerned faces.

"Correct, General."

"Why is it just you with this information?"

"My life has been devoted to this field. I work with the best special telescopes and travel all over the world. I give research grant monies and keep fingers and mind on every astronomical pulse."

"You're quite pre-eminent, Dr Zari?"

"Quietly and humbly so."

A different service uniform spoke. "Here in the states. Are we the best at looking for. . . .?"

"We are by far the most the most technologically superior. LINEAR search with US Air Force and NASA. The NEAT program in Hawaii with NASA Jet Propulsion and Air Force help. Arizona and Spacewatch survey and at Lowell Observatory and the LONEOS survey. New Mexico installations. Arecibo and its Cornell ties. A lot is going on gentlemen. If we don't find things here, than no one really does, but I still travel around the world to make sure. I have a lot of friends all over. Astronomers are a tight little community."

"Like a Union?" The Navy spoke.

"Exactly; it's the International Astronomical Union."

Air Force stood up. "We know through your preliminary memo about some of the effects and defensive proposals including *Ahab* which you've been part of from the beginning. Tell me again Dr. Zari, defensively speaking and everything is conjecture in those piles of paper, what's the time element?"

"Well sir, there'll be sufficient lead time or not." Alex spoke with a hand over mouth as if he'd prefer no one really heard well or absorbed.

"In those piles of paper, any mention of approximate size?"

"No, but maybe large, not sure. Sorry for the vagueness gentlemen."

"If we're in agreement, you too Dr. Zari, then it's time to begin thinking of getting the President involved. Firstly, keep doing your thing here and abroad. We'll all continue to observe security protocol and containment. Let's target March to sit down with the President and that means, Dr. Zari, all those piles of paper become a couple of sheets that he can look at quickly, so get your ass organized. Pardon my French. Everything understood?"

"Done." Alex wanted to smile using Elvin's favorite word but dared not. The train station and Shark River seemed hundreds of million miles away or where that thing may be coming from.

"Say Dr. Zari. We've got a jet flying up to McGuire, want to hitch a ride?"

"Does sitting on a step in front of a college building make you feel younger, Simeon?"

Alex, with fist in palm, resting a chin, elbows resting on thighs, watched Rutgers students walking across a sprawling lawn.

"You're right. I do feel younger, but why are we here?" Simeon Morris positioned himself the same way.

"Geology Hall is security and timelessness. Elvin loves it. On the way to see your father in the hospital, we stopped here. He singled out this brick and perseverated about the man who cemented it in place a hundred seventy years ago."

"Why'd he do that?"

"A typical thing to do. He's got this love affair with Rutgers. He comes to New Brunswick for lectures, basketball and football. Actually we were here in October. Rutgers played West Virginia, lost forty to zero. He doesn't think they'll win another game this year, but he still wanted to bet me that in five years Rutgers cracks the top ten in the country."

"Why?"

"It's an Elvin thing. He saw coach's first press conference and listened to words, saw eyes and a smile and told me the coach knew something. For Elvin, particulates of spiritual energy become gut feeling. New Brunswick is waiting to explode. The town is being fixed up in anticipation. Cobblestones on George Street. Rutgers flags on buildings. Train station waiting for more passengers. A new hotel. Some unknown power, politician or company President wants this to be. Elvin even brought up an Islamic concept that Rutgers prominence is Qadr, pre-destined."

"Along those deterministic lines of thought."

"Pentagon meetings finished Monday. They flew me back to McGuire. Simeon, they're concerned."

"Should Gabriel be?"

"Not yet, but you'll be there every step. At least they gave me an audience, so that's progress. We're scheduling a meeting with the President in March."

"Don't get one of your headaches on me now, but we'll be at war by March."

Simeon jumped off the step, facing Alex, shaking circulation back into his legs.

"Iraq?"

"Alex, do you fast for Ramadan?"

"I do a little of everything because of my parents and Christine. Coptic, Catholic and Muslim, but you know that. I'm a religious dilettante, but nice change of subject." Laughing, shaking circulation back as well, Alex was on the sidewalk.

"There's a student bar nearby. Elvin goes. Want to feel younger? It's called the *Olive Branch*. Sandwich and a beer?"

"Young works."

For Alex, hearing things in the middle of normal conversations that people won't know about for months or years, no matter how nonchalant, usually constricts cerebral blood vessels, giving the feeling of a judge's gavel on both temples. He'd never get used to certain things so the best he could do was force a smile.

He did whisper, "Iraq" as they sat at a booth with old student's names or initials carved into the tables.

Elvin's favorite time of the year was Thanksgiving. Leaves change to vibrant colors just before falling and crunching beneath feet, cars or rakes. Everyone celebrates the holiday because there's always something to be thankful for.

Indian summer interrupted winter's march with a seventy degree forecast. Saturday morning was quiet. Nelson slept at a friend. Evie slipped out of bed. Cascading shower water, like a Guadeloupe waterfall stirred Elvin's subconscious. Startled, randomly tossing shorts and tee-shirt, he rolled a Newsweek into a cylinder, and before reaction response, opened Evie's shower door to a plunging magazine attack.

"Must you recreate that stupid movie, *Psycho*?"

"Wrong movie, try *High Anxiety*."

"Shit, there's black ink all over the shower. Why are you here?"

He picked her up, and since bathroom remodeling a few years back, there was more room in the shower. "Let's do it right here. Like our first time."

"The water's getting cold, but the bed's still unmade."

Shower doors nearly came off the tracks, carrying her away. "You're still strong."

"And virile; no pills for me. Jack never needed that kind of help either. Martha once let it slip out, that he was still chasing her around. I told Martha to keep that information from you. I didn't want great expectations or pressure."

"Cute."

A few minutes later, Elvin rolled off. "I've got an idea for the afternoon-indulge me. We'll pick up Nelson and take a ride on the Parkway."

"And where might that ride take us?"

"New Jersey Vietnam Veterans Memorial."

"Why such a random place?"

"Because we've never been and Nelson has no clue about that time. There's a visitor's center with films and stuff. It'll be a good learning experience for all of us."

Nelson sat between parents. Era pictures, newspaper headlines and artifacts were on the walls. Eyes emotionally stared into space and at the ceiling. Elvin drifted. Both Evie and Nelson knew it was time to let his eyes fill. They walked outside. Another man was walking around inside the exhibit, opposite direction. An MIA- POW sweatshirt approached Rutgers.

"Do you know someone who died there? Is that why you're here?"

Elvin's voice had to be cleared, giving it a chance to recover. "I knew everyone, but no one. Something said to me this morning I had to come here."

"That's heavy man. I'm Mike. My son's name is on the wall. Thanks for coming."

"And thank you and your son especially." Turning around to pick up his Rutgers hat on a bench and to say something more, but Mike was gone. He went to find Evie and Nelson. "Sorry for drifting inside. Too many died with so much to live for. Life is precious. Listen to everything I say. We need to respect how precious each life is. Do you know the odds of being born; staggering, billions to one, a miracle?"

"What do you mean, Dad?"

"Sperm and egg get together to make us unique at conception. Odds of existing and birth probably can't be computed. When you were little, sitting with me by the Shark River, I thought of this because I realized you're odds of existing was billions to one."

"Only you, Dad."

"That's why life is precious. Earth people don't get it, but maybe one day, but probably not. Alright family, next project. We'll walk around the circle of the memorial. There are 366 panels with 1560 names, all Jersey men and women's names on panels arranged by the day they died. Look at every name and whisper each one, then we'll each pick and remember two names forever. Two brave wonderful people who gave their lives. We'll think about them from time to time, like contacting their spirit. Nelson, you start."

"I love you, Dad."

"You bring tears." Evie was looking for a tissue.

"Let him get a head start, I want to tell you something."

"Are you going to make me cry?"

"Probably. In this place of reverence and remembrance, I need to tell you how much I love you. I thank spirit and heavens above for having sunburned testicles the day we met. There you were and I was dressed, standing on a rock and the only one around to help you. Life is so fragile. You are my life. Look what we created."

"You planned this day to tell me that?"

Nelson turned at the right time, watching his parents kissing as they corner eyed him watching.

Thanksgiving dinner waited until Louis and Rick, Bogart finished taking out Major Strasser at foggy Casablanca airport. Black and white movie watching was still holiday tradition. The Stone dinner was a thirty minute feast, somehow never reconciling preparation energy and time with rapid consumption. Both Jack and Adel, aged patriarchs, faded into amino acid and wine stupor and needed to go home. Both fathers lived near each other in Marlboro senior active life style developments. Last month, Alex asked the administrators if both fathers, at ninety, were still paying for tennis court maintenance.

"It's midnight, fathers tucked into bed, Christine and Evie dozing in the den. Ready?"

The Matawan train station was twenty minutes away, serving the Jersey coast line and like Maplewood, trains stopped running around midnight. Benches were comfortable, ambience not the same, but keeping tradition was worth effort and enduring cold wind.

"Alex."

"This is the third time in a row you broke silence."

The sign was immovable and high so no squeaky pushing.

Alex was pacing, "Cops drive by at midnight and see two older guys messing with their train station, are we OK?"

"Of course we are, but are you alright? Something is bothering me because it's bothering you. I know you probably can't talk. I understand things as they are, but don't really understand which means I really do understand; you understand?"

"I do. Remember our Memorial Day chat at Shark River about something I think I found up there?"

"It's still there, you think and that's what's bothering you."

"I'm going to talk to the President in March."

Elvin's hands waved erratically, "Enough said, I don't need. . . ."

"Done."

"Done."

A police cruiser slowed, and then disappeared.

Elvin started pacing, and if one looked closely, there were also wrinkles on his forehead, which prompted Alex, "And what's bothering you?"

"Spirituality. I keep meaning to tell you, but this angelic stuff, *Malak*, as Aarif described, has been all over my life lately. It seems the more consciousness, the more depth and awareness. Alex, I'm so not alone anymore. And if angelic intervention, I say to myself, what content of my character, or deed brings me to deserving such a spiritual honor?"

"Numbers are still in your life?"

"Yes, *444* and *111*."

"Are you consumed?"

"Yes, and I wrestle with my soul, conscience and righteousness."

"Sofia?"

"Part of the wrestling."

"Don't think I'm shrinking from you, but I don't know what to say."

"I know. I don't either. What I do notice, the more I open and receive, the more I am given and how perfectly simple and beautiful the communication is. I could be drifting across the Atlantic on a raft, concentrating on surviving, looking at the stars for navigational guidance, then fall asleep and all of a sudden, something gets me up, makes me look at a watch, and it's 4:44 and there's a ship in the distance and I shoot my only flare and I'm saved. The key for me is what makes me feel things."

"Do you chronicle everything?"

"I do." Elvin jumped up, walked south until the station ended, head cocked to the right, glancing at the track, then he turned around. "There are two of them together, like us, close, and stems intact. Be back." He handed a leaf to Alex.

"Thanks and it's still green."

"Something else you want to say?"

"Yes, our fathers were at Thanksgiving dinner tonight. Christine and I have been part of your family for so many years, but never your sister Judy, real family. I've never brought it up like this before. You know what I'm saying?"

"I know how sensitive you are; you see so much. Maybe I thought your silence is an extension of your visions and that you've never had a long range vision of me with a sister. You just said she was real family. I think *real family* is a made up word of convenience, describing the by-product of sperm and eggs and sharing of genetic material. Family is bullshit; it's not a perfect world. Does family belonging make a sibling or cousin more caring or responsible or does every earth resident start the race at the same line? If you did a statistical study, half human close relationships are with friends, like us, the other half, with family members. If someone adopts a child, one of two things happens, there is infinite, perfect love between parents and child, a family or there isn't. Judy was just never and that's alright. Remember, family is a made up world. It's a statistical fifty-fifty. Could you or I be any closer? Judy exists and I'm happy. She's the other side of fifty-fifty."

"What I hear is we're all a human family beneath the surface, so dependent on each other, especially now, this generation, for basic survival."

"And it's suddenly cold."

"Done."

"Done."

"Do you know where you're going, Elvin."

"Since the day you told me about Solchiali and selling eyeglasses."

"I meant getting us to the restaurant before Christmas."

Sofia was wearing a fur coat which Elvin refused to acknowledge, then, in a scolding voice, "Stop, please no more about how you're kept warm because of some poor animal."

She defended. "I can't turn down a gift from my father."

Philadelphia in early December was layered in its own holiday energy, different than New York. For Elvin, there was nothing on Earth quite like New York at Christmas time. If the planet put all their resources together and had an unending supply of concrete and steel to build a better city than New York, maybe in a warmer climate, Elvin knew it could never be done, not in the entire universe. Regrets lingered about not being able to walk around New York with Sofia at Christmas. Elvin pulled to the side, pretending arrival at destination.

"That's not the restaurant. It's an auto parts store."

"Emotion made me do it. I love Christmas season and need to say a few things. Don't worry, I'll leave the car running to keep you warm in case your coat stops working."

A gloved right hand touched his cheek.

"Thank you for my middle age."

"Excuse."

"You've been part of it. You gave me a new career where I thrived. You've been a special teacher and friend and I'm grateful."

"And I'm touched."

Several more stops to check directions and finally, "Over there, Viola's."

Ethnic restaurants imbedded into city fabric are hard to find and if there's a small neon sign in a front window, according to Elvin's theory of relativity, some of the best real food was served. Small neon signs are essential. A quiet little table was surrounded by just two dozen more. Antonia, who was taken there by a European Prince, about to inherit lots of money, told her about Viola's.

"Antonia gave him three months and if no inheritance, then thanks, have a nice life."

"Gold digger?"

"Realist."

"How?"

"Knows she likes money and does amazing things to please, but she's very impatient. Too bad you can't meet her."

"Why?"

Eyes rolled. She motioned to a passing wine steward, "Castello Banfi Brunello. What year?"

"1996."

"Grazi. You taste first. It's an old wine but good year. Italy had a really bad wine harvest, worst in forty or fifty years. My father said the winter was too dry and summer wet. He owns a few vineyards so he might lose a few dollars."

"There's nothing in the world like dining with a real Italian woman."

"Can I ask you something? You're so into Christmas, but you're Jewish."

"Spirituality of the holiday; been to Midnight Mass with Alex and Christine. It's a beautiful service. Been to a Mosque too. I've never said this to anyone, but after my first Mass experience, I knew I'd go to Midnight Mass again but it has to be in Montana, in a snowstorm, at a small church and town, walking all bundled up to pray and find a special spirit in the universe."

"Do you really mean that? You'd go to Montana just to go to church and pray on Christmas Eve?"

"Of course."

"Why Montana? Why everything?"

"I honestly don't know. A vision was just there one day. A spirit. An angel."

Seemingly overcome by Elvin, she asked, "Let's get another bottle."

Glasses were filled higher than protocol.

"To your Christmas in Italy. I'll miss you. Happy, Healthy and Merry always."

Free hands touched briefly.

"How do the holidays work with your parents?"

"Christmas with my father in Lake Como, New Years with Mother in Rome."

"Can we talk a little business? I'm in the mood, teacher. Does your father worry about government interference with the growing they're doing?"

"Father hates Americans and most lawmakers in Washington more. He laughs at how ineffective and stupid they are. They talk too much and take donation money for everything including getting local or state laws passed so Adolfo can hire non-optical professionals and save money on cheap labor." She winked.

"Money from Adolfo directly to officials to lobby to get laws favorably changed?"

"Who knows? Adolfo Zahl laughs at all lettered agencies, especially the FTC; perhaps the most ineffective and blind agency in American history. The FTC looks the other way, comes up with the most ridiculous definitions, and has let the eyewear industry spiral out of control. Either they're stupid or like a few Jersey mayors and you know what I mean. Those are the only two explanations.

Maybe they need to get rid of the whole crew of geriatric, prune juice drinking administrators and bring in a new gang, but all under thirty. To my father, there's such stupidity and no motivation to look into things or just simple laziness or maybe they just don't care that my father, who hates them all, is raping American eyeglass consumers and carrying the money far away. No caring or insight into the eyeglass business exists, so American's get raped or as you like to say, get herded into cattle cars. My father worries that a caring President will come along one day and defend the American consumer. Adolfo has a file on every law maker. He dislikes women lawmakers. Of course he hates Blacks, Hispanics, Jews and old people. Did you ever notice how few of those work for us? My father even lobbied state representatives here in New Jersey, to change laws to allow anybody to make glasses so he doesn't have to pay state licensed opticians. He still pays me and you, as an independent contractor, so he saves taxes and benefits. How many mistresses does he stash all over the world? Whatever suits himself."

Elvin broke protocol again refilling wine glasses close to the top.

"Our business is a best kept secret. Adolfo likes control. Nobody knows and I'm not talking trade secrets, just everyday simple things."

"Do I want to hear more?"

"Solchiali does whatever they want. They spit at official legal things. Someday government might get smart. Right now your President let's foreigners do and buy whatever they want. Major price fixing? Restraint of trade? Hiring and firing discrimination? To my father, Americans are stupid. Every time they walk into Eye-FYve to buy glasses, they're screwed. Nobody knows what the hell's going on. Lenses people buy from us; no brand name marker but a piece of glass or plastic. God only knows where and who. Throw in senseless American vanity."

"You don't like your father."

"He's hard to like."

"I never realized the depth of greed."

Eye-FYve sells one thing, eyeglasses. Rent, operating overhead, employee costs are a tremendous expense. What happens when an American customer buys our eyeglasses? If we only sell eyeglasses and people need them once every two years and we finally get them to come in, then we have to rape to survive. Somebody has to pay overhead and rent. What about a store that sells twenty-five thousand items? Potato chips. Aspirin. Toys. Eyeglasses. Do they charge less? Eye-FYve sells one item. Adolfo loves unsuspecting, trusting Americans and weak government officials who let the industry do whatever they want. Did you ever see Eye-FYve advertise low prices? Excuse me, it's the wine. I'll be right back."

He watched her walk away; a movement of finery, beauty and confidence. As if a fog rolled in from the Atlantic or the Delaware River, and covered his face, it was hard to envision Sofia Zahl with him. Different worlds, upbringing, religion, age, doing more to repel, yet something kept them close. Elvin wanted to understand, and remembered Qadr, pre-destiny. Sofia walked back; he watched every movement, arms swinging wildly and sexy.

"You watched me so intensely. Do you stare at my ass when I walk away?"

"I do."

"So where was I?"

"You know, I'm not in the mood anymore? Another bottle of wine?"

"How about a glass? But there is one more thing, student of mine. Two months ago I was in Germany for meetings. Remember?"

"You were away two weeks."

"They were heavy duty meetings, plotting out a course for my father's two hundred stores because of rumblings of national health insurance one day and perhaps changes in buying habits of Americans, so Adolfo is beginning to think someday of franchising all his stores. It's about recouping all the investment and sitting back and taking a percentage of the gross from the franchisees and not worrying about the business changing and leaving him in a bad spot."

"He's really thinking ahead."

"Greed makes you think a lot."

Elvin fumbled around overcoat pockets. "Merry Christmas, Sofia, something for you. And no more lessons tonight."

"I thought we said no gift giving."

"I had to."

"*The Pieta.* You brought a tear, sweet friend. Too bad we're both going home tonight."

"I know."

"Tony." A long index finger summoned the waiter.

The waiter hovered. It amused them that Italian speaking patrons somehow got hovering waiters. Every so often he'd stroll by, talking in Italian, not thrilling Elvin, who scowled when foreign language left him sitting like a schmuck.

"Averna, please."

Caught between languages, Tony shook his head.

"Averna is special Sicilian liqueur, rare in the states. Antonia said they had it here."

"Special?"

"It's a secret recipe, Sicilian, started by monks over 200 years ago. You might taste herbs and roots. It's a spiritual drink for me."

"Spiritual?"

"Because it's Christmas and we're together as friends."

SIXTEEN

The rear door of a bland colored Taurus was about to be opened, when the opener pretended receiving a cell phone call and roamed around talking to air, fussing with a red tie, but really checked out the license plate. Finding car ownership was easy if deemed necessary. Tim Damper sat in the back, waiting; two non-descript men sat up front. Whenever Alex Zari thought *non-descript*, it was a face with nostrils, eye sockets, no brows, oral cavity, all recently transplanted, sewed on. Maybe science fiction or humoresque, but government security people looked alike, with minimal human qualities. Working for a different organization, with the same job description, the men in the front would've been tagged as goons. Alex smiled. Tim Damper stared at his smile. The car burned rubber peeling out. Maybe they knew Alex was smiling at their goon status and decided to live up to expectations. When they ran an orange light, Alex smiled again.

Astronomers observe small celestial minutia. Alex watched rear view mirror eyes of the driver watching a tailgating car, doing their same abrupt turns without signaling. Arrival at final destination was routine as best as he could determine, passing through a gate, stopping at a side entrance. Rain was heavy, but they were whisked inside dry. The tailgating car cleared security meaning it was a friendly car all along.

"Dr. Zari, welcome to the basement of the West Wing. You're a Harvard grad so pretend we're in Filenes if you want."

A long handshake with General Safton and a smile about the Filene's remark was as demonstrative as Alex thought he'd be the rest of the night.

Alex sat where asked; between CIA director and Chief of Staff. The Situation Room reminded him of Nolan's library minus book cases, but with the same mahogany paneled walls. Just behind the head of the conference table, where the President sits, was a panel with his Seal. For a room with so much weight and responsibility, the conference table only had ten seats. Almost bleacher like, a row of seats were behind Alex's shoulder. Safton sat there. Familiar faces entered, greeted Dr. Zari as if long time friends or enemies and opened notebooks. An image of the Godfather's marionettes flashed around an analytical, nervous mind. National Security Advisor sat opposite the President. Hers was the most enthusiastic handshake. Defense Secretary, last in, made a coffee cup coaster by folding a piece of paper then reached across the table. "Dr. Zari. It's a pleasure to meet you."

Finally the President walked in, circling half-way around the table. Alex got the handshake most Americans only dream about. He wanted to feel a special emotional tension, that the most powerful man in the world just shook hands with him. For one of the rare times in a spiritual life, there was no feeling. Why was he suddenly running on empty with the President breathing on his face?

"I've heard a great deal about you, Dr. Zari."

"Thank you Mr. President."

"I would say, been looking forward to meeting you, but let's hear what you've got to say first." Familiar chuckling lasted until he sat down.

"We'll go right to Dr. Zari. It's been a long day."

Alex could feel Iraq war tension, remembering Simeon telling him on the steps of Geology Hall way back that we'd be in Iraq today. Now he was in the war room with the main players, passing out a six page report.

"If you turn to the third page, bottom, it summarizes the two hundred pages discussed at my recent Pentagon meeting."

"Ominous box, Dr. Zari. All your projections and estimations?"

"Yes."

Protocol slipped from memory; now all of a sudden he was unsure how to address people sitting and staring at him.

"Any other scientist here or abroad, in your opinion, that has this report or similar information." National Security was leaning back and forth, hands rubbing face, all seemingly gyrations of grave concern.

"Appears we have a good head start."

The President cleared his throat, "Let's jump ahead. Years ago, I think it was called Clementine. A satellite launches armed rockets into intruder, then Ahab, which you started working on under my father's direction, where a satellite travels into deep space, and hooks up or harpoons- I think is the term- then opens up a solar collector. It travels alongside, causes deflection. Are these viable options?"

"Well sir, depends. Some options need a ten year window."

The President was looking at him, perhaps through him. Now he felt those missing emotions welling up intestinally. The gavel headache came out of nowhere. The President just talked to him, Egyptian-American, Alex Zari, now at the pinnacle or depths of power, however you look at it. Alex wanted a train station. Could he close his eyes and be there? Could the last year be a nightmare or a misdirected television episode?

Please, Mr. or Ms. Dream, if you are, just get me up and out.

The Defense Secretary leaned back with coffee cup in hand, "Does anybody know what Congress has done with respect to pertinent investigations?"

"Hearings back in 1993, 1998 and last year. Make no mistake and I'm sure Dr. Zari will corroborate, no one has our technical capability to find, look and deal with."

Alex waited for Chief of Staff to get involved. He'd been shuffling papers next to him. What impressed Alex was the depth and knowledge sitting around the table. The enormity of the situation had everybody on toes; some grasping and all in denial, but still an impressive group.

"Agreed, Mr. Secretary, we stand alone at the top in this field."

"Recommendations, Dr. Zari, as a scientist?"

"All outlined in the box on page six."

"Serious?"

"Indeed."

CIA Director turned to Alex. "If we didn't know about the existence prior, time wise, what would we have?"

Alex could feel words hitting him in the face- the Director was leaning that close.

"Well sir, that scenario might mean a week or so, of course depending on angle."

"Trajectory."

"Exactly. Another problem, before hand; the object moves directly towards Earth and doesn't really have much motion across sky. If it doesn't move fast, then it's hard to identify and not to confuse everyone, but if the object was in or near the plane of the Milky Way, it could even get mixed up with background stars at night. Scenarios get complicated. To specifically answer your question, by the time it was somewhere around the moon, our deep space radars might find the object, and depending on speed, give us thirty six hours or so."

CIA leaned away, maybe to get a better viewing perspective of Alex. He rubbed his chin prior to answering, "Oh. Thanks."

"Dr Zari."

"Yes, Mr. President."

"I just read your notes again and what I'm coming away with, is a second meeting in six months. There seems to be room for more calculations and projections. I like preparedness, on front end and back and we're still at the front. Can you devote the next six months to fine tuning? I think you should put together an intimate committee to help you and CIA will assist. Then give me a larger box at the end of the report with more contingencies and elaboration, go to ten pages if you have to. Agreed?"

"Mr. President, I honestly believe what you see here is what you'll get in six months with little variation anticipated. Time is a critical component so I hoped we could avoid denial in whatever form it takes."

"I understand your concern Dr. Zari. Presidents weigh and modify for the common good; that's why we're back with this in six months not in a year or two." Presidential palms motioned elevation.

Alex had a second Presidential handshake. The room slowly emptied. A chilling few words slipped from the President just before clearing the exit. Alex appreciated a keen sense of hearing inherited from Adel.

"And no bearing on Iraq strategy."

General Safton reached for Alex's shoulder. "So, Dr. Zari, you've been in the Situation Room, the mountain top or basement, however you want to describe it. I think you impressed everyone and perhaps everyone impressed you too?"

"Correct, you're perceptive General, smart group."

"If you had to sum up in a single word, rate the meeting, the boss at head of the table, reaction response and the way he dealt with things, like coming back in six months, give me a word."

"Well, taking into consideration *time,* there's a favorite word a friend taught me but think maybe I'll just demonstrate the next best word."

Shoulders were dramatically shrugged.

"How do we get out of here, General?"

"Should I order two sandwiches for us?"

"No, I'll have Pastrami, you do Corned Beef. Maybe we'll share?"

Mark Severance thought back a few years, breaking his jaw and getting wired shut for three weeks and asking Ann to buy a minimum amount of Corned Beef for olfactory purposes. Meat stayed for two weeks before greening edges, but it satisfied an urge to smell and dream. In the midst of only fluid intake, there were serious thoughts of putting Corned Beef in a blender with stock liquid to see if that unmistakable taste could be captured through a straw. When he finally did it without telling Ann, there was rapid regurgitation in the bathroom sink with the realization, some things are not meant to be.

A broken jaw and being wired was ultimate punishment for a Presidential interpreter. Mark followed in father Ted's footsteps, from speaking five languages and going to Princeton to winding up in government service. Ted, the Bolshevik, quietly retired to Key West and Montana.

A few weeks back, Mark was told to be on twenty-four hour call until such time and at moments notice, would be asked to get to Washington with a weeks clothing. At nine a.m. that morning as they were consummating, almost perfectly finishing together, cell phone *interuptus*, as Ann moaned, conspired.

"Yes sir, eight p.m., Connecticut Avenue, park in front, there'll be a space, only two days clothing, then midnight, understood. No, I'm fine. I just ran up a flight of stairs to get the phone, thank you."

"So, Ann, where were we and do we go back easily?"

"You're flaccid. We're done. When are you leaving again?"

"Tonight."

"I'll shower now and you can take me for an early lunch. You'll want to nap most of the day. I know the routine; preservatives in cured meats help you nap, so the deli is fine for lunch."

"The woman behind the man."

"No, the woman behind the flaccid Bolshevik. I like that nickname borrowed from your father. Do you know where you're going?"

"No."

As Executive Branch briefings go, this was particularly short and satisfying to Mark. Six men left the premises. Three others hung around the front door, two more on the other side, two on the street, chain smoking and tossing butts with a flick of a finger, like an Olympics event.

"Still time for a little gin, Mark?"

"Drink or cards?"

"Funny; deal."

Four men sat at a dining room table playing gin, throwing a few dollars around and checking watches. Four cell phone calls in quick succession prompted running around, retrieving, tightening ties, and washroom stops.

"Leave everything."

Lights stayed on; cheese, crackers, an empty milk container lay on the table, a bottle of blue mouthwash, at the far end. A gin bottle look abandoned from a game of spin the bottle, pointing to a doorway opening into a dark hallway.

Two bland cars waited outside, idling. Card-playing men paired off into back seats; front seats were filled.

Officially early morning, air traffic around the airport had ceased. At a deserted unused corner of the airport a Continental Airlines 747 waited. Cars surrounded the plane like a Conestoga wagon train fending off an attack. Back seat men proceeded up. Mark sat near the front and immediately closed eyes. The briefing explained the jet was just another Air Force One, disguised, completely fitted, but in matters of special needs, impressed into service. Mark liked the word impressed; it felt like he was, since there was no orgasm that morning because of a quick pull-out. Air Force One made a trip earlier to Texas.

At two a.m., Mark's eyes, barely functional, saw the President briskly walk by, escorted by two men front and back. An unknown sat down next to him.

"Buckle up, seat back, tray table, you know the routine. There's no help on this flight. It's a good idea to sleep. I'm Neil."

An awkward handshake followed.

Mark was nudged out of a deep sleep by a gentle rubbing of a bicep. A few moments passed before processing humming of jet engines and an image of two rectangular blocks on top each other. Neil's head and middle torso looked like wood blocks, flat crew cut hair, level jaw and wide square shoulders.

"Half hour. Familiar with Iceland?"

"Been."

"Interesting place; always thought icy, but actually quite temperate."

"North Atlantic current."

"We've had a military presence there since World War II. Brits were there until 1941, then our Army. Think we're going to leave in next few years, but as long as we're there, guess that's why. . . . "

"Assume my talents are needed where we're going?"

"Most of them. The overnight suitcase, don't worry about it, we're not staying long."

"No sight seeing."

"Just the drive to House of Parliament in Reykjavik. Protocol review; John, yourself and the President in the meeting room, that's it. John stands to the right at all times."

Mark shook his head and wondered what languages were needed.

Six cars and an equal number of Army vehicles waited below the window. Far in the distance was an Aeroflot plane. Neil and Mark joined a third body in a back seat. Just before bending down to get in, he saw two American fighter jets passing overhead.

The air almost felt warm by the time they walked into the Parliament at noon. Was warmth due to tension or remnants of the Gulf Stream? Mark's watch flashed eight a.m. They walked up a flight of stairs where a dozen erect military personnel were positioned in the hall, spaced a few feet apart. Mark, John and the President entered a large room. A dozen men stood up which meant four countries, now fifteen souls in an intimate circle, exchanging handshakes. Mark intellectualized that the scene was as tense as ever encountered and tried to think what current events might account for this group standing around in a circle in Iceland.

"We've all been briefed and read reports. Our purpose today is policy and implementation, security and acting together in a unified way."

Russian response was translated. Mark knew the German and French translators. He flashed a reserved smile of recognition. The young Russian was new. Russian translators always seemed new, making him think there's a remote Gulag somewhere filled with *retired* translators.

"We'll communicate with those not here when appropriate." Britain spoke.

"Did everyone get a chance to thank Prime Minister Oddsson for hospitality at such short notice? I meant to say that before. I also congratulated him on their work with hydrogen powered vehicles."

Translation took a few moments to catch up to the President's grin but the group barely smiled.

Russia spoke. "America is fortunately far advanced technologically in the field. Do we expect any third world interference?"

"Not at all. The policy we have to agree on is preventing and handling discovery." America looked to Germany for a response.

"Mr. President. Think I speak for all of us. We'll support outlined initiatives and direction."

Britain and France concurred. Russia made it unanimous after a slight translating delay.

Lunch was served by military personnel. For Mark, it was the lightest moment of the day so far. He tried to imagine what boots and fatigues would look like with an apron. Sitting around the table, John was still on the President's right. Local dried Haddock was lunch without much culinary imagination. Bland, no garnish, the plate had no greenery either. Mark wished upon Corned Beef, but the fish smell killed the dream. For the first time in his career, he questioned why he never went into teaching, but the fault was with a father who pushed the joys of Princeton academic life and all the doors it could open.

Discussions after lunch were like someone poured an accelerant into a raging fire of candor and brutality. Words going back and forth weakened Mark's knees and stomach. Hearing words difficult to translate made him dizzy and nauseous. Was he doing too much thinking in between foreign words? What the hell was going on anyway? There were actual translating delays, trying to process everything going on. No one was sharp enough to notice, but he was having a hard time digesting and formulating words.

America stood up and the rest followed, re-assembling in a circle. John was still on the President's right. "This has been difficult but historic. We can do positive things working together like this. I have a good feeling. We'll be in close communication; maybe we'll all get the same colored phone just for this." The President looked for smiles of acknowledgement, but soon thought impromptu humor was probably lost in translation.

Final thoughts translated indicated everyone agreed with the President's initiatives. Hand shakes between the leaders closed the meeting to pre-arranged departure choreography, with America leaving last. A room down the hall was used for an hour, so the President could close his eyes. John followed him everywhere but never closed his eyes.

Back aboard the jet, everything started to spin for Mark as if Icelandic water swished around with intestinal contents and wanted to come back up. Was the Haddock back to swimming again? Half an hour before take off in the head, partially alleviated sick feelings, but he sensed being some kind of sick for the rest of a life. Interpreter's lives were strange and hostile. Walking down the aisle was like being stuck in traffic, not being able to move or find a short-cut. Relief wasn't anywhere on the plane or most importantly when they landed. To add to the despair of the day, the President never said good-bye.

Bad dreams and hopeless fatigue filled senses by the time Mark was chauffeured back to Connecticut Avenue. The same men, who earlier situated him into a back seat, were there to get him out of another back seat. Before disappearing into Washington early morning, the group shook hands on the sidewalk, littered with fresh cigarette butts.

Dave, from last night's session, spoke before Mark's get-away. "I apologize for the early phone call yesterday, catching you running up stairs and out of breath."

"I remember."

"You live in a ranch house; good night."

It was too late to call Ann. A half hour drive was ahead, but at least there was no traffic. At a red light which seemed frozen, he didn't pay attention to a large truck approaching the intersection at great speed, not slowing. Impact was head on; death was immediate and bloodied. The truck driver jumped out into a waiting car.

Police investigation revealed a stolen truck carrying thousands of dollars in bootleg cigarettes without tax stamps.

Waves broke closer than thought. Sitting was moist, watching the sun lift off the horizon. Elvin kicked at a wall of sand in front.

"Do you think this can stop a wave?"

"Not even a sand crab." Elbows leaned back into the sand. "I love ocean and beach, especially with children playing all around."

"Children?" A wave rolled to Elvin's wall.

"I dream about motherhood, children and watching them grow into the world, just like you and Nelson. I think about you at that Mosque and Qadr, things that are meant to be and how one can't change that. I could never change Adolfo, who mentally brutalized my mother. As a child, it messed me up; actually I want to say fucked me up."

"You just did."

"I guess the term is dysfunctional; pleasing Adolfo and wanting his money which is a kind of servitude. Somewhere in my life, there was a point of no return, so I'm stuck at Solchiali. You've helped me find some kind of normalcy. I date Italians mostly, some come to me by way of my father, the pimp, remember?"

"I've helped you?"

"Like now, sitting, caring, being gentle and letting me into you, you into me. We're a special closeness and it sustains. Sure I get laid when I want; like a month ago in Manhattan near the UN. Three limp inches and three minutes. A minute an inch and he's on Forbes list of richest and that's all he's got. Imagine the wealth of the plastic surgeon that comes up with penis transplants that really work and get erect when they're supposed to!"

In response to her shiver, Elvin's arm wrapped around.

"Hope you don't talk about me like that?"

"I don't talk about you. Did I ever say how perfectly you fit inside me? Your anatomy's so perfect, it rubs my spot naturally. Some day, before I go back to Italy without you, I'd like to bring your thing with you in it, to someone who can make a working playing latex copy for me."

"You're serious?"

"Of course.

"Then I'm touched."

"Be touched."

Walking into the ocean up to his knees then backing up if a wave looked threatening, watching the horizon, Elvin thought about the departed and Sofia, trying to understand everything going on. Philosophical dilemmas made Elvin clench fists and close eyes to summon inner troops.

A foamy wind gust sprayed his face. Ayn Rand came to mind. The gust was a warning; now he was stubbornly wet thanks to a rogue wave. *The Virtue of Selfishness* became a wet epiphany. In order to be the best husband to Evie, he'd have to be selfish and that was virtuous, because thinking of his own needs first would make him happy, then it would be much easier making Evie happy if he was already happy and isn't that what it's all about? Or was it all bullshit. Now a beautiful Italian woman wants to replicate his penis for posterity.

Sofia's arms outstretched for lift up. Instead he jumped into the sand next to her. "Look at the horizon, fifty nine years ago, right about now, we were landing on Normandy beach; those brave Greatest Generation soldiers. Guess what's in the glove compartment?"

"Must be a black and white movie."

The Longest Day."

Late morning was spent on Ventnor Avenue; miles of quaint stores, beach things, exclusive dress shops, foods and sunburn items-preventative and treatment. Soft summer rain left a clean street smell. A last purchase was a brightly colored polka dot blanket for spreading on the bed.

Henry Fonda was on screen as Theodore Roosevelt Junior. Grapes were fed to each other.

"There's a famous child following in a father's footsteps."

"Ready for business lessons?"

"Am I your protégé?"

"I've been preparing you for years. I'm going to quiz you one day. Everything I'll ever teach you about Solchiali and Eye-FYve can be expressed in one word. That's your final exam. Someone needs to know and understand. Why not you? Do you know what happened to those two west coast managers?"

"Not really."

"Forced out. One's wife was dying and he couldn't work enough time to make more money for my father. There's no feeling for an American anywhere in the company; no honor, respect or reward for loyalty. Americans can't be loyal, not to my father."

"Not an ounce of caring. American workers are a just a business expense that your father would like to do away with."

A voice came muffled from the closet. "Correct. If he could eliminate our whole sales force tomorrow and put commissions into his pocket, he would. If he could change state laws so an optician or store doesn't need a license and hire cheap tech labor, he would. If there was an ultimate eye exam machine to replace eye doctors, he'd be thrilled?"

"It's called an auto refractor. A friend of mine uses one when he goes on missions to Africa and South America."

"If he could eliminate eye doctors and sell his own contact lenses, he would. Anything for a dollar; there's never enough money."

"I bumped into a salesman the other day from a new frame company, Gratis Eyes, and he told me they're using one of the same factories in China that Solchiali uses. Their overhead is negligible so they're able to charge our same accounts twelve times less for basically the same frame. That's staggering!"

"No, Elvin, that's just Adolfo, raping unsuspecting eye care professionals, who pay twelve times more for the same frame. And what do you think happens to the ultimate American consumer when the optical store has to pay twelve times more?"

"Rape. He's a bad man."

Sofia smiled.

"Adolfo would fire any American with a family to support if they cost him a dollar. *Eye-FYve* store managers get pulled aside after secret memos are sent. Our managers are responsible when customers return eyeglasses. Their job is to clean, adjust and integrate returned glasses back into stock. In other words, eyeglasses worn on someone's diseased face gets sold to another customer's face; real sanitary conditions. The rest is for your imagination."

"You've taught me so much. I think about other companies that affect human lives. Americans take so much for granted. Look at my piece of shit SUV. I've been loyal for years, even recommending them. When I drove it out new, it wasn't right. First three years, three transmissions. The rear wheel fell off on the Parkway. They close plants, make garbage and don't give a shit. I wrote countless letters, made phone calls and not one response and I think about all those ads on quality and service. They'll probably have to merge to stay alive because they don't get it. A great man from Arkansas got it. He preached always taking care of customers, wanting their business for life. Are we talking too much?"

"Are you saying we should be under the covers now? Well, soon. I pity suppliers in China. Adolfo mistreats and misleads. When we do 50% off glasses or lenses or buy one get one free, Adolfo gives nothing away. Costs are so microscopically low, customers run to our stores thinking free, but get nothing of value except getting nailed on the front end. Americans run without thinking. But you know what, if they did know, it wouldn't make a difference because people are herded. Nobody cares and my father knows that. Elvin, you could contact the ombudsman at the best paper in Washington or New York and offer all this knowledge but they wouldn't give a shit either. Adolfo is safe and he knows it.

"I don't know what to say."

"One day, I'll be gone and that's all I can say now and there won't be anyone with your knowledge. That's why I tell you all this."

"Gone?"

"Gone!"

SEVENTEEN

Two wooden stools faced each other across a kitchen counter. Stool design was free form with black and white spots and an almost anatomically correct pink cow's udder underneath. Unusual stools happen when you cross the Delaware River into Pennsylvania on a Saturday of antiquing and stumble into a store dedicated to the American cow and so birthed Christine's mild obsession with the giver of milk. Black and white cow themes were all over the kitchen. They were sitting on cow stools, drinking coffee from cow cups and stirring cow's milk around with cow teaspoons.

"Alex, aren't you supposed to call Ian Fielding in Cape Town today?"

"I am."

"What time is it there now?"

Alex never looked up from the Times, half on counter and lap. Without looking at Christine, almost trance like and speaking in monotone, mumbling, "Six hour difference. Three p.m. Shoot. I better call him now- thanks for reminding me."

For most of an adult life, perhaps even going back to early family histrionics, Alex wore slippers around the house. Once Christine, also from barefoot persuasion, asked Alex why he always wore slippers. Alex had no idea. The following morning he showed up for breakfast, barefoot, smiling.

A toe nail clipper came out of a catch all draw in his desk. Bare feet on desk, phone at ear, he played Podiatrist, waiting for South Africa to answer.

Ian Fielding was an "Ichabod Crane, tall, gangly, long skinny proboscis, who walked on tip toes, never wanting to come down hard on heels and disturb anyone." Quoted verbatim from a local magazine, that's how Ian described himself. Alex argued he was one of the best astronomers on the planet. Their friendship began at Harvard graduate school and if there was one iota of Alex criticism, Ian needs to appreciate himself more. One recent birthday, Ian opened up a package from Princeton University. Contents were wrapped in a local Trenton newspaper. The gift was a mirror from Alex so Ian could see what others see, *sheer reflective genius*. "Know yourself but first see yourself," was captioned on the card.

"Ian!"

"Alex Zari, as I live and breathe! Are you in Cape Town, looking for a ride to the Observatory?"

A couple of throat clearings reverberated into the phone; whole cow's milk sometimes gave him phlegm. An oncologist friend once told Alex, to lose the milk because it causes intestinal mucous and cancer loves hanging around that medium. Throat clearing was meant to be; Alex wouldn't be able to explain that there was never a vision of cancer in his life. Who would ever understand, except Elvin and Christine?

"You're not around the corner from me Ian, so there's no such thing as a surprise visit to Cape Town."

"Wishful thinking on my part."

"Why wishful? Do you want scientific company or just miss me?"

"Little of both."

"On the astronomical front is there anything that can't wait until October or you've got something for me now?"

"I'm not sure. I'll email you the notes but mostly inconclusive."

"Anyone else working with you?"

"Of course not."

"Then plan on my coming in October. I've been busy with a couple of committees and projects. You folks had some trouble with gang violence recently?"

"All the way in Jersey you hear about those things, quite the electronic information world. It happened back in April, mostly when gangs killed a few kids."

"How's Margaret, send her my best."

"Thanks, she's fine. I could've been in trouble or worse years ago for being with a colored girl, especially in a serious relationship or marriage. I think I'm too old for the formality of marriage and going shopping for towels and dishes."

"Bless your expressiveness."

"Best to Christine."

Alex looked at his appointment book; during the upcoming week there was a meeting with CIA for *routine matters* and another with several new special committee members as per the President. Housekeeping issues were where to hold group meetings. Arizona and California won out. The six month deadline imposed by the President hung over everything. What amazed Alex is the trickle down power of the President. Arranging, contacting, and simple everyday dealings involved with putting people and agendas together and all he had to do was say "Dr. Alex Zari", not even invoking the President directly, and everyone couldn't do enough, almost in a panic to help.

A half-eaten bagel with cream cheese waited in the kitchen. Toe nails were trim. *Why did it take so long to appreciate the joys of barefoot living?*

By June, Cape Town, South Africa was in Mediterranean like winter. Frequent cold fronts off the Atlantic brought wind and heavy rain. A late model Volvo drove around a block several times before a car left, freeing up a parking space. Two men sat, smoked and joked about waiting for rain to subside.

"Bet another half hour of rain?"

"Pointless bet, look over there, our friends are arriving."

Two white men in trench coats walked inside the Moulin Rose, a food and strip joint. Rain came down harder.

"Fuck this heavy rain."

"Let's go. We're getting fucked one way or another."

Two black men ran across the street, soaked by downpour and a speeding car that swerved purposely, splashing a puddle.

"Come back you bastard. I'll give you something I've got in my pocket."

Runway seats were all filled. The two whites were front center, drinking loudly, and trying to place valuable paper money in female anatomical orifices.

"Go tell them we're here in the back and when they're done with the women, we're waiting. Maybe tell them to wash their hands."

Stale alcohol aroma, dim lights and scratchy recorded music set mood. Sounds of inebriation and bad misogynous language were everywhere meaning no sanctuary available on premises. The two black men whispered about their discomfort being there. Years ago they'd never even be allowed in. The two white men asked permission to join them.

"Errol and Winston at your service."

"Have a seat."

Errol, the taller white man spoke. "There's a few new one's up there tonight. I have to get to know them better so I can go for a record alright; been with a dozen over time already."

"Impressive record." Black response.

"You sound sarcastic, maybe a little jealous, but you don't know what you're missing. We'd better get back soon; they won't hold our seats all night, so let's get to it." White response.

"Next day or two, take care of things." Black.

"And the girl?" White.

"Keep her for a few days then let her go but don't. . . ."

"Why not?"

"It's not what we're about, follow?"

"Too bad."

A business envelope exchanged hands. Whites stood up, mockingly saluted goodbye and resumed their place at the runway front. Two white palms pulled away from each other as a demonstrative measure of length. Naked breasts from a red headed stripper moved close to the show of length.

"Is that really true?"

"And are yours?"

"Back in the seventies and eighties, Long Street was known for anti-apartheid theatre. Ever been to New York and Greenwich Village?"

"Why."

Ian Fielding turned around in his seat. "Atmosphere is Bohemian in Greenwich Village, just like here on Long Street and this restaurant, Raz's. It's dark, Casablanca fans, smoke, drugs all around and of course marijuana so I feel like we're in New York. I've been there twice with a friend from Harvard, whom you know."

"Alex Zari?"

"Of course. Smart you are."

Margaret reached across the table. "Some day take me to New York. The seventies you said. I almost wasn't here then, born in 1978 in Cape Town and been here ever since."

"This restaurant might've been a theatre originally then they chopped it up."

"We should go Ian; I've got a bit of a trip in the morning and no doubt we'll be up late."

Camps Bay was one of the more exclusive neighborhoods of Cape Town, overlooking beach and ocean. Cape Dutch architecture dominated with distinctive design; elaborate gables made you think middle of Amsterdam. Ian's black Mercedes pulled in front of an H shaped house, with thatched roof. The street was quiet, drizzle lingered. The racially mixed couple held hands, stopping to kiss before the front steps.

As he was looking for house keys, a car pulled up and called out for directions. Instantly, two men ran around from the side and pushed Ian and Margaret into the house. Her mouth was taped and face covered with a pillow case. The butt of a gun knocked them both unconscious. Eventually, a car drove away with the girl wrapped in a Persian throw rug, still unconscious.

Three bullets were deposited into Ian's cranium- a silencer doing what it was supposed to. He was stripped naked, penis cut off and dropped on his chest. A pail filled with slaughtered animal's blood was carried in. The house was ransacked, blood thrown over downstairs walls. The letters XT was blood painted with a brush on a dining room mirror.

Two days later, Cape Times reported another incident of gang violence with possible racial overtones; white man, colored woman, now missing. Several suspects were brought in for questioning. The girl, Margaret Reed was found several days later, hospitalized and suffering from cranial injuries and shock and remembered nothing.

A mirror helped adjust a military tie then a few steps back for a squinting, perspective look. General William Safton's bifocals were on a Paris hotel's night table. The General's wife went shopping at an Alexandria mall a week before and came home with a chain which kept eyeglasses hanging, so they're not left on night tables. Sally was trying infantile bribery to get an invite for an upcoming trip to France. Safton responded abruptly. "Not at this time, so stop with gifting and bribing. It used to work darling, especially when stationed on military bases. Now I'm a decorated, almost retired Army man."

On Friday, Safton accompanied the American delegation to the D-Day Anniversary remembrance at Normandy. His own father passed through Normandy as a reinforcement, but not first wave. It was Safton's fifth time back; each time visions of his father as a soldier and later with dementia did battle with tears standing near the embattled beach. Before his father sunk into the lonely world of mental deterioration, he managed to sit down every afternoon for a week, getting him to recall as much as he could from war days. Much came out that he never knew; a dozen German soldiers shot, two bayoneted through the heart, a medal awarded, but was left at their last house in a hidden safe. German hatred was still evident in his father's thinking.

"Why lingering hatred, Father?"

"William, we're part Jew, but no one knows. It's better that way for advancing military careers, like yours. Forget I told you."

Echoing in his mind, the conversation became a permanent fixture, mostly as a last lucid chat with a father- shortly thereafter he faded away. How were they part Jew? Strangely he never thought Jewish roots again and it was a better military career with certainly more Presbyterian advancement.

Most days in France were different venues for military meetings with French counterparts. Their official translator was jokingly but seriously told to spend time at the Place Vendome to shop for jewelry for his bride of two months. Safton was fluent in French.

This Monday morning a small military convoy waited outside the hotel to shuttle the General's entourage to the Parisian countryside for a final meeting.

"General, we'll check out and pack up. Colonel Coffee is waiting."

"Speaking of coffee, I could use some. That's a tough name to walk around with in the morning after a late night."

Forty minutes from Paris on a country road, where Safton pictured General Omar Bradley's invasion headquarters might've been located, was a farm house, a few French military vehicles parked haphazardly and camoflaged helicopter off in the distance.

A mirror image stood in the doorway and saluted Safton.

"Jean, missed you on Friday."

"William, come in."

The living room seemed too big for a farm house, but maybe refitted for military use; walls broken down, all bedrooms plowed under, then again with the French maybe not. On two uncomfortable chairs facing each other, speaking French, and no one around, they talked.

"Everything is running smoothly." Safton leaned closer as if Jean forgot a hearing aid.

"We're all on the same page, William." Perrier was twisted open.

"Important that we are."

"Do you sense a special kind of cooperation?"

"Camaraderie?"

"Sense of purpose, needing each other and way past typical diplomacy."

"Way past."

Mirror space was fought over in a small hotel room. Three topless men tried different things; shaving, hair brushing, and putting on a bullet proof vest- each nudging the other away from viewing space. Soon after, the vested man pounded the bathroom door.

"Hey, two of us need to get in and if you don't hurry it won't be Monday morning anymore and we'll piss all over your new white shirt lying on the fucking bed."

Two men tried squeezing through at the same time. The heavier man got to the toilet; the skinnier used the bathtub.

"Why the look; are you pissed that I pissed where I did?"

"Yeah, pissed."

"What's the difference, we're out of here, never to return. It's a flea bag Parisian hotel that'll never have any rating stars."

"Not if you keep pissing in the tub."

Another man walked next door, yelling through the door, "Almost ready in there?"

A door opened with a gun pointed.

Everyone spoke French.

"Put it the fuck away."

"Come in, there's a problem with a vest."

"Well fucking fix it. Get the cars in half an hour."

All six gathered in the room with the clean bath tub- all were vested, wearing shirts and ties. Two pulled guns out of ankle holsters, waving them erratically.

"Go ahead Ibra, why don't you fire a couple of rounds into the ceiling, and get off a little to relieve tension."

"Fucking funny. Just look at us, presumed Arab terrorists speaking French. What blending in."

"You three, car one; rest second."

"Do we know they'll be there?"

"They will. The one who excuses himself and disappears is French Secret Service."

"Who'd they get for the suicide car?"

"Some Palestinian student on visa- parents got three thousand."

"Life is getting cheaper, or was it a sale price from Dillon's?"

"Fuck off!"

Early June sun lifted Paris temperatures to eighty degrees- actually above average. Sidewalk venues were crowded all over the city on a perfect spring day. The Le Marais section was continually evolving into chic and culture hip instead of Gay and Jewish.

Five men sat together outside at Villa Antoinette, a new café on Rue des Archives. Outdoor tables were filled while inside mostly empty. Why bother being in Paris if you can't breathe its real air? Four of the men, all around thirty, drank white wine and spoke Hebrew. Marten, the fifth, obviously older and not Mediterranean, sipped a Perrier and managed to fracture the Hebrew language.

"Appreciate your hospitality, Marten. It's been a very productive week; your software impressed and we've already let Tel Aviv know how much."

"I wanted to make sure all the kinks were worked out; we've been playing around, testing for six months before we showed you."

"We're all in agreement here and ready for next step, if that's OK with you."

"OK with me and Henri. I speak for him. Please excuse, I'll be right back."

Marten reached down, finishing his Perrier, before leaving. The bottle rolled off the table but somehow didn't break and it should've. Four men spent several seconds staring at a bottle, now resting at center table. Ari's name was called out so he was the one who gave it a healthy spin, until slowly stopping, pointing towards the sidewalk and a passing priest, busy crossing himself.

Two Citroens approached the café, windows rolled down, before the cars stopped short. The four Israelis saw drawn weapons at the windows, hitting the sidewalk in an explosion of gunfire but not getting to their concealed weapons in time. Two cars sped away as a third car plowed into the cafe, exploding at impact with the building, shaking city streets blocks away.

The Israeli secret service agents were killed. Twenty other tourists and restaurant patrons were also killed by Arab terrorists linked to Hamas. Just five innocents on the sidewalk survived. A month later, Israel retaliated; four suspected terrorists on the West Bank were killed in a pre-emptive strike. Marten disappeared out the rear of the restaurant.

EIGHTEEN

A lex threw both arms out like a school crossing guard.
"Does anyone think we're walking into a painting?"

Elvin, Evie and Christine thought humoring him, by concentrating on a crowded boardwalk scene. Lately time spent with Alex was premium. He was still running all over the country. It bothered Christine, confiding to Evie and Elvin, how worried she was, not so much about Alex, he was resilient, but what was causing the running. She partly blamed the President because of Harry Truman and bucks having to stop somewhere. Alex knew about her resentment; she had every right to be upset with the President, but could never imagine why. Life was about running, meetings, CIA, observatories and Situation Rooms, ironically related to the President, but no one would suspect anything.

The group was silent and clueless. He was impatient. "Answer is obvious, you guys. Nine p.m. Sky is dark blue. Point Pleasant Beach boardwalk. A dark mysterious ocean. People are still lying on the beach, but not making out, because ten thousand people are walking by. Tongues licking ice cream cones. French fries doused with vinegar. The painting is called, *Jersey Shore, Fourth of July.*"

"The whole buildup, that's it, Alex?"

"Never mind."

"Girls, can you get the French fries while Alex and I walk ahead?"

Evie and Christine were guided to the back of the line.

A miniature train ride sounded an alarming whistle. Turning to watch adults sitting with knees near jaw and an infant squeezed between, Elvin remembered Nelson was a passenger a few blinks ago. "It goes around to nowhere, keeping lives entertained and never gives money's worth. If you computed distance travelled with cost, this train ride is the world's most expensive form of transportation."

"A minute or two in the life of a kid, forgotten the next day; maybe remembered if the kid comes back before September again. Does Nelson remember?"

"Only after I remind him. He says, yeah right."

"Elvin, time and universe mean nothing. Time doesn't exist. For a kid, parents, our planet, time has meaning. But in vastness of space which was built with infinite wisdom, time is nothing, but everything is intelligent design."

"We're doing too much heavy thinking. If we keep talking like this, the China syndrome will melt us all the way down to Beijing, Tiananmen Square. There's an empty bench! I have a question."

"About the make believe race I refer to all the time; two participants, one finish line and a vision."

"Exactly."

A cigarette lighter fell at their feet. Alex moved to recover. Elvin whispered, "Wait, there's no reason to encourage the habit."

Bulging breasts with asymmetrical tan lines bent down, picked up the lighter and walked away. "A Jersey beach girl, showing off burned tits, clueless why there's no gallantry left in the world and why we didn't pick it up. Watch, she'll turn around and stare, maybe discharge a middle finger."

"Alex, you hint about the race all the time."

Perfectly scripted anticipated behavior carved out smiles where none existed. The girl turned and threw that elusive finger.

Air was sucked in and expelled. "I recently read another classified report. Glaciers are disappearing; maybe a billion people in Asia lose fresh water. There's evidence that the water table in Northern India has lost a foot over the last decade. Ironically, Asians will go to war and fight over water not oil. Carbon dioxide is making the ocean acidic. There are not enough antacids in the world. Bats and bees are disappearing."

"What about future sex manuals for kids?"

"Funny. Not funny. Ever wonder why ADHD and childhood cancer is increasing? The planet can't support our life style anymore; there's not enough land per person for our throw-away kind of living- a real shortfall. You know me, I complain every time I see plastic coffee stirrers that get used for two revolutions and thrown away. Sometimes they're wooden. It's sick. No more races and finish lines today. We're on a damn *amusement* boardwalk."

A basketball shooting game of chance seduced. The rim was fixed, inflexible, ball conveniently too big and Elvin was out ten dollars. Friendly scolding between friends followed a teen barker hawking Elvin into another try.

"I'm surprised at you suckering for that game. You've never sunk a boardwalk shot anywhere."

"Stop me next time. Can I ask you something?"

"About meeting the President?"

"You know me so well."

"The meeting was alright. The President's just a man. I told the gang sitting around a table in the basement that I was concerned. Top level advisors felt the same, but the President wasn't as moved."

Two girls bumped into them with no excuse or pardon, leaving a smear of chocolate ice cream on Elvin's white tee shirt. "See that, we don't exist, no eye contact nor apology. So here we are, talking about your visit with the most powerful man in the world, and two Jersey high school girls leave a fresh chocolate stain on my new tee shirt, and everybody keeps walking nonchalantly-a nearly perfect definition of America. Alright, so the President wasn't moved; was it denial?"

"Of course denial. Do you want water for that stain? There's a fountain over there. We're destined to a life of stains, you and me, but mostly from pizza marinara."

"What now?"

"I've been working with scientific teams under the President's direction. He was moved enough to grant a return engagement in August. The team has to put together a final report. Next week, we've got Arizona and then California before the White House meeting. Do you think the women saved us fries?"

"Do you really like vinegar on your fries?"

"No. I take each one and wave it around to dry the vinegar off."

"Alex, how long?"

"To dry the French fries?"

Their eyes were close to each other, noses nearly touched.

"No."

"Then years and years."

"Carl Sagan stuff?"

"You mean when he used to say, billions and billions?"

"Yup."

"Not that long."

Flying west, Alex thought about Arizona adventures after high school, a rattle snake shooting and the great white light night. Uneasiness settled in at 35,000 feet. Thoughts about red mountains, God, spiritual energy and cactus, the defining symbol of the American west helped him nap. For unraveling reasons, the American west was loved. Blue sky, red rocks, people and clouds were all brighter in Arizona. Forest and mountain silence was purer, deeper. Lately he listened to Native-American flute music; sounds haunted, calling a soul to metaphysical communion with centuries of Native peoples. Was it realistic, that he felt his soul being pulled and beckoned by flute sounds, like a pied spiritual piper? Arizona was a Godly place to be; spiritually gifted more than anywhere else on earth and now there were Godly reasons to absorb extra spirit.

The airline magazine featured a cover story on Saguaro cactus; impassive, slow growing, reaching out and up as if they knew what they were doing, but surviving with stoic patience. Gabriel recently bought the Zari's a home near Sedona and another outside Kansas City of all places. The Kansas purchase was inexplicable, even discouraged and gently refused, but done nevertheless. Laughable moments would be telling Christine they'd partially retire to Kansas City. Sedona was different. Christine loved it, discovering the Chapel of the Holy Cross. Once she spent three hours staring at red mountains through a crucifix window at the same time Alex hiked to the summit of a favorite vortex.

Smooth landings brought graphic facial relief as in never liking flying and to think, whenever asked about going into space, he always responded, "Perhaps if they asked me." The truth was simply that no desire ever existed for space travel, but how would it look if a pre-eminent astronomer was afraid of heights.

After a few steps from the gate, three men surrounded and escorted Alex to baggage. After a short trip to the Tuscon Arizona Inn, there were a few handshakes in the lobby. Seeing distant colleagues would be the best part of the trip.

As meetings got more intense, sensitive and classified, Alex noted double rooms didn't happen. Extra communication was not desired. Alex tossed all night long, got up near four a.m. and twisted off the cap of a red wine bottle from the mini bar. At six a.m. he was on knees, facing east, deep in prayer. At seven a.m., one of three red tie choices was made. At eight a.m., Christine was told how much he loved her.

At nine a.m., the meeting began promptly. The Westphall Center for Studies in Public Policy on the campus of University of Arizona was taken over days earlier by security arms of the federal government. A six story brick building and acres of parking was expected instead of a small, un-assuming, white with blue trim, one story building, that a half-sneeze and blink made you miss.

Alex sat at leader position, looking at the table of scientists shuffling papers and still thinking back to the Situation Room. Why such affinity for astronomy as young boy? Where the hell did it all come from? He was smart and there were other things in life that he could be involved with at this precise moment in time. Too much real milk in coffee meant clearing his throat. "Gentlemen, no further introductions necessary, except for a late addition, Samuel Coutros- astronomer extraordinaire from NASA's Ames Research Center."

"Thanks, Alex. But, extraordinaire?"

Coutros was a second coming of Ray Bolger from the *Wizard of Oz* and with such remarkable likeness, there was a need to expound in new situations. "*Wizard of Oz* fans. There must be some here. I'm perfectly aware of a likeness to the scarecrow and I even went through genetic testing to see if Ray and I were related. Stop me if I get carried away; the truth is I'd rather be somewhere else."

The meeting leader was quick to respond. "We all would."

"Dr. Lansing, you're itching to talk."

"We're scientists and I think we should acknowledge our colleagues work, even if it doesn't necessarily pertain to what's on our agenda."

Alex glimpsed the back of a suit standing outside the window, wondering about feeling safer since security was present.

"I know exactly, Dr. Lansing." Robert Stander, from Jet Propulsion waved his hand.

"They found a body circling a distant star, resembling Jupiter, some ninety light years from this table." Lansing was demonstrating using a coffee mug and a bottle of spring water for props.

"And a planetary system much like ours."

"And don't forget interesting work going on at our old friend, Tunguska." Giacomo Custode, with heavy Sicilian accent and Alex's closest friend in the room, had close ties to Italy. Tunguska took place in June 1908, when a fireball exploded above remote forests in Siberia. Scientists are still guessing whether it was an asteroid or comet, flattening more than eight hundred square miles of trees.

"My friends from the University of Bologna are hell bent to figure out Tunguska. They're constantly traveling up there with unique ideas. Wish they'd hurry."

Ray Bolger's look alike walked to the window, knocking gently. "Well trained security, not easily distracted. Say Jack, anything in particular they're looking for in Siberia?"

"Most of the time is spent around a lake."

Physicist George Terranova leaned back too far, catching his balance, grabbing the table cloth, almost pulling it off. "Tunguska fascinates. Basic physics tells us the largest, fastest traveling objects penetrate deepest. I know what they're looking for."

Packets of papers were handed out by Alex. "Two hundred pages originally, down to a hundred now so read it over. We'll talk during the next month. I'll be spreading my wings to some of you. The President wants closure to findings and individual approval stamps, if you get my drift."

"Refresh our memory."

"Schedule?"

"Yes."

"Early August, Jet Propulsion in Pasadena and bring extra clothing even if the President changes his mind about our Washington get together."

"He'll want all of us there?"

"For theatre, drama and effect. The group was his idea in the first place. Yes, all of us, if it all holds up."

Terranova rifled through the report.

"Want to say something, George?" Alex felt forehead wrinkles coming out.

"Impressive work with mathematical entries, but I'm not seeing room."

Alex thought tactile reinforcement, so he walked over and patted George's shoulders. "Stop speeding. Delve and throw it into your software. I'll see you in two weeks. Digest and inhale."

The rest of the scientists looked at the mathematics that George referred to. Alex allowed himself to drift like Elvin, all the way up to Sedona, where'd he'd soon be with soulful spirit, searching for mostly questions and not necessarily answers anymore.

Giacomo and Alex sat in a fast food place on Sedona's main drag, eating a contraption for breakfast.

"What the hell is a contraption, Jack?"

The Sicilian was tiny in stature, bald, and elf like. Eyes were myopic, close together, and linked by a thick brow. Lips were thick and unnaturally red. Jack was obsessed with women, such that it impacted a career that should've won him awards and fortune, instead was interrupted by law suits and bad marriages.

"Different earth colors layered between round bread that looks like the moon's surface, but what really defines is the oily residue on the wrapping and packaging, hence contraption."

"The coffee is good."

Oak Creek canyon, with picturesque mountain stream slicing through boulders, was a few miles away. An art deco hat took money for parking. At waters edge, they watched bathers splash and slide off slippery rocks.

"Reminds me of the National Forest near Belluno, where I used to hike and camp."

"Reminds me of a Jersey shore river, where I still go to think, meditate and pray."

"Powerful word."

"Prayer?"

"For sure."

Airport Road was a mountain vortex known for special spirituality. Vortex was part relationship to Christ and healing of mind and body. Climbing was slowed by holding hands for steadying support. The summit was small. Miniature trees were scattered; panoramic view breath taking, making him think back years to Elvin, Steven and Carl. Could this be where they camped out? Energy that changed Elvin's and his life, leaving magical traces of something, birthing deja-vu was here, airborne, sensual, absorbable and non-transferable. He felt it.

Hiking boots and socks off, now barefoot, eyes closed, he asked God why things have to be the way they are. A mind raced with thoughts and prayers for understanding. Sura's name was whispered, asking for help, with thoughts of how much she's missed. How strange the world of spirit. An hour of rubbing bare feet on red dusty rocks, half the time with eyes closed, produced random images and feelings of been there, parallel worlds, universe, mathematical equations, the Holocaust, KKK lynchings, children born with cancer, a plane crash, starvation in Africa, polio, billionaires descending list in a magazine, Mid-east unrest, whale hunters, oil and cigarette companies and a distant vacant lot. Every item fired into conscious thought. Images were powerfully there, but who initiated the actual firing?

What a potent mountain.

For Elvin, this all had to be remembered.

Glancing over to Jack, he saw mimicking of his meditation, right down to bare feet. The sanctuary was invaded by a loud couple who couldn't keep their hands off each other.

"Why bare feet?"

"Absorption through soles."

"S-o-u-l?"

"That too."

Downing of a mountain is easier if you're pushing sixty and rocks are ledged conveniently. You sit and move to the next ledge, still sitting, and keep moving down slowly.

"Jack, red dust stains mean magic is clinging to our rears."

"So, we've done well?"

"For now."

The last three meeting days in Pasadena were the same; sunny, warm and boring, making Alex realize the need for meteorological variability, seasonal changing and equinoxes. Distant Thanksgiving thoughts with colors of orange and brown and farm stands selling harvest were thought about instead of special scientists, looking to him for leadership. Holidays were memories, family and sanctuary. Pasadena Jet Propulsion Lab was harsh reality, but CIA insisted on the venue. Alex was partial to Hilton Hotels for meetings. CIA not.

The group was now assembled back in Pasadena. Last moments of meetings always seemed to grow quieter, every one spent and tired, bewildered and frustrated over inability to change or reach consensus.

"Are we officially done?"

"We are." Alex's response seemed atypically brusque.

Early morning pastries and coffee were brought in by aides; one wore powerful looking stomping boots, so perhaps not an aide in the traditional sense.

"The final pages we hammered out last night will make it easy for the President."

On either side of the door, two security agents stood at attention. A gentle knock preceded two different suited men entering; one whispered in Alex's ear for several minutes.

Alex thanked him, shook hands and spoke. "Gentlemen, the men who just left and rudely whispered in my ear, left a message. The President wants us in Washington tonight. White House at ten p.m. They work fast because Delta just bumped people off an eleven a.m. flight. Bags from our hotel are already at airport. It's an amazing world."

"That's it?" Four voices harmonized.

"Done. You shouldn't be surprised, it's been foretold."

The room reflected. Senses were keen; fatigue sometimes heightens. A mild odor, due to malfunctioning air conditioning, brought in a Propulsion aide to play with electronics.

"One other thing."

Alex waited for the aide to leave the room. Sam Coutros stood guard. Jack stood by the window.

"The report, and remember, each one of you has a copy and that's all there is, so keep it closed in a brief case on your lap. Security accompanies us everywhere. Wouldn't it be purist paranoia, not trusting security and requesting security for them?"

"How are we supposed to feel?"

"About security being with us, secure?"

"About earth life, Dr. Zari."

"We can talk about life on the plane, George."

"Do you think there's enough time?"

"Where's Einstein's entourage when you need them?"

A mini bus waited outside a rear exit. Two cars parked at front and bus rear. Police cars and motorcycles idled nearby. An image of an ice cutter on frozen Hudson's Bay flashed as Alex smiled about their traffic cutting detail. Official Washington maneuvers was still getting used to, but it fascinated how everyday life, from getting on sold out flights, to easing through Los Angeles traffic and having teams of people pack everything including your toothbrush and check you out of a hotel was routine. Power does corrupt but makes earth life so much easier. Twelve scientists scattered throughout the bus. A security agent sat with each one. The bus, cars, police and motorcycle units all got together in a straight line.

Airline tickets were handed out by a professorial looking man, average height with Ben Franklin rimless spectacles. "Attention everyone. You'll go through normal security check and the plane is a little delayed, so relax in the waiting area and if you need anything, just ask for Jonathan. That's me. I'll be floating around."

Airport waiting areas were as congested as planes on the tarmac and long lines to nowhere. Noise levels peak when planes are delayed; bumped people going through stages of realization that they're screwed again. A man, looking like he needed more than one bumped seat, severely obese, pounded on the agent's counter.

"My father died, they're burying him tomorrow, a fucking veteran, sorry, a veteran, but I need to say goodbye to my father. Does anybody understand?"

"Sir, we'll do the best we can, please."

"I'll stand five feet away; maybe I'll just drop dead right here and then, you'll have to get me back. How about flying me in a casket, seat belt me down, leave the casket open so I can breathe, then I'll be able to get to Washington on time."

"Mr. Feld, we'll make an announcement to the passengers. I'm sure someone will take a free ticket offer. Please be patient."

"Tell that to my family." *Mother fucker* snuck out under his breath.

Feld was round with large belly, white shirt, pony tail and goatee. A minor delay for the connecting plane was posted, perhaps caused by thunderstorms or turbulence, but nobody really knew. In this age of communicative gadgetry, you were still never certain about delay causal factors. Alex headed for the bathroom.

Nine white urinals flushed electronically by timer and despite the crowded waiting area, Alex stood alone. Urinary solitude was welcomed because it was easier to get the flow going. Almost immediately, someone unzipped next to him. Alex looked right at Jonathan from the bus.

"Alex, recognize me? Stay right here at the urinal and don't move."

"Are you serious?"

"Real serious. I'm from Gabriel and we're here to help you, so listen carefully. There's not much time. We've got to keep you off the plane and don't say a word. If someone comes, follow me."

Just then, two men in urgent mode, unzipped as they approached. Alex followed Jonathan, half paralyzed with more fear than he's ever known. Sweat dripped into eyes, now salty and burning, but he calmly walked down the aisle, away from the gate. Standing by a gray metal door with keypad, an airport employee punched and opened for them.

"There's really not much time but you'll trade tickets with a Mr. Feld."

"The large man?"

"He'll be waiting outside this door and gets on the plane no problem. Everything's been cleared; just turn left and walk with two waiting friends; they'll explain later."

"What's happening- tell me that, please?"

"The plane's going down."

"What?"

"No time now. This is your life. You're part of us so just do."

Hands shook tremor like, fists clenched, wiping eyes and brow. Alex's normally rock steady voice cracked. "I don't understand. Dear God."

"Let's go."

Tickets were traded not before Feld slipped a hundred dollar bill into Alex's hand. Words of thanks fell empty from non-functioning ears and eyes as Feld lumbered away. Alex was escorted to an hourly parking lot and a back seat, still clutching a brief case. When Sura died, he shed the first of life's adult tears and again now.

NINETEEN

"Nelson, trust Dad, the twenty yard line can be a magic place to sit."

"Dad, you're talking to me, not selling eyeglasses. Why season tickets on the twenty yard line? "

"A few things come into play. It makes perfect sense."

"Right Dad. The Earth, sun and moon have to be in proper alignment."

"Exactly. Rutgers moves the ball in front of us then the quarter changes. Buffalo's back here at the twenty yard line and every game has the same scenario. Teams get stuck right here. It can happen like that."

"Silly, Dad."

"I like when you call me silly. You've been calling me that since you started talking." A peanut shell hill between old worn Nike sneakers was Elvin's work in progress.

"Want something to drink?"

"Anything diet."

"I hate diet."

He waved a ten, Nelson grabbed.

"A diet toast to gut feeling. Rutgers will be National Champions one day. Remember last year at Monmouth Racetrack, when I said to watch money bet on horses just before post time, called smart money?"

"Rutgers is a horse race?"

"Exactly. Time is needed for coach to develop and for New Brunswick to get the physical plant ready for the after party. But I'm worried about something."

"What?"

"When Rutgers wins the championship, we'll be there, cheering. Energy expended in passionate loyalty is awesome, sometimes a life time of devotional waiting. Imagine when any team wins a championship. The team is on the field getting the trophy. Fans are hugging one another. Strangers kissing. Tears of joy all over the stands. Coach speaks. Everybody yells until their hoarse. The team heads to the locker room. People head for the exits and that's it; a lifetime of waiting for ten minutes of post game glory. A few words are mentioned on the eleven p.m. news and everybody's sleeping within the hour. Of course, we've got memories and videos."

"Why so introspective? How long have you been thinking that?"

"Since you were eleven and we started going to see Rutgers. Winning a National Championship is a microcosm of life. You study all your life to a get a college diploma and it takes two seconds to hear your name called. You go with a girl for two years and get married. How long does it take to say, I do? Life is a process and it's important to enjoy, treasure and savor every moment along the way. Live each day. The only thing relevant is what's happening right now. Yesterday is a memory and tomorrow uncertain. Everything is now, so my son, live it fully and richly."

A sea of red sweatshirts and hats marched to scattered parking lots. Nelson shot an empty cup into a trash can.

"Hungry?"

"Grease Trucks?"

"Then I want to show you something. We'll walk and eat at the same time-called a simultaneous burn."

"Simultaneous burn?"

"Caloric burning of grease while in motion is almost the same medical principal as chemically blocked absorption of fat."

Geology Hall warmly invited so they sat on the steps, near the third brick on left. Strangely, Elvin was certain, he'd been here already with Nelson but it was their first time. Trees were moving and bending, yielding to wind direction. Shadows were the same as last time. The same people were walking again. This precise moment happened before. Nelson stroked the back of his neck and said he loved him. Elvin smiled at the repeat performance. An irretrievable web site confirmed Sedona energies leave some with senses of having been, like a favorable side effect just like an anti-hypertensive drug was found to have a side effect of promoting hair growth.

Why think of all this now?

Elbows resting on thighs, Elvin drifted.

"Dad, you're far away."

"Geology Hall means something deep to me." Elvin squeezed his hand.

"It's cool that you came here with Uncle Alex to reflect and wonder; kind of like a permanency to life. Now I'll always wonder about those things which moved you, like the human life that cemented this brick and guess what, I'll come here someday and show my child this special brick."

"It's continuity."

Sitting on hard steps, Elvin pulled Nelson's head close and kissed an approximate soft spot. Both stared across the lawn, at a historic church with precious steeple and a high speed train just crossing the Raritan River, heading south somewhere, maybe to Kilimanjaro eventually.

September mornings are idyllic if you jog and come from Louisiana, where morning heat and humidity start things off sucky and sticky but you're really up north, not down south. Kevin Hollingsworth raved about forty-five degree morning temperatures and running countrified streets in upstate Rome, New York. An LSU shirt had sweat circles under arms. Running partner Lowell Canto, a Buffalo man, used to cool Septembers, perspired the same way. Seven mile jogs do that. Turning up a driveway, they were back to an old, one story, spread out-because land was cheap back in the early fifties-motel, Inn at the Lake and conference center.

"Shower first Kevin, I'm calling home. Tuesday morning, a week after Labor Day and my mother's getting dressed right about now."

"She still teaches?"

"Still."

Both shared a mirror with a full length crack down the middle. Kevin pulled a lamp draw string, reducing room light by thirty-three percent. A horn sounded once. Odorous curtains parted.

"They're here, got everything?"

"Yeah."

"Hey Kevin, what's this?"

Lowell threw a small, thin case.

Kevin swiped, caught it mid air and opened for re-assurance, *Federal Bureau of Investigation.*

A van drove out of the motel grounds. Lowell and Kevin sat in the second row. A third row and rear were filled with suitcases and large bulging black plastic bags. The driver and passenger spoke Spanish until the second row commented that George Washington would've pressed number one.

"You FBI guys are fucking funny. Isn't your job description, learning and speaking a second language?"

"We speak Norwegian, so fuck you Castillo."

"And you too, Lowell."

Second row patted the shoulders of the front row, all laughing robustly as they pulled into a Dunkin Donuts parking lot.

"You Spanish guys know what a bagel is?"

"You telling me they have bagels in Louisiana- maybe fried green tomatoes."

An elderly couple seated next finished quicker than they wanted. Lowell commented on a recent article that in small towns like Rome, the average sitting time at a donut shop in the morning was three hundred percent longer than the rest of the country.

"Why?"

"Well Castillo, what else is there to do here?"

Back in the van, front row turned to face second row.

"Review time, you too Mingo; you're always too quiet."

"Bad language turns me off."

"Mildred and Victor Senko, sixty something and both sickly so they're retiring. Kevin is designated driver to Florida. He'll follow moving truck, which should be at the Senko's house in two minutes." Castillo spoke perfect English.

"Who'd we get?"

"Originally wanted Felice Trucking, a local firm, but they backed out a few days ago. They're much too busy and didn't want to tie up a truck for so long. Do people really need trucks way up here? Anyway, we got Frank Peace and Son from Syracuse, the Peaceful Moving People."

"How come there isn't a moving company anywhere with somebody and his daughter?"

Maple Street in Rome was mid-America with mid-sized cape houses, trees and lawns. A mid-size Mercury Grand Marquis was in the garage. Even the Senko's, standing on the lawn watching Frank Peace's team load their worldly possessions from forty years together, were mid-sized people.

The van pulled up. Lowell and Kevin walked with the Senko's around to the backyard.

"We're impressed with your town; it's so country and peaceful. It must be hard after all these years to leave."

The old man sighed before speaking. "The body starts to fail and things go wrong and it's a hard winter with all the snow and cold. No children or relatives. No reason to stay except for friends and some are gone now or in Florida and the decision was easy. And you're driving us to Florida?"

"My pleasure."

"Did you ever drive a Grand Marquis?"

"Life's filled with first times. Today there are two; Rome, New York and your car."

Mildred Senko slept in the back seat. Victor's head was bobbing like a dash board hula doll, every few minutes, another startle reflex.

Kevin was too tall for comfortable driving- a right knee massaged the ash tray. Like clockwork, every twenty three minutes, a Marlboro cigarette was lit, smoke expelled out of an opened window. Each puff was followed by making sure the Senko's were still sleeping just in case of emphysema and their telling him to stop his passion.

"Say Victor, push the seat down and stop fighting sleep."

"Are you on the New Jersey Turnpike?"

"Just got on, the moving truck is right in front, why?"

"We've never seen New York City in person so maybe we can see the skyline. Can you let me know, I'll wake Mildred."

"You're in your sixties, lived six hours from New York and never been here?"

"No reason, happy and content with Rome all our lives. We had Syracuse and Buffalo and Toronto. You get comfortably stuck in a place, then pass a point and it's never going to happen."

"But some people get to that point and decide that it should happen."

"Some, we're not."

"Well, wake her, start looking left."

Kevin felt like a bus driver for an elementary school outing; both wide eyed faces were pressed to the window with exclamations and realizations that perhaps they did miss something. Kevin asked if they wanted a quick trip through the Lincoln Tunnel, but old people are funny and just wanted to keep eyes on the truck with all their belongings.

"Mildred, Victor, there's a rest area and gas station in a few miles; your furniture is pulling in for gas and so are we. Do you need to use a rest room?"

"Prostate problems. We both will."

Kevin thought cute couple, humorously stereotypical, right down to prostate and hearing problems, so he smiled at them and asked three times about a soda and stopping later at Exit Seven at a truck stop restaurant for dinner. Kevin carried three sodas back to the car on a tray made out of compressed recycled materials. In a few minutes, they were sleeping soundly.

After twenty minutes south on the Turnpike, rush hour traffic slowing pace, the Grand Marquis got off at Exit Eight, paid the toll, while the Peace moving truck continued south. Kevin drove through Hightstown, quaint, historic and former home of a Ku Klux Klan chapter, right in the heart of central Jersey. Gentle gurgling noises emanated from the sleeping couple and for a brief moment, his late parents were sleeping, on their way to Little Rock for a cousin's wedding. That Arkansas trip was one of the best times ever spent with them. His father had depth and keen understanding of the world and mother came from aristocratic lineage. Parents and Kevin promised to spend more time together, bonding, talking and using the word *love* more often but both died within six months.

Route 130 South reminded Kevin of a story he read to his five year old daughter, *The Little Engine that Could*, or something like that. The lengthy highway went from south Jersey, somewhere below the Mason-Dixon line to New Brunswick with virtually no traffic, therefore, a highway that could but didn't. Heading south, they passed an occasional garden store, generic gas station and a few road signs to Camden and Burlington. After several minutes, a left turn took him off the highway onto a semi-deserted road, becoming more deserted and eventually all dirt.

A mail box read G. Kennedy and the road led to a farm house, barn and dilapidated silo. A rusting tractor seemed like it was growing into the road and partially obstructed the drive. By the barn was a truck, *Washington Homeward Trucking*. Four men walked out of the farm house, exchanged handshakes with Kevin. Two stretchers were wheeled out of the barn and sleeping Mildred and Victor were placed into the truck, IV and oxygen hooked up.

"Good work, get some dinner, enjoy Florida."

"You too."

A day later Frank Peace and Son's moved the Senko's into Exeter B, Century Village, Boca Raton. Hours later, Kevin left the Grand Marquis in designated parking spot forty-four and was back in Louisiana the next day for more time off with wife and daughter.

"Why cut vegetables so fine?" Sofia wore a white top, no bra, and an apron, depicting the Italian boot, with a gold star over Florence. Pasta was tripped through a colander, broccoli still simmering by itself.

"It's called Israeli chopped salad. The steam is having anatomical effects on your projections."

Cargo shorts were covered by an apron as well, but with cucumber, scallion and tomato.

"Did I tell you how silly that apron is?"

"Just did."

A second glass of blonde wine was poured; anything not red was blonde, even white.

"September eleventh means a serious toast. To an hour glass that's filled with sand, and emptying slowly as if time is infinite and things should go on forever in a perfect place under a perfect sun with a perfect friend. Salud!"

"My goodness."

Espresso from a shiny machine accompanied them into the living room after dinner.

"Bet that espresso machine cost plenty?"

"Much cost, how is it?"

"Wonderful." A raised cup saluted the preparer.

"We usually finish dinner and run upstairs and. . . ."

"Screw the night away. I said it before you, but it's something else and we both feel it."

"I've been seeing a man, not serious but serious. He's older than you and is with the Italian consulate. His family has money. He asked me to marry him. I said no for now, but I know it's time."

"It's been time for you for a long time."

"It's also time for me to go home and leave Solchiali. They're heading in different directions. My father's partners have strange connections to diamonds in Africa. Last year, quietly, my father bought a few high end jewelry stores on the East coast, Chicago, Arizona and California. Remember how uncomfortable I always feel around them because a vagina doesn't have enough killer instinct for Europeans. They need that instinct now. Maybe I'm too nice. They asked me to run the jewelry chain and move to Atlanta."

"They're moving you out."

"It's strictly business, not personal- sound familiar?"

"But he's your father."

Elvin inched closer, eventually retrieving her hand, with a gentle kiss.

"Whatever longings and dreams I've been having, things are getting accelerated, making it decision time soon. And why aren't you in the mood to drag me upstairs?"

"I've been worried about Alex. It's not like him to be out of radio contact with me for so long. We did hear from Christine; she's visiting relatives. You know me, I sense things. It's more of a curse that takes sleep and peace of mind away, waking me some mornings at 4:44, tossing and turning. Something brings me downstairs to the computer. I stare at clouds and grass on the screensaver. I surf around at that ungodly hour, looking aimlessly and then I find things."

"What do your find?"

"You. Tomorrow. An angel. Evie. Nelson. Alex. *Lamplight.*"

"Lamplight?"

"An amazing song that sends my soul off into the universe. It was early *Bee-Gees.*"

"Sometimes you gently scare me. There's so much inside you but it attracts me. I'm looking for things too and the challenge is to look deep inside, but not sure if I'll ever find."

"Look at us, two adults in a crazy mixed up world, caring about each other with too much intuition about life to go upstairs and simply screw the night away."

Sofia lifted Elvin's hand for a return kiss.

A dark ocean that they couldn't see but hear held them silent for a few minutes.

"You're going to say goodnight now and head north on the Parkway."

"Funny, isn't it? Timing is uncanny. We ran out of words. Thank goodness for ocean sound effects."

Elvin intellectualized about strip mall parking lots. Why are the closest spots never vacant? Do stores pay cars to be there from open to close, making it appear busy, creating imagery that you picked the right popular place to shop? Stubbornly driving around, refusing to walk extra, Elvin thought it all made sense. If most shoppers were *amiable* according to sales courses, and it's perceived that stores are popular, then amiable personalities don't want to be left out. Finally, Elvin mumbled, "To hell with it," and drove to the empty back lot.

Evie and Nelson were meeting him at David's Deli; a favorite place for potato salad. No other food mattered, just potato salad. Waitresses finally figured him out, ordering potato salad with everything else on the side.

Life was beautiful; potato salad dinner and shopping for antioxidants and vitamins. Cashiers always asked if he found everything. Somewhere there was a perfect answer. Leaving the store, a plastic bag satisfyingly swung over his shoulder, almost clipping a man smoking a cigarette just beyond the door. The cigarette was quickly heeled to extinction.

"Elvin Stone? Why don't you keep walking to your car; it's far enough away so we can talk."

"What?"

"I'm a friend of Alex."

Walking continued briskly without a break in stride.

"Friend?"

"Am."

"You've been following me if you know my car's far away."

"Have been. You spent a lot of time driving around to get close then you park far away."

"Reverse psychology. Do you have a name?"

"Serge."

"Now what?"

"Do I have your trust? If not, Alex said to mention the vacant lot where you guys met and the game you played."

"I'm trusting."

"Good. I can't explain much more. We're at your car."

"There's still time, Serge. I'm meeting my wife and son at that deli and if you care to join us, they have great potato salad."

"Alex said you'd be charming and funny. It's Tuesday September 16th. On Thursday September 18th at two thirty p.m. meet Alex at your river, but be on time, there won't be much time."

Serge forced a hand shake, lifting Elvin's frozen arm. Watching him get into a car and for whatever reason, Elvin wished being closer to get a peek at the license plate, like he'd ever do anything. His heart was racing, legs rubberized, cerebral pathways, synapses and everything else up there was screwed up and deteriorating. He felt dizzy, leaning on his car. The fear was like getting that notice from Selective Service agent Bessie Daggett back in the 1960's, worrying about winding up in Southeast Asia, and dying in some flooded rice field, alone, or worse, being captured and having to play Russian roulette everyday to survive. Fear was top to bottom, intestinal, ocular and cerebral, so the mood for potato salad passed, maybe forever.

A clock radio's face, barely illuminated, still had luminary energy to tell Elvin it was 4:44 Thursday morning, so quietly, without disturbing Evie, he tiptoed downstairs. Four framed pictures leaned against a mantle wall. All four departed parents, in later years, looked at Elvin, sitting, hands folded together, breathing into the space between palms. You look at things for years and don't necessarily see. Evie's mother Anne was next to Jack. On the other side, Morty was next to Martha. Evie must've had reasons.

"Are you alright? I felt you get up. Now you're sitting and staring. What's going on?"

"I can't say much because I don't know much."

"Alex? Is he alright? I spoke to Christine last week, so I assume."

Elvin tried to laugh, thinking of Roosevelt Dix and a past lecture about assuming things. Roosevelt surely has been gone for a long time. He never knew whether Roosevelt had family, kids and could he track them down at this late date and tell them how much he liked their father.

"Evie, never assume anything, but Alex is alright, whatever that means."

"You're going to see him later?"

"Later. By the way the pictures on the mantle are paired wrong."

"Not really, you assumed but its just random- a by product of dusting haphazardly."

Perfect weather for mid September, 2003 at the Shark River Inlet was cloudy, cool, westerly breeze at seven miles per hour, with a few sprinkles. Elvin thought like the hour early weatherman, he wished being at this time. Any profession, which would drag him far away from this ridiculous excuse of a river, to another world, where he wouldn't have to deal with curve balls of life, would be acceptable at this moment in universal time. Thinking curve balls, he thought about his father, a month before his death, talking baseball and that Jack said how much he loved the old New York Giants. "But Dad, I always knew you were a Dodger fan; that's why I loved the Dodgers, because of you." "No son, always the Giants." Elvin smiled and kept his head from moving in any direction.

Nothing skirted the horizon. Usually there's a ship going to Kilimanjaro or Guadeloupe. Was emptiness a sign? Just like Martha used to do on occasional Friday nights, observing the arrival of the Sabbath, Elvin covered his face. Martha's name was whispered three times. How he missed her strength and love, no matter how many times they fought about skin color. It wasn't her fault; it's what Rebecca instilled in her daughter just like he instills in Nelson. Foreboding feelings made skin tingle, almost like a niacin overdose. Elvin got up, walked back and forth, and then down along water's edge.

Alex approached from the street. Water's edge was too wet and sloppy for meaningful speed but Elvin started running. Alex reached to help Elvin up on the jetty, then into a hug.

"I love you, Elvin Stone."

"Me too, Alex Zari. I don't need the Doctor in front, do I?"

"You're nervous, I can tell."

"Well. . . ."

"You met Serge, a good friend. Let's go sit at the end."

Hands touched, mostly for steadying over slippery sections, but subconsciously, for something else which they sensed.

"Elvin, please just listen and absorb. I don't have a lot of time. Look on the bridge."

"Funny, Serge up there looks like George Bailey about to jump off the bridge in Bedford Falls in, *It's a Wonderful Life*."

"Stop rambling."

"Sorry."

Alex wore a back pack but not noticed until just taken off.

"There's a report inside; the only one left on Earth. I want to show you something."

At least a hundred pages were rubber banded together.

"Read this page then look at me."

Hands started to tremble. Words were trying but not coming; it was the closest thing to a stroke he could imagine. Finally, "I don't understand."

"It's denial, not lack of comprehension. Denial is powerful medicine." Like an infant finishing strained carrots and needing burping, Alex patted Elvin's back. "Now let's put it back. As I said, you have the last copy. You could make millions selling it, but you won't and you'll put it in a vault and forget it exists."

"OK."

"Remember starting college? A professor or dean hit you with a speech; *see the kid on the right and left. They'll be gone, flunked out.* But what happens if you're the one on someone's right or left? Maybe Earth is on the left or right? Actually what we've got now, is that finish line to the race I've been talking about all this time. Remember when we sat on your attic roof and said how we're a silly species, making such a big deal over skin color and all the wasted energy and resources differentiating skin and God. God is God. There for all of us and so simple. Maybe prejudice and hate is a profitable cottage industry? Nothing changes over time, killing and hating goes on. No one cares. Everybody is fatalistic and says *why bother, I'll be gone anyway,* so they let the globe warm and animals become extinct and fish disappear. Everybody lives for today. We're told the sun will shine for billions more years so we go on terrorizing, hating, perfecting killing, being greedy and drinking plastic bottled water because it's cool even though the bottle takes a thousand years to decompose and is made out of evil bisphenol A." Alex stood up, shaking circulation back into legs.

"*There's still time brother*, from the movie, *On the Beach*, one of my favorite scary movies with lingering recurring nightmares. It feels like Gregory Peck and

Ava Gardner are right here with us, *On the Jetty. Waltzing Matilda* was such sad movie music. I don't want to start listening to it now. Make the world go away, Alex."

"You're a movie romantic. Do you think God ponders the same things we are right now; there's an infinite wisdom and things like a Noah's ark? Are we mathematically coming back? Don't we seem further away from Peace on Earth? Killing, murders and inhumanity is on such a grand scale now. Because of technology, the world knows everything in minutes, but does nothing about it or pretend tries when it's too late. Don't we love after the fact protest signs or rallies after a million people are murdered?"

"Alex, do you think God's words, decisions, are in the back pack?"

"I don't know, don't know. God is so much of my life and yours."

"I know."

"My time is running out."

"What do you mean?"

"Remember the plane crash near Los Angeles last month." Trying to stand, but Alex's palm nudged Elvin back down. "I was sort of on that plane, but a friend told me it was going to crash and helped me disappear."

Elvin jumped up. "My God."

"That's just what I said, *my God*." Alex gently motioned him down again.

"A friend?"

"For all these years, we talked about my sliding into something at Princeton. I've been part of an invisible society, called Gabriel- old with more power and money than you could imagine. For sixty years, they've infiltrated every aspect of life in America and even abroad, but that's not important now, besides you've sensed."

"Sensed and it made me feel secure that my friend was protecting me. Did Nolan bring you in?"

"Yes. Simeon too."

Elvin was staring skywards, eyes searching for words and thoughts. "That means 250 people were killed, but why?"

"Because there were scientists and agents who knew too much- scientists with this same report. We were on our way to talk to the President that night. Someone very deep in the government, powerful, decided policy and that's it; cold, brutal, with no turning around, changing, mercy or stopping before it's too late. Mercy is one of man's greatest possessions. If you've got that inside then you're on top of the spiritual world. It's like a little kid playing on train tracks. A train is coming full force. Do you think that innocent little kid can reach up and stop the train before it hits him?"

"Who saved you?"

"The slide folks at Gabriel. They know everything going on thank God. There's more. Do you remember that Paris terrorism last month when the four Israeli secret agents were murdered? That was really a diversion. Four scientists were at that cafe too. They were the real targets. Two key Italian astronomers were gunned down by police because they were suspected bank robbers. Remember Ted Severance?"

"Sure, the blond Bolshevik language specialist from our discussion group."

"Son Mark followed in his footsteps, became an interpreter and died in a car accident after coming back from an assignment and there's more. My South African friend Ian Fielding was a victim of gang violence and murdered recently."

"What does it all mean?"

"Policy, coincidence and maybe a little of both. They think I'm dead. Notice how final casualty lists from the plane crash were not published."

"What's going to happen to you and Christine?"

"They'll find out. I can only hide and run for so long."

"Where's Christine? Should she be with us?"

"Safe for now. I'm targeted, probably her too. Now listen carefully, my Princeton house will be sold and the money will eventually work itself to you. It may take a year to get laundered properly, but use the money, enjoy, be frivolous and buy Nelson an old Mustang."

"Why's the money coming to me and not you?"

Alex sat down close to Elvin. "Remember our friend Michael Lauzone? He shaved his head because his father went bald, wanting to cheat destiny."

"His father died at forty-five, a heart attack. We worried he'd tried to cheat again by suicide."

Nimbostratus cloud color was being absorbed by Elvin's skin.

"Michael succeeded with destiny, controlling his own fate, all in his hands."

"He did commit suicide at forty-three." Breathing was labored, gasping, deep inhalations mixing with sighs of wanting closure.

"But *his* control of *his* own fate."

"What are you saying, Alex?"

Something made them both stand; mostly an approaching climax to a scene, both knew had arrived.

"There's Serge, he's coming for me. I love you always, Elvin. A most perfect friendship. You know me so well. I have to be in control of my fate and life. I have to go. What happens to me has to be on my terms."

"Well where, what, can I do something?"

"They don't know about you. Shit, he's here. The best and only way I can explain- do you remember *MASH*? A dozen times we saw the movie together and you know my favorite scene."

Hands rested on Elvin's shoulders.

"The suicide. No, Alex! Not that! It's the craziest thing you ever said. It's ridiculous. It doesn't make any sense. I won't. . . ."

"Just think about it, you'll understand, please don't get emotional, it's all part of life. The whole thing is easy. Christine and I are alright and accepting of everything. I have to go."

He waved to Serge, buying a few more seconds.

Tears overcame them both.

"Alex, please."

He started away then ran back. Elvin was motionless- like an erect dead body. Alex did all the hugging. Serge and Alex disappeared just as the drawbridge started up. Rain started to fall. Elvin sat frozen, stroke like, getting wet, but conscious enough to zip the back pack securely. Hands covered his face so none of the gulls or the small fishing boat entering the inlet would see a grown man crying.

TWENTY

An hour before sunrise, Elvin sat in den silence, as he'd been doing for two weeks. Morning's first light cast a hazy pall; pictures on the mantle slowly focused as he realized that Evie had rearranged parents together. A loving smile temporarily flicked away lingering sadness.

Washing hands in the kitchen sink, he stared out the window at a row of evergreens separating a neighbor's backyard from his. Nolan's endless yard came to mind, walking around with Caye, who'd never seen obscene opulence before. Newark's backyard was measured in sneaker lengths. Maplewood's was so small that when it came time to sell after Martha died, they got seventy five percent of what the house was worth because there wasn't even room for a wading pool. Splashy hand washing was better in the kitchen sink. Ever since Merrie wiped out tiles in the Maplewood bathroom, he'd been a kitchen sink aficionado because Martha said it would take half a year for new bathroom tiles to adequately dry. Wild random thoughts filled long days; inner senses said fire away on thinking deeply, keeping a fragile mind occupied.

One early Saturday morning, Martha sent him to Kravitz's grocery store to pick up a *Silvercup* white bread, which used to be Grandma Rebecca's favorite. Alex came along. A refrigerated open case of foods had a row of pre-packaged hors-d'oeuvres. Two winks signaled Alex slipping the package under a tee shirt. In the vacant lot, it was tasting time. Quickly, they both spit contents out and read the label; it was something called anchovies. Promises were sealed with a long handshake; never to take anchovies that didn't belong to them.

Days were degrees of cloudiness and dull just like after Dr. King died. Fists were clenched frequently. An occasional inanimate thing was punched or slapped. How can Alex not be around? Was there a place to wake up, maybe on top of a red mountain and everything would be restored. Was restoration just a matter of squinting real hard?

"Alex." Whispers were frequent.

A single egg was scrambled and a small glass of orange juice forced. Acid problems followed juice. A recent medical article linking juice's antioxidant powers with dramatic Alzheimer's onset reduction made acid tolerable. Intellectually, did Alzheimer's make a difference anymore or could it be a blessing?

Keeping a pair of jeans and sweatshirt in a down stairs closet was not to disturb Evie at ridiculous times when gallons of fresh air were needed. His walking route occasionally passed the same dogs on leashes. Passing life forms in suburbia was a *Seinfeld* episode; nobody said anything to each other, mostly pretending no one was there because you didn't want to get involved. Caring was a dog sniffing sneakers and getting yanked away before scent recognition.

No words circulated from any source since Alex's goodbye, not even spiritual signs. How could anything really happen to Alex, with three different houses of God, living piously, loving and accepting all people? Alex's last words reverberated while trying to make sense of every word. The mysterious report was put into a local bank vault. Security cameras must've had a field day when he walked in with a back pack, asking for the largest box. Bank tellers would always stare at him, he sensed, but didn't really care anymore about how others viewed him.

During dinner sometimes, he'd disappear, usually to the basement, because he forgot to put in a new furnace filter or some other excusatory reason. Knowing emotional tears were ganging up, Evie and Nelson let him go without a word.

The last six blocks of this morning walk turned into a light jog. Turning the corner, Elvin saw Evie on the porch, leaning on wrought iron railing and holding a newspaper. Elvin knew from her ashen face.

"New York Times, Saturday.

Noted Princeton Astronomer, Wife Dead in Fire.

Kansas City, Missouri.

The bodies of Dr. Alex Zari and Christine Zari, of Princeton, New Jersey have been identified after a recent house fire. No cause for the fire has been determined. Dr. Zari graduated from Princeton and Harvard Universities and taught astronomy at Princeton. Christine Zari graduated from Rider College and worked for several New Jersey accounting firms. A University spokesperson mentioned Dr. Zari's several religious affiliations and ongoing studies of Eastern religion and culture. No funeral plans have been announced."

Elvin dropped to the steps.

"Dear God, this all can't be."

Trancelike, mostly with fixed eyes, aimlessly staring, Elvin spent most of the day on the recliner. Fists clenched, arm rests were pounded occasionally; reality needed abuse. Life made perfect sense growing up with Alex- it was all meant to be. Spirituality and God comforted them both. When you hear about tragedy, it's out of body, not real. A man died in a car crash on Route Nine, close to his age. Once upon a time that man was behind Elvin on the bagel store line. He wasn't real now; the universe placed him in life to give substance and consciousness to the world around. People dying, passing from life was not real. Newspaper obituaries were fiction by creative writers. No one died; everything was props in a universe, helping to explain his life. Alex was part of his soul. Did part of him die? Something was dead inside. If excruciating pain found him, would he feel anything? Was extreme sorrow a powerful opiate analgesic?

On a cluttered office desk, a small triangular red rock sat on top of a memo cube. Leaning back, he stared at the rock, a gift from one of Alex's trips to Sedona's red mountains and spiritual vortex. Explained at the time, it wasn't a real gift but something on loan so whenever Elvin had reason to go to Sedona, he'd return the rock to the mountain, borrowing another.

"Alex, sitting here every day thinking of you, it doesn't get easier. It's bullshit what they say about time and healing. Last week, I went to the Maplewood train station. The sign squeaks again. I don't know what Evie thought about my rushing out of the house at ten p.m., to drive an hour and sit on our hard bench. I want to say I felt you, but I can't. All I feel is a strange emptiness. When alone, I talk to you like this. It makes me feel better, maybe. I don't know. I don't know. I'm staring at the red rock, squeezing it now because you touched it and some of your molecules are all over it. This Monday, October 6th is your funeral. You and Christine will be with Adel and Sura in Freehold, at Maplewood Cemetery. Life is strange, it's called Maplewood."

Later that afternoon, Elvin needed air and drove twenty-five miles an hour to a small strip mall that dealt in money, stamps, bagels, Chinese, pizza, lottery tickets and clean clothes. Two fingers, like Nixon's old dual victory gesture, which made Elvin laugh in later life, thinking how preposterous Nixon was, really meant two pizza slices and a diet soda. Tom Romeo knew his fingers well. Elvin drifted back to pizza in Maplewood, marinara stains on sweat shirts and abundant amounts of water wasted over the years for stain removal. Alex was in every thought, motivation and visualization. Life was vile, angry, filled with disbelief.

The bank next to pizza was empty. He'd been thinking, hesitating about bank business. Maybe doing it now, meant coming to terms with Alex's death. In thirty minutes, Elvin finished twenty one signatures with a mid level bank employee. In a back office, the employee was probably rubbing hands together and cackling like the wicked witch or Aunt Evelyn. A three hundred thousand dollar home owner loan was easily secured for Nelson's future college tuition and other things.

Maplewood Cemetery dated back to the late 1800's. Years back when discussions focused on funerals, Adel and Sura knew they'd be together, but different religions and cemetery requirements could keep them apart. Alex and Elvin jumped into the conversation, in stand up comedic timing, that being the silly species we were, even in death, they separate, segregate and still discriminate with no peace on or below earth. Non-sectarian Maplewood Cemetery didn't care, so the Zari family signed up for internment. Zari's would be together.

An hour before, he stared into a mirror and whispered Alex's name. A red tie, Alex's gift from a last birthday was knotted. A strange pain started in his left abdomen but he knew it was alright and why it was there. When so close to ending a life, the same pain urged him on with seductive persuasion. Pain was a life form, a banshee, a temptress, wanting him in the coffin with Alex. Heavy breathing fogged a mirror. A bottle of open chilled Chardonnay was tipped to fill one of Evie's best wine glasses; some kind of annoying jewelry gadget hung on for dear life at the base. Held up and examined closely, it looked angelic with wings.

"Remember Belmar, Alex? First time we had Chardonnay. You got back from Indiana. They found three civil rights workers dead. We chugged and hugged. I miss you."

"Dad, are you alright?"

"I didn't know you were there. I was just thinking out loud about Uncle Alex. I'm alright."

A son knew when to hug a father- half environmental, half heredity and half situational need.

A hundred people gathered at grave side services for Alex and Christine Zari. Some came from Princeton and Harvard, making the long trip to pay respects. Evie and Nelson stood on either side, bolstering Elvin, busy looking around to see if he recognized anyone. With this new world, he wasn't worried about those he knew, but rather those he didn't. There were too many scenarios to ponder, especially with the strange contents of a knapsack, sitting in a bank vault behind curious tellers and cameras.

Did a bank employee tip off a federal agent about the knap sack? Alex reassured that no one knew anything about him. Was there someone photographing funeral guests from a distant black van? Feds knew all of Don Corleone's guests at Connie and Carlo's wedding, even writing down license plate numbers. Warm winds of paranoia blew from the southeast into Elvin's face, shoving aroma of coffee or chocolate from a nearby factory into confused nostrils.

Simeon Morris wasn't anywhere to be seen. Elvin would've worried about Simeon if he was there but better not; there were too many strangers around. Fifteen earthly minutes were left for Alex and Christine; that's what a recently repaired gold watch said. Christine's uncle, a Catholic priest from Connecticut performed the service with help from Coptic and Muslim clergy as per Alex's wishes. At the service end, caskets were lowered and legs turned rubbery. Nelson kept him upright. Up in the sky, a family of cumulous clouds presided, blocking sun and dimming sober light of the day.

Aarif saw Elvin lingering by the grave, borrowing a shovel and throwing soil on top of both caskets; for Jews it means respect and honor.

"I thought of you through all of this. Not a day has gone by since, when you and Alex weren't in my thoughts."

"Evie, Nelson. Meet Aarif al Hakim. A good friend to Alex and me. I need to come see you."

"I know, anytime."

A flashback remembered Alex's beaming face when they hugged and how happy his face. Now, there was a longer hug. Maybe Alex saw it and beamed again.

The red rock was clutched, fist tightened and squeezed. George Reeve, the first TV Superman back in the 1950's used to do the same thing with a hunk of coal, transforming it to a diamond under pressure. It was a favorite show of Elvin. The only special effect used in those by gone days was imagination and it worked for the kids on the block. After the show, you ran outside, yelling, I'm *Superman* or *Jimmy Olsen* or *Perry White* or a terribly inept bad guy. Girls were never around so they played without a *Lois Lane.* Alex was still in Michigan.

Last night was special. Nelson was at friends. Evie ran downstairs, offing lights. A twist open bottle of Manischewitz Cream Red Concord and two plain glasses stood with Elvin in boxer shorts at the bedroom door. Knees finally looked six decades old.

"Wine is wine, why the look?"

"People say sixty is the new forty. When we were forty, wine was from Italy or France, not Goldberg's Liquor Store but I'm guilty too. I should've lit moody candles."

"We got the money from the home owner loan which takes care of Nelson's Rutgers tuition."

"If he gets in."

"This is going to be hard for me to express." Eyes rolled towards the ceiling for divine intervention then back to Evie. A pair of deep breaths dramatized unfolding tension.

"Love me, trust me?"

"Always, Elvin; what is it?"

"Always trust. Alex used to say that all the time. There are things I have to do now. It's hard to explain because I don't know what has to be done, if that makes sense. Maybe there's too much time for me to think and mourn."

"Are you alright?"

"I'm giving notice, leaving Solchiali. With my heart and mind in upheaval, I can't concentrate or do a credible job. I don't want it anymore. It's not relevant. There's nothing for you to worry about including money. Always trust."

Evie climbed on top, tears rolling down and Elvin fingered each one, kissing them away.

Two black sample suitcases slid out of an SUV and became an uncomfortable, probing kind of seat. For a few minutes, Elvin looked up at the sky and watched construction vehicles heading to Solchiali's rear.

Parsley sage. Rosemary. Gladys. I never knew a girl that I wanted to fuck named Gladys, so here I am apologizing spiritually to all the world's Gladys'. But why didn't I ever fall for a Rosemary? Maybe I missed out. What if Sofia had been a Rosemary? Maybe next thyme. Martha and Earth. How I miss my mother. You spent a lifetime molding, loving, teaching, working two or three jobs to give us a little more material things and pieces of your heart and soul. Sitting on this bag, hurting my ass, I realize, Martha, that you were the quintessential mother, giving everything you had to me

Calvin Schwartz

and Judy. And yes, you tried to push Jack too. I know that now. But going forward, not looking back. My poor soul is being led in so many different directions. This is all hard; unimaginably so. Alex, you're not around to guide, to listen or sit next to on a hard bench or boulder. We've learned from each other and your spirit is always inside. I'm thinking there's enough left. It's going to be all right. A journey is going to begin in a few minutes. 'A rest of your life' decision. Let me suck in as much air and schlep these sample bags inside.

Sofia ran around her desk. Hands shook cordially. Nathan Knight lurked.

"Elvin."

"Sofia. Nathan."

Self assured, egotistical Nathan looked nervous and tentative. "We're beyond saying, have you thought it over and any chance to reconsider even though I'm saying it again?"

Elvin stared, focusing on rapid baldness onset and no traces of the Afro hair cut, synonymous with Nathan. "Let me collect my thoughts for a minute."

"Take your time."

It couldn't be that long since seeing the phantom National Sales Manager. Maybe he's got some kind of ravaging alopecia. That miserable guy and he was a miserable fucking guy. Funny, I never asked Sofia if he ever tried to get a piece of her. Most everyone did at one time or another and how I loved hearing stories of all their failures, especially when I was inside of her, which is when she loved to tell me those things.

"Your kind thoughts are much appreciated. It's just time for me to move on."

"Can I ask you where you're moving?"

"Sure you can ask, except can't answer cause I really don't know."

"Well then, only the best to you. I speak for Sofia and Mr. Zahl. You'll always have a home here."

For whatever reason, Nathan's limp handshakes never meant much but he still mustered the most cordial smile available. Once Elvin was tempted to violently shake his arm, but he'd never get it, so why bother. Nathan was now gone from his life.

"You never liked Nathan much."

"That's cheating, you know me too well. Do you think he ever felt it?"

"He doesn't feel; that's the problem. When God gives things out, there's always a balancing in nature. If you're a genius with off the charts IQ, then you've got a shortfall in social, communicative skills, called humanism. Plug it in and see if it doesn't work all the time. God is fair and a lot of other things too."

"Never thought of it like that. Why didn't you tell me ten years ago?"

"Would it have made a difference?"

"Maybe. I'm officially gone. My sample bags are in the hall. When are you leaving for Italy?"

"Back to Italy before Christmas. Mother's excited. I'm not getting married, well not for a while. Marriage is a big step especially for Roberto, being sixty and stuck in routines; maybe too hard an adjustment."

"I'm almost sixty. Do you think I'm all routines?"

"You don't count. How are you? Is this sudden upheaval in your life mostly because of Alex and Christine?"

Deep breaths meant change of subject and she knew it.

"Spending Christmas in Rome is going to be a natural thing for you."

"Natural?"

"Natural, means no travel, you're there already."

"And you Elvin, what about your Christmas?"

"Do you know something?"

"I feel you."

Feet nudged each other under the desk.

"Depending on the weather forecast a week before Christmas, I'll be in a small town in Montana for Midnight Mass. But there has to be snow in the forecast."

"You never told me why?"

"I honestly don't know. One day the vision was there just like you were there one day. Sofia, when. . . . ?"

"For us to say goodbye?"

Her right hand meandered across the desk, crossing mid point; just their fingernails touched.

"Yes."

"We'll figure it out."

Life would never be the same. Thoughts were barricaded behind eye sockets. A gold watch was massaged. Late walks at night, alone, whispering, calling Alex, spirit, God, Martha and Jack. Neck creaked to sky, staring, hoping to see a sign. Elvin wanted something. He deserved it, being a believer. On a recent Sunday morning, perspiring and restless, he tossed and turned from 4:44 until before seven a.m. Evie lay next. Maybe it was a cardiac fibrillation, but his body was out of whack. On his back, staring at the ceiling, he whispered, "It's all too much for me."

A soft voice spoke. "Trust."

"Evie, are you up?"

No response. He rolled out of bed and checked Nelson, also sleeping. Life now had a purpose, with strange support and direction. Life was a gift and you needed to show gratitude. For the rest of a life, trust came from spirit. What had to be done was understood thanks to the National Championship of Epiphanies. Everything was suddenly clear; a rest of life journey, ticketed with places to stay and miles to go.

The night before Halloween in New Jersey is designated mischief night. Soap abstractions on car windows. Toilet paper draped on trees. Raw eggs like a Jackson Pollock.

Martha once hosted a costume party even though she had a hard time with symbolism of the holiday, not being a Jewish thing. Adel had the best costume, coming as a doctor with pretend blood droplets on hospital green. Alex and Elvin recreated characters from the original *Invasion of the Body Snatchers*. There were no special effect characters in the original black and white movie, just occupied human bodies, so there was no need wearing smelly uncomfortable costumes, just jeans, a baseball hat and faded college sweatshirts.

Halloween morning was Indian summer like. A large sign was hammered into Elvin's side lawn facing Wyncrest Road. The eight foot long sign proclaimed, "An Un-Celebration: Some American Companies finally collectively surpass and break the record of the Third Reich(Nazi Germany) of fifty million and one people, dead, killed, murdered and counting since end of World War II. Money, profit and bottom lines, not people are important to those companies. Please read the candles."

Fifty signs, made to look like black burning candles, with messages contained in the flame, were staked. Neighbors, friends, and strangers stopped to read candle flames all day long.

"Cigarette companies. They've been lobbying journalists to ease up on the second hand smoke issue. How many millions dead?"

"Companies that recall anything including food, drugs and cars. Why bother with a recall when actuaries tell companies to wait; keeping products on the market an extra year would generate more sales and more than pay for the extra law suits."

"Trans Fat. Fat tastes good. Makes you want to eat more and clog up."

"The power company in California that used hexavalent chromium for years knowing that it kills in so many different ways once it gets into water. Hollywood made a pretty good movie about that. Thanks Erin."

"When drug companies do "off label marketing." Persuading doctors by paying them, wining and dining, taking to resorts, getting them a massage; all to get them to prescribe medicines NOT for what they were intended, but to make extra money and putting the poor patient at great risk or worse."

"Billions of empty plastic bottles of water end up in land fills every year which requires forty seven million gallons of oil to make, equivalent to one billion pounds of CO_2 released into atmosphere. It takes a thousand years for plastic bottles to biodegrade and when they do, they leak nasty things into groundwater, like phthalates. Think of the fuel required to ship all that water to your local store."

"Hot Dogs contain nitrites and amines. You cook them and the heat reaction creates nitrosoamines, very carcinogenic, which means they kill over time and the hot dog makers know all about this."

"Malaria kills three thousand African children every day and it's simple and cheap to fight. A five dollar net helps keep insects from a sleeping child."

"Some health insurance companies profit by denying treatment as much as they can. It's a literary art form to send rejection, denial letters to people who would love to live. Bonuses are paid to executives for profitability and panel doctors who find reasons to deny."

"Companies since the end of WWII that dump nasty poisonous things into waterways or landfills; know what they're doing. Remember Love Canal."

"Chlorine. A few plants are still left that make it the old fashioned way using outdated process with tons of highly toxic mercury which evaporates from giant vats while the EPA looks the other way."

"The artificial sweetener aspartame has been shown to cause cancer in lab rats and should be banned for human consumption. I wonder who was president of the company who owns aspartame and were markers called in to get the product approved? What's scary is that the product is present in 6000 food products. Two hundred million people use the product. A lot of cancer to ponder."

"Ships are painted so marine organisms stay away. Part of paint is Tributylin, nasty stuff. Paint chips and sinks to the bottom and fish aren't smart."

"Polar Bears and Arctic birds have flame retardant chemicals inside them. Retardants are used in electronics, furniture and clothing."

"What about *endocrine disruptors?* The chemicals poison frogs, fish, amphibians, little boys (leaves testicles un-descended) little girls, fetuses and adults too. Chemicals mess with endocrine functions; it'll take a hundred years to understand. Plastic water bottles contain phthalates which are also endocrine disruptors. Disruptors are killers, world wide and in our water. Companies hide info. EPA is probably scared out of their pants and dresses. If they could get some of these chemicals out of our water supply (people who take medicines also piss some of them into water cycle), they wouldn't, because it's too expensive."

"Some restaurant chains dump salt into their meals making food taste better, but salt is brutal and kills."

"Coal power (plants) soot kills twenty four thousand Americans annually. Currently available emissions control technology could prevent, but it probably costs too much money to install or use. So let some people die. Big deal."

Setting sun was blinding. Elvin stood with Evie and Nelson facing the sun so that Channel Twelve news, a Jersey based mostly news channel, could interview them. The long day brought a healthy supply of cars passed the protestation. Elvin kept looking out the garage door. At three p.m., they called to interview him.

"Elvin. Can you tell us why you did this? It's not everyday someone takes time, energy and money to make a statement."

"It's an expression of freedom, to reach people and make them think. Thinking is the most important thing. A close friend of mine was concerned with the environment. Actually he was confident, that we've passed the tipping point, and there isn't much that earthlings can do to stop the degradation. It is too late. I've already given my son that talk, not about sex, but I apologized for the environment and advised not having children. If all your viewers intellectualize what I've done here, and get out a calculator and add up how many people these companies have killed, that fifty million and one number is rather real. Good old politics let's it happen. The purpose of all this is to yell that time is running out; the whole human family needs to do something, but I worry, we're addicted to energy, bottled water, microwaves, remote controls and smoke stacks. Somebody needs to look at the insanity and in Asia and Europe too."

"Evie, Nelson do you both support what's on the lawn?"

"Of course. I'd like to say Elvin is eccentric."

"You just did Evie and on New Jersey television."

"Well, it's a caring eccentricity. He cares about people."

Nelson was shielding eyes, trying to sneak behind Elvin.

"What do you think of your father?"

"Proud."

"Any plans for the future, Elvin?"

"Well I think I'll spend the next few years discovering America and see what other issues are worth fighting for."

Watching *Shane*, a favorite western, in bed, Elvin needed reassurances from Evie, that the expression on the lawn was alright, and he wasn't losing it.

Now lying down, facing the television, his feet were close to her. "*Grafton's*. A long time ago I wanted to open a store with same name, like a modern suburban general store, but nobody would ever know where the name came from. I wanted everyone to know that I love *Shane* so much, I went to all the trouble of opening a store because of the movie's effect on me."

"They're called convenience stores now."

"It's almost the end. Little Joey yells for Shane to come back. *We want you Shane.* Now it gets really heavy, full of meaning and symbolism. I've got the goose bumps. Shane is riding off into darkening skies with lonely scary mountains all around and terrible uncertainty at the end- like what happens to him, lives or dies. He's hurt and bleeding. Did you know Alan Ladd was short? He wore special elevator shoes and they probably used special camera angles too."

"You're rambling, which means you want to say something."

"I'm at a point in life."

"Alex and Christine's passing moved you?"

"Yes."

"And you have things to do and I keep telling you, it's alright."

"And I love you."

TWENTY ONE

C old spotty rain fell, wipers used intermittently. Wiper utilization was a matter of principle. If it wasn't clear cut rain, Elvin kept turning them on and off while armies of droplets slowly snaked down the window embankment in a race of life and death, but mostly annoying vision. Perhaps it was reminiscent of the game played with Alex all those years. Who talks first and gives in to temptation- a sign of weakness, like turning the windshield wiper on before its time.

Meteorological thoughts entertained. Early November cold rain was now intensified, so wipers were enlisted full time. Rain changed to wet snow in December then in January, an accumulating snow. A week prior to snow events brought typical media coverage. Elvin smiled at television survival segments; how to dress for outdoors and don't shovel if you're in the latter stages of congestive heart failure. When was the last time someone in Jersey was snowbound and waited days for rescue? Eight million close neighbors in a state that's more densely populated than India and they're worried about a car abandoned on a Jersey non-existent tundra.

Heading north on Route Eighteen for a meeting with Adel and Alex's priest at St. Marina Coptic Church, thoughts still battled with denial and reality. Alex can't be gone, and what about pathways to spirit- where are they now? The parking lot was empty. In classic Bogart fashion, a trench coat collar went up, beret secured, and a quick glance at as much sky as he could absorb.

Looking around the church like a wide eyed kid walking into Madison Square Garden for the first time, he was surrounded by serenity and beauty- a special view for his eyes only. Piety and holiness eased him into a drifting state, almost taking him away from the reason why he was there.

"Father. Thank you for making this time. I was drifting into the beauty and peace of my surroundings."

"It's easy to see your meditative state. Alex was a great loss for all of us. We miss him."

"Do you know why I'm here?"

"To feel your friend and be close to his spirit."

"Exactly. Not many people read me as well as you do. I'm comforted by that. From my time in college, I believed people have an aura- a kind of invisible energy, presence, spirituality and so much we don't understand. Alex was all that. He imparted so much to me."

"Spirituality is wonderful. To recognize that it's part of your world and being able to feel it is a gift from God. Elvin, you are blessed in many ways; most importantly to have had a friend like Alex."

"My being here would've made him happy by this opening mind and heart to seek God and understanding. He compared different ways of getting to Yankee Stadium as similar to the journey of man seeking God. I suppose there aren't many like Alex with as many roads as he used?"

"A very unique soul. My sitting with his Jewish friend, who's thrilled to be here and learn; that's the real testament to Alex's life. Come Elvin, let me show you around."

Entering the sanctuary, Elvin asked to sit in the last row.

"May I sit for a while? I won't disturb anything planned?"

"Take all the time and come back. I have a few more things to show you."

Beautiful reverent silence helped him hear a gust of wind push rain against the stained glass window. For years, absorbing energy from the departed was part of a quest. Vichy Water touched by Bogart. New Jersey Vietnam War Memorial. Now, Alex's Coptic Church sanctuary.

Cold rain lingered into the next morning. Elvin yelled to Evie, busy drying hair, that the season's first sweater was needed. Life is a first and last. Today was a first seasonal sweater wearing day. A few weeks ago, meeting a former Rutgers basketball player at the *Olive Branch*, the athlete remembered to Elvin the day he last dunked a basketball. An aging body wouldn't let him dunk a ball ever again. How many former players remember their last dunk? Henry's was at a playground in Somerset under a sunny blue sky with a young son watching, proudly cheering. What about inviting the athlete to sit on the steps of Geology Hall with him, Elvin thought for a moment and about writing a short story called *The Last Dunk*.

Shoulders adjusted, his sweater stretched over mid rift changes. Was there a hidden meaning in recognizing this was the first seasonal time wearing a sweater? Sitting at the edge of the bed, Elvin wondered how nature knew to birth him in New Jersey. Snowy Christmas scenes and autumnal bright colors are life experiences that didn't happen in Mississippi. Imagine being born there. What would've happened if an enlistment gang came to his house, some on horses and told him to start wearing a sheet and carry around matches. But he was a Jew so that wouldn't have happened; instead just a few cross burnings on a recently hand mowed lawn. Thinking back and forward, Elvin whispered, "We really are a silly species. Look what we waste time and energy with- getting people to wear sheets and terrorize despite all the real problems facing the world and the rest of our silly species."

Evie finished drying hair, now standing topless and ironically it was that first time that Elvin noticed the effects of gravity and age on female breasts.

After a moment of thinking that Elvin was staring at her breasts, she spoke. "What you're doing today is wonderful. I've been teaching fourth grade all these years and you've made several brief appearances. Now you're going to spend a full day observing, listening and caring about what I do."

Slowly beginning to understand behavioral things from the depths of a stomach to a soulful conscience, he began to understand what his life meant. There was purpose, journey and a new end. Evie was demonstrably happy while thoughts drifted to reliable Ayn Rand.

"Who are you?"

"Mrs. Stone teaches fourth grade. I'm her husband, Mr. Stone and one day Mrs. Stone will be your teacher and who are you?"

"Eric."

The little boy's face was happy, filled with anticipatory wonder and thirst for knowledge. Why did it take him so long to do this day? The school was four blocks not ninety three million miles away.

"Can I ask you a question, Eric?"

"Yes."

"Do you remember my name?"

"Mr. Stone. It's a funny name."

"Why?"

"We have white stones around our house. My mother doesn't let me touch them."

"Did you ever watch a movie called *March of the Wooden Soldiers*?"

"Mean *Shrek*?"

Over a brown bag lunch, Evie went on about pride and colleagues, thinking it such a positive experience to have Elvin spend a day interacting with children. Kids are especially impressed by over six footers; an event to be perseverated about all week and beyond.

Kid's facial expressions were absorbed. Words fired cerebrally; innocence, hope, learning and trees. Now re-thinking trees, watching children laugh, all with shining faces, and by four p.m., something told Elvin to plant trees in the spring on the lawn where environmental protest signs stood for two weeks. Was it the same spirit that was directing him to Montana for Christmas Eve that made him think trees? Does everybody have this soulful energy but most don't know it? Maybe life's precious gift is awareness and it keeps getting heightened. You suddenly turn and look at the clock. It's 4:44. A look at the passing truck on the right; the telephone number is *4444*. Those numbers and how and where they are absolutely exist and are part of real life. What's so haunting for Elvin was being made aware of their presence. The universe shares angelic intervention. Sedona is a building block of awareness.

Larry King was back at midnight for an encore. Evie pressed volume up and secured the bedroom door. Entry back into bed was into a straddling position for kissing and thanking.

"Do you know how touched I am with you? The whole school will be talking about it for weeks. A little thank you, so get comfortable."

Elvin assumed the old attic position, hands folded behind head, smiling, pondering, still wondering about trees in the spring, where the thoughts came from and deciding that he didn't give a damn about gravity and breasts and actually liked the wholesome, mature look. Larry King in the background wasn't helping mood and elevation. The bedroom went dark and silent.

heavenly concept, being able to start again, making things better each time or if undeserving, not getting that second or third chance.

"Ah, Mr. Stone, order ready. You said no fortune cookies today."

"I'm tired of fortune cookies. They've stopped working for me. You might not see me for a long time. I love your food, but I'm moving far away."

Elvin never liked irreversible farewells and being a perpetual, cock eyed optimist, thought that maybe one day, Sofia would return to vacation on the Jersey Shore instead of the pretentious French Riviera or Lake Como. Two greasy bags with handles were in the trunk, not front seat, where a lonely single rose refused to trip the seat belt light. Soon three garage doors lifted.

Elvin stood with food bags and a lone rose in mouth, wrapped in several yellow *Wendy's* napkins.

"Don't laugh at me. I finally figured out what button goes to each door. I did this to make you smile. Is that rose for me?"

"For you, just *one* rose and *one* means it's been *one* hell of a ride and *one* special lifetime filled with memories and you're *one* amazing person, *one* of my life's highlights."

"No *one* makes me blush like you do. I know you have to get back, so it can't be a long dinner."

"I couldn't wait to see you but on the other hand, actually there's some dread too but not in a bad way. How do we say goodbye? How do we do this; run upstairs and go crazy?"

"Have dinner. I'll finally use chopsticks. I think we need a hit of blonde wine. After dinner, I'll make some espresso. And. . . ."

"And, you're right, say goodbye."

Dinner talk was about the farewell tour which ended an hour ago and Sofia's Italy plans. Money was sitting in Swiss banks so there was nothing ever to worry about and when she offered Elvin monetary support, he got up and kissed her, but promised he'd never have financial problems.

"You invested wisely?"

"Just a lifetime of frugal living."

Each sensed sadness and finality. Whispers deepened mood. What faced them was a mountain of emotional goodbyes which are always incomplete. Lifetimes are spent thinking about things you wanted to say, but never did. Elvin stabbed.

"We're never going to be able to say everything to each other."

"Why?"

"Because we both feel sad and it's impossible. There isn't a book that comes close to us at this moment- the perfection we shared. Maybe some things are *better left*."

"Think I like that, *better left*."

She reached for his hand, holding it tightly.

"Things are always *better left* because we can dream no matter how old we are and wonder about everything finished or not, so let's leave things to wondering."

Espresso cups clicked. "To the wonder of what we had and endless perpetual wonderful wondering."

"It's like future, present and prologue."

"Our eyes say so much. When you say goodbye to your accounts, what do you tell them you're doing?"

"Looking for America. Always looking."

"Will you ever come to Italy?"

"Probably not, but I will leave the country one day."

"Guadalcanal?"

"You remembered." Elvin grabbed her hand.

"Does the offer still stand?"

"Actually I've been thinking about it. We'll see."

"We'll see."

"Time."

"Time."

"Let's do this easy and simple."

They walked into the kitchen holding hands.

"I almost forgot about the quiz that I've been promising to give you about Solchiali and the business. All you've learned these years can be answered in one word. Have you thought about it?"

"For years, teacher."

"And."

"The word is *fragile*. The whole business is *fragile*. National health insurance looms. The company is *fragile*. Industry regulation is *fragile*. FTC and SEC are *fragile*. Both FTC and SEC people are not really smart. No invention. No caring about Americans being raped and overcharged. No imagination. Sometimes you think they're so bad, it has to be more than stupidity. If you fill a few buses with SEC and FTC people, take them to New York to the old Waverly Theatre in Greenwich Village and make them watch *Animal House*, not a single one would understand what the movie is about. Born is a new definition of stupid; out of touch lazy people who don't have the slightest concept about the eyeglass business. Your father's few hundred stores that sell just eyeglasses and nothing else are *fragile*; maybe that's why your father wants to franchise and get out. One day Americans are going to stop spending hundreds on a stupid plastic eyeglass frame with a couple of inane rhinestones and alphabet letters glued on the temple and that part of the business becomes *fragile*. Actually, one day smart Americans are going to realize that eyeglasses are best purchased at small independent stores and offices-my last *fragile* thought. Now I'm really done."

"And you passed the test even with lots of unnecessary rambling."

"And you've passed my heart and you know why I rambled."

She put a finger to his lips. They kissed briefly. Sofia reached around the doorway, pounding all three buttons, lifting three garage doors.

TWENTY TWO

A black wool hat pulled down over ears made Evie and Nelson laugh at Elvin, sitting on steps, squeezing rubbers over old shoes.

"Dad, you look like a poster boy for vagrancy or a man sitting near a bon fire by train tracks. Woody Guthrie is singing *This land is my land*. Huddled men, trying to stay warm are un-employed, dreaming of the day."

"Say Nelson, that's a pretty good description but what's so funny?"

"Scarf, hat, coat, rubbers and gloves- all for an inch of snow. Looks like your about to climb Kilimanjaro?"

"Not climbing, just clearing lungs."

Life was strange. Lungs filling meant cold fresh air was working its way to all his cerebral lobes. People go through life without caring about the world. Thousands of years ago, Moses parted the Red Sea- maybe the biggest historical visual event. Modern civilization doesn't see urgency to life. Most let the globe warm. Alex's environmental thinking was inspired by the Gabriel gang. One scientist friend thought global warming was so bad, meaning irreversible, advice was just like a doctor's for a terminal cancer patient, to make the patient (Earth) comfortable; there was nothing more to be done.

How do you get the message out? No one listens. Elvin's mind was firing defeatism, walking in cold air. Firing was a mental game; just let anything random shoot, never knowing where or why, like a roulette wheel. Was random firing due to mysterious spiritual subliminal suggestion? Random was being five years old when Martha took him downtown Newark to Lorstan Photographers. For ten minutes, they manipulated his resting arm on a piece of driftwood because there was nothing better to do in those days before computers and remote controls. There wasn't global warming, but actually there was. That picture from Newark stayed on Martha's coffee table until she died. Evie just added it to her mantle collection.

Flurries were coming. You could see the cloud responsible. He was sitting in Mr. Townsends' office, the Maple Avenue Grammar School principal. Seven years old and the principal had to reprimand Elvin for talking too much. An old grandfather clock ticked loudly next to his isolated scolding chair. Mr. Townsend would always be that mustached clock, just like Eisenhower's bust was always the capitol rotunda. Today seven year olds bring box cutters and central nervous system stimulants to class without reprimand by a grandfather clock. Random firing felt good and purging.

Standing outside a morgue window at the Beth Israel Hospital, he smelled formaldehyde. Climbing on a ledge, he looked down into the dark room. A table was in the middle with something covered up; a tag dangled from what looked like a toe. Olfactory memory would linger a lifetime. Maybe the thing covered up could somehow be related to the mason who cemented the third brick at Geology Hall?

Old folks were gathered under a single roof, living days simply; morning seated exercises, afternoon bingo, monthly podiatrist visits, and Atlantic City excursions with walkers temporarily stored underneath the bus. Aging is part of life because we do and until they find that stupid switch which starts the process, we always will.

After Valentine's Day, Elvin phoned Monmouth View, an assisted living residence nearby and asked permission to interview a few residents. Much to his surprise, he had lingering celebrity status; facility administrators still remembered newspaper and cable interviews on his lawn at Halloween. He was the crazy environmentalist without an apparent motive.

"Do you still have the signs up, Mr. Stone?"

"Call me, Elvin. I took them down after a few weeks."

"What would you like to talk to our residents about?"

"Life and after."

Near West Monmouth Hospital was a quaint three story, colonial motif building, assisting old folks with living. Elvin signed the visitor sheet and was led to a room in the back. A left hand clutched a yellow legal pad. Now seated in a conference room with ten chairs, he felt being taken seriously. The administrator made small talk. Elvin randomly switched talk to the virtues of prunes, handed down from Mesopotamia.

"It's really that old a fruit?"

"Part of my research here today will solidify the theory."

"Why do I feel, not knowing you, that. . . ."

"Yes, I'm teasing, but I really am appreciative for your cooperation and generosity."

A heavy set, slightly hunched woman, supported by a walker and two tennis balls cut into the bottom, making movement easier, smiled her way into the room.

"Elvin Stone, meet Sylvia Grabelle."

"My pleasure young man and happy 2004."

"I'm not that young, a year from sixty."

"Then you're pretty well preserved."

"Thanks."

"So, how can I help you? I saw you on local television and remembered you. My memory still works, legs a little shaky."

The director left the room.

"I have a few questions about life and. . . ."

"Death."

Elvin was doodling, in between, smiling back at her constant smile.

"What are you going to do with this interview- *Sixty Minutes* maybe?"

"Truthfully, I don't know. I just needed to do this. I'd love to know how people feel being at this point in life- about tomorrow and what you think about the day after today. What you look forward to? Do you think about heaven?"

"Let me talk. My husband died twenty years ago. I'm eighty five. He was a pharmacist. We lived healthfully and comfortably. He died in his sleep and I miss him every day and yes, he's waiting and no, I'm not rushing to him. Plenty of time for that. I read everyday and accept that I might not get up the next morning to finish a book, so do you know what I do?"

Her smile never diminished. It was constant, making Elvin comically think there was facial nerve damage, leaving Sylvia in a permanent smiling state.

"What do you do?"

"I read as much as I can everyday. There's a force within me; maybe it's within all of us and maybe we're built that way on purpose."

"What force."

"Good force, optimist force. I'm eighty five, why not ten more years for me? Ten years is a long time, so I exercise every day, even with this walker. I even went through two tennis balls. I think it's a record here and a challenge. I'd like ten more years."

"And if. . . ."

"Well if, then it's alright. One second I'd be here then I wouldn't, so for a brief second in time, a gasp of regret then maybe on to another adventure. Philosophers say next part of life begins."

Elvin wanted to agree with her but he sighed and spoke. "Did you ever go to college because you're amazing? So much insight and the way you talk."

"I never finished high school. My parents were poor and father died early. I had to help my mother make clothes to support us. The director here came to me first. She knows how I feel about things and don't get spoiled, not all the residents here are like me."

"I figured that. Where are you from?"

"Newark."

"Me too."

"What high school?"

"Weequahic."

"I would've gone there too. Promise me something."

"Sure."

"Come visit me while I'm still able."

"I promise."

Her words, *Well if, then it's alright, it's like one second I'd be here then I wouldn't, so for a brief second in time, a gasp of regret*, were circled along side a prodigious exclamation point. The best thought about the day, was that a smile would always be there when he thought about Sylvia Grabelle and vice versa, he was sure.

Life is ebb and flow. Music stores that sold different speeds, 33, 45, 78, then cassettes and CDs, must be having a hard time with the internet and digital electronics. Elvin thought disappearance like the corner grocery store in the 1950s. Joe the milk man drove that funny truck. Joe was long buried but not his memory. May 2004 and he still remembered milk delivered to a box by the side door. Is it part of defining long earth life? Sitting at the Shark River wasn't the same either; cement was poured years ago to fill spaces, taking away a sense of natural adventure. Evie and Nelson were shopping for Rutgers dormitory things, so he decided on a Shark River sojourn.

All this time, Sedona was still in thoughts and dreams, but with no urgency to get back, especially without Alex. Was extra spirituality baggage really needed? Perhaps introspective practicality kept him from going back. Would memories set him back, especially the one, holding Alex's hand on the mountain, looking into reassuring eyes and knowing this was a special friend for life, who so cared about him?

In the same place when Alex was still on earth, he spoke softly. "How could Alex's life force be gone?" Maybe it wasn't too late to study physics, Einstein and time. Would his being a physicist help cope with loss and sense of future loss?

"Alex, I'm still not feeling you in a way I would've expected, if that makes sense. Maybe it's an experience thing, not knowing what's it like without you most of my life. Remember when we talked about Emmett Till and his mother and one day doing a tour of respect and honor and how amazing that would all be, opening our spiritual souls? Maybe I do sense you, because sitting at our river now, with two ships almost side by side skirting our horizon, I decided it's time for Chicago and Emmett."

The front hall had rows of shopping bags lined up and judging by what protruded, looked like an arrangement according to the floor plan of a dorm room; sheets, a pillow, desk lamp, power surge and finally a poster of John Belushi wearing a *college* sweatshirt. Nelson ran downstairs into a hug.

"Did you see the poster?"

"*Animal House.* It just hit me. My little boy is going to be a freshman in college and not any college but my alma mater."

"What do you think about our son, a Rutgers man?"

"Are you all happy right now?" Elvin's arms folded, prompting Evie to make reference to *Mr. Clean*, but with plenty of sandy brown hair, temples tinged gray.

"Are you poised to get serious?" She copied the folded arms.

"I need to know you both understand. Of course, I'm not sure if I understand. Feelings and an aura come over me. My gut physically hurts. I have to do things like it's the call of my wild. Unfulfilled parts of life, like Heathcliffe wandering around Pedyston Crag without Cathy. I need to gather a bunch of heather near the Crag. Would you guys like to smell the heather?"

"You're rambling darling."

"That reminds me. You tricked me, Dad. When I was eight, you made me watch *Wuthering Heights*, saying it was a ghost movie. For three seconds at the end, Heathcliffe and Cathy fade into a snowy mountain and they even added that scene, months later, after the final shoot. See Dad, I know stuff. You're a good teacher of tech noir."

"You're not sorry I made you watch that movie, after all you're still talking about it?"

"No. Kind of glad you did. I added it to my resume. It helped me get into Rutgers."

"I'm going to disappear for a few days. Both of you fill my life. You know that."

"Where to?"

"To the grave of Emmett Till in Chicago. Alex and I dreamed of paying respects."

Four arms wrapped around Elvin, settling themselves into a group hug, rotating, swaying and accepting the man.

Two mid size suitcases bordered knees. Elvin pressed *six*, to a hesitation and jerk and looked frantically for the emergency phone. Doors opened to smiling cousin Bob, Jack's first cousin's oldest son and family competitor all these years. Taunts and challenges used to come from Jack all the time.

"Your Cousin Bob made little league all star team for Chicago and did the same with swim team and made honor roll. Guess where Bob is going to school?"

"Well Dad, just by your tone, must be in New England somewhere."

"That's right, Yale."

Temptation was to say, "Let's see what happens in a few decades. Who winds up where, how and with whom?" Nelson just got into Rutgers while Bob's son left after a first marriage broke up and last heard, was on a Harley somewhere between Jerome, Arizona and Great Falls, Montana, bypassing higher education. After a second marriage failed, Bob bought a bicycle shop on Diversey near Lincoln Park.

"Cousin, are we too old to use that prefix?"

"Never too old."

Bob's metamorphosis from a lean, athletic, swimming body, to mildly obese and baldness was lamented that Jack never had that chance to compare cousins now; Bob was out of a second marriage and no wonder, and Elvin, with a long time Italian blonde friend who could've easily graced the cover of most magazines, while he still looked a trim twenty years younger than supposed to.

Modern minimalist highlighted the apartment, which meant stainless steel and uncomfortable places to sit. View was Lake Michigan and downtown. Quietly, reflectively staring and blinking, Chicago's lights blinked back. Shaking his head at the city's breathtaking beauty, Elvin asked, "What the hell took me so long to get out here?"

"What did bring you here?"

"I've become a hippie of sorts, looking for America, whatever that means."

"Be careful cousin, sounds like my son; maybe it's genetic. You'll find yourself on a Harley one day, hanging out in Jerome, Arizona at the *Spirited Rail* with female bikers bigger than you."

Now they were laughing, reminiscing, and drinking White Russians; it was the last thing they did together at Sarah's wedding years ago.

"How is Sarah?" In boxers and Rutgers tee-shirt, Elvin absorbed more skyline and lake.

"Still a gynecologist, divorced twice and it makes me feel good to talk about her; the twice divorced commonality card. I had a growth on my back, nothing dangerous; a sebaceous cyst, so I went to see her last year, professionally. You should've seen the looks on patients reading Cosmo and People when they called me in. Bet half of them thought I was *tranny* in training."

"You up for this Elvin, meaning are you in shape?"

"Just give me a boy's bike and point me towards the Lake and Park. We'll do a nice dinner later."

Elvin pedaled while a smile lingered because of a cousin's concern and things in life you never forget doing. Approaching Diversey and North Clark, heading to Lincoln Park, and not forgetting how to achieve motion with balance, an Elvin worldly blackout rolled in like a dense fog off the lake; there was no future, past or sadness, just endless pedaling. *Endless* was becoming a favorite word concept.

A volleyball ball bounced just in front. He handed it back to a tall thin man in cut out tee shirt who asked in Sofia's accent, "What's a Rutgers?"

"State University of New Jersey."

"Why not call it Jersey State."

"Because we're different."

"Guess so."

Couples on a blanket near a tree were wrapped in each other's arms. The sweaty helmet was removed to watch, knowing it wasn't privacy invasion, just observing the miracle of young love. Young love reminded him of Marlboro Grammar School, spending a day, seeing kids with faces of hope and awe. Sylvia Grabelle welcomed aging in awe and hoped to grow older. A few days before coming to Chicago, Evie saw the Star-Ledger newspaper obituary section. Sylvia died. Using the same note pad when he interviewed her, Elvin doodled at his office desk for two hours. Doodling didn't make sense. Chardonnay didn't make sense. A last thought about Sylvia, was hope that she finished reading whatever and if God was good, kept her around, so she could finish that last book. Maybe someone could do a mystical last dunk in memory of Sylvia and he'd be there to watch. Are we a silly species of hope and awe? Finally as biking was nearly done, it was time for soda and a hot dog with a just conceived Lincoln Park constitutional preamble that all hot dogs are not created equal. From wherever the hot dog stand was, the bike was now pushed all the way back to Bob's shop.

"Why dress up for dinner? Ties and deep dish pizza?"

"Pump Room. I called for reservations from Jersey."

"How come?"

"You know my fascination with *Casablanca* and Bogart?"

"Family legendary stuff, everybody knows."

"Well Bogart and Bacall celebrated their wedding sitting in Booth One. Of course we can't sit there. We'll be close and I'll notch another thing to do."

"To do?

"Since I'm kind of retired, I've got all the time in the world to fulfill things."

"A little crazy, then again, it's consistent."

"Tell me how to get to Burr-Oak Cemetery in Alsip?"

"Alsip's easy, but I never heard of the cemetery."

"Ever hear of Emmett Till?"

"No."

"He was a young teenager from Chicago who went to visit relatives in Mississippi in 1955 and may've said something to a married white woman in a general store. He was a sweet innocent kid, happy, full of awe, hope and life and would've been around our age now but was brutally murdered. That horrendous act, his death and his mother's brave outrage helped start the American Civil Rights Movement."

"You're going to pay respects?"

"I've wanted to do that for a long time. Part of the reason I'm here. The cemetery is Chicago's first African-American."

"When?"

"Tomorrow, it's supposed to be sunny and warm."

The weatherman forgot windy. The passenger seat had maps, camera and a yellow legal pad for remembering. Elvin was confused, passing by a guard rail blocking the entrance to Burr-Oak Cemetery. New Jersey common sense dictated staying with the periphery until a new entrance beckoned. A stomach was queasy; strange feelings travelled up and down, cerebral to feet. Truth being, he never felt this way and if a life depended, it might be hard to accurately describe. A hand with five fingers dug into his abdomen, squeezing hard. Throat was scratchy parched; eyes dry and hard to blink. But of course, he was here before but not. Everything was as pictured; feelings of warmth, love, God, reverence and fear. Fear was real, but not deleterious, more about the unknown and it tingled until goose bumps jumped out. Goose bumps were great to have around, especially when a spiritual presence was near. So fast the bumps came, like an all knowing dermatological rescue squad.

Inside the main gate, he stopped and got out of the car. Hands folded on chest, inhaling cautiously, not wanting to disturb what he couldn't see but felt. Cemeteries were as billed, deathly, but something special was here. The next inhale was for extra oxygen, just in case.

"Alex, I'll narrate for you. Strange, but not since you passed have I felt you like this. Now you're sitting next to me." Passenger seat paraphernalia was thrown to the floor.

The crypt of Mamie Till-Mobley, mother of Emmett was just in front. She died last year. Standing near a mother who loses a child that way, he thought about what unbearable pain she endured. Life with Nelson flashed and things he could never imagine, like a world without. How did she live and endure the pain of her son's brutal death?

A soft voice reached her marker. "I never knew you, but respect, admire everything you did. You fought for civil rights and equality. My heart is heavy right now. It really is. I've come a long way for precious moments with you and your son. Maybe the hardest thing I ever had to contemplate is another universe out there, but maybe you and Emmett are together and wouldn't it be perfect, if you never sent him to Mississippi that summer. I know what you said after they did that to Emmett. You wanted the world to see and left his casket open. A brave amazing woman, you were. So, Mamie Till, I wish you love and peace always. I regret never meeting you; the same sorrow in not knowing Dr. King, Humphrey Bogart, Albert Einstein, Ghandi or George Washington. Pain dwells within me about life taken away so soon; it hurts and my fists are clenched, convinced standing here, we're a silly species and I just realized that *silly* means *fucked-up* more than anything else."

Bending down, he touched pink and gray stones semi circled around. Driving slowly, barely moving, looking in the rear view mirror in case anyone behind was losing patience, Elvin hoped to stumble on Dinah Washington's marker.

Finally by Emmett Till, he saw a small, unobtrusive and simple marker with a picture of Emmett, probably underneath an adornment and inappropriate to touch.

"A humble tribute to a life taken away senselessly; a precious life to live and accomplish, feel the warm sun like I'm doing now. To love and hope; it was all taken away because of ignorance and hate. Emmett, I've come a long way to stand here and say I care. Peace and love to you and as I said to your mother, my hope is that you're together, maybe deciding you shouldn't go to Mississippi. I wonder how many come here with spiritual telegrams. You're part of me now."

A tear, waiting since Mamie, finally traveled and disappeared naturally. For twenty minutes, he sat a few feet away, knees to chin, deep in thought, internalizing where he was and how close to spirit. How many Americans even know who Emmett was, much less visit his grave? Happiness wasn't an appropriate emotion, but gratitude was- being grateful to the universe for giving this time with Emmett and Mamie.

The next hour was circling, walking, looking at the wide expanse of grass, trees and markers. Trees bent in the wind, bowing in reverence, respect and sadness. He took a last look, deep breath and whispered, "Goodbye."

Elvin smiled; maybe somehow Emmett heard.

A gardening truck, pulling a flatbed of two driving mowers, parked in front of the Stones'. Jesus Sanchez made Elvin the last stop of the day. Meek hesitancy to come into the house kept him at the front door.

"Grass all over shoes."

"You're like family, come in."

Evie and Nelson slipped into the den.

"Say Mom, what's Dad doing now?"

"He'd like to plant a few trees where the protest signs were."

"Should I ask why?"

"You know Dad these days."

"Jesus, how about four fast growing trees, maybe in a circle?" A yellow legal pad illustrating planting designs, tree names and growth feet per year was on the table.

"How about two Summer Red Maple and two Hybrid Poplar? Fight disease and good if doesn't rain."

"Do they grow fast?"

"Faster than your son."

Two weeks later, the Stones stood near four fledgling trees; Elvin held an old-fashioned watering can.

"Trees are life and give life. They bow in the wind. I think it's a gift all the way around to plant and nurture especially for. . . ."

"Remembering departed loved ones." Evie kissed him.

"Who are you remembering, Dad?"

"Alex and Christine and two others, Emmett Till and his mother, Mamie."

An SUV pulled into the driveway of a center hall colonial. The passenger walked around, opened the trunk, and got into the back seat while the driver pretended immersion in the editorial page of the Washington Post. A weeping willow tree shaded a rusting bench in the middle of the lawn. Patches of flower arrangements scattered about looked wilted and neglected. Near the front, along side the driveway, a large brown boulder was poised to roll away. At boulder top, displayed in white paint, was wording, "From GT 4581 with love."

"Do you think anyone sits there?"

"Bench or boulder?"

"Both."

"Never."

"Why not?"

"Ask the ex-wife."

"What about the boulder? I never noticed the paint job before."

"If you find out what it means, let me know."

"A mysterious man?"

"No shit."

The far right garage door lifted. A mountain bicycle accompanied a biker over to the trunk.

"Les, good morning."

Strangers thought Les looked like Harrison Ford and they constantly annoyed him about it. In restaurants, they excused themselves and asked, "Aren't you him?" For the first time, Les understood the trappings of celebrity. To deflect similarity, he took to the military crew cut look, even entertaining the shaved bald route; it was all that annoying.

"Moore. Phil, we've got perfect June weather today. Throw me the Post. Sixty years ago today, D-Day. A cousin died at Normandy."

"An Offenholt?"

"No, on my mother's side. By the way, any comments on CIA Director Tenet resigning?"

"He said for personal reasons." Moore clicked the seatbelt.

"Too much pressure and intelligence lapses." Les clicked.

A few minutes away from Burke was Wakefield Park, probably the most popular biking spot in Northern Virginia. Les Offenholt told his world, that a routine cardiac assessment a few years ago motivated him to take up biking and get rid of an incompatible first wife at the same time.

"I'm in management Doctor, so it's all work and no play. I'm sure you've seen similar. . . ."

"Too many times, same physical specimen, so take up biking and listen to your physician; it also saves your knees for golden years, if you ever get there."

Still considered novice or whatever inexperienced biker status was, Les and Moore took to what locals called *Creek Trail*, behind softball fields and power lines and the easiest of the biking trails. Both men hung at the same level even after two years of Sunday mornings. Phil preferred walking. Job description for both was hovering around Les.

Always within visual contact, Moore hung back, cutting Les slack and space for eventualities, a term used for opposite sex machinations. For the past two months, a blonde model type, wearing tight aero-dynamics, invariably passed him by or vice versa. At best, they smiled at each other in passing. Sexual dreams gave Les something to look forward to each week.

Today he caught up to the blonde biker and when they were handlebar even, slowed to keep pace. Moore dropped back further, nearly out of visual biking rules range, he humorously thought.

"I was wondering when you were going to stay even with me. It's been a few months of passing the other by. See you next week."

In a burst of acceleration, she was gone. Les decided not to accelerate, savoring a first titillating verbal exchange.

"Melting butter on a frying pan before beaten eggs are scrambled," was Les's description of how she made him feel.

"Sounds like you got the thunderbolt."

"Hey Phil, do you think this is Corleone, Italy and she's Apollonia? Stop quoting that movie. You're dating yourself."

"All these years Dad, you and Uncle Alex came here. I remember when you brought me here for the first time."

"It's not the same, Nelson. Boulders were filled in with concrete. It's easier to walk but Shark River inlet changed. I used to like walking on boulders with the ever present chance to slip beneath a crack and disappear into the world of *Alice in Wonderland*."

"Are you stoned?"

"I'm teasing you. Dad doesn't have to do those things."

"Angels?"

"You bet. How does it feel to be a high school graduate with Rutgers University in the fall?"

"Feels like following in your footsteps. That Fishing Club building is neat. Architecture reminds me of a war movie in the African desert."

Staring at Nelson, watching his eyes take in the universe, a brow rise in exclamation, or squint in comprehension, each moment spent with him was gifted and precious. Martha was prayerfully reminded that he was a good father, right down to bonding with a son on a jetty under God, close to the horizon. A few whispers to Martha also reinforced that it was the right thing marrying Merrie, despite her strong admonitions and tears. According to the universe, if he hadn't, then where would he and Nelson be? Merrie begot Evie and Nelson.

Late June meant fishermen, some seriously working on dinner, and local kids looking for pieces of concrete to throw into the water and piss off the fisherman by scaring dinner away. The whole process became a constant battle for territory. Elvin rambled, "Just like a scene from *Shane* when cattleman battled the ranchers."

Ships skirted the horizon, heading left to right, never going the other way, making him wonder if there was another horizon somewhere for the other direction.

"You have a serious look."

"Nelson, you've reached a point in your life where four years from now you'll be a Rutgers graduate. It's a serious life and career station with no more summers off for the next fifty years, so look at the horizon, life and future; all there for you. One moment you sail even keel in calm seas under sunny skies and another moment, waves thrash and ships can't sail because it's dangerous and rough. Life changes just as quickly, so use every moment. Clench your fists with determination- love life, learn and grow."

Hands squeezed together, smiling at each other.

"Heavy."

"Remember the boy that Oprah had on her show? He's thirteen years old now and an advocate for peace and an amazing poet."

"The kid in a wheelchair?"

"Mattie Stepanek. Oprah did a wonderful thing by bringing him into our lives, making us think, really think and that's why we're here now at the river."

"He died dad?"

"The other day. He loved life, wanted to live, but accepted and made something of everyday, every moment; that's why I'm serious today."

Father and son hugged. A fisherman nearby watched.

An hour into biking, with Moore far back but still within visual, Les Offenholt waved, signaling rest. Late September was too warm; sweating became profuse. Chest pains were dispelled as dehydration. Water was squeezed from a bottle, while the mysterious blonde was looked for. Over the last few months, words went back and forth when their handlebars were even. Each time, she accelerated from sight. Moore thought the scene was similar to *American Graffiti*, when the blonde in the white Thunderbird did the same thing to Richard Dreyfus, Curt, teasing him unmercifully.

The first of two water bottles emptied, Les looking behind at Moore, spotting the blonde passing him and his waving in code. Game plan was to be cool with folded arms, crossed legs, leaning on his bike which was doing the same to a tree.

"It's kind of hot today, mind if I join you?"

Cool worked perfectly, excitement needed containment. "How many months did we pass each other? Maybe I speak for myself, but it was a hard verbal restraint task."

She was much taller than thought which fueled allure. "Almost a year, I think."

"It took us that much time!" For Les, so much was hanging, balancing on every word.

She smiled. "It's called building trust."

Her every word and body language movement was assimilated; he wasn't sure how much of each was left.

"You think this is a trust issue? I guess there is an element of trust to stop and talk to a stranger in the middle of Wakefield Park. I'm Les. It's a pleasure to finally meet you." A shaky hand shot forward.

"I'm Jennifer. Me too. Finally."

"So, Jennifer, do you hop back on your bike and speed away soon."

"Still time before soon."

The mating process took months of hard work to get where he was. This blonde ravishing woman who melted him was completely worth it and so unlike any other. Les quick glimpsed Moore sitting by his bike. She caught the glimpse.

"A friend of yours back there?"

"How do you know?"

"I always see him first then you, but he never keeps up."

"I don't think he wants to keep up."

"Why?"

"We like our space. Biking is our meditative time. If we were riding next to each other, we'd be bullshitting and it's not why we ride."

"What about us?"

"Different."

"Cause it's the sex thing, a single woman and you without a ring."

"You don't miss much. What do you do?"

"Dental hygienist."

"Management here."

"Well Les, time to get back on."

"Can I. . . ?"

"Next time."

She accelerated out of sight.

Moore couldn't wait to catch up, already poised on his bike ready to roll down the path and find out status level to intercourse.

"Is she the stuff dreams are made of?"

"If I get her phone number next time."

Six tourists and guide hiked, snowshoes flattening fresh fallen snow. Everything around Lewis and Clark National Forest, in Montana's Little Belt mountains was covered with white cold. Snowshoes for a Jersey boy were a strange sensation. Elvin couldn't help think what a duck feels and expressed it to guide and group when they started out an hour ago. Fending off questions why a Jersey boy was in Showdown, Montana a few days before Christmas, walking around in rented snowshoes, he still made the group laugh.

"Part of life is to experience. I've got a sign over my desk. *Get to Montana for Christmas, wear snowshoes and stuff a lot of cold air into my lungs.*"

The group choired, "Really?"

"Of course."

"Is Jersey as bad as they joke about?"

The guide, a senior at Montana State, towered over all. Elvin kept thinking, Ricky, a seven footer, almost abominable, was a by product of a hundred percent Montana raised beef; there were proclaiming signs in some restaurants. What if Elvin Stone had been brought up on pure Montana food instead of Jersey off the supermarket shelf things; he might've grown a few extra inches, and played serious basketball? As grateful as he was to God and universe, Elvin had no problem lamenting on what an extra five more inches would've allowed him to do; Rutgers basketball, New York Knicks with headlines that local Jewish boy attracts throngs to Madison Square Garden. Enough times he'd say, "I could've had class. I could've been a contender. I could've been somebody. And credit to Bud Schulberg's screenplay."

"Pardon Ricky, you asked me something. I was day dreaming. Cold air makes me do that."

"About New Jersey."

"It's not that bad. I really think negative publicity is a conspiracy to keep people from Montana away. We've got it all; snowshoes, skiing, New York, Philadelphia, ocean, and mountains. Unfortunately, there are too many people. Eight million of us. Try calling up for pizza delivery on a Saturday night, it's a two week wait."

"Really?"

The notion of a hundred percent pure Montana raised made him smile. Maybe eighty percent would've given the kid a tougher outer skin to deal with eastern strangers on a hike. Sun peeked through clouds. Nature and creation came to mind. Nothing ever seen could compare to the white purity of where he was. Silence was pure. Clouds even seemed a whiter shade of pure. God and universe were thanked for being able to experience.

Showdown was sixty five miles south of Great Falls. Heading down that morning and now back to Wilson's Mansion Bed and Breakfast, Elvin opened the window for cold pure air ingestion.

Look where I am. I did it, really did it! A Jewish guy from New Jersey, far from home and culture, soon a walk under a north star, maybe. Christmas Eve, solemn, holy night, taking me to spirit, hope, peace and love and everything is real, nothing make believe. I'm really here fulfilling. No one could ever understand why I have to be here.

Alex, Christine, thinking of you both. Mom and Dad, you too. Evie and Nelson how I love you both but I'm so alone here.

A deserted roadside produced an animal that ran back into the trees. All he knew was large and four hairy legs. Imagine driving to work on this road everyday with almost no signs of life, remembering years ago, on the Parkway in August that two million other cars headed to the shore, taking five hours to accomplish what thirty minutes in Montana could do.

The bed and breakfast was quaintly rural; everything Elvin expected from remote, lonely, almost top of the world ambience. Yesterday was spent pretending to be Lewis or Clark, exploring in a rented Conestoga SUV with two yellow legal pads on the passenger seat. Maps were sketched from the internet; one guided thirty miles to Power, Montana and St. Anthony's Roman Catholic Church, where he met Father Smith, contacting him weeks back, asking to spend Christmas Eve, explaining about dreams, destiny and fulfillment.

The church was an eye closure of what small town religion should be; a one room school house on a prairie, Michael Landon standing on the porch calling kids home. A white weather beaten steeple stood proud as in pure Americana. The service schedule sign was on the right. Power was a small town. An eight square block area back in Jersey was more densely populated. Father Smith, bespectacled, graying wavy hair, looked like a fast food combo dinner between Bing Crosby, Pat O'Brien and Cary Grant.

"I've been a priest a long time, coming from Minnesota; born, raised and never been down south or anyplace warm, so cold is comfort for me. What I'm doing now, talking with a Jewish man, traveling fifteen hundred miles, wanting to share Midnight Mass, is wonderfully ecumenical and of course never happened before."

"And you've been so gracious. The Pope has been a wonderful spiritual influence for me too and I love the word ecumenical. What time are services, Father?"

"Little before midnight and it's supposed to be snowing, so leave enough time driving up from Great Falls."

Elvin chuckled, "Silly question. It is *Midnight* Mass."

Mrs. Conant walked around her bed and breakfast wearing an apron and head covering. Overly effusive and accommodating types annoyed Elvin; then again this was Montana, and the lady probably always gushed, like a nearby oil well.

"Mr. Stone. . . ."

"Mrs. Conant, please call me Elvin."

"Why don't you try the *Bluegrass Grill* tonight; meat and fish, pretty good food? It's not New Jersey."

"And the fish are from Montana's streams and lakes."

"Actually fresh fish is flown in every day from Hawaii."

"Think I'll do meat, flying fish bother me."

Christmas Eve day brought sentimental visuals of the past; Uncle George and Aunt Witch, Alex, Christine, Adel and Sura, St. Leo's, the choir at Maple Avenue School in Newark walking around, singing, *Feast of Stephen, snow laying round about.* Laying snow and Christmas in the fifties was different. Snow was always deeper, maybe perceptual, but he was half size and a foot of snow reaches different body parts. Then again, global warming holds down snow depth accumulation. A sweater, tie and shirt were adjusted in a mirror. When he left Power yesterday, Elvin turned and Father Smith yelled, "Come as you are." Two days in a row at the *Bluegrass Grill* made entry on the yellow pad, because it's safe and already proven the night before. One hundred percent Montana raised beef was spectacular, though he was slightly curious about the fish and what they did with it, bringing it from so far. Beef eating days for Elvin could be winding down. The world loves beef. Five hundred million plus cows in one Asian country alone, leave behind a lot of methane which stops carbon dioxide from escaping, so even holy and innocent fast food outlets help heat earth up. Then again, diet change could be moot. Elvin was on a thought roller coaster. Sofia used to talk about the Italian tradition of fish on Christmas Eve. He remembered to e-mail Sofia, Merry Holiday greetings from Mrs. Conant's kitchen table.

Ten thirty, light snow started falling and the local radio played Christmas Carols. Pavarotti just finished Elvin's favorite, *Adeste Fideles.* No one knew, but he made a CD for himself; all twenty four songs were *Adeste Fideles*; theory being, if you like something in life, then really like it and enjoy. Why does the best part of a song and melody last a few seconds? Maybe it's the same principle as an orgasm's just a couple of seconds. Best feelings, best friends are gone too quick. Why couldn't an orgasm last an hour, which was a good point for a universe suggestion box?

Dear God. How amazing is all of this. Snow. Christmas Eve. Small church. How I hope, pray and wonder and I'd go anywhere, climb any mountain, if only. If only. If fucking only.

Elvin drove around Power, a few square blocks, parking at 11:11 p.m., down the road from the church, leaving a short walk in falling snow, which is exactly what he dreamed. A few people were about; some called out, *Merry Christmas*. Images of a post card came to mind; Currier and Ives and the last scene when Tiny Tim was hugged by Uncle Scrooge, Alistair Sim who was the only movie Scrooge that Elvin cared about, ranking just below Stan and Ollie for holiday memories.

Since the church was small, he sat in the last row, not wanting to take a good seat away from regular parishioners. Father Smith nodded warmly. Sixty people prayed. Silent Night was poignant. Elvin sang along thanks to Simon and Garfunkel's, *Seven P.M. News*. People noticed when he didn't cross or kneel. Father Smith briefly introduced. Drifting was realization of where and what an accomplishment. He did feel spirit and Alex and gratitude to have been conceived and born into a wonderful Garden of Eden, and paradise soon lost.

After the service, many thanked his effort of being there. Several invitations for food and drink followed. Elvin wanted some time to walk around Power and maybe find the elusive North Star. Snow stopped falling; stars became holiday decorations.

A couple waited at their open front door. Many from the congregation were inside. Small pieces of a foodstuff with toothpicks piercing what looked like a cooked organ was served by an official looking waiter. Life was a circle. Bottles of wine, brandy and beer were put on the dining room table. Muscatel was mysteriously right there on purpose, label facing front, so there was no synchronistic doubt.

A speech surged from an overjoyed soul. Elvin raised his voice. "You've made me feel so at home, welcome, comfortable. It's Christmas and Jersey is far away. I'm Jewish, but a long time ago, the image of spending Christmas Eve here came to me. I never knew about Power so it's entirely magical. There's not enough time to delve into spiritual stories. Thank you all. Merry Christmas and Happy New Year. Oh, who put this Muscatel wine here? Salud."

More toothpicks piercing and holding mysterious foods together were served. An old piano in the living room played Christmas Carols and when the *Feast of Stephen* was sung, he drifted back to Maple Avenue School in a snow storm. A head felt explosive, no doubt from all the sensual input and Muscatel wine. Eyes blinked, head bobbed and nodded, sitting in a corner, alone on a chair probably born in a local garage workshop.

"Are you alright?"

Startled up, he saw the same woman who was shyly eyeing him before, in a scene like high school study hall. She was Haight-Ashbury hippie looking, long red hair, bespectacled, beautiful and concerned about his health.

"Actually, I'm more than alright. Sometimes I drift off, especially when fulfilled dreams all gang up on me at the same time." They shook hands. "Elvin Stone. Merry Christmas."

"Rebecca Little. If you're dizzy from the burning incense and multiple glasses of Muscatel, there's a North Star and others outside for cold revival air and deep breathing. Maybe a walk is just what the doctor ordered, although I'm a pediatrician. I don't know if this changes anything, but I put the Muscatel in front of you."

Too many coincidences with deep breaths and Muscatel haunted him, so it only took seconds to be lured outside. The North Star has been on his mind for forty years since Christmas Eve with Aunt Witch and Uncle George and finding that special girl.

"Lead the way Doctor. I'm a compliant patient."

Biting cold, near the top of the world, no wind, starry skies, a beautiful doctor holding his hand while they walked around Power, all conspired to induce deep drifting.

"Are you sure you're alright?"

"Sorry, this is all amazing, what's happening, so I drift, daydream. Sometimes it's a defense mechanism."

"For me too, it is all amazing. A perfect Christmas Eve. Snow. Friends. Church. A mysterious Jewish stranger. Remember the holiday, so it's easy to figure why I found you enchanting and why we're walking."

"My grandmother was a Rebecca. You're my second one."

As they passed last vestiges of Power; a Cape house, shutters, a pick up truck with prominent gun rack like in *Easy Rider* and a small snowman with Cobb pipe, they found themselves holding hands.

"How long are you in Montana for?"

"Two more days. Been to Showdown and hiked with snowshoes. Most importantly, what I'll come away with and take back to Jersey is how a duck feels walking."

"May I ask, why'd you do this trip? It's certainly not conventional."

"If I only knew. Energy, spirit or something leading me beside still waters. I'm a regular all around guy; no fanaticism, no nothing, except respect for the universe and things meant to be. Maybe it's the wine talking; then again I'm here, aren't I? So everything is real."

Stopping forward progress by holding his hand, she took a deep breath, melding both their exhaled vapors.

"It's too cold to walk anymore. People do get frostbite up here. My husband died in a small plane crash in Alaska two years ago. No children. No more husbands. You have a wedding ring. There is something deep and charming yet there's sadness in you. I'm not in the habit of making speeches like this. There's not a lot of time. I heard you say Wilson's Bed and Breakfast. I know Mrs. Conant; her kids were patients. I live twenty minutes from Great Falls and. . . ."

"I'll follow you home. Don't lose me or you will lose me."

Back in Jersey, a long drive from the road to a house meant estate, but in Montana, it was routine. Rebecca's ranch seemed a mile off the road, with rolling hills in the background; a barn and silo nearby and no neighbors.

"Let me get a fire started."

"Was this a working ranch?"

"More of a dilettante ranch. My husband dabbled out of boredom. He came into a lot of money and so did I."

"How'd the crash happen?"

"He was heading up for a week of fishing. No radio contact. The plane just went down. His best friend died too."

"I'm sorry. I know about losses like that."

A fire crackled and lit the room. Rebecca turned and threw arms around Elvin.

"Why is it, you grow up to adult status, live in New Jersey, but nothing close to this ever happens especially meeting you. Now I'm in a ranch on top of the world staring at a beautiful woman. Your eyes could seduce whatever they gaze at. Do you know that?"

"Ground rules before you take me to bed. I won't ask anything personal about your life back home and we'll never talk, write, email or communicate ever again once you leave."

After a business handshake, they kissed.

Imagination runs wild when you're not sure who and where you are. There was a four poster bed, layers of fluffy blankets, perhaps inspired by Louisa May Alcott or J.D. Salinger. A mind was firing, thinking irrelevant things, like what the hell was he doing. He never saw a driver's license or medical school diploma and what if, he'd be lost forever, with no trace, except for snowshoe footprints in Showdown. Perfect form nudity makes one forget about licenses and other things.

The sun was coming up. Rebecca stood with a breakfast tray, coffee, juice and of all things, toasted bagels.

"We're so alike- same breakfast preferences but I'm surprised you have bagels here."

"You'd be real surprised about Montana, if you ease up on the stereotypes."

After an hour for digestion, they went back to passion. Elvin thought Belmar, and how Martha always cautioned about jumping back in the water after eating. When he was five years old, Martha used to tie him to the garage while she cleaned. Even then, he was a freedom fighter, got untied and walked around the block, got on a bus because the women waiting thought he was the other's kid. Cops found him at Newark's Penn Station about to board a train to New York. Now he was in Montana, about to re-board a beautiful woman, at her request.

"Did you ever snow mobile?"

Laughing at her random question, he chuckled, "Never did anything in the snow except shovel."

"There are two in the barn and three inches of snow. Why don't you think about all your sexual fantasies? Things you'd like to try. Places on my body you'd like to explore. We'll never see each other again after tomorrow and you're a wonderful lover. If both of us fulfill deep fantasies tonight, it'll fuel visual memory for the rest of time. Think about it, but not on the snow mobile."

All Elvin thought about for nearly a thousand air miles was precisely what Rebecca said he would and it wasn't going away. Drifting made it visual, and there was no escaping. How does a woman living in the middle of nowhere come up with all that? Saying goodbye, they kissed, thanked each other, said Happy New Year, and she told him, that last night had been for him alone and those things never happened to her before and never would again.

A flight attendant asked for his drink order.

"By any chance do you have Muscatel wine?"

"Excuse me, what kind of wine?"

"Never mind."

TWENTY THREE

Building shadows, filtered sunlight through high clouds and late February afternoon dulled Elvin's visual acuity, sitting on the steps of Geology Hall. Was Nelson waving from a distance? The main gate was too far. Two students excused themselves walking out of the Geology building. Elvin heard their after thought. "What the hell is he doing, sitting, blocking steps in the middle of winter."

It was Nelson. Seeing Elvin, he jogged into a father and son hug.

"Dad, aren't you cold sitting like that, its freezing."

"You're the third person in the past two minutes to address my step sitting."

"Where we eating?"

"Behind the student center, our favorite place, The *Olive Branch*. Being an old timer, walking in, hanging with college kids, there's an instant rush of youth. Maybe it's healthy, opens arteries up and makes you feel alive."

"Opens arteries up? Silly, Dad."

"No, I'm serious Dad."

College Avenue had pockets of students, some at bus stops, others hovering at Grease food trucks. Walking by Brower Commons and the Military ROTC building, Elvin pointed. "Uncle Alex had a meeting there once, around the back. A mathematics professor had an office there. When you get a chance, check out Professor Josef Simmons for me on the internet."

"When you're step sitting, what do you think about?"

Two Rutgers buses lumbered by. Elvin's eyes followed them until gone. "Life and if only I could go back in time, back to the future or back to yesterday."

"That's silly."

A hand rested on Nelson's shoulder, followed by a squeeze, which meant affirmation of love. "I think about what I'd change, do things different. Use time better. Take advantage of every gifted moment. I wish more people thought about changing things and paying attention to global warming and hugging a child everyday."

"Is that a ramble?"

"Maybe. We're a silly species, Nelson. So much opportunity at our finger tips; promise, hope, chances to make life better for everyone but we never learn. Asking God to keep forgiving us because we don't know what we're doing has been going on since that couple messed around with forbidden fruit. Everyday there's terrorists, murders, starvation, bombs and companies killing Americans just to maintain profit."

"Like what you did on our lawn?"

"Exactly. Just once, I'd love to hear a company admit there could be a problem and work with authorities instead of trying to keep a deadly product on the market. Do you think cigarette companies would ever stop by their own choice? Nobody gives a shit. Humans are a cheap renewable resource with too many of us walking around."

"Why so serious, because of Alex and Christine?"

"Partly and I'm going to be sixty which means responsibility to the next generation coming up."

"Who said that?"

"Me."

They sat in a wooden booth, generations of names carved, including a "Nelson and Elvin." A dozen televisions showcased college basketball.

Watching the rise and fall of his father's diaphragm, he exclaimed, "You're sucking in a lot of air?"

"Thinking about far away places."

"Which ones?"

"Guadalcanal, an obscure island in the Pacific and important battleground during WWII; our first offensive action in Pacific."

"That's a lead into the nightly news. When are you going?"

"Soon."

"Are you taking Mom this time?"

"She said no already."

"Why there? Is it because of Uncle Alex?"

"I need to pay respects to Americans who died for us. I'll take my yellow pad along, and yes, partly Uncle Alex."

"You're going to journalize things."

"Partly."

"Do you cry at graves?"

"I've been known to."

Laying in bed, restless and glancing at a clock radio face at 4:44 a.m., Elvin thought about the *Olive Branch* and Nelson's sensitivity which was a miracle of heredity and environment. Nelson's question about crying at graves and knowing a father was sucking in a lot of air was comforting, that a young son has the sensitivity to think and observe. It comforted him back to sleep.

Elvin sat on the porch step, palms supporting face, neck tilted to a quarter moon, remindful of the serenity and peace of Islam and seeing Aarif the other day. Their growing friendship was bound tightly by memories of Alex. Apprehension always simmered with upcoming long jet flights especially to Los Angeles and eventually Guadalcanal. Like Alex, he wasn't a big fan of air travel, in part, because you defer control to a pilot instead of making a sharp turn yourself to avoid oncoming traffic. Was the Pacific as far away as he'd ever go? Europe sat on the other side of the Atlantic, filled with precious world history, but somehow the continent didn't beckon him like North America. For whatever reason, he was especially nervous this time about being away from Evie and Nelson. Ironically, they did most of the insisting that he go and fulfill. Cousin Steven in California was thrilled when Elvin called to say, *Guess who's coming to dinner* and Steven answering, "Sidney Poitier."

A group hug with Evie and Nelson in front of Continental Airlines terminal was cut short by airport police. First class was a by-product of Alex's money from the Princeton house sale. Muscatel was not to be had on the plane. A mind was firing images of growing up, making decisions, mostly feeling some unknown force was directing. A seatmate slept, occasionally expelling a snore.

Elvin stared at the flight attendant; pretty, effervescent, accommodating and not much older than Nelson. When you think you recognize someone, and time is finite and knowing you'd always regret not pursuing, Elvin pressed the assistance button.

"May I help you?" She leaned down, exposing a name tag, Elaine.

"This isn't urgent, so if you have a passenger who needs oxygen from the overhead, please tend and come back when you're free."

"I'm still leaning."

"Well Elaine, I don't know how to ask, so I will. I've been watching you, nothing devious, so don't worry and it's probably something you've never heard before. I can't explain all the spirituality surrounding me and why I have to ask, but do you have a mother originally from New Jersey, maiden name Cathy Cassel? We were in sixth grade together, a long time ago and of course, you're exactly what I remember of her."

Gentle laughter lifted her out of a lean, into upright status. "Not ever in my flying career; this was a first, you're right. My mother's from Iowa and you're funny. Something tells me there's a wonderful story behind that question. I think someone does need oxygen but I'm just kidding. Perhaps after dinner over Arizona, come up front and tell me more."

Cathy Cassel and Elvin Stone sat next to each other in Mrs. Bornstein's sixth grade class at Maple Avenue School. The prettiest girl in the school and everybody knew it, was sitting so close to him and if he only knew what to do. Talking would've been good. Even in sixth grade, little boys nonchalantly managed to steal looks. If Cathy could only feel the same way about him but that was impossible in the state of his world and he wasn't too young to know about things out of reach. She was a number one dream. Number two lived a few blocks away and for years, Elvin walked by her house on the way to the Osborne Terrace library, hoping just once, after checking out and reading all those unnecessary books that she'd walk out of the house and know he was alive. One day at the end of class, Cathy handed Elvin a note and told him to keep it secret.

Walking home, alone, crossing Lyons Avenue by the Beth Israel Hospital, and at the ledge by the morgue window, with terrible deathly smells, Elvin read the note. Cathy was in love with him and thought he was the cutest boy in school. Did he have the same feelings about her? The bottom of the note was filled with a few drawn kisses. Martha and Jack would never understand; therefore no problem keeping it a secret. Sixth graders of all generations have flowering feelings of parental estrangement; maybe it's chromosomal. An underpants draw was a good place to hide things because there's always a pair or two left. Martha was laundry efficient.

The following morning before school, Martha found the note. She yelled about why the note was hidden and who's Cathy? She couldn't be the kind of girl that Martha wanted for her son, besides there's plenty of time for girls and he'd better ignore her. Something must be wrong with both of them for hiding/ writing a love letter and not coming to parents first. Martha kept it to show Jack and maybe the mustached principal, Mr. Townsend. Before discovery, it was Elvin's brief certificate of existence, value and instant credibility in the world of Newark's young Jewish social hierarchy. Cathy loved *him*. He was finally somebody after six long years of grammar school. Martha made him swear not to bother with Cathy. A week later, he saw her hand a note to Larry, the tallest boy in class. Elvin never saw the note again. When Martha died, he still looked amidst papers, old photos and in a small pocket prayer book from World War II, inscribed: *To George. God Bless always. Your sister, Martha.*

Smiling at the vast blue sky out the window, Elvin was content, hands folded in lap. A seatmate was still sleeping. Sitting at a jet window, he realized what a lengthy, multi-decade recovery from an inexperienced and first time mother's handling of a little boy's first love and squashing of any existing self confidence. Did his constant fucking-and that's all it was-of a beautiful, worldly, unattainable, blonde Sofia, finally free him from little boy, growing up demons?

"Two beers, two open turkey with gravy and pick any two potato sides for us."

A waiter slid a pen behind an ear.

"Forty-two years ago, Steven; seems like a couple of yesterdays."

Both cousins knew only one lunch option existed, *Pando and Ernest,* though not for six potato sides.

Steven probed. "How much retracing steps do you want over the next few days?"

"Some. Tell me about Carol. I still remember. So Pacino comes here?"

Steven initiated beer glasses clicking. "Carol never made movies, moved to San Diego twenty years ago. Burning question for you and I'd never e-mail or phone, but had to look into your eyes; did you open the bottle of Vichy Water yet?"

"Nah."

"Tomorrow we'll go to Van Nuys Airport. Pacino sits at table twenty eight over there. Hemingway, F. Scott, Chandler, Faulkner all drank here. I'm sorry about Alex. It upset me for a long time."

They sat in a black Lexus, windows down. Bogart shot German Major Strasser somewhere near them. For the first time, Elvin expressed sympathy towards Conrad Veidt, the actor who cast himself into nefarious history by superbly playing that role. If Elvin met Conrad a hundred times since 1942, he'd still look at the actor as a Nazi who spoke English well, and wouldn't have been thrilled if he moved next door in Marlboro. That's how good an actor he was.

"Nothing here reminds me of Casablanca. It's too California. Bogart was right around here for the scene when Strasser got shot. *Louis, I think this is the beginning of a beautiful friendship.* It was said right near here. Let's walk around." A chest went in and out, comically sucking in as much air as he could. "Maybe I'll catch a particle that Bogart breathed."

"I said you were screwed up forty years ago."

Heads tilted up, plane after plane buzzing, landing, taking off.

"It's a busy airport!"

"Van Nuys is the busiest general aviation airport in world."

Back in the car, Elvin pressed face on the window as they left the grounds, thinking about journeys and goals. Hard to admit, but something was lost since they filmed the movie in 1942 to now. Rambling, he thought it was like seeing a dull knife not being able to cut a banana. Was it aging, emotion, or the hour glass borrowed from the *Wizard of Oz*, quickly losing grains of sand?

"All these years I thought about standing at Casablanca airport and I just did. Part of me feels empty. Going home is hard."

Steven patted his back. "The word is fulfillment. Look at me, retired from medicine three years ago, read, go to theater, still live in the same house for thirty years, play tennis twice a week, got a wife who still knows how. For you, it's a youthful attitude, still manifesting itself and it's powerful, because it's better than taking age defying antioxidants. Think about what you do. How many of any generation pick themselves up and fly to Guadalcanal or any historic military battle place to pay respects to fallen soldiers or run around the country trying to capture molecules of air from expired role models? Don't despair cousin. Don't feel empty. It's kept youth stuck inside."

Two days later at the airport, before getting chased away by airport police, Elvin thanked cousin Steven and issued a standing Thanksgiving invitation to come east, see leaves turn color, fresh cider stands, a parade where you have to wear a coat, watch *March of the Wooden Soldiers* live on Channel 11, and be together with his East coast family.

"Watch *March of the Wooden Soldiers* live?"

"Live is anything not on tape. It's better live."

"Is it?"

Two hours into flight, Elvin tilted his neck at the window, trying to get face perpendicular; an unusual position for a flight attendant to remain silent about.

"Is everything alright sir? It's almost as if you see something on top of the fuselage."

"Everything's fine, my friend was an astronomer and since we're 35,000 feet up, I wanted a closer look at things."

Seatbelt was undone, propping himself to pull a folded wrinkled paper out of a front pocket.

"Dear Elvin. I'm breaking silence. Had to. Your Guadalcanal invitation touched me. You've touched me. Not a day goes by. You know what I'm saying. Life is complicated, so not now. I know you'll find places to go and invitations to send. I'm going to say love and goodbye. Just those two words. Something. Special. Magic. You'll understand. Always. Sofia."

Words were barely visible; repeated folding, sliding back and forth, dulls printed material. The paper was ripped, a right fist squeezed tightly and remnants were dropped into an emesis bag. Emesis was a neat word, sounding softer with fewer convulsions and heaving.

Strange, wonderful feelings helped close eyes, killing time over the Pacific on a bastardly long flight. Elvin's been to Guadalcanal before thanks to Sedona side effects. This whole flight happened before. Passengers were scattered around the fuselage. He saw all this before, but not. A black man, across the aisle, by himself, sleeping, helped him drift back to New Brunswick a few months ago. Peace on earth exists more now than ever before; he was settling into that notion. Humming of tired jet engines eased him into memories.

Alexander Library on College Avenue, in the heart of Rutgers, had book stacks beneath the surface and quiet places to talk, almost like Rutgers Newark, decades ago. When an email arrived from Peter Simmons, son of the mysterious mathematician Josef, suggesting they get together finally, perhaps when Peter guest lectures on campus, Elvin was thrilled.

College dinner hour meant solitude in places of research. A few misplaced books and a Targum, the Rutgers college paper, were scattered on a small table.

Jeans and sweater met Peter's suit and tie in a warm show of greetings. Peter, a lawyer and professor at Rutgers Law School, met Elvin once, a few days before Nolan died. Not quite as tall as Elvin, graying wavy hair and an exaggerated handlebar moustache, he looked nothing like his father, as Elvin remembered.

Peter was loosening a tie, hands shaking noticeably. "Thanks for coming on short notice. Synchronicity brings us together. Alex and my father were close in later years, sharing goals and visions of the world. Then Alex was involved with my uncle John, who's gone now too. Uncle John saw the universe in a special way. So did Alex, as you know. Their time together was precious and heavy like metal. Words fired around me about concepts far above us civilians. A few times, I joined them, but it was over my head. Alex spoke about you incessantly. The bond between you two was as special as the gifts they possessed."

"Alex told me briefly about Josef and the universe, life and death. When he was telling me, we were both sipping wine. Alex gets hysterical laughing. So I asked, what's so funny." He said, "There's nothing more to worry about." And I said, "Define." He said, "We'll need a year, no showering, cots set up, no budging from the room."

"So I laughed and said never mind."

Almost a staring contest, they leaned on elbows, close to each other.

"No, this isn't a journey to understanding departed. My Uncle John was African-American, long story, not now. He had a son, my first cousin, Brandon, also a lawyer, who'd like to meet you, continuing a special journey begun by loved ones, not with us now, but out there, beyond comprehension. If you like, how about joining us for dinner next week? I live in Maplewood. See the synchronicity?"

"I'd like and I do."

The Maplewood train station was crowded. Late afternoon passengers were arriving and waiting. One seat was vacant on the bench. Elvin pretended going to New York, sitting, dreaming. Two trains came and left without him. Bench personnel changed twice. A few whispers, *Alex,* snuck out, but nobody heard. For a brief moment, he was alone. The sign was pushed, still squeaky. A Maple leaf, recovered from the tracks was held by the stem and left on the passenger seat, next to a yellow legal pad. Peter lived two blocks from his old house on Elberta Road and when Maplewood was mentioned, he knew about visiting the station before dinner; like an aperitif, warming his inner soul.

A woman, who looked too much like Rebecca Little for comfort, prompting a flash of guilt and thoughts about universal retribution, answered the strange musical sounding doorbell. "It's from Nessun Dorma. Welcome Elvin, Laurel Simmons."

"Turandot. A favorite. I feel at home already. A friend used to listen all the time."

Walking briskly from the living room, a tall black man, approached and stopped, allowing seconds and eternity, to symbolically tell each other, this was a special meeting, ordained and meant to be. Souls were about to be linked for a long ride together, and their smiles, leading into a hug, sealed fate and vehicle.

"Elvin."

"Brandon."

"Why do I feel like we've been doing this for thirty years?"

"Heritage. Magic. Loved ones. Spirit. Universe."

Dinner was pretend Thanksgiving; turkey, stuffing, trappings and cranberry sauce. Laurel explained that Alex spoke about affinity for the holiday and they wanted this to be a comfortable night, touching Elvin's soul and making him miss a friend even more. Later Elvin held a glass of Grappa, telling Brandon about his new life and mission. Brandon proceeded to his mission.

"Rutgers Law trained me well. Newark inculcated feelings of poor and disenfranchised. I heard about what you did on your lawn, castigating companies and fighting for the environment. That's part of the reason I wanted to meet; your extreme sensitivity. From Alex, I knew about your life long involvement speaking out against racism, hearing Dr. King talk and I was so moved at dinner, to hear about your visit to Emmett Till's grave, which segues to us perfectly. A few decades ago there were three hundred thousand people in American prisons. Now, there's about two million, three hundred thousand. Many are of color and poor. America loves to throw people in jail, even thirteen and fourteen year olds, who the courts say are adults. Imagine throwing a thirteen year old in prison for life. If there are over two million in prison now, what are the statistical odds enough of them are innocent, on death row, going to die for something they never did, but are too poor for legal counsel? Maybe it's better to be rich and guilty then poor and innocent?" Brandon walked over to the dining room table and brought back Italian Grappa and filled Peter and Elvin's glass.

"Next time Peter, Brandon, try Averna, a Sicilian drink. Brandon, this is all haunting."

"Well, I love to light fires. You love fires. There's so much injustice and so few people know what's going on. Did you know that there's no right to counsel in America after a case is tried and appealed in the initial court? Most people on death row can't afford counsel. America is the only country known to condemn young teens to imprisonment until death. Elvin, why not make signs for your lawn about equal justice? You've got an audience now. All kinds of people education helps the cause."

A lifetime of thoroughly enjoying and needing hugs, Elvin knew Brandon's and his, closing a special night, would last forever. After the hug, looking into eyes, they said how much they liked each other, as brothers in a crazy world, and probably would never see each other again, and they knew why and it was alright.

The announcement finally came about trays and seats. Guadalcanal was closer. A seatmate still slept. Elvin looked to see if his diaphragm was active.

Frederick Mar waited by baggage at Honiara Airport, Guadalcanal, Solomon Islands, with a sign, *Elvin Stone Welkam*.

Walking around in circles literally, Elvin couldn't take in enough sights, after all, he was on the other side of the world, near where they made *South Pacific*, feeling like world problems and his didn't apply here.

Innate sense made two men smile at each other. "The *Welkam* threw me off. I thought it was someone's last name; then again how many Elvin's pass through here. You must be Frederick." Being wired, hands shaking, far from home, Elvin apologized for not paying attention.

"Long flight, welcome, that's the English version. Let's get you to the hotel; we'll start fresh tomorrow."

Japanese cars flooded the roadways. So did a tropical rain, giving way to peeks of sun. Central Market Honiara was crowded with fruit and vegetable displays and other food stuffs. Frederick was a perfect guide; a friend from Rutgers History department recommended him.

"Natives are called Malaitans, originally from a nearby island. In 1999 there was violence between Gwale and them. Malaitans forced from remote parts of island to here in Honiara then Gwale left here."

"What about the island itself?"

"Mountainous. We're on north coast, south very rainy. More than what you already saw."

The car pulled over, windows manually opened. People congregated on the sidewalk, talking, gesturing a few feet away.

"Make anything out?"

"Of course not, what is it?"

"Melanesian language, Pidgin."

"Your English is perfect, Frederick. Funny, my image of Guadalcanal is confused; such a turning point of the war, Americans stopping the Japanese here and so many died. I expected something more American; maybe even Americans settling here. It's so beautiful with real jungle all around. This place haunts me.

Believe it or not, I saw a movie and that's why I'm here. I know that very few Americans come here to thank the brave soldiers who died for them."

"Few Americans come. This is not Club Med. What you hear in my accent is Pacific Islands, Australia, Hawaii, a few years in California; meshed together language with no homeland really. Maybe I'm like you, trying to find something. You are special to come here. Maybe by end of week, I'll understand why. You'll surely ask, so I'll tell you now. My father was Japanese and mother is many things."

Elvin asked to stay a little longer. "The people outside my window; I've got a feeling no one really knows what happened here a long time ago, meaning the war and ultimate sacrifices made."

"People might talk about when yellow fought white but it doesn't concern them."

The King Solomon Hotel had thatched roof, lush gardens, and small lobby with composition floor, scattered cane chairs and pastel sofas. Loving tropical air, his pulmonary collection process began in earnest.

"Rest up for tomorrow."

Elvin circled the hotel lobby, pinching a left arm, realizing where he was and why, whispering *thank you*, looking beyond the ceiling, and randomly digesting a passing thought of Brandon Simmons, wondering why it was there.

Intense tropical blue skies amazed because he always felt skies over Jersey were rubbed out, old and worn from all the planes flying over from Newark, Kennedy, LaGuardia and Philadelphia. A few years back, around eleven p.m., on a garbage-out night, he counted thirteen planes overhead. Waiting until it was safe before closing the garage door, he seriously thought about making an emergency phone call to the FAA.

An old Volvo, with four coats of paint, judging by a naked rear side, weaved erratically in and out of traffic. Frederick's response to Elvin's island emission control question was sarcastic laughter.

"Where are we?"

"Edson's Bloody Ridge. In September 1942, Japanese, led by General Kawaguchi attacked Americans on Hill One and here too. Marine and parachute troops led by Colonel Edson held. Battle here was maybe the most important."

"Be back in a minute."

Looking down a dirt path, everything was green, like nature was caring enough to make signs of war disappear completely. Gazing at the sun, Elvin said, "God bless you brave Americans, everything you did. I'd love spirits to know, that's why I'm here. You guys at Edson's, God bless, always."

Until composed, he looked away from Frederick. An emotional moment needed healing time, feeling strangely, like he was back in that bathtub with a cutter at his wrist.

A most perfect island because the word *island* means by itself, standing alone, separated on all sides, Guadalcanal was so far from everything. He relished being alone, standing on embattled soil and grass, sending spiritual waves to departed soldiers. Stomach muscles tightened and chest hurt from deep inhaling.

After parking again, Frederick stated, "I know you're from New Jersey!"

"Is there anyplace else?"

Mar was worldly enough to laugh at Elvin's response, which impressed that Jersey's reputation was so far reaching.

"Follow me."

Tropical breezes kicked up; a warm breeze slapped his unshaven face, making it feel less itchy. Elvin decided not to shave for the week- a sign of respect.

"John Basilone earned his medal of honor here."

"Wasn't he from Jersey?"

"You know your history. He served in the Phillipines, was called *Manila John* and was honorably discharged in 1937. War was coming and he felt it, so he re-enlisted in the Marines, think in 1940. Right here Elvin, in October 1942, Basilone was in charge of machine guns. He defended a narrow pass to Henderson Airfield. Outnumbered by Japs, but he held and got the Medal of Honor and was sent home a hero but had to come back to fight and at Iwo Jima much later, that amazing man died."

"I'll be back."

Frederick smiled watching Elvin walk down a path. From a distance, he saw him sit and stare at the sun or sky or something else up there.

Drifting deeply, a myriad of synapses firing, every past relative remembered as well as obscure, ridiculous things that meant nothing or something. Newark was getting a heavy snowstorm. He was across the street from Decker's Candy Store, throwing snowballs at passing cars, challenging Alex to watch his accuracy. A crowded Public Service bus pulled up. A monster snow ball was tossed at a passenger window but the door opened and Elvin's aim misfired right into the bus driver's head, who immediately chased right after him, leaving an idling bus.

More fear than ever felt before propelled him down Clinton Place but he was losing ground. A quick evasive left turn down an alley, but the driver, as big as Boris Karloff in costume, was closing in. Fear became panic. Like a scene from a movie, Elvin approached a dead end. An only escape was a tall fence with semi-barbed wire. A quick look behind and the driver was almost at him, now beginning to lunge and reach out.

"God, please help me", he yelled, so even the menacing bus driver would hear his divine enlistment and perhaps have second thoughts.

Not ever again could it happen. Elvin sailed head first like an Olympian high jumper over the fence, landing in a snow drift. The driver stopped at the unapproachable fence. Elvin looked at him, still stuck in snow, knowing he was safe, so a middle finger was emphatically pumped a few times.

"May I?"

A few seconds passed before leaving the snows of Newark and returning to Guadalcanal. A beautiful blonde woman, green eyes, wearing a strange hat, almost what a flapper wore in the 1920's was standing next.

"Pardon."

"May I sit down?"

"Sure. Pull up a piece of grass. Do you speak English?"

"Thank you. I do. I've been watching you for a few minutes. You were quite engrossed, thinking, if that's what you were doing?"

"I am a thinker. I think it gets me in trouble sometimes."

She sat down; a hiked skirt revealed long thin perfect legs. Elvin concentrated on her face.

She spoke much too softly to hear clearly. "Who are you here for?"

"Every soldier who died here."

"What do you mean?"

He sighed. An appropriate answer was too daunting and involved with no time or energy to attempt explanation but he tried. "It's to pay respects to all who died here, even Japanese, after all, we drive their cars. Is there someone here for you too? Are you from Guadalcanal? You can't be. Forgive me if I stare. It's old, but you look familiar."

"A distant relative of mine is here. I'm Dutch." She sighed as Elvin did ostensibly for the same reasons.

"I keep staring at your face. Please don't think. . . ."

"It's alright. For these parts, it's not a common face."

"Dutch. You're even further from home than me."

"East coast?"

"How do you know?"

"Just do."

"You are familiar. It just hit me. Two months ago, I went to a cousin's ninety-fifth birthday party. I've only seen Hildy once the last twenty years. She's completely with it, meaning sharp as anything. There was this blown up picture of her from the 1930's in the lobby; she's a beautiful blonde curly haired woman. It's exactly you. I'm sorry for going off. Forgive me."

She stood up. "It's late."

"It is."

Elvin let her walk a few steps ahead. Frederick waited by the car.

"Nice talking to you."

"Likewise."

A man sat in the passenger seat, she drove. Elvin watched frozen-like as the car pulled away. The license plate caught his attention, as goose bumps covered both arms. *444.*

A quick look to the sky before speaking. "Let's go Frederick." *Angelic intervention* made the yellow legal pad with an exclamation mark.

The following day was another head raised to sun and sky day. Frederick sat on a rock while Elvin stood in front of U.S. Memorial on Hill Seventy Three, overlooking the Matanikau River.

Three days to get here so I'm going to stand for a long time. I told Frederick to get comfortable and be patient. To all you precious spirits, Thank you and God bless.

Standing at attention, looking around, he felt like a soldier guarding the Tomb of the Unknown Soldier. All the soldiers on the Island were unknown to him; strangers yet kindred spirit. That night they dined at a Yacht Club. Elvin never asked what menu items were but only if they were cooked the old fashioned way, stove or toaster oven.

On the last full day, Frederick arranged for a boat trip across Iron Bottom Sound, around twenty miles, to Tulagi. Every few nautical miles, he whispered, "Tulagi." It was probably from a past but he couldn't place. Skin tickled when he whispered the name. Maybe it was Sedona, making him think about Tulagi. Could he have died or fought there? Just a little juggling of stacked-up universes and he'd been born in the twenties and maybe? Looking at pastel Pacific and blue sky, he drifted to Mr. Roberts, Henry Fonda. Even though the movie was made years after the war, it had the same poignancy as the war itself. An old movie was bittersweet like real war, with memories, people, actors and times long gone, never coming back or could they?

Several military landing spots were visited. On a beach with gentle waves, Elvin excused himself and played with sand, collecting and letting it slowly slip through fingers. Eyes closed, wondering what it was really like to have been here, landing in gunfire, maybe imminent death or death itself and taking that last breath, calling out for mother, father or God.

He whispered, "Thanks guys. *Guys* is a new modern term, meaning affection and love, like I feel now. Please just know I was here."

As his plane lifted and circled back around, Guadalcanal natives disappeared and impressive mountains faded fast. Yesterday on the boat, leaving Tulagi, Elvin threw a flower into the ocean and told Frederick, if the flower floats to shore, he'd come back; if it floats out to sea, he won't. Saying goodbye at the airport an hour ago, they hugged. Elvin knew the flower went out to sea.

Rutgers Stadium was sold out, yet it was inexplicably quiet, right out of the *Twilight Zone*. Elvin speculated that it was brief disbelief that the team was finally going to a bowl game after so long. Part of the explosion that he always thought about was going to happen. Nelson kept leaning into him for body warmth. The skinny kid had no chance in cold temperatures especially as the sun fast exited.

"It's brutally cold, my toes are numb."

"Rutgers is beating Cincinnati forty four to nine and is bowl eligible."

"Have we lived, Dad?"

"Watch this." A left coat sleeve, then a red sweat shirt was rolled up. "Pinch me!"

"Are we going to the bowl game?"

"Of course."

Driving home, Elvin drifted, looking at a late November sky and cirrus clouds tinged pink. Spending time with a child, no matter how old, and still finding ways to look at life through those eyes, is a gift, and recognizing it's a gift, is everything. Martha used to read him a book about a circus, and setting up big tops in the early morning. Pictures showed pink sky and clouds which meant anticipation; something loved was going up, and kept on going up each time Martha read the book. Love of that story was stability, continuity and things not changing. Did the pink sky over his car belong in another time, place or universe or in Martha's picture book decomposing in a Newark land fill? There were thoughts about attending a recent lecture on environmental justice that made him think about the land fill decomposing his favorite childhood book and more importantly, about incinerators that were built in poor people's Newark and Camden but not rich people's Short Hills. Injustice is weaved into the linings of political expediency coats. Politics is a synonym for injustice. The window was down for deep cold air inhalation. Rutgers was going to the Insight Bowl, so at least he'd pleasantly dream in a few hours.

Christmas in Arizona falls short of expectations if you're from New York. You need to see car exhaust in cold air with tell tale plumes, Rockefeller Center ice skating, wall to sidewalk crowds at ungodly hours, chestnuts roasting and miracles all over 34th Street. Elvin and Nelson absorbed sedate Scottsdale Road.

Checking into Scottsdale's Chaparral Resort, everyone was wearing Rutgers and Christmas red. A few people were ahead in line.

"Alan DeMarco?"

"That sounds like Elvin Stone."

"Holy shit. We meet again."

The two eyeglass salesmen, former competitors hugged.

"Nelson, Alan worked in Jersey when I was at Solchiali and one of the few guys on the road I liked. Merry Christmas."

"You too. Lets go Rutgers. Beer later?"

Elvin lay in bed, hands behind head, staring at a napping son. For a kid to see his college play in a bowl game is special. Spirit permeated everything. Rutgers fight songs echoed everywhere without provocation; everyone was ready to yell and sing preferably with a beer in hand, randomly hugging strangers wearing any kind of red.

Later the hotel bar rushed to close for Christmas Eve. Two alumni nursed beers in red plastic cups. Elvin tipped his Rutgers hat. Joe and Jerome, the last two at the bar, promised a return tip of the hat before they headed back east. The foursome decided to hang together and meet Wednesday after the game for sightseeing.

A Ford Taurus had an unexpected benefit; the seat went all the way back giving Elvin more leg room than an old Volkswagen. A Scottsdale convenience store loaded them up for the day of exploration.

"So, Nelson, they lost the Insight Bowl, it's a process, wait till next year."

"But Dad."

"I promise, next year, better."

"How do you know?"

"Because Dad knows things. There's the sign for Montezuma's castle."

Just off Route 17 north, a winding road led to a parking lot. Joe and Jerome waited. An eerie presence made them feel they were alone despite other tourists. Nelson called it *anti-silence*, when extreme quiet makes it seem noisy. On the right, was a mountain, tall as a New York building, with caves built into the face, forming a series of special dwellings. Blue sky touched the mountain; heaven and earth joined together.

Elvin became tour guide. "These were the first condos built four hundred years ago. Sinaqua Indians lived here. Look at the intricacy of their work and high up, so no one got mugged or bit by four-legged things."

Nelson's forehead wrinkled. "What happened to them?"

"Nobody knows. They had a good thing here, expensive condos, protection, security, running water except Sinaqua means without water, so it's a mystery."

Joe kept staring at the sky. "How do you know so much about this place?"

"I was an historian."

"I want to yell as loud as I can, tell spirits I'm here, from New Brunswick and go Rutgers."

"They know."

Small signs with altitude and population welcomed to Sedona. At two p.m. they'd meet up for a pink Jeep tour into the forest, leaving time for Elvin and Nelson to explore. Alex gave Elvin a red rock and told him to return it one day to the rightful owner; a special Sedona red mountain. The Taurus seemed to know where to go. Nelson asked, "How come you know how to get around without a map?"

Off Airport Road was a vortex; a place to energize the soul, mind and spirit. For Elvin, there were some trepidations about coming back. He thought how a life was energized by spending time here in the past. What would more feelings of deja vu mean? Where would it take him? Rock formations were studied for hidden messages. Would Nelson come away with something and sit with a beer at the *Olive Branch* and discuss soul, spirit, and strange feelings of angelic intervention? Would he get it? Was it genetic? Could it happen to him? Was there enough time? Why was Elvin in receivership or is a soul always open, waiting for intervention? Time with Nelson was a good laboratory test.

"Uncle Alex, Cousin Steven and I were around here a long time ago, when I was your age. We camped up there, maybe. Don't remember exactly. One night we went to a girl's house. Cousin Steven and a friend got laid. Uncle Alex and me hiked around outside, talking about President Kennedy."

"How come you didn't get laid too?"

"Because we weren't ready. Times were different back then. Upbringing. Grandparents. Parents. All this talk reminds me, to tell you to be careful out there."

"You've been reminding me since my Bar Mitzvah."

"I'm supposed to. It's my job."

Elvin, barefoot, slowly followed Nelson to each red rock level. Near the top, Alex's rock was returned to the mountain in an emotional ceremony. Cute miniature trees were scattered randomly; some actually grew out of the rock. Nelson made it to the summit, pounding his chest. Just below, eyes closed, hands by his side, Elvin felt warmth of the sun and serenity of spirit filling him up, like a car at a gas station. Quietly, for half an hour, he pinched both legs, standing, almost looking, according to Nelson, like he was pissing on the mountain with prostate problems blocking meaningful flow.

"Where'd you learn to describe things like that?"

"You of course and why barefoot?"

"You absorb energy, spirit through the soles of your feet, into your body without hindrances of socks and shoes. It might do you good to kick off."

How he loved the boy, so much a part of him. Scenes of youthful discovery on a mountain summit with innocence and thoughts about freezing time were firing all over Elvin's drifting mind. One of God's greatest gifts was enjoying every moment together with a child. Seconds were precious. Fuck the universe because it didn't care about time. Every second on Earth for Elvin counted as in being with a loved one that meant something and not just any family member because of title but a family member that cared and was in the other fifty percent. Going back down was a slow dusty process. Elvin sat at each ledge and slid to the next. Another small red rock caught Elvin's eye and pocket.

To be returned, promise, I hope.

An open pink Jeep tour took Joe, Jerome, Elvin and Nelson and a couple from Salt Lake City into silence and beauty. About to go straight down precarious rocks, he asked out of the jeep because it was much too steep for comfort, but the tour guide reassured. When they made an abrupt U-turn in the middle of beautiful scenery, the sophomore guide from UCLA mentioned the government wouldn't like it if they went further. Elvin remembered being near with Alex, Steven and Carl Wyler, who said the same thing, that government erases you if you trespass. Jeep passengers all felt the extreme silence of forest and mountains colored red. Nelson joked that it looked like a cheap painting sold in motel parking lots. Back in downtown Sedona, Joe and Jerome, Nelson and Elvin hugged like brothers for forty years. Dynamics felt right and meant to be and they decided to see each other again back east. Suddenly Brandon, beseeching equal justice in America, fired across his field of vision again.

At the Taurus ignition, the digital clock in the car read out *4:44*. Elvin stared then kissed Nelson's soft spot. Sedona had worked its magic so quickly.

Elvin squeezed a new borrowed red rock through take off and right up until the New Jersey Turnpike toll booth at Exit Nine. Tight squeezing, soft whispers thanked his spirit.

TWENTY FOUR

April showers lingered. Les Offenholt couldn't make up his mind. A right hand rested on a door handle. A gift umbrella from a Bloomingdale's cologne promotion two Easters ago lay conspicuously on the back seat. Window watching, Jennifer opened her front door just as he got there.

"Were you contemplating that umbrella in the back seat?"

"You don't miss much."

Les looked around, following Jennifer, thinking about a single woman living in a large house, while each sensed the other's sensing. A still life painting stopped him: a fruit bowl, bottle of wine on a table, a window with draw string shade half up, and night time beyond.

"It's an original, no one you know- an old boyfriend actually."

"I like it, not because of some old boyfriend. I was going to lay some impressionistic, minimalist bullshit, maybe to impress, but decided to tell you what I was thinking instead."

"Original."

An ornate coffee table was lost in an expansive living room. Behind a sofa, curtains tied with sash had a Broadway theatre look. Wine, cork unscrewed, resting comfortably, cheese, crackers and sliced apple, were on a silver tray.

Les poured and mumbled wine year.

"Was it a good year?"

"It was and it's a good vineyard too." Les toasted, "To the process which finally got us together, cheers."

"Cheers, not so much for the process, but the processors."

"Good point." He was still busy looking around.

"You'd like to ask how a dental hygienist affords all this."

"Would've, but it's impolite. I just realized one thing that attracts me. . . ."

Her legs uncrossed. "To me?"

"Free spirit, you say what's on. . . ."

"My mind, always. My parents are gone. I was an only child. Out of Darwinian principles, I had to be a free independent spirit to survive. The *fittest* rules. Les, we finished a bottle of wine, both are intellectually stimulating, so where's dinner?"

"A friend of mine owns a small neighborhood Italian restaurant near Burke, so we don't have too drive far in the rain. It's called *Louis's*, best veal in the city."

"Thought that place was in the Bronx." She jumped up, reaching down to Les.

Our first date; strong arms to go along with strong great looking biking legs which cross and uncross like a traffic light changes. She knows about the Godfather and Louis's. Maybe this is heaven's gate.

A waiter called out house specials. "Our veal selection brings people from long distance."

Jennifer didn't flinch.

"Of course you need to like veal."

"You're an observant waiter. A while back I heard about tetracycline and baby veal. A dermatologist used to give me that for acne."

"I would've assumed a tall healthy woman was into. . . ."

"It's the only meat I don't eat, but since you might, subject is officially changed. It's rather interesting that it's April 2006 and Chinese President Hu Jintao is dining with Bill Gates as we speak."

Fascination with a dental hygienist was surprising after dates with models, government attorneys, surgeons and executives. Chemistry with Jennifer was there but it tickled in a funny way. Maybe her career, which didn't fit into the overall picture then again maybe it did. Remembering the last time he smiled broadly on a date and trying to imagine what she looked like nude was difficult, probably because it never happened until five minutes ago. Along with nudity think was a sense of urgency or horniness and would urges change the flow of a relationship, born long ago, smiling at each other from bikes?

A bathroom mirror was leaned into and backed up from, then three separate mirrors in the bedroom were used for perspective and side views and finally a full length mirror downstairs at center hall- all part of the process before meeting an old friend. From a distance Nelson observed, shadowing Elvin.

"Dad, you're carrying on like it's the President. You never talk about Calvin Graham."

"Uncle Alex and Calvin were part of a discussion group in Princeton. He's a Brit, arrogant, cocky, but we liked each other. He was the one who taught me all about blue balls?"

"Dad!"

"Never mind. He's in from London for a few days."

"Calvin, do you remember, one night four decades ago, all three of us, slightly inebriated after a party at Nolan's walking around this same street?" Elvin pointed to a *Hulfish Street* sign.

"Operative word is *slightly*, don't think any of us ever really tied it on." Calvin Graham was a half step behind his taller friend.

"I'm thinking about Alex now and can't dispel circumstances. Do any of us ever have a right to say we don't understand and be angry about it?"

"It's personal, we can feel anything."

"You two were so close. How do you cope?"

"That's just it. I don't know how. Coping is nebulous, can't distinguish what is or isn't. Everything comes out of the wash with different degrees of wrinkles."

Elvin felt emotional welling- a feeling all too familiar. Chest tightens but not cardiac and a side abdomen hurts with heavy breathing. Tears are there and you can't let go, certainly not on Hulfish Street despite abundant memories and molecules floating around Princeton.

"What do you think about my *Travels with Elvin*? and the experiences I've been keeping you up to date on."

Two friends e-mailed regularly since Calvin rarely physically crossed over the Atlantic, but when he did, it was always to Princeton, not for sentimentality, never for homecoming.

"Impressive Elvin, especially the Solomon Islands bit. What bloke in their right mind goes there?"

"No one right minded and no bloke either."

"Did you like it?"

"Pretty place, natural and almost untouched in a non-commercial virginal way. Virginal means no mile long malls or fast food or hardware stores that take up half the island. War is covered over, forgotten about. They just had all kinds of rioting in the Solomon Islands. Lawmakers elected a new prime minister, but he's linked to previous corruption which could've put a damper on my stay, so my timing was perfect."

"Where we eating?"

"Two choices, both fish on Route One."

"You pick old chap."

A fish restaurant in a local mall made them wait an hour. The vibrator that was handed to Calvin if you decide to wait and walk around made him laugh.

"Why order veal in a fish place?"

Calvin defended. "Cause I like the way they bread things in Jersey."

"Shiraz?"

"Sure. Have you been following CIA things?"

"Some."

"Just fired Mary McCarthy; she leaked things about secret prisons."

Both men reaffirmed how much they liked each other from that first meeting about Kennedy's assassination at Nolan's and if the Atlantic Ocean hadn't separated them, they might've become better friends.

"Why bring up the CIA all night? Am I missing something?"

Whenever Elvin thought about close friends, he smiled, like now, thinking people close to him did things they couldn't talk about. Was he a magnet with a safe deposit box for cloak and dagger exercises? He knew about being a magnet for an angel.

"Leak is a fascinating word with so many interpretations."

"Speaking of fascinating old chap, I'm going to buy a three wheeled vehicle which runs on natural gas and gets a hundred miles per gallon. Quite interesting how they glib over global warming. High placed friends of mine in London tell me how bad things are. No one cares because they'll be long gone and buried when the ocean rises over coast lines, giant squid move close to shore, more intense storms and diseases, droughts and starvation- real nasty stuff. Global warming has won; game over with declines from here on and no power on Earth can stop Arctic melting, animals dying off, because they won't adapt in time, and wait until millions more Asians burn fossil fuels or need a drink of clean water. Sorry for going off."

"Maybe it's that least of our problems."

In front of the Nassau Inn fireplace, friends said goodbye with a long hug. Over the next hour, Elvin roamed the streets of Princeton; places of youth, innocence, and tender memories. Passing Einstein's house on Mercer Street, he remembered that Alex truly thought he was out of the realm, almost from another dimension of consciousness but still aware that the universe was created by amazing intelligence, God.

A church with an old white steeple where they went to a meeting about Kennedy's assassination was open for business. Last row pews were favorite places. Elvin sat, hands folded tightly. Two women walked by and sat in the first row. One was blonde, and if he stretched imagination, she was the Dutch woman from Guadalcanal. A factory whistle in a defense plant sounded quitting time. It was a week before Christmas and he wasn't sure what to buy Rosemary. Money was tight. Not a day went by lately when he didn't pray for his heart murmur to disappear so he could fight Germans. It would be uplifting revenge because of what they were doing to Jews. More and more stories were leaking out. Martha and Jack were working when two soldiers came to their house in Newark to deliver a telegram about Kenneth. His only brother died in North Africa, all by himself, away from family and army buddies in a surprise air attack. He'd never be the same again. Life without a real loved one was unbearable. A loved one could be a friend too. There was much hurt in a life. How do you purge or soothe it?

"Come to Key Largo with me Evie, just for a few days. You've got enough sick days coming."

"It's mid-May. I can't leave my classroom near school end. Besides, your sojourns should be just that, yours."

"But."

"Don't you remember asking for space? I do have something to ask."

Stopping their nightly walk under a convenient Maple tree, holding hands while a leaf was pulled off a branch, Elvin apologized to the leaf, then handed it to Evie, stem intact.

"Most things you do since Alex and Christine, they're understood, sort of, but this Key Largo fascination, I can't figure that out."

Relief was subtle. "I thought it was serious, couldn't imagine. Key Largo might take time to explain, so let's finish walking."

"I like this tree."

She rubbed the leaf between fingers. Elvin said leaves don't like loud noises and kept whispering. "Before you, divorced, living alone, never finding peace and so unhappy. I was in a downward spiral. I never told this to anyone. People close to me were passing away. I couldn't even find an empty boulder at the Shark River. There was no sanctuary. No place for me in the universe. Alex was in Massachusetts. One morning my side abdomen really hurt- a strange opiate kind of pain. It was pain, if you visualize, that I controlled and it made me feel sorry for myself, so I cried. It was strange; the pain felt good. I don't know why, but I loaded up with wine and found a box cutter and went into the bath tub."

"Elvin!" Evie hugged him, letting the gifted leaf slip away.

"I didn't do anything, but close, too close. All of a sudden, I heard Bogart's voice. A movie that I never saw or knew about was on. *Key Largo*, in gut wrenching black and white. You know how much I love tech noir. So I jumped out, watched the movie, frozen and nude the whole time. It was a sign and here I am, still in love with a woman who I met right after that."

A late afternoon flight into Fort Lauderdale became a later drive to South Beach to buy a newspaper, a bottle of low calorie beer and a walk on the beach.

Roller blades scantily clad. Dogs leading masters. Endless procession of cars and not just cars but events with four wheels. People dining. Leaning on a car now and watching diners watch, called watching back. They're staring at me and they're the ones with a schmuck sign around their neck. And it's even the way they hold their forks like a conductor of a symphony. No one is eating anything identifiable; all the food is covered with home grown weeds to enhance presentation. What ever happened to egg salad on white? Wonderful material for my yellow pad and why am I drinking beer that's low calorie?

"Hi, you have great eyes. Can I take a picture?"

Elvin thought she's another hippie from Haight-Ashbury, reincarnated, long hair right to mid ass.

"Well. . . . "

"It's legit. There's an art show, party and exhibition later. A picture gets you an invitation. There's a cover charge."

"I'm not too old?"

Holy shit! It's a scene right out of Midnight Cowboy but I'm not Joe Buck. Cover charge. Entrepreneur. She's taking a college course. I'm a summer assignment.

"Don't worry, forty is not too old."

"Try sixty."

"Never mind."

It was two a.m. Two cell phone calls driving down to the Chesapeake Resort in Islamorada, Florida Keys, alerted a night watchman that Elvin Stone from Nueva Jersey was still on his way and where could they meet because the front desk closed at eleven.

A balcony overlooked gardens and tennis courts. Grass grew in court cracks meaning there'd be no problem getting court time. Lungs filled with tropical aromatic air. The Keys were loved so quickly.

Modest key dwellings seemed to say, worry about ocean, sun, fish and nothing else mattered. Calm pastel water on both sides defined the four block wide spit of land. Maybe the air, sky or something undefined was creating feelings of dull, surreal, or was the sun too bright, making you squint dull? Key life was slow motion; even gentle breezes were laid back. The more exploration, the more regrets having never been. Was it a conspiracy of Key residents to keep others away? Don't give Key interviews, or spread words and just keep Keys low key. First impressions told him nothing on earth was as perfect as the Keys if informality was a life choice.

Somewhere there was a small dock where Bogart and Bacall stood.

Several pools surrounded the Chesapeake. Elvin sat at the smallest, alone with a regular beer and yellow pad, scribbling Key things. The Morada Bay Restaurant, suggested by an old woman at the pool was ethereally picturesque; plastic chairs, tables scattered on the sand, everything facing a setting sun, that you wanted to reach out and hug for its beauty. A group of people at the next table were drinking *Jagermeister*, so he pretended cool and ordered. Imagination dictated being there with Evie, sunset dining, kicking off shoes, rubbing feet in the sand, dipping calamari into red sauce, drinking a woody chardonnay from California and going back to the room. Instead he was alone, doing too much thinking.

In the movie *Key Largo*, Matecumbe Key was mentioned a few times and he loved the way it sounded, so he kept whispering, "Matecumbe Key", feeling a pulling inside that he couldn't explain, but almost like having to be somewhere, so he kept looking at his watch. Lauren Bacall was still around, looking wonderful and that was good. The late forties were black and white magic. The world was a better place. War was over. Bogart was part of Hollywood elite, making you feel good, uplifted, wanting to be just like him, cool and unaffected. Life was simple. Sprinkles on ice cream cones were a big addition to quality of life. The globe wasn't appreciably warming and no three dollar a gallon gas or terrorism because people didn't learn to speak up yet. American companies didn't kill for profit and there was no stack of paper, rubber banded together, resting comfortably in a vault in New Jersey. Fists clenched but nothing changed. A breathtaking sunset reinforced Earth's beautiful creation.

Like a tiger in a zoo cage, pacing back and forth in classic stalking behavior patterns, Elvin did similar, driving around Islamorada and Key Largo.

For Age Art Gallery, Upper Matecumbe Key was off the main road, set back in what looked like an old garage, Newark vintage. It deceived, having endless browsing space and displayed art works that went into another attached garage. Still life was never Elvin's thing. A painting with fruit, bottle of wine on a table, shade half pulled down in the night background caught his eye. The draw string seemed in motion, like someone was just there.

"I like this painting. Do you ship?"

"Only to New Jersey."

Elvin laughed. "My accent gave me away?"

"Since I'm a native, sure."

"Can you tell me about the artist?"

"Fairly young, from Burke, Virginia. Slowly becoming popular. Even though it's a still life, it manages to tell you things."

"It does. Can you put a card inside the package?"

"I do all the time."

Arms folded, head was reverentially bent for those who died in the Labor Day Hurricane of 1935. Elvin wondered about life in the 1930's, without Doppler radar. The Hindenberg exploded at Lakehurst and a radio announcer called out, "Oh the humanity." Standing there at a memorial, Elvin thought about humanity and future, whispering "Matecumbe Key" again and a few more times in a row. Then more whispers, "Matecumbe Key."

The sojourn, built around where Bogart and Bacall stood in the movie, came down to a bar on a main highway, with prominent sign, that out back was a wooden dock, from the beginning of *Key Largo*. Early next morning, bars still hadn't opened and Elvin found his Bogart place; a spit of a dock by the water, wood decaying so badly it probably scared tourists away. Five bare right toes eventually rested on the wood.

Bogart and Bacall touched this dock. Makes no difference if it was a soundstage, maybe. Hell, I've got the Vichy Water. They've got the dock. It's small yet looms so big in my life; my existence on Earth and the first thing I saw when I jumped out of the bathtub. Dear God, thank you. Humphrey Bogart, thank you for filling my senses all these years, giving me reasons. What a great screen play this could all make; just need time, time. Amen.

Maybe an inhalation record, deep breaths were taken again and again, not wanting to miss atoms, protons, electrons, whatever. No one came by while he was there; toes still rested on wood. No one driving by heard of the movie anyway; he didn't originally until the bathtub. Like a celestial wink, the sun brightened. Elvin thought something funny amidst heaviness of the morning. The last thing on his mind as he walked back to the car:

Sixty.

Never mind.

Thoughts of sugar plum fairies, a Vermont ski lodge, and how Jennifer Kraft uses a body, contracts important strong muscles, enhancing sensations, prolonged a smile on Les Offenholt's face, lying nude under covers. A bottle of Caymus Cabernet Sauvignon, two long stemmed wine glasses were points of focus, not a six foot tall nude woman walking into the bedroom.

Reaching for the bottle, he sat up. "1996 Napa Valley. Good year, opened and ready to go."

"Little game darling. I brought the cork with me too. You have to find it."

A distorted voice brought Les to serious thought. "You sound like Don Vito. They stuffed tissue in Brando's mouth to create that sound, so the cork is in your mouth."

She spit it out as he reached for her swollen cheek.

"You know your *Godfather*."

"Play that cork game again with me?"

"But the cork will be harder to find next time with different rules."

"Toast to Christmas in a few weeks and to January in Vermont."

"And how perfect we are together. Cheers."

Wine glasses clicked and were drained fast. Night tables took over glass responsibility so Jennifer climbed on top, maneuvering around.

"Stay like this, don't move."

"Can't move anyway."

"Let's stay exactly, for as long in closeness, perfection."

"Lets."

"Nice teeth Les. Braces?"

"Of course."

Fingers maneuvered inside his mouth, around lips, catching a few kisses. Bodies still locked together as she leaned for a closer look.

"It's a hell of a time and penetrating position and maybe the most unique diagnostic spot in dental history, but darling, you've got gum problems."

"What?"

"Your gums are pretty inflamed. When's the last time you were checked?"

Completely caught with more than pants down, Les quietly stared until whining, "Jennifer, this dental shit just shrunk me out of you."

"Felt you slide out, sorry."

"Well, let's finish what you started. A couple of years ago, I had a cavity filled."

"A smart man like you; we're a month from 2007 and did you ever hear that gum disease can lead to heart disease? Bacteria travels from gums, settles in blood vessels, become a focal point so clogging plaque builds up."

"You know your stuff."

"Good at what I do; also with legs, hands and all kinds of lips but you know the routine."

"So, Ms. Hygienist, what do we do about it?"

"First Saturday in January, you can be my last cleaning appointment. Let's say two p.m. Doctor examines you first, then your lover here cleans your gums and then we go to Vermont with your clean oral bill of health. Are you happy?"

"Been happy since you first smiled at me."

"And I'll bet you knew we'd be like this."

"Hoped."

TWENTY FIVE

A folded overcoat sat next. A gold watch reminded, thirty minutes past a lunch appointment. Ian Eon wasn't necessarily annoyingly late, after all Elvin thought, that he was on the eighth floor bar at the Marriott Marquis in Times Square with enough visual distraction, so who gives a damn; therefore just continue people watching in the capital of the world. Five days into 2007 and patrons looked like they've been hanging at the bar since New Years Eve; pale gray skin, bloodshot eyes, no facial animation. The funniest observation was, most of them had no clue they were revolving around Times Square.

New Years Eve was a phenomenon for Elvin; sixty years on earth, thirty five miles away the entire time and never saw the ball fall live. As a teen working at Kraft Pharmacy, taking the bus, always wanting to be the first on the bus and if necessary, walking a mile out of the way to accomplish that, really meant dislike of standing in crowds.

All this pensive time, he couldn't help but think about the name, Ian Eon, sounding more theatrical than surveillance detective work. Why would anyone use a name like that in a supposedly invisible profession? Was it a father's last name? Even Sam Spade blended. The more he thought about Sam Spade in *Maltese Falcon*, maybe author Hammett influenced his detective, Ian Eon too.

That man walking over to the bar. Large, round, bald. Sidney Greenstreet maybe? Ferrari? The bar isn't the Blue Parrott. Where the hell is my detective? God I love that movie. Think tonight after this revolving bar, I'll go home, cuddle with Evie, and watch Casablanca again.

"Elvin Stone?"

"Ian Eon?"

"Good, that's done."

"How'd you know it's me?"

"Remember what I do. You've been looking at your watch nervously. I walked around once. You're a thumb standing out. Sorry I'm late, only excuse, New York City."

"No problem, not as if anything else to do."

"You're retired with lots of time."

"You checked me out? By the way. . . ."

"My last name?"

"How'd you know I was thinking that?"

Eyes rolled. "Eon is a contraction from my father's last name. Russian immigrants need another generation to assimilate before certain lines of work are accepted easier and mostly detective work. Maybe it's a knee jerk to the letters KGB? Ian Eon has a nice sound, a bit like Sam Spade."

"I love Sam Spade and Bogart. Don't tell me you know that too?"

"I'm not that good. I thought your insisting on a public place, with people around was a little dramatic."

"Not insisting, just mentioned, but was kidding. It's actually a line from a movie."

"I know."

Imagination had Ian Eon in mid five foot range, pompadour hair, moustache, maybe bushy eyebrows like Breznev. Instead Elvin was surprised by a retired Russian Hockey Player look; broad, tall, bald and no facial hair and eyebrows looking tweezed which intimidated. Elvin picked up a muddled accent; Russian mixing with Brighton Beach Jewish old timers, still walking the boardwalk on Sunday mornings.

"How can I help you?"

"As I mentioned, it's not critical, life or death. With everything on the internet, maybe I could've done it myself but time is especially important. I just made up my mind to do this."

"Say no more. Since you're friends with Magda and taught with her a long time ago, she asked me to help you. Let's see what you've got."

An overcoat pocket was relieved of a thrice folded manila envelope.

Ian scanned, letting an index finger guide eyes down the single sheet of paper.

"Easy, give me two weeks."

"Would you like a check now?"

"Now and full. Another beer? You were in Guadalcanal recently; tell me about it."

Three men walked out of an Alexandria office building. Since it was Saturday morning, pedestrian traffic was confined to just them. Cold wind shuffled flurries, making it look worse than it was. An SUV pulled up and the three male pedestrians became passengers.

"Where to Les?"

"Let's get breakfast."

"What time's your appointment?"

"Two p.m. Both of you can take off the rest of the weekend."

Les Offenholt turned around. Moore and Phil, shadows extraordinaire, as he called them, sat in the second row.

Phil downed a window, expelling dragged smoke, coughing words, "Taking off means you're safe and sound in bed with a woman for the whole weekend."

"For me to contemplate options and eventualities. Remember, we started out at Wakefield Park at the same point. You all had the same shot. Say Phil, didn't you read that intelligence report the other day? They've now got a million Chinese dying each year from smoking related diseases. Efficient aren't they?"

"I read it."

"Key word is *related*. Throw the fucking cigarette out of *our* car."

A bottle of gold mouthwash was pulled from under the front seat.

"Swig and spit."

"Great name for a down to earth, back to basics mouthwash, swig and spit."

"Why was it there?"

"My appointment's with a dentist. It's called proper grooming."

"No it's called love with the proper stranger."

"Funny, Moore."

The wind kept Phil's rejected mouthwash stuck against the passenger door.

"Mr. Offenholt, please sign in."

Ten minutes before two. Les thought doing a study about dental appointments and the percentage of patients arriving early versus late.

The magazine rack was a viable source of patient demographic information based on what they read. A woman, about to leave, dramatically swirled a scarf while thanking the receptionist behind sliding glass. Warm colonial motif and a television tucked into custom mahogany furniture took a mind off the fact your mouth was soon going to be opened, probed, injected and drilled for three units of dental time. Sound dental practice management also preached leaving a television cable remote in the waiting room. Sights and sounds took a patient's mind off the swiveling chair and drill with spittoon on the left. A local cable news channel had a lead story; two area government scientists died overnight in a small plane crash near Marietta, Georgia. Les never looked up.

"Mr. Offenholt."

Four pages of patient profiles and insurance forms were filled out. Signing off on who was going to pay if all else failed was laughable. Just once, a recently deceased mother should be guarantor.

In the chair, distance glasses were relinquished to a young assistant in exchange for an overhead television remote. Les smiled. "No thank you. Saturday's are mostly cartoons anyway." There was a strange numerical tattoo on a left arm.

"Dr. Speller will be with you shortly"

Two minutes later Dr. Speller arrived. He was short, slight and sight tricked an undiscerning eye into thinking Woody Allen, but the voice was deceptively deep, hoarse and with an accent which Les didn't think was from Northern Virginia. When Jennifer was riding him later, he'd ask about the country of origin.

"You were referred to the office by Ms. Kraft."

Les was impressed that Speller took time to scan all the pages.

"We'll do a full set of x-rays and see what we've got going on, then take care of your gums."

Jennifer walked in. "Mr. Offenholt, welcome to the office. I'll take x-rays now." It was the same smile when she first passed him on a bike in the park.

Dr. Speller re-entered, voice deeper, more concerned. "Two cavities. We'll address that whenever convenient."

"Any emergency with the cavities?"

"Over the next month, we'll take care of them, but you shouldn't experience any discomfort. Let's have a closer look."

Gloves removed, hands were washed again. New surgical gloves were pulled on like a rubber before sex, amusing Les, with similarity in motions. A probe worked around gums and teeth. "Let's start to get gums healthy. You've got some pockets."

Smiling Jennifer was back. "Do you like our meticulous wonderful dentist?"

"I do."

"Good. Let's go into the gum cleaning room." Jennifer slipped his glasses into a lab coat pocket. "Relax Les, you're stiff. I promise nothing hurts, actually enjoy yourself, close your eyes and think of new positions for later."

A laugh was muffled by suction and high pitched whirring. Eyes closed in anticipated pain. Suction slowed, causing a swallow reflex. She rubbed his cheek- not normal procedure but he liked personal touches. Lastly, there was scraping and more probing then a final rinse out.

"Now the best. People have been known to only come for this. Jet spray cleaning. You'll feel warm bubbling action all over your gums."

"Bubbling?"

"Flavored sodium bicarbonate releasing oxygen."

Right after she started, Les gasped for breath, slumping in the chair. Jennifer positioned him back to the head rest. With gloves still on, she turned off the room light; office lights were already off. The staff waited at a rear door, all still wearing gloves. The receptionist yelled, "Be right there," and finished re-hanging an office Christmas picture next to the patient file cabinet. The rear door slammed shut. A waiting Explorer drove off.

Elvin walked around a red dumpster in the driveway. With his palm came a slap of solid steel composition, and thoughts about human technological advances, like this incredibly impervious iron dumpster, slowly filling from a basement construction project.

"How much longer, John?"

"Two weeks, long before your vacation. Come on down, a lot of changes, I want to show you."

Life is acceptance of your place in the world and coming to terms if you're either handy or not around a house. Elvin realized *not* after moving to Maplewood as a teenager. A slow drip in an upstairs bathroom sink brought pliers and wrenches. He probed. A corps of plumbers had to finish what Elvin exacerbated and promises were made to parents, about never using plumbing tools again.

Sitting on basement steps, he watched John and helper go back to work, and thought about a sales training session when they were told about an executive who cost a company fifty million dollars because of a wrong spur decision. Next morning promptly, he was called into the President's office, expecting to be fired for the fifty million dollar mistake, but instead was told how valuable he'd become, because fifty million was now invested in his training. For the first time in his life, Elvin would have a finished basement. He knew exactly what he was doing and it would never be a mistake and still, he had no desire to pick up plumbing or any kind of tools.

Thanks Alex, for the basement. It's funny how things in life you want and never give in to yourself unless it's someone else's money. I miss you.

Evie slept against the plane window, shade half down, letting slivers of warm sun beacon through. Elvin leaned over to catch a glimpse. The Caribbean was too far below to see if refugee boats were headed to South Florida or if military surveillance ships were near Cuba.

Two houses away in Newark, a Jewish Cuban couple moved in but had no children so no extra stoop ball or street hockey players. Since the foreign couple was older, neighbors talked. Why were they really there? Irv Gash, from across the street, told the kids to keep eyes and ears open. Maybe they were commie spies. Playing *Sneaky Joe* with flashlights one summer night, Elvin snuck into the Cuban's dark basement, figuring the gang would never look for him there. All too clearly, the lady was yelling at her husband, part in Spanish and English. The man cried, begging forgiveness. She was hitting him. Yells were for him to get out. What if they came into the cellar and found Elvin? The old man ran out the side door a few feet away. No one ever saw the meek husband again. The old lady moved a month later. Curiously, she singled Elvin out, paying him five dollars to bring empty boxes from the grocery store. Staring at each other, she *God blessed him.* Born was a promise never to raise a voice to a woman, so she doesn't do the same to him. The worst verbal with Merrie, was a whispered *fuck you* while she slept on the sofa on their last night together and of course the night before they got married.

A kiss was left on Evie's ear lobe, "I love you."

"Where are we? Did we start initial descent?"

"Near Tiperrary, a small island near Guadeloupe."

"Does anybody ever know what the hell you're talking about when you say Tiperrary?"

"Only you and Alex."

"I want to tell you how excited I am about our second honeymoon where we met. I've never been away on Spring Break before. You're still a romantic. I love you."

Club Med Caravelle underwent a twenty-nine million dollar facelift back in 2006. Jokingly, Evie asked on New Years Day if she was ready for the same kind of lift. Elvin said no to her face but booked a vacation, getting the Grand Terre suite because they were older with different needs, mostly way past roughing it.

"Let me open the door."

A cosmetics bag held the door. Evie was carried across the threshold and dropped abruptly on top of a red bedspread. For the first time, deep inhalations became medical necessity. Dark wood fixtures and three separate roses in a picture frame over the bed confirmed things changed since the facelift.

Looking to recreate their first time, they checked-out the shower while still dressed and laughed. "We can't do this. Look at the physics of positioning. Your back went out six months ago trying something crazy like this and knees feel like my meniscus washed down the drain into the Raritan River."

"What are you saying?"

Evie pointed in back and forth motions to the bed.

Two a.m., walking hand in hand near palm trees and pediatric waves with moonlight guiding, they settled into plastic contoured chairs on an almost deserted beach except for a prowling stray black cat. Elvin giggled. "Think we should head back."

"It's not bedtime."

"Not what I had in mind."

"We've been doing that all day."

"That's right, but I didn't finish my thought. Let's go back, put on bathing suits and go back to the ocean. All the lubrication in the world and the best natural candlelight, the moon, is waiting for us."

"I'd like that."

Always thinking of himself as brave and imbued with pioneer spirit, so messing around at two thirty a.m. in an ocean far from Belmar was fine, provided they didn't venture too far from shore, but deep enough for the impending attachment to be beneath the water line in case of any pain in the ass spectators.

Steven Spielberg's creation kept him close to shore for the past thirty years as well. *Jaws* played at the Maplewood Theatre. The ocean and moon looked just like it did in the opening scene, so despite Evie's suggestive prodding, they stayed close to shore, locked inside each other, revolving around like figurines in a Fifth Avenue holiday window.

"Is that what you think we're doing? Figurines on Fifth Avenue."

"Just loving each other and I've got no problem staying like this until the sun rises."

"Me too."

"Some say life flashes in front of you at some point. Well right now, as close as two people can get on Earth, there's a lot of flashing. I've never been happier and more fulfilled, in love and content. I'm so lucky we met here and have so much to thank you for, especially the last couple of years, running around like I do. Every time I come home, it's to your open arms."

"Because it's you. You're a deep man. Your son and I talk about you."

"Behind my back?"

"There's so much inside of you, going through re-discovery, releasing all that inner energy. It's hard for both of us to explain. What you just said to me, will last forever. Thank you."

"It is hard. Your eyes glisten. I just want to look at you. Do you know that if there wasn't a full moon, I'd never be brave enough to be in a dark ocean now? The moon helps me see shark fins heading towards us."

"Stop teasing."

They revolved like a minute hand for a dozen revolutions.

"It really is spirituality these last years; a constant feeling of deja vu. All day long, driving, looking out the window, thinking I've been there, everything's familiar. It happens a hundred times a day. Maybe it's just a tree next to a house or a couple of stores or a street full of houses. I know the store, been there, but I haven't. Maybe it's a shadow hitting the side of the road or a lawn a certain way. I've seen it before, but not. Constant feelings are with me all the time of having been, but not. It's strange and wonderful. I never feel alone ever since Sedona with Alex and Steven."

"I love you. What you're saying is kind of scary. Love me more."

Still locked together, they remembered childhood at Belmar, playing in the sand then going in the water for hours until a mother yelled to get out, making them look at their shriveled fingers resembling an eighty year old.

Evie giggled, "Can't wait to see what it looks like when we get back to the room. Promise you'll show me."

Elvin was fast to reply. "Promise, but I have to look first to make sure it's still hanging at the right angle and hasn't shrunk from sight."

Last nights in the tropics are sentimental. They walked on the beach well past midnight. Cargo shorts concealed a bottle of wine smuggled from dinner.

"Let's drink the night away."

"There's so much to say to you. I need to close my eyes for a few minutes first. Hold my hand. I want to think about our life, hope, Nelson, tomorrow and the day after."

"Close your eyes."

A hand passed over her eyes. She kissed the hand that closed her eyes.

A sunrise aerobics class woke them. An empty wine bottle was almost covered by sand. They jumped-up, embarrassed, holding hands running back to the room, laughing like the kids they hoped everybody thought they were.

Elvin remembered some Rutgers students go home on weekends so it's easier finding parking around campus. At Rutgers Newark a long time ago there wasn't a campus, unless you include department stores like Bamberger's, Woolworth's, or Hahne's, which students used for shortcuts with prior acceptance by the stores because it was good for traffic building. Elvin loved the first floor smells of cheap cologne sprayed out of counter-top atomizers. On a campus with trees and dorms, loss of virginity might've happened sooner. Idly sitting in his car, a mind was firing and drifting.

Woolworth's in Newark had a sign on the window. *Try something new in Newark, from Italy, called Pizza Pie.* He was twelve years old and went downtown to see the latest Japanese monster movie at the Branford Theatre. A few years later, near downtown, in a store front fraternity house, late on a Saturday night, no one was around except Ronnie and himself. One of life's highlights, a first bra removal attempt, was fumbled around with. When almost removed, a few hooks away, banging on the outside window interrupted the last few and that much anticipated grand slam home run. James and a few others told Elvin to get out in ten minutes; the Black Student Guard was going to fire bomb a few stores. "Elvin, you're like a brother, go man, go."

Getting back to that point of undone hooks would take a long time. Ronnie disappeared to upstate New York and according to an experienced fraternity brother and baseball player, had no chest anyway.

Satisfied and smiling, he pulled out of an empty parking lot and headed towards Route One. It was late September. The main gate at Rider University in Lawrenceville forced a stop to tell security, he was a history teacher, doing Saturday morning research and like Rutgers, he drove into an empty parking lot. Security never bothered to see what he was wearing. Cargo shorts were hardly appropriate for research by a member of the profession.

At the far end of the lot, a cluster of cars close to buildings meant someone was around with academic pursuits. College campuses could be a lonely place. Before getting out, he used a shot of the same breath spray used to kill a big spider- half the size of a basketball- before it disappeared into a car vent and ruined the rest of his car life. Elvin was anticipating, not researching. A white Honda approached. Pennsylvania plates were the objective.

The Honda driver stood with a right hand over mouth. Looking at each other, with no motion, but suddenly, facial emotion exploded. Elvin ran over, arms open, poised to hold dearly.

"Caye, my goodness."

"Elvin, same for me."

They hugged. Her left hand escaped for a renegade tear.

Caye backed up. "You're as handsome as ever. Men age so well."

"And you, still so beautiful."

"Beautiful? I'm a grandmother, twice. What are grandmothers? I mean they have Mrs. Contests all the time but do they for grandmothers?"

"You're rambling. I bet nerves. I get accused of that all the time. You're a beautiful grandmother."

"Thank you. Of course nerves. Forty years just got wiped out. When you called me a few months ago, I gasped for breath, got dizzy and almost fainted. Our time together was cut short by society, so I wonder why I almost fainted. It's not as if we had years of history between us."

"No, because of the unexpected."

"You went through a lot of trouble to track me down. A detective is big time impressive. Imagine a black grandmother getting a detective."

"Not just a detective, a Russian."

"What was his name, just curious?"

"Ian Eon. Spelled E.O.N."

"You're wearing shorts. That means a Shark River expedition."

"Yes."

"Thomas Wolfe said something about not being able to go home again."

A same animated, glowing face, large searching eyes that hadn't changed in four decades sat next to him.

"Not home, just a place with wonderful memories, so strong, they endured until now."

Laughing, driving back to the security post, he wondered if they'd question such fast research. Forty years left a void. Caye graduated from Spelman, became a teacher, got married, divorced and re-married. Daughter Serena got married after a PhD. She was able to follow Elvin for a while. Her friend Tasha-the boys took her to a hospital during the riots in 1967- was in Elvin's class. Cancer took her husband two years ago and she still teaches elementary school in Yardley, Pennsylvania, just across the river.

"I read about Alex a few years ago. I felt so bad and wondered how and knew you were close. Men keep their names, so it's easier to look. My name changed twice and address a dozen times, living in too many states. My husband did government work. This societal rebel had a wonderful husband messing around in government and there were times I felt like asking Gene to look you up with one of those fancy George Orwell computers."

On the back floor was a basket with grapes, bread and Pinot Noir. The weather was the same as forty years ago, getting cloudier, cool, out of season.

"But not Muscatel."

"You remembered that wine. Confession Elvin. I wasn't impressed with your wine selection back then. Muscatel was the wine people drank out of brown bags and empty bottles thrown into a vacant lot."

"Over there, look familiar?"

"The fishing club. Implied by architecture, no Blacks or Jews."

A blanket was unfurled. They toasted, laughed and stared at the horizon as two ships sailed towards Africa and Kilimanjaro.

"Are you sorry not having been to Kilimanjaro or Paris?"

"Not really, but I'm going to look you straight in the eye and tell you that being here with you now completes something in my life; a quest, purpose and a fulfilled feeling."

"Do you really feel that?"

"I do and it might take a month of sitting here to fully explain."

"It's in your eyes. I always knew you were happy being with me. We're old enough now to ask mature questions."

"Hundred and twenty years combined old enough."

"Do you think we could've, should've?"

"We were perfect, did whatever the sixties let us. Perfection filled part of the last four decades with wonder and made me think about you, eventually hiring a detective so we could be here like this."

Elvin let their hands touch.

"We're not going to run off."

"But we are going to walk to the river now."

Same gulls and warning to cover head was followed by laughter as they walked past a couple of fisherman who never bothered to look up and notice white and black together. March of time was praised. Waves were rough, smashing into the end of the jetty, spraying mist.

"I think about Dr. King all the time and listen to his *I have a dream speech* on the internet. My Rabbi spoke right before Dr. King back in 1963. God bless the internet and progress, tolerance, and a changing world. How I wish, really wish Dr. King could see where we're at. Every headline of achievement or political accomplishment of African-Americans and everything I read and hear, wish he could see, but deep inside, I know he does."

"Why so much thought?"

"It's inside of me; a spirit. Can't deny who I am."

Like years ago, it was time. Elvin helped her up, holding hands and again, she surprised Elvin with a kiss.

"I was wrong. I said way back that was our last kiss, remember?"

"Never forgot."

"Let's not say anything now."

A boat waiting in the inlet honked.

"Was that for us?"

"Think so and I think I know the name of the boat. Let's go before we see the boat name so we'll always wonder."

On the sand, a few hundred feet away, both turned around at the same time and looked at the future silently.

TWENTY SIX

S tanding sideways in a downstairs bathroom mirror, gut sucked in, tee shirt dropped back over dietary failures, Elvin turned to face himself, promising sweeping changes in six hours, when 2008 descended on Times Square. Just out of sight in the hall, Evie thought a campaign speech for town council was taking place.

"I love to hear you accost yourself and ready New Year resolutions."

"How long were you standing out there?"

"I heard the campaign promise to lose thirty pounds by summer equinox. You love those equinoxes; besides I'd love to see you a bit healthier for Nelson's graduation."

Elvin felt satiated from a bowl of wheat flakes an hour earlier. Sitting in the den, staring at mantle pictures, thinking certain things about life on Earth were rock solid by resisting change, like breakfast cereal and the only timely difference was the size of the bowl. As a Rutgers student, a pressure cooker pot took a full box, now a small orange bowl barely held a fistful. Maybe they didn't have to go out for New Year's Eve dinner but on second thought, he wouldn't change tradition. Several years ago the Stones settled into Chinese dinner, all by themselves, no friends or relatives. Evie felt it was reclusiveness but Nelson was allowed a Rutgers girlfriend.

Two bottles of wine, one Muscatel, one Merlot rested on a white table cloth next to hot mustard and duck sauce.

"No offense Dad, but who the hell drinks Muscatel?"

"So, drink the Merlot."

"I don't drink fucking Merlot either."

"Wise guy, that's a line from a movie."

"You bet. Sarah and I stopped for Chardonnay from a South Jersey vineyard. It's in the car."

"South Jersey!"

"Just teasing. It's California, relax."

A mirror's reflection in the back of the restaurant let him watch Nelson walk out; it was like gazing at an hour glass filled with genetic sand. Lately he was into absorbing Nelson as much as possible. Ploys were impromptu phone calls and a quick *Olive Branch* sandwich, beer and Rutgers basketball game. Life was not destiny anymore, just a dream.

A few weeks back, lying in bed after showering together, and that's all they did, meaning they were older, wider and didn't fit, Evie started crying. Tears were a mother's joy, to see a father and son so close; friends hanging out at a college bar together. She was never happier. Elvin ran downstairs for a monotonous bottle of Manischewitz to enhance the moment.

"Elvin."

"Yes, Sarah. I'm glad you're finally calling me by the name by mother picked out and not that Mister stuff."

"Nelson talks about you guys all the time, especially the way you hang out together."

"No big deal. It's just what we do. I never think twice about it."

Nelson returned with Chardonnay and in a blink of an eye, it was looking at himself in a mirror.

"Toast to Nelson, Sarah and your graduation in May. A word to you both; *plastics*. To Evie, my everything, always. Happy, Healthy New Year everyone. Love. Peace. Hope."

"It's funny Dad, every time you toast, there's always *hope* thrown in."

"It's funny Nelson, you noticed that."

Times Square with five minutes left to go before the ball comes down was on all the local channels. Elvin reflectively announced, "I should've been there this time."

"Why?"

"Because I've never been."

"That's a reason?"

"I think so."

Back in the fifties. Guy Lombardo and his Royal Canadians band played *Auld Lang Syne* at this holiday juncture. Martha, Jack and friends were in the living room watching television with an antenna sporting a teaspoon hanging from one of the ears by a string. Jack swore it helped reception. Elvin was in a door way in pajamas, rubbing eyes. Aunt Gert noted that his cute thing was hanging out through the big hole in front so Aunt Lillian took the pleasure to pull pajamas all the way up, almost severing it off. Someday he'd write the pajama manufacturer and ask about the reason for openings and why did they stop making them. Adults started kissing, hugging and crying. Crying bothered him. Old people weren't supposed to.

"Elvin!"

"Sorry, I was back in Newark."

"Well, happy 2008."

The ball was down. The foursome hugged. Nelson got the longest hug.

"Are you alright Dad?"

"I am now. Say Nelson, do you remember wearing pajamas with an opening in the front, so things could slip out?"

"Nah."

Two men leaned on a van, smoking, joking about Vermont's scenery change from winter to a spring day and how everything was once white, desolate and foreboding. The taller man questioned the usage of the word foreboding. The smaller man assured him that it was proper usage and reminded about growing up in Burlington, graduating from the University. A woman, about thirty, leaned out of a window, saying how much she loved Ben and Jerry's from Burlington and what she'd do for a pint of *Phish Food* right now.

"Sex? All kinds Mary or are you ATNA right now?"

"ATNA, George?"

"All talk, no action."

"When have you known me?"

"That's just it Mary, we don't know you like that."

"And you're not supposed to. We don't want to get federal now?"

"We are federal lest ye forget."

Mary, nearly six foot, got out of the back, stretched along the road side and walked over to surveyor's equipment twenty feet away.

"Say Mary, that Patriots hat, with your hair tucked underneath, and no tits, sorry, I call them as I see them or don't see them, kind of makes you look like one of us."

"Steve, fuck you. What's gotten into you this morning? Too much sexual innuendo, so stick a sock in it."

"Sorry, nerves."

"Then run into the woods and take care of things. There's a white towel from the motel in the back seat."

Tall George flicked a dying cigarette before looking at fresh art work signage, *Fahr-Cole Surveyors, Burlington*.

Ode to Joy chimed on a cell phone. Steve answered, "Understood, we're on the way."

A few miles down the road, and off a quarter mile, a solitary farm house was perched on a hill. A brick building behind the house seemed out of context. Slamming its door, making sure it was shut, a middle-aged man walked away, adjusting a cowboy hat. The house front door opened; a small girl ran down the steps.

"Mommy said get white bread too. Can I sit up front?"

"Jessie, you know the rules. If you want, let Abigail sit up front with me."

"Abigail's a doll."

"That's why she can sit up front."

Mud, salt stains from winter, covered the rear and side names on the van, idling for the past five minutes. Up close it read, *Sherman Brothers Farm*.

Ten minutes of winding roads, some changing to dirt, the Sherman van veered off to another side road, finally pulling into a dirt parking lot in front of *Hank Callan's General Merchandise and Deli*.

"Hobbie, Jessie. Happy May Thirteenth."

"Thanks Hank. Happy spring to you too. Do you think we hit seventy degrees today?"

"Supposed to. Say Jessie, how's Abigail."

"Sitting in the front seat waiting for me."

Hobbie Sherman took a small wicker basket and began walking around the half dozen aisles. Jessie knew her routine; at the side rear was a display of white and wheat breads, used as building blocks. When they fell, it was soft and never made noise, so Dad never knew.

A van pulled up, almost blocking the front door.

"Ah, the surveyors from this morning. You're back. Coffee? Lunch? We make pretty good deli sandwiches for Milton, Vermont."

"Hank, we'll have three turkey sandwiches on rye with mustard and regular coffees."

"Coming right up."

Mary strolled around the store with real wooden floors- the kind you could still get a splinter from-watching Jessie building a fort out of bread. Hobbie put a half gallon of milk into the basket, excusing himself, so that a stranger wearing a Red Sox cap could get by. George ran behind the counter, interrupting sliced turkey. Mary picked up Jessie, and took her into the bathroom as George put a gun to Hank's head and fired a shot. Steve did the same thing to Jessie's dad. Mary left the bathroom, Jessie's cries still heard. The cash register was opened, all the bills and one partially wrapped turkey sandwich was removed. The surveying van drove away slowly.

College graduation represents fruition, hope, dreams, legacy and the harsh, abrupt end of three month summer vacations for the rest of an adult life unless you teach something. Before Nelson's graduation from Rutgers, Elvin made a CD. All twenty four songs were *Pomp and Circumstance*.

At red lights, window down, sound up, *Pomp and Circumstance* blasted, so that the microcosmic world around could hear his music and maybe feel just a little of what he did. What a great name for a short story about a son like Nelson, *Pride and Swollen Chest*. A dozen times between WaWa for a gallon of one percent milk and pre-cut mango and Sunoco gas, Elvin whispered Nelson's name to the background music of a repeating CD.

Evie and Elvin sat on the steps of Brower Commons, waiting for the graduate. Women with parasols, fancy hats, strolled down College Avenue promenade.

Dresses were layered with all kinds of fluffy stuff. If you were trying to make a baby and the basal thermometer said hurry, you've got five minutes but could you get it all off in time? Maybe that's why birth rates were lower back then. Men with handlebar moustaches and tall hats pompously walked a few steps ahead of the women. Today women wore jeans under graduation gowns and guys who pompously walked a few steps ahead, were labeled assholes by popular magazines.

"Elvin, come back! You're far away."

Nelson approached waving a facsimile diploma and handed it to Evie. "You earned it more than me, so you keep it."

If only the Tavern restaurant or Claremont diner were still around, how fitting and proper to show Nelson cheesecake, health salad and pure Newark seltzer. Better days were back then because Alex was around breathing the same air. Nelson's graduation gift was a week in Washington, not a car, trip to Europe or Australia. He was wonderfully, magically, spiritually his son, even deciding to teach college history.

At the Holocaust Museum, there was mournful silence everywhere. Silence permeated everything. Elvin remembered Rabbi Prinz's speech at the March on Washington in 1963 when he said the worst thing mankind can be is silent. A black and white photo of Hungarian Jews, women and children, marching to gas chambers at Auschwitz in 1944, showed sadness, bewilderment, abandonment. One mother, holding an infant was the only adult in the group staring at the photographer- haunting eyes asking why. Another mother was squeezing her young son's hand, maybe tighter as they walked inexorably. The little boy stared at the photographer too.

"Why, Dad?"

"Because fanatics and people who follow them. It's easier to go along and be silent, less confrontation."

"Are you hinting there's good in people but they make stupid decisions?"

"Maybe. I know people get lazy or don't think terrible things could happen and when they do, they're more relieved it isn't happening to them, so they look the other way, turn cheeks and let people suffer, die or even help murder. Sometimes there's oil, money or power underlying."

"Like Darfur?"

"Exactly. There's an old Hebrew saying, that he who saves a life, saves the world but our world lets people die in Darfur. Quite a world we've got. I think the big four television networks averaged about ten minutes each for an entire year covering the genocide in Darfur, but spend a hundred minutes covering any celebrity who's DWI and parties too much. It reminds me when a prominent newspaper covered the early Holocaust way back. A couple of articles here and there mentioned some Jews dying, buried towards the back of the paper, so I'm not surprised about ten minutes television coverage for an entire year. Look how long it took the President to even define what's happening as genocide. A few million people could die while coming up with a working definition which took a year; quite remarkable in this information, digital age. What are we doing to the world; definitely not saving it and what's God thinking now? Do we forget what life is about? Alex used to tell me all the time. He went to three houses of worship to be with God and try to understand this picture we're looking at now. It could be Darfur instead of 1944."

"Did Uncle Alex finally understand?"

"His last few years, maybe."

"What does that mean?"

Elvin had a list of Washington things to do. Vietnam War Memorial was on the second day.

"Let's split up now and meet in an hour. Pick two names to remember for the rest of your life, just like we did at New Jersey's Memorial. Always think about their sacrifice and lives snuffed out, like mothers and children marching to die in a gas chamber."

A light drizzle felt good in oppressive Washington heat. Nelson was about to pass Elvin by at panel 17E, when he pulled him to the side and kissed his soft spot.

"I love you son."

"Me too, Dad. Do you have your names?"

"I do."

"Mom's crying over there. Did she know someone who died in Vietnam?"

"The fifty-six thousand- like all of us."

A white Buick made several parallel park attempts, backing in partially then pulling out, starting all over. On the third, half try, a gray haired woman switched with a younger woman who started over, but parked on the first try. A passing pedestrian saw a daughter helping her mother. Two women started to cross Cannon Street in Hibbing, Minnesota, waiting for several cars to pass. Koerner Pharmacy had a small sign in the front window; *parking in rear.*

"Mother! After all that!"

"Don't say it, Jackie."

A long center aisle passed greeting cards, laxatives, first aid, and paper towels. Some greeting cards were hand made by a local women's club, according to a small sign.

"Let me look, how perfectly quaint. *To my Husband of all these years. In snow, ice and bleakness of unforgiving winters, now it's springtime, Happy Anniversary.*

"Surely hand made. There's nothing better to do here in winter solitude than to make cards."

"May I help you?" An impressionist picture of white greeted them. A white haired, white lab coat, white sneaker wearing pharmacist stood at attention.

"Prescription please."

"Let's see, Roland Hagle, Cherry Township. A long way from here. Phone number? Oh, it's written on top already. May twenty fourth. Any allergies?"

"Penicillin, sulfa."

"Age?"

"Forty-five, next week."

"First time here?"

"First prescription in years; he's a healthy guy, just can't sleep."

"Fifteen minutes."

"Thank you."

Jackie decided to get the car and continue driving duties. Mother's cell phone rang.

"About fifteen minutes."

Driving on Route 37 on a deserted stretch, the Buick pulled over, a trunk popped open, a tire jack was dropped on the roadway, with Jackie and Mother practicing frantic gestures and waving hands. A pick-up truck from the opposite direction approached, crossed over and pulled in front.

"Ladies, need help?"

Jackie sassily answered, "You think we look like we're in trouble?"

They laughed.

"Roland Hagle at your service."

"Gertrude and Jackie Damon. Is it flat sir?"

"Way flat."

"Thanks for stopping."

"It's alright. A couple of minutes, I'll have you on your way."

Jackie walked around and yelled, "Nice pick-up."

"Thanks, it's new. Just three weeks ago. I've been waiting for the snow to melt before I break it in."

An approaching black van was the only sign of life the past few minutes, pulling behind Roland's pick up. Two men, tee-shirts rolled up, exposing tattooed biceps, both of the *mother* variety, jumped out.

"Is everything all right?"

Roland hollered, "Thanks, got it covered."

Tee-shirts approached fast, and covered Roland's face with a moist cloth, holding tight until unconscious. Gertrude opened a purse, pulling out a vial and syringe. One of the tattoos removed Roland's left boot and sock. Jackie injected him between toes. A sleeping body was carried to the van. Jackie finished changing the tire and drove back towards Hibbing. Gertrude got in the van which turned around.

Twenty minutes later, the van pulled into a dirt drive, leading to an old two story house, with barn and a garage like brick building a few hundred feet away. Another truck, *Catchings Plumbing and Heating* approached.

"Everything's done. The dog's dead on living room floor. House is loaded up since this morning. You've got a hundred twenty seconds. Upstairs, second door on right."

Gertrude leaned over. "Four sleeping pills taken out of prescription vial. Matches what was injected. Give or take."

"He'll sleep then really sleep."

"Have a nice night."

"You too. Good timing, sun just setting."

The other tee-shirt, driving Roland's pick-up, followed the tire tracks to the side.

Unwinding of a garden hose was interrupted by a daddy long legs spider traversing Elvin's sneaker. In a James Bond movie-the only real Bond for Elvin was Sean Connery- a poisonous spider with hairy legs was deposited in his bed; then it crawled slowly up his stomach, towards neck and face. Exercised restraint, sweat beads forming on forehead, was priceless. Suddenly Bond brushed the intruder off, jumped out of bed, and pounded relentlessly with a shoe. Nature would take Elvin's spider away.

The hose was unwound, keeping a cautious eye to feet, before stretching out to four thirsty young trees. It was late June and Jersey was in a drought. The drought made it to the Presidential campaign, when the front running democrat and likely nominee commented on global warming, its effects and a promise to keep it high priority. Elvin watched intently with dreams that Dr. King was looking down and seeing America mature. Somehow, the only thing that mattered in the presidential campaign circus was if Dr. King spiritually knew what was going on. Like a folk song, it was Elvin's reason to believe.

Now in front of trees, he forgot to turn on the water, so a cell phone came out of an exaggerated cargo shorts pocket. "Nelson, sorry to bother you. Please turn on the outside water for me?"

"It's sick how you abuse technology."

"And it's sick, how you're going for a Masters Degree at Rutgers in two months and you're sequestered in your room on a beautiful summer Saturday morning with all those letters around you."

Water shot out. Nelson walked over.

"Letters, Dad?"

"E mail. X-box. I-pod. F-book. IM."

"You love those trees don't you?"

"You're changing subjects on your old man?"

"Exactly."

"Are you going out with Sarah tonight?"

"To Belmar, we're going to hit the boardwalk then a couple of beers."

"These trees will always remind me of Alex, Christine, Emmett Till and his mother Mamie."

"See you, Dad. Oh, a favor, don't call me."

Elvin looked around; cars passing by and a black bird circling overhead, finally settling in a tree across the street. Water was flowing, with leaking, creating a wet groin stain. Producer David Selznick got fined a couple of hundred dollars for letting Clark Gable's Rhett Butler say the word *damn* at the end of *Gone With the*

Wind. Atlanta was burning to the ground. Miss Prissy couldn't find the doctor. Spending four hours watching the movie was worth it by the time Rhett told Scarlett, he didn't give a damn. Music swept you down south to a problematic innocent time. Drifting had liabilities; he didn't like the south.

"Sorry Nelson. I just got an inspiration. Could you find me the tape of *Gone With the Wind.* I'm suddenly in the mood. Want to watch?"

"Bye Dad."

Groin wetness stains evaporated sitting in the den with feet up. Music transported him back to when brothers fought each other. Since Goodman, Schwerner and Cheney were murdered in Mississippi, the south was never a place he wanted to see. *Easy Rider* didn't help southern loving either. Little Bonnie Butler just died on screen after getting thrown from a horse. Music was so strong and evoking, it almost made him want to hitch hike through Alabama and Georgia on a new sojourn looking for Tara. Deep in his heart, he wanted to go back and live during the Civil War. Life was simpler. The future looked better. There was more of it.

The front door bell chimed a few times. Evie must've been napping while Nelson played with loud letters in his room. New front doors were thick glass, so objects standing and ringing came through wavy unclear. Standing outside enough times, he made sure outsiders saw the same.

As the door opened, he mostly stared at a bearded man and froze, eyes fixed. A left hand reached to lean on the door, then gasping, eyes departed, body slipped to the floor. The beard ran in and yelled, "Evie, Nelson, come here, we need help!"

Evie first, then Nelson, stopped before the bottom step, in shocking recognition of the beard. A hand covered her mouth then a scream, "Alex, Christine!"

"Let's get him up."

"I'm alright. Nelson, get me some water and turn the TV off."

Elvin's head was propped on a few throw pillows, feet stretched out on the den sofa. Alex hovered. Christine and Evie continued hugging, not wanting to let go.

"Get up slowly. Let's get you some color."

"Your voice is the same. You've got a lot of hair on your face but fairly gray." A slight smile appeared.

"Good, your color is back, humor too."

Alex sat on the next section, reaching for Elvin's hand. Christine held Evie's hand.

"So, Alex? Talk to us."

"There's a lot to say. How about I make some general statements, then maybe we'll do a reunion tour?"

"Reunion tour sounds good."

"You're staying for dinner of course."

Christine eased up on Nelson's hug. "Can we bring in Corned Beef and Pastrami; it's been a while?"

"Nelson you go to pick up. Think I want to keep my eye on Uncle Alex."

"It's easier to say I've been working on projects for the government. You know my security clearance. To be perfectly safe, I needed to be invisible all these years. What better way than for people to think I'm eternally resting in Freehold, while I've grown a gray beard and done my job."

"Pass the mustard."

"Pickle?"

"Half sour?"

"Pass the potato salad."

"We'll be living in Freehold. We bought a house with a pool. I'm done, retired now. We can relax, but very important Nelson, we're going to ease into things, so we're not really broadcasting and publicizing. Get my drift?"

Three heads shook.

"Nelson. Later on when you're with Sarah and you happen to be on the boardwalk at Belmar and see two older guys near the water on a blanket talking and they look familiar, just keep walking. Pretend you don't know."

Air conditioning was turned up. Night heat was unseasonably stifling. The car turned onto Route Eighteen towards Belmar. "Do you feel like listening to *Pomp and Circumstance* twenty-four times in a row?"

"I missed your rambling the most. Did anyone ever tell you how amazingly unique it is? You fainted on me; a hell of a reaction and I'm a little confused."

"You're confused?"

"Now I'm really confused, Elvin. Everything was carefully orchestrated and words chosen. You should've known everything with no confusion. Saying goodbye at the river was so only you could've ever known and figured it out. We've been sending cryptic messages like that since we met in the lot in 1960. I knew you'd never be confused, relieved obviously."

"I'm still confused."

"At the Shark River, saying goodbye, I told you about recreating the suicide scene from MASH; the same favorite scene I loved for thirty years, when the dentist wants to commit suicide because he can't get it up."

"Sure, it was always your favorite."

"The suicide was staged in the movie, it never happened, only in the dentist's mind that night. The following morning he was fine and started a jaw reconstruction. Staged, make believe, just like what I had to do. "

"My God, you did tell me at the river and said I'd figure it out. Those words reverberated for years. I cried after you left the jetty with so much emotion. I never looked beyond what you were saying. All these years! I really messed up. You did explain everything. Do I laugh or cry? My goodness."

"Messed up! Elvin, that's a major under statement. You and the rest of the world believed. We wanted the rest of the world. Actually, it's almost fortuitous that you believed we were dead. It probably made the whole plot workable, fooling who we needed to, on a more plausible stage."

"Walk me through everything."

Chardonnay, two bottles, plastic cups, and a container of almonds rested on the blanket.

"The house in Freehold was bought and furnished for us but we haven't even seen it yet. What about the report?"

"It's still in a vault. Did anything change all these years? I never thought anything would."

"Nothing changed, except the timing; maybe Thanksgiving night."

"We'll that's good. We'll go back to Thanksgiving dinners together and I finished the basement with your help."

Each held a bottle; bases clicked.

"Gabriel was born after World War II started and grew to be part of secret American life. They're everywhere and around the world and have all the money they could ever want. Since they're everywhere, they know everything and are the ultimate inside traders. Imagine someone knowing everything, like a crystal ball. So much money came from inside trading information. It's like having your own legitimate mint."

Spontaneous hugs led to bottles resting in the sand.

"Our first hug in years. You got the money a few years ago from the Princeton house and you've been using it."

"Simple thanks is never enough. You helped me finish things in my life; more than a brother forever. Most things you knew I'd do. I borrowed a few hundred thousand from the bank. Fuck them. I couldn't have done anything without you. I love you, Alex."

"I love you too. Remember Chicago when you were at Emmett Till's grave?"

"How'd you know about that? We always talked about going there."

"When you were there that windy sunny day, I waited outside for you to finish then I went in. You spent a lot of time there."

"That's so strange. It was the only time since you died that I actually felt you. Talking to Emmett, his mother and you, I felt something about you more than ever before and you were right outside. All this is too haunting for Belmar beach. How'd you know I was going?"

"Gabriel."

"How did Gabriel?"

"Back track. The plane crash killing two hundred fifty people. I was supposed to be on it. Government policy is secured in Iceland, at a secret meeting and all life things are to continue as normal. Everything going on is forgotten about. Those who knew too much had to be eliminated because there can't be any leaks. They want people to live normal lives and no chances taken. The world is clean, neat and simple so they wiped out a plane to eliminate a couple of dozen scientists, aides and security people. They keep going through security people. Maybe they'll run out."

"You're presumed dead?"

"For a while but Gabriel knew that wouldn't last. I had to be eliminated especially with vengeance as a motive. I knew way too much. Gabriel had to buy me time. They found a couple in Rome, New York. Gabriel made me buy a house in Sedona and also in Kansas City of all places. This is going to sound terrible but they kidnapped that Rome couple and put them in a medically induced coma and shipped them to Kansas City. The rest you can figure out."

"DNA identification and everything else?"

"Gabriel. Our DNA was substituted."

"Where've you been?"

"Gabriel is a travel agent too. Remember when Christine and I went to Churchill, Hudson's Bay and Winnipeg? Those were some of the places for us after my funeral. Of course, there were never problems with passports."

"Gabriel?"

"Sure. We also spent time in San Francisco and Northern California mountains. A nice fellow took care of us. John Patch, an Alaskan, involved with something like Gabriel which I've been a liaison to. Nolan introduced me and pushed me to be a liaison. Remember that Rutgers mathematician Josef Simmons with his office behind Rutgers military science and his son, Peter? Same group as John Patch."

"I had dinner recently with Peter and Brandon."

"So you've been busy innocently interacting but not knowing much."

Elvin walked an empty bottle of Chardonnay to a refuse container. Always thought of as refuse not garbage, refuse was a beautiful word, sounding kinder and gentler. A thought of how he'd love to just drift away now without any more knowledge was suddenly there, almost like trumpets, heralding the arrival of royalty.

"Question; how and why are you here now? Aren't they, whoever the hell they are, still after you?"

"The major policy obstacle was eliminated last year. Elimination helped to smooth things out with assurances and guarantees. Gabriel negotiated everything. The poor fellow was permanently put to sleep while his gums were being cleaned."

"Gabriel?"

"Don't ask anymore. What else, Elvin? I'm getting hungry."

"Great pizza nearby. Remember one slice is like a half pie. Are you safe now?"

"Sure, all is well. We'll all be fine, plenty money to tide us over."

"Are they still going after scientists?"

"No one's left who has a much of a clue. They did a thorough world-wide cleaning job but there were some lingering problems with a few amateur astronomers. Recently amateurs in Vermont and Minnesota that might've posed security threats were eliminated."

"They?"

"Them." An eye winked. "Carl's erasers, remember?"

"Hey Alex, you won't be able to vote in the Presidential election in November."

"All my years involved with Gabriel, they knew things, sometimes years ahead of time."

"What do you know now?"

"Be surprised."

"Life is funny. I've been thinking about Dr. King lately." Elvin finished the bottle with a last healthy drink out of a cup.

"Same here."

"We were always similar thinkers."

"And always will be. Dr. King would've been brought to tears of joy. *The Eyes of the Prize* and making life struggles worth it."

"How about heading out to Sedona in the next few weeks?"

"I was just going to ask the same thing."

TWENTY SEVEN

New York City on a summer Saturday was deserted. A strong breeze, absence of vehicular traffic on east-west streets, paper blowing in tornado-like circles, no street people, all conspired to ignite imaginative science fiction. Eventually power fails, neon signs in a nearby coffee shop window go dark with the hope that stale brewed coffee can still be found inside. Alex laughed at Elvin's narrative. Earlier that morning they parked at the Maplewood train station and let the swaying motion of a New York train ease them into a nap by East Orange.

After covering all floors of the Metropolitan Museum of Art, they eventually found the coffee shop; tuna sandwiches were substituted with turkey when Elvin warned about rising mercury levels. Eyebrows lifted but Alex let his friend manage the food tray. Later, Central Park seemed more alive than the rest of the city with *anti-Hampton* people- the rugged individuals who stayed city-bound on summer weekends. The park reminded of the cemetery in Chicago, with trees bending in the wind, showing reverence. Elvin returned an errant Frisbee to its owner. A long time ago a Rutgers bus went out of its way to flatten a Frisbee on College Avenue while Alex watched with John Simmons from an office window.

"Why are these microscopic irrelevant pieces of cerebral minutia still floating around? Sometimes I worry, that I'm clogging my gig memory space with such bullshit, so there won't be room for relevancy."

Elvin pointed to a sofa-like boulder. "Relevancy? Does anything matter?"

"It might. Are you still doing Rutgers football with Nelson?"

"And women's and men's basketball, wrestling, hockey, lacrosse and baseball. Keeps me busy. I finished doing a host of special things thanks to you. Spent time with Cousin Steven, ate at *Pando and Ernest* and inhaled Casablanca airport.

Steven's coming for Thanksgiving. I journalize my travels, thinking of publishing it. *Concentric Circles and Maple Leaves-Stem Intact by Elvin Stone.*"

"Sofia?"

"Invited her to Guadalcanal- the last meaningful time we contacted each other except for Merry Christmas but that's alright. Everything is the way it was supposed to be. Wonder is a beautiful word. Helps you get to sleep a thousand nights in a row. I hired a detective to find Caye. She's an amazing grandmother. Looks and spirit never changed."

"Guadalcanal?"

"Probably like Churchill, Hudson's Bay, remote, poignant. I cried by soldier's graves."

"Of course you would."

"A strange spiritual thing happened there. Wish I could go back but the flower drifted out to sea."

"Flower out to sea?"

"It's a custom which means I won't go back to Guadalcanal but we know that anyway."

A Greenwich Village basketball playground was crowded on both sides of the fence.

"Hey, you two old guys want to play half court? We'll take one of you on each team."

"Only if the offer was heartfelt."

"What the fuck you talking about?"

Half a block away, they found a small pizza shop, reminiscent of Maplewood center. Elvin fingered the hot marinara and rubbed it on a polo shirt. "Just like when Michael Lauzone shaved his head because his father went bald. I know before our day is done, there'll be a stain, so I'm cheating destiny too. Wouldn't it be nice to really cheat?"

"Maybe."

"The kid back there called us *old*."

"It's my gray beard bringing your age up. Guilt by association. Tell me about St. Anthony's Church."

Two middle aged women in tee shirts and shorts sat table next. Corner eyes were going back and forth between Elvin and a smiling blonde. "Stop it, Elvin."

"Montana was soulfully moving. I whispered your name enough times hiking in snow shoes. Services reminded me of St. Leo's. A North Star led me astray at one a.m."

"Astray?"

"Later. I did feel a powerful presence inside myself; a warm contentment and angelic spirit close by."

"And I've been back to my worship places."

"I know. Was anything ever said?"

"No, they were respectful of privacy so it was business as usual except they told me that you came to see them both. I never knew that. I was teary, knowing you believed I was gone and tried to feel my spirit in a Church and Mosque; a great definition of friendship."

A last train from New York stopped in Maplewood. Walking under the tunnel, making sure they were alone, they yelled, "WEEQUAHIC HIGH!" The bench was empty and the sign *to New York* was rusty squeaky. Elvin pointed to carved initials, *ES and AZ.*

"When did you do that?"

"After you died, one night late."

Alex got up for another sign push. "You whispered God before."

"Can we get help? You've got more connections."

"I don't know. We've seen things together, come full circle and been involved in struggles for freedom and equality- that's how we became friends. Everything's meant to be and deterministic, even sitting here like this. Thinking, dreaming, wondering, all these years and searching for spirit and now, most importantly, knowing it's there. A key to life means knowing spirit exists. Sure, we don't understand beyond."

"Forces still make me aware. I constantly feel something and even look for numerical signs that I'm not alone. Something makes me believe that I've been and done. Spirit listens, loves, cares and it makes me content, with no fear or regret. I find ways to talk to that angelic spirit every day. You've helped me get there. What about afterwards?" Elvin slid closer, always starting further apart but by session's end, they almost touched.

"We know spirit exists so after is there, we'll just never understand until we're there after. When we get to Sedona, we'll have time to ponder. I've got things to tell you, Elvin."

"All these years, you've seen things. I remember the day we met and went by that orphanage in Newark. You knew our parents would live long because you saw them as old and never wanted to take a child to a mountain and look at the sky because you were afraid of what's up there. You've seen so much all along."

"Yes. Some images were vague, like when daylight is wiped out by a solar eclipse or the way a movie scene looks, if it was filmed in strange, foreboding black and white. The race I talk about is when one contestant is the environment. How many more atrocities can the planet take? Billions of people need water, food, shelter and energy, and the best we can do is get kindergarten kids to color a green poster or bring a new energy saving light bulb to market. I saw bleakness, no trees or flowers, no children playing, barren mountains in a background and couldn't even see myself after a time; that's what really scared me. But only on this earth. Maybe in Sedona, things will make more sense."

"I've sensed you saw a future. Do you feel like leaving our train station now? Funny, I used to think it was ours from eleven to four exclusively."

"Do you want to go?"

"I never do, it's a security. Trains keep coming, stop for the night, start running again in the morning. Life's continuity."

"Wait, there's two leaves with stem intact."

"Let's do the tunnel again."

A single forty watt bulb was the only light on one whole side. "We should've marked the bulb, like they do a black bear or whale sent back to habitat for study. It could be forty years old."

"Ready!"

"WEEQUAHIC HIGH!"

"Done."

"Done."

A Scottsdale hotel pool at two p.m. was nearly deserted in unyielding heat and off-season sparse August attendance. Sitting on a lounge chair, towels covering lower and upper torso, Elvin yelled, "Feels like the surface of Mars but it's not dry anymore. Phoenix civilization makes them bring a lot of water down from the mountains which throws humidity into the air. There are clouds."

"Leave Mars out of it."

"What are you reading?"

"Bill Clinton's book."

From the pool, Elvin's voice found Alex nearly napping. "The water is too hot to cool the skin so it feels heavy but there's no other sensation. Maybe it's like the womb except I can't remember."

"You may get another chance."

"You've been dropping hints like that for weeks, wise guy."

"Where's dinner?"

"Furizi's. Italian."

Croutons were carefully segregated around the plate periphery. Two anchovies joined. Alex watched. "Why bother with Caesar?"

"I'm searching for the perfect dressing with flakes of Provolone cheese."

Glasses clicked, "To the universe, our friend."

"Elvin, Josef Simmons was an amazing mathematician with a black brother, John, whose son Brandon you met. John and I had that same mysterious ability. Some call it a gift, others a burden. When our commonality was realized, we spent time together. John knew about dying young, even wanting to be cremated because it was temporary and didn't make a difference. Josef and John were part of a secret world that studied oil supply issues for the government which started with Eisenhower. Josef's office at Rutgers was a headquarters of sorts and John's peculiar vision of the future fueled the whole project. Fuel is a funny word to use if you're talking about oil."

"Are you ready to order gentlemen?" A young girl, brunette with striking pink highlights, chewed gum voraciously between interrogative words.

Elvin whispered, "Welcome to Phoenix and the American west," then louder, "Two cavatelli and broccoli, heavy on garlic. Bring another wine please. Do you have Averna for after dinner?"

"Yes."

"Averna?"

"Sofia turned me on. Good earthy stuff. Secret oil supply?"

"Yes, secret oil issues, but not important. Josef taught me about the mathematical universe."

"Mathematical?"

"Well first you should know that everything possible happens. Think about the implications."

"Is that true?"

"Well if it is, think. Many believe it can be."

Wine glasses were filled past protocol. Elvin spoke, "If our waitress can chew gum, then I can fill glasses until they almost spill." Elvin eyed two women seated at the next table. Alex gently kicked him under the table.

"Well, think."

"Everything possible happens. Maybe it's a definition of God."

"Good thinking. Exactly the thought I had. Josef explained ideas from a Princeton math PhD candidate in the fifties and which are still very much around today. Without getting too technical, maybe there are parallel universes. There are two worlds, micro and macroscopic which is the world we see. Quantum mechanics is the world we don't see. There's something called universal wave function which is a mathematical list of all possible positions of an atom and there's a lot."

"You're losing me."

"I know but watch where all this goes over the next week. Now take a gram of an element, anything. It's made up of microscopic systems (atoms, electrons, etc.) that are in super positions, but we don't see all the billions of positions in the gram, we see only one. Could copies of us see another position that we don't and keep splitting to see each position? Are you beginning to grasp the notion of parallel worlds and us?"

"I like that definition of God. Everything possible happens. Let's eat before *me* in another position eats *my* cavatelli which would piss me off."

"Split Tiramisu for dessert?"

"It's like splitting me to see each position."

"Elvin, you're getting it!"

"What now tour director?"

"Well Alex, thought we'd stop at the hotel bar, listen to some jazz."

"I want to finish Bill Clinton's book. See you in the morning."

Cooler evenings brought out locals, starved for cooler night air. The hotel lounge was almost crowded. A jazz trio set up in front of a massive fire place.

"Do you ever use that fireplace?" Alex asked sarcastically.

"Wintertime. It does get cold."

"I'd come back just to feel Scottsdale cold after today's heat. Red wine please. No Merlot." Elvin smirked at perfect timing as the musicians set up.

A few years back, Elvin started wearing a red rubber band around his right wrist. When questioned, always honest, he wasn't sure why, but thought it was probably directed by a spirit. Suddenly, the band was snapped hurtfully. The culprit on his right was a woman with crew cut black hair and large gold earrings swinging with laughter.

"It was an invitation waiting. Hope I didn't hurt you. What's the significance?"

"I wear it when I go to bars. There's always a woman who snaps it, so I call it the great segue."

She raised a hand. "Guilty. I'm Marie Gold, the segue."

"Elvin Stone. You have an interesting name combination."

"I'm from Boston. Moved here after my divorce. I've been single here five years. And you?"

"From Jersey. I'm here to climb mountains starting tomorrow in Sedona."

"Impressive. Do you climb a vortex?"

"Just the vortex."

"Should we get close to the fireplace? Better acoustics."

"Sure. Are you here a lot?"

"Twice a week. Single girl and all. I love real Jazz. I don't do drugs so I like coming here after working hard all week, getting a little buzz, going back to my apartment and if I can, fuck the night away, as long as I can sleep late the following morning. Here's my number."

"I'm an old movie fan. You just performed Bo Derek's scene from *Ten* and made my week. I'd better go now; too many reasons to stay and that's a real bodacious problem so I'll say goodnight, but may I keep the number?"

"Sure."

Traces of cirrus clouds from yesterday in Scottsdale disappeared by Montezuma's Castle, leaving a stark blue sky above and rushing water sounds from a nearby brook. A couple with two small children, led around by hand, caught up to them.

"Excuse me; my wife whispered that she saw you both by the Plaza pool yesterday."

"So who's following whom? Actually I do remember. You had a Chicago Bulls cap on." Elvin tipped a Rutgers cap.

"I did. Hometown loyalty. I suppose you're heading to Sedona?"

"Actually we split here. Jerome today, eventually Sedona. Your kids would like Jerome; an old copper mine and ghost town."

The family walked ahead, watching the water flow below. A little boy tried reaching the bed with a rock.

"Elvin, refresh the history here for me"

"Sinaqua Indians disappeared four hundred years ago. No one knows why."

"Prophetic, isn't it? Indians then, earth inhabitants now. Life is a tower of Babble. Not, B-a-b-e-l. The race with the environment. Do you know earth's worst culprit? It's all the different languages, which really means every country has a different agenda or language so it's hard to sit around a table and come up with protocols, treaties or guidelines. We're a funny species. We can't process urgency. Every political leader is more interested in today, getting votes tomorrow, but the damn day after tomorrow is the tower of Babble."

A nude couple emerged from the water. Smiles lingered all the way back to the parking lot. On the steep road up to Jerome, Alex pointed out the mountain's thirty degree incline and that gravity literally pulled buildings down the slope including the town jail. During the heyday of the copper mine, as many as fifteen thousand people lived in Jerome, now a few hundred. A walking tour took them through a historic back alley called *prostitution row*. On Main Street was a local eatery, dispensing chili in a plastic cup. Across the street, a panoramic view of distant mountains with snow capped peaks made them sit on a brick wall taking it all in. Two heavy duty Harleys parked just behind; the bikers headed for chili.

Elvin walked empty cups to refuse. "Continue with multiple universes. I think best with beans and beef, from a plastic cup, now colon bound."

"Such an eager student impresses teacher. Infinite universes means there are other copies of earth, so there are copies of us, maybe with every possible outcome like a multiverse, same life and different lives. Maybe you never met Evie. Maybe John Lennon is still alive."

"It's a hard rain."

"I know. Picture this; the universe shape is perfectly flat or curved. Maybe if flat, an infinite number are sitting on top of one another. An experiment once shot laser beams into space and the angles added up to one hundred eighty degrees, so it's flat. There's also a level two universe theory, kind of like a giant soap bubble. Strange material inflates. A little piece stops inflating, eventually forms galaxies, planets and people."

"What about the big bang?"

"Out of chaos comes existence. Amazing intelligence created us. God. Simple isn't it?"

"Einstein, Alex?"

"He's the relativity and gravity man which fights with quantum mechanics theory. Some think the universe exists in eleven dimensions or it's a membrane and we're adrift on one. Another level deals with electrons disappearing and reappearing, so we're at multiple places at the same time. Remember everything possible happens."

On cue, representing cerebral fullness on the part of Elvin, they hopped off the brick wall and walked around the parked Harleys, letting eyes fill with dreams and regrets, having never experienced motorcycles and wondering why. A biker arrived; a bean remnant was clinging to an upper lip, so Elvin motioned. A voice was surprisingly deep. "You guys virgins?"

Elvin spoke. "In what sense?" He observed that in this new foursome, everyone stood eye to eye.

"Ever been on a bike? We can tell the answer's *no* and that you're longing for an adventure."

For Elvin, it was like Bonnie looking at Clyde. In a brief instant, they smiled and knew death was imminent as machine guns exploded filling their bodies. Elvin and Alex's look at each other was also instantaneous with a smile, that said, seize the motorcycle moment. "What's next?"

"You guys give us fifty dollars apiece and we'll take you on a two hour tour and meet back at the *Spirited Rail* over there for a couple of beers."

Elvin's cycle pulled out first; arms wrapped tightly around, helmet annoyingly constraining, yet a body still felt the rush of power and seductive speed. Alex's cycle wasn't over his shoulder yet. The thrill of speed on two wheels obviated paranoia that both of them were being taken for separate rides. Bikers were gentle people, with bad reputations. Nothing was wrong with Marlon Brando in *The Wild One* except generational misunderstandings. Rocky in *Mask* had a collection of biker friends, so gentle and caring, that years back, fixated Elvin in trying to find Rocky's gravesite somewhere in Monrovia, California. An image of

Cher's poignant face about to shed tears at Rocky's grave made Elvin's growing list of life's haunting images. Now he was with a new biker acquaintance exploring. A forest appeared after a long eye blink, at the same time the road became dirt bumpy. A few minutes into oblivion and slowing down, the biker's deep voice asked if he wanted to walk around for a spell. No one in New Jersey ever used the word *spell* to equate a measurement of time, making him realize, he was a long way from home. Whispers of Evie and Nelson softly passed pursed lips.

"Sure."

A small clearing in a dense section of wooded majesty had a pair of boulders, one painted with a white *Helen*.

"That's me." A finger outlined the name.

"Huh?"

"Helen." Removal of helmet and sunglasses led to a long blonde hair explosion like the machine gun explosion killing Bonnie and Clyde that he thought about earlier, which helped him get on the bike in the first place. "An old boyfriend painted that a few years ago. We'd come here all the time, camp out and you know the rest. He wanted to memorialize mostly the sex. Sleeping was too silent; sometimes you heard a bird or felt a four legged creature's vibration."

"I hear something now. How old are you if you don't mind me asking?"

"Forty-six. Would you like to talk? I've got some joints in my saddle bag."

"That's the first time in my life anybody's ever had a saddle bag, so I think a few joints with inhalation works. By the way, where's my friend?"

"Probably in a forest like this, sitting on rock and lighting up about now. You have an aura and powerful sad eyes."

"I'll be right back." Sliding off the rock, he walked over to the cycle, looked at the license plate, smiled and came back for another drag.

"Why'd you do that?"

"Do you have a week?"

The morning after, a telephone rang, and was banged down, words repeated for an audience, "Ten a.m. and sunny."

By eleven, waiting for a breakfast table at the Coffee Pot Restaurant, more words for his audience. "Feels like we were here."

"Maybe that waitress with the red stain on her left breast worked here."

'That was an eternity ago."

"We've got to finally order grits with all due respect to *Easy Rider* promises we made." Heads turning gently back and forth, absorbing locals and tourists, Elvin suddenly froze, staring at a woman walking by.

"Are you alright?"

"It's her, that blonde woman from Guadalcanal who looked like my cousin in 1930. She talked to me in the middle of an island in the Pacific Ocean then got into a car and disappeared. I knew her license plate would show a spiritual sign, so I watched the car leave; *444* and some letters. That's her but not. I've got to follow her when she leaves."

"A typical day?"

"Yesterday?"

Eyes concentrated at each other. Deep breaths and exhales annoyed coffee cup steam. A smile was shared. The blonde woman walked by. Elvin followed and waited as she got into a car. Arizona license plate, *444*. Watch time was 11:44. Goosebumps started their heralded trip down his arm.

"Good time to talk. Agreed. There are multiple universes, flat, stacked up on one another."

"Agreed."

"Elvin, we've both experienced rampant deja vu since Sedona as teenagers. Souls have been opened like receptors because some kind of attachment was made to us. The more open and receptive, the more given to you just like that blonde woman before. Angelic intervention is all over your life and I see things. One more thought needs to be passed along over an empty grits bowl. Angelic intervention has been part of your life for years. You've chronicled everything."

"I have."

"Here's a thought for you. The guardian angel that's within you, communicates, watches, sends you to Montana on Christmas Eve, puts you in a restaurant at the precise time that blonde woman walked by our aisle, made you swerve our car away from an oncoming car at the exact precise second, makes you see *444* and *111* all the time and everything else that brings goose bumps and tears. Did you ever think maybe your guardian angel is you; your energized spirit from another universe, dispatched? Who better to watch over you then you? How many times do you hear that everyone has a guardian angel? Shoot, I hope those people at the next table aren't eavesdropping. With what we're talking about, it's called getting arrested and put away for lengthy observation."

"Let's go."

Airport Road vortex arrival timing was perfect as a rare parking spot just opened. The climb to the summit was slow, stopping often for breath and view.

"Stand with feet, shoulder width apart. Loosen your knees, Elvin. Sway back and forth until you're comfortable. Sway until you're balanced. Breathe deeply, like you did in Greenwich Village at Christmas time. I still remember that. You'll feel your body inflate, like a separate universe or bubble. When you exhale, your body deflates. Feel energy and power of breathing. Bend your knees, getting closer to earth's energy. Grab some of the energy radiating up and squeeze it tight. No more talking."

The summit was invaded several times over the hour. A young couple kissed for almost as long as they stood. When alone, they sat, facing each other, like at Belmar beach, feet kicking at sand, discovering a gold watch. "Where is the watch?"

"In the room, in my attaché case."

"Elvin, what if there are multiple universes? What if deja vu is an energy that some people feel, like us? Remember, it makes us feel that we've been some place before. What if that energy leaks into our universe from another universe and that leak is right here in Sedona and this energy is a lock and key, knowing to find us precisely. We've got receptors or a spiritual delivery service."

"Some call it vortex."

"Precisely. We know there's something here. We've lived with it most of our lives. What if, when we're feeling deja vu, you or I are also in another universe, doing something at that moment, and we're also feeling this same something in another universe at the same moment in time. Deja vu is there for them too, of course meaning us. A complicated thought but nothing comes easy."

"But leaking universes?"

"Sure, remember the mantra, everything possible happens. Some scientists think someday, a long time from now, that they could be able to get from one universe to another through what they call a wormhole. Of course sliding through one of those things in a hundred thousand years, what the hell are you going to find at the other end? What about the idea of shooting a satellite through the hole with just our DNA so it could save the human race. Optimists, aren't they?"

Like everything around Sedona, the world was casual and unassuming. Walking into the *Heartline Cafe*, small mountains and a forest surrounded. The sun was setting, colors were still vibrant.

"There's over a hundred thousand shades of green that the human eye can distinguish."

"I can't stop thinking about deja vu and what you told me. It makes sense but you fight with yourself not wanting to comprehend."

"Let's sit by the fireplace."

Champagne toasts were to God and the universe.

"The universe is amazing. We recognize now, everything possible happens so what if there's the next universe waiting to pick up when this one leaves off. What if you and I are sitting on a fateful day at this same restaurant and we're both quiet for a few moments and deja vu tells us, we've been here and we have, right now, so everything is alright and earth and our universe are back in business, rolling along? Josef and John knew about this. Josef thought about God, infinite wisdom, taking care of us like children and giving us immortality that we ponder about. When terrible, inconceivable things happen and we don't understand how God could let it happen, God's infinite wisdom created the universe and knows there are many universes to get things right. Maybe moving on, which is like a heaven, depends on getting things right. Maybe it's a graduation; if you've passed courses in forgiveness, tolerance, charity and mercy."

Elvin refilled champagne glasses, looking puzzled. "Then time on earth should be devoted to learning and getting things right, obeying God's and man's laws or condemning yourself, to the same outcomes later on?"

"Doing righteous things."

"Science, universe and God are all together."

"More than coexistence, but reality."

Alex laughed as Elvin ordered breakfast at a fast food restaurant. "What's so funny?"

"You've ordered a contraption."

"A what?"

"A few years ago, I was here with Giacomo Custode, a colleague and friend. I mentioned him before. He was on that ill fated airplane. A sweet man. We were here once, and he explained why this English muffin is a contraption. Look at the grease on the paper and all the different colors."

Twenty minutes from Sedona, passed Oak Creek Canyon was a mountain overlook into valley, forest and heaven. In a parking lot, dozens of tables were set up by Native-Americans, selling wares and jewelry. A bus emptied tourists with Northeastern accents, original Bermuda shorts exposing men's bony knees and high dark socks. Elvin and Alex stopped at each table, whispering just before, how women's skin was weather beaten, tired, and wrinkled, looking well past their years. Eyes were sad and yearning. Maybe it was the effects of two hundred years of pain, discrimination and injustice; now standing behind tables in a flea market, trying to sell the ancestors of the people who kept them on reservations. Easterners bargained stereotypically and loudly.

Elvin and Alex spent thousands at each table, walking to the next, spending thousands more. Enthusiastic handshakes followed each purchase. One old woman looked at Elvin, walked around the table and hugged him like it was a perfectly natural thing to do.

"You're special men. I see it in your eyes. I know what you're both doing. I've known about you for a long time. Does that make sense?"

"Actually it does because I know about you too. That's why we're here. What's your name?"

"Maria Moon but reservation papers say Maria Smith."

"We're Elvin Stone and Alex Zari."

"You're going home the day after tomorrow."

"Yes we are."

"You see with your eyes as I see and that makes me feel good." Alex's voice cracked.

"May I hug you both again so this feeling between us lasts for a long time?" She made Elvin open his right palm and handed him a smooth reddish rock with the number, *444* etched.

They hugged the old Native American woman. Voices back and forth used the word *love* again.

TWENTY EIGHT

What always defined Thanksgiving for Elvin were cloudy, ominous skies, foretelling the coming of winter, Christmas, Hanukah, hope and family memories. Just as the sun was supposed to make an entrance, the radio alarm went off to *Kathy's Song,* so Elvin could get a handle on the day. It was perfectly cloudy.

Elvin used his cell phone.

"What Dad? You're two rooms away."

"It's going on."

Nelson, in a cut out tee-shirt, boxers, stood at the foot of his parent's bed. "Move over."

"*March of the Wooden Soldiers.* My sixtieth straight time. Thanks for indulging your old man."

"My twenty second. I hate that expression. You hang out at college bars, notably the *Olive Branch*, so you're not old."

"Thanks for the vote of confidence. I never said this before but when I was your age, I made up my mind not to age in the traditional sense."

"What do you mean, there's no control?"

"Actually there is. It's a mindset. Knowledge. Nutrition. Exercising mind and body and never seeing myself age the way other people do. I know, it's hard to explain but I've been conscious of aging all this time."

"That's heavy for Thanksgiving morning before watching *March of the Wooden Soldiers.*"

Channels flicked obsessively during commercials between the Macy's parade and Stan and Ollie.

"I meant to ask you; why are we doing Thanksgiving dinner in the basement?" Nelson rested his hand on Elvin's shoulder.

"I'm trying to recreate the difficult times when our forefathers celebrated the first Thanksgiving."

"Is that bull or do you mean it?"

"Half bull."

"At least you're honest and you're still silly, Dad."

Arms wrapped around Evie but she pushed him away. Carrot peel flew recklessly around the sink, some pieces landing up on the drain board. Leaning at the window, she saw a snow flurry. Back with arms around, her ear was gently kissed.

"Stan, Ollie and Toyland are around for another year. And more good news, the boys disposed of the boogey men again, except just one time, I wish the cannon of darts doesn't wind up in Ollie's rear. I suppose you need cider?"

"Get two gallons and I'm so happy about Stan and Ollie."

"First, I'm going to catch a couple flurries."

Dressed in heavy coat and Rutgers cap, Elvin ran outside with outstretched tongue leading the way. A dozen flurries were caught lingual, well off his record set back in Newark. A gaze went skyward, like needing divine verification for the dozen flurries caught.

"Mah. Dad. I've been thinking of you. Miss you. Grandma, you too. Mah, you were a real mother with total devotion and love. As a father now, don't think I've ever forgotten what you did and the sacrifices for your children all your life. Just look at me now. It's all you. My fists are clenched which is serious for me. When I clench, I want to go back and hold tight those days and want nothing to change. I want you all back, laughing, holding, and loving. Suppose later and this is what's so confounding and I'll never understand everything despite all of Alex's teachings, I'll want right here and now back. Judy's coming today and I know that makes you happy."

Back inside, arms wrapped around Evie again as she scolded, "Go already. Get the cider and come back. It's a lot of work schlepping everything downstairs because you want to show off your finished basement and that bullshit you told Nelson about experiencing what our forefathers felt on the first Thanksgiving."

"I told him it was half bull."

Christine and Alex, still with gray beard met Elvin in the driveway.

"Cider expedition folks. You know the routine; I've been running for cider for decades."

"I figured it's a cider run. There's a twenty dollar bill sticking out of your coat pocket. I think you need help carrying and schlepping."

"All right you two boys, we came early to help Evie. Go for cider but don't stop at a train station."

"Such an amazing woman. I prayerfully thank Nolan all the time for inviting Rider girls that day and God for giving us celery."

"But that would've happened anyway."

"Determinism. It did happen so it's written and done."

"Glad you're back. I don't know what. . . ."

"We're alright. Let's just look at autumnal scenery. Before I forget, I've got a surprise for you. Last night I drove back to the train station because I needed time alone. After midnight, I saw a solitary lonely leaf on the tracks, stem intact but brown, tired. It had just landed so I rescued it. Take care of this for me." A winter coat pocket produced a leaf, stem twirling right up until the transfer to Elvin.

"I don't know what to say."

"Don't go off on me now."

During the cider run, Judy, new husband Andy, Evie's brother David and Ellyn arrived. Everybody hugged in the foyer, briefly reminding Evie of the day Alex and Christine returned from the dead. The tradition of black and white movie watching on Thanksgiving afternoon was explained by Nelson who took votes on movie choices. Early returns were for *Casablanca*. Theory was pure Elvin that black and white would've been closer to being available two hundred years ago and the ambience went better with cloudy skies.

Judy was in the den, staring at mantle pictures of her parents. Elvin walked in and pulled her into a hug with thoughts that maybe things could be different in their relationship. An image flashed by of Jesus near Jerusalem on top of a boulder in a clearing, preaching forgiveness. Forgiveness was a powerful force and curiously, it seemed the older you got, the more room you had for the force.

"Let's not say anything Judy, just hug tight again so Mom and Dad can see."

The door bell, recently changed to a Beethoven melody, chimed.

"Dad, I think cousin Bob from Chicago and wife number three is there."

Bob, seriously emaciated, stood with a woman decades younger. "Meet

Alice everybody. Our three week anniversary is Saturday. We don't call ourselves newlyweds. No strangers to divorce, we're actually *resume–weds.* "

Bob and Elvin hugged.

"Confession Bob. I never said this to anyone before but I was so pissed off when you got into Yale because I knew Jack was going to bust my chops about that for years and he did right up until a few years before he died. Actually I don't know why he stopped nudging me."

"Confession Elvin. I was pissed off when you got into Rutgers. The school was called the *Berkeley of the East* back then; free speech movement and unpretentious life experiences. Rutgers is intelligentsia and real world."

Chopped liver, crackers, broccoli, carrots perfectly peeled, Chardonnay, Merlot and tiny hot dogs wrapped in dough-Nelson hated the other animalistic description-were served.

"Everybody meet Sarah."

"How long have you two been together? Thanksgiving dinner usually means dating at least a year."

"Cousin Bob, you're right on, somewhere in the year family."

Cousin Steven and Susan were opaquely standing at the front door; Beethoven was chiming away for the second time. Elvin and Alex went running.

The three Arizona explorers and *Pando and Ernest* potato men hugged.

"Steven. Susan. We're a whole family now that you're here. I couldn't wait for you to breathe our Jersey Thanksgiving air."

Nelson looked around. "Everybody is paired up like Noah's Ark."

"Does a Rutgers Masters degree program help with that observation?"

"Yeah, Dad."

Late afternoon was filled with *Casablanca*. Nelson took over the reigns of narration. Elvin finished a bottle of Merlot before disappearing outside with Alex.

"Dinner everybody. It's also the christening of our finished basement; another Elvin dream. Where is the dreamer?" Evie wore the same apron Martha did at Nelson's bris.

"Dad and Uncle Alex are outside walking. Hey Mom, I think Dad had too much fucking Merlot."

"Watch your language."

"It's from the movie."

The corner was turned; the same corner when Elvin saw Evie with Alex's obituary.

Alex was massaging his beard. "Ten twenty. I checked this morning. Are you OK?"

"Sure. I miss Martha, Jack even more these last few hours. Why do memories of departed parents well up inside so powerfully all of a sudden?"

"For me too. Most of emotion is the holiday. Adel, Sura. It does hurt. I never dreamt after all these years working with telescopes that I'd wish I was a dermatologist, a grocery bagger at a supermarket or an eighteen wheeler tractor driver. Traveling around the country is romantic; you eat well, sit high in the cab, earn a good buck and live carefree. What about you Elvin- any career change dreams perhaps for the next time?"

"Think maybe an astronomer."

"That was fucking funny and I never use that word."

"Do you feel irony in our lives? Our new President elect. A long dream. Every consciousness all these years."

"I think about Dr. King too and all the struggles and what'd he say now?"

"It's the thrill of seeing the promise of America. So what to do when we're back at the house?"

"After dessert, lots more wine."

"Just let."

"Just let. One more major thought." Alex stopped talking abruptly, seeing Nelson at the door.

"Hey guys, Mom's ready. We're waiting in the basement or should I say down in the prairie?" Nelson put an arm around father and uncle.

The basement looked like a twenty-five thousand dollar remodeling project and it was, but Evie never knew. The room had two attached aluminum tables decorated with fine china, sterling silver, stem wine glasses and a lace Italian table cloth. Six candles did most of the illumination; real lights were dimmed. Curtains were drawn on small casement windows. Three original paintings, all still life, were on the side wall. Dishes steamed aromas of basted turkey, stuffing, brisket, vegetables and freshly baked breads. Everybody was sitting, poised for the holiday blessing. Alex stood up for a blessing. Christine put her arms around him. Soup spoons angled down.

"Wait! Wait! Wait! I forgot. Don't do anything. I'll be right back."

Elvin ran upstairs. Nelson figured it out, leaning back in his chair, whispering to Sarah and loudly said, "Sarah doesn't know the history".

Back downstairs, shaking tremor like, the refrigerated bottle of Vichy Water was opened. Fourteen long stem glasses were passed out.

Elvin's voice wobbled and he remembered, sounding like Jack whenever they passed the *Buena Vista* hotel where he was conceived. "No more *nahs* about opening this bottle. Forty-five years, I've been waiting to share and now looking around this table, about to open this special bottle, I feel love, peace, and God. I love you all. Most importantly, please tell me if you like the water. I'll pass the bottle around; you can still see, but barely, Bogart's signature."

Water was rationed to fill fourteen glasses. Everybody lifted and clicked. Elvin smiled and whispered, "Thanks Humphrey and Claude too."

"That's it, Dad? Forty-five plus years of aging but it's not bad."

In the background, selected music from Elvin's computer played music softly, mixing holiday, a few pre-Christmas songs, eclectics and sixties, which Elvin considered ancient, almost like Benny Goodman, while the eighties now took responsibility for the *oldies* category.

Elvin sat across from Alex, stealing glances, throwing occasional calm winks at each other. Whispering across the table, Elvin thought it was the same wink from back in the vacant lot, when he said, "We're all Americans."

Conversation bristled. Family memories abounded. Everybody was growing up all over again. Memories were the matrix glue holding a wine laden post dinner feast together.

Alex kicked Elvin under the table, prompting. The table was cleared. Candles had burned a third down. Elvin might've been the only one paying attention to *Waltzing Matilda* playing on the computer, sending a brief chill. Suddenly the room shook and vibrated. Basement lights flickered. Shaking got more violent, almost like an earthquake. Lights went out. Women screamed. Bob, passed out, awoke, falling out of his chair. The room was less than candle dim; dust was everywhere. Nelson jumped up and reached to pull a curtain open. Elvin looked at Alex, hands reached across the table. Dust made everyone cough. A single lit candle was left. Elvin and Alex smiled at each other, squeezing hands tight while they still could see, before everything went dark.

"Remember *TTE* from a long time ago when we met? *Till the End.*"

"I figured it was something like that."

"Done?"

"Done."

They were still squeezing hands.

Ocean City, New Jersey is a smaller, toned down version compared to Maryland. Toned down means a dry town along the Jersey shore. Alcohol is pretend smuggled in, with no legal penalties for crossing city lines. Imagine the gutsy principles of a town in the twenty-first century, sticking to its dry guns. Ocean City is touted as one of America's greatest family resorts by their own tourism department. The bridge over bay heading into downtown Ocean City was deserted. Most pull up stakes after Labor Day, leaving a handful to live, die and shop on the main street.

Elvin spent the last month pretending rock singer on farewell tour, needing to say goodbye to optical friends and accounts. Beachcomber Vision Center was the tour last stop for a big reason; proximity to Sofia. Jeans and a sweater were worn for the first time in a sales career, on the last official day with yet another opportunity to remember a life's first and last.

Noticeably emotional, words were slow to form as Elvin took multiple deep breaths, finally settling down. "I'm going to miss you guys for a lot of reasons; a low key approach to life, eclectic eye glasses and loyalty to a human being- a sales rep who serviced you all these years. Simple things in life move me. Did anybody ever say that your store belongs in SoHo?"

"Just you, Elvin, thanks. So what are you going to do?"

"I'm going to look for America."

"Wasn't that lyrics from a song?"

"I've got the CD in my car as we speak. Do you want to listen?"

A few miles away, in Margate, near Sofia's Longport, was their take out Chinese restaurant, staying open all year for an imagined monopoly on Asian cuisine for miles around. Leaning on the steering wheel, chin nearly touching, looking at the emptiness and abandon of the Jersey shore when season died, Elvin was overcome with a strange loneliness and it felt stifling and not that far removed from Bogart's rescue from an evil bathtub. Sometimes during summer, crowds lined up all the way outside for a table inside. On the right, a seagull hopped, skipped then flew towards the ocean, a block away. A fist pounded the dash board, impacted from previous poundings. Intestinal lining refluxed a twittering sadness. He was sixteen years old. Alex was standing with him by the orphanage fence. To be able to start all over and then hold tightly each day was a universal gift and dream. God was universe and wisdom. What if, as a spiritual entity you can and are supposed to start all over again? Maybe that's another